Toward the Bad
I Keep on Turning

Toward the Bad
I Keep on Turning

A Novel Confession

Stephen Paul Foster

Stephen Paul Foster is a world traveler and philosopher (Ph.D. St. Louis University). His writings cover the world of politics, religion, and contemporary culture, and his lifelong fascination is with totalitarian tendencies in modern life.

A native Midwesterner, he grew up in Michigan, married in Missouri, and currently resides in Ohio, with his wife of forty years.

He may be contacted at: **nephets.foster@gmail.com**

Also by the Author

AFTER HARRY MET SALLY (July 2021)

> The sequel to *Toward the Bad*, concerning the parental investigations of a tortured young man, who never knew his father and knew his mother merely on a first-name basis. *After Harry Met Sally* is the story of a son's growing up, a compelling confession of a tortured young man struggling to understand his brilliant, driven, but self-destructive mother and to come to grips with the mystery of "Harry," who disappeared when he learned of "Sally's" "family way." The careers of Harry and Sally — their names changed to protect the guilty — as captured by their son, compose a chronicle of disillusionment and deviance — a droll and sardonic commentary on the darkness and corruption that marks the modern world.

FATAL FRIENDSHIP (Aug 2023)

> The age-old Rousseau-Hobbes debate solved, merely requiring a grisly murder (or two). The novel begins when Frank Bradley learns that his best friend, Rich Wahnfried, has brutally murdered his girlfriend in his Florida condo and fled to Europe. The ghastly news that his good friend was a closeted monster detonates Frank's confidence that he knows anyone, starting with himself. This philosophical novel follows Frank's self-torturous path to understanding the darkness in the human condition.

FALLING MARBLES PRESS
Marble Falls, Texas
www.fallingmarbles.com

"Cascading Worth, One Work at a Time"

For the "Little People"

And, for Barbara

Quis custodiet ipsos custodes?
(And who will guard the guardians?)
Juvenal, "Satires"

In our country, the lie has become not just a moral category but a pillar of the state.
Alexander Solzhenitsyn

Whatever it is, I'm against it.
Groucho Marx

CONTENTS

CHAPTER ONE   19
An Invitation

CHAPTER TWO   23
FDR in Terre Haute

CHAPTER THREE   33
How to "Lose Your Religion"

CHAPTER FOUR   39
Invidious Comparison

CHAPTER FIVE   46
Attainting Alliteration

CHAPTER SIX   58
Camelot Crumbles

CHAPTER SEVEN   67
Hey, Hey, LBJ…

CHAPTER EIGHT   73
…What Really Happened with JFK?…

CHAPTER NINE   77
…I Still Want to Know

CHAPTER TEN   85
Philosophy Bakes No Bread

CHAPTER ELEVEN   90
Bought and Paid For...

CHAPTER TWELVE   99
"I Might Take a Train, I Might Take a Plane"

CHAPTER THIRTEEN   106
An Enchanted Evening

CHAPTER FOURTEEN   111
Enchanted Days

CHAPTER FIFTEEN   119
Then, What?

CHAPTER SIXTEEN   123
Incarceration

CHAPTER SEVENTEEN   129
Government Criminality

CHAPTER EIGHTEEN   136
Lansky or Dulles

CHAPTER NINETEEN   145
Relocation

CHAPTER TWENTY   151
Radicalization

CHAPTER TWENTY-ONE   158
Decimation

CHAPTER TWENTY-TWO   168
My Friend, Fidel

CHAPTER TWENTY-THREE   174
Assassination Destination

CHAPTER TWENTY-FOUR 184
Ennui on the Island

CHAPTER TWENTY-FIVE 190
Agonistes in Argentina

CHAPTER TWENTY-SIX 197
Fake Cristina

CHAPTER TWENTY-SEVEN 202
Conception in Concepción

CHAPTER TWENTY-EIGHT 207
Kant's Crazy Disciple

CHAPTER TWENTY-NINE 216
"Slippery" Little Rock

CHAPTER THIRTY 221
The Man from Hope

CHAPTER THIRTY-ONE 229
Selling Heaven

CHAPTER THIRTY-TWO 236
Holy Toledo

CHAPTER THIRTY-THREE 245
Dandelion State University

CHAPTER THIRTY-FOUR 251
Superiority Ain't What It Used to Be

CHAPTER THIRTY-FIVE 259
"Racism," I Hardly Knew You

CHAPTER THIRTY-SIX 269
Sunny Cynicism

CHAPTER THIRTY-SEVEN   274
A Gay Confession-Profession

CHAPTER THIRTY-EIGHT   278
Pyramid Diversity

CHAPTER THIRTY-NINE   285
Diversity'd Up

CHAPTER FORTY   290
Diversity'd Out

CHAPTER FORTY-ONE   296
Hitlerization

CHAPTER FORTY-TWO   303
Bully Boys in the Balkans

CHAPTER FORTY-THREE   311
Kosovo Catastrophe

CHAPTER FORTY-FOUR   319
Lieberman's Lesson

CHAPTER FORTY-FIVE   325
Nuremberg Two

CHAPTER FORTY-SIX   329
Escape and…

CHAPTER FORTY-SEVEN   335
Homecoming and…

CHAPTER FORTY-EIGHT   341
Blown away in Bozeman

CHAPTER FORTY-NINE   348
The War Party

CHAPTER FIFTY   357
Juneau Tops Little Rock

CHAPTER FIFTY-ONE   363
Que Será, Sarah…

CHAPTER FIFTY-TWO   371
Sarah Barracuda

CHAPTER FIFTY-THREE   377
Striking Through the Mask

CHAPTER FIFTY-FOUR   384
Pain with McCain

CHAPTER FIFTY-FIVE   387
In the Kingdom of the Pretenders

CHAPTER FIFTY-SIX   394
Kingdom Crumbles

CHAPTER FIFTY-SEVEN   399
Disintegration

CHAPTER FIFTY-EIGHT   406
Vindication

CHAPTER ONE

An Invitation

I went to a garden party
To reminisce with my old friends
A chance to share old memories
And play our songs again
When I got to the garden party,
They all knew my name,
But no one recognized me,
I didn't look the same

Rick Nelson, "Garden Party"

What good are "old friends"? Ones I haven't seen, thought of, or cared about for decades sent me an invitation — to our 50th high-school class reunion. Hold on. Wait a minute! Why would I or anyone else want to go to it? That seems like an obvious question. It was not addressed in the invitation. Why not? It should have been. Do gatherings of this sort serve any useful or entertaining purpose? Why waste a perfectly good afternoon and evening? But, then, maybe I'm missing something crucial. It's possible.

But, no. I must speak truth-to-stupidity. Risky, I realize, but someone has to. Think about it for a second, boys and girls. People are at the top of their game, physically speaking, between ages eighteen and twenty-five. After that? Downhill.

19

On a bell curve plotted for looks, you have the few — the beautiful and handsome — perched at the right end. Those occupying the far left? Well, you get the picture. Most of us range across the middle. We bear a multiplicity of disappointing defects and imperfections courtesy of mom, dad, and their whole ancestral crew. They make dating and mating highly competitive, agonizingly unpredictable, sometimes frustrating, and often disappointing.

Fifty years added to your eighteen with simple arithmetic gets you to sixty-eight, if you're lucky — and to Social Security. It is absolutely axiomatic — apodictic, no less — to say that, at sixty-eight, no one looks particularly "good" anymore without that condescending, humiliating qualifier, "for his/her age". For those lucky dogs who, for a season, occupy the right end of the curve, the bloom is long off the rose. They're a disappointing crew now, visually speaking. As conversationalists, they don't churn up much interest or excitement, either.

Meanwhile, the elderly left-ender, looks-wise, is not likely to have advanced toward the right. Coping with a lifetime of rejection, however, may possibly, though not necessarily, have resulted in an improved personality. That's fine. I hope so. But who knows? I don't really care that much — not at all, to be honest, which is hard for me, being honest, that is.

Those of us in the middle? Do you remember mom and dad at middle age and beyond? Did you want to look like them back then? Now that you do, are you happy about it? Be honest! I thought so. Cruel, depressing confirmation of this axiom is all that these sorts of reunions will offer.

But this admittedly nasty and mean-spirited riff on looks aside, there is still more — much worse — to be said against these reunions. Someone should, and I am about to.

Twenty years or so post-HS-graduation, for most of us,

are all it takes. That is, all it takes to obliterate the delusional optimism that typically percolates away in the not-yet-mature brains of gullible teenagers — "She was going to be an actress; I was going to learn to fly," Harry Chapin; RIP. The preposterous ambitions and the ridiculous aspirations? Over and out, Good Buddy. The rust-iron jaws of reality have clamped down hard. They grind them up and leave the inevitable, soul-corroding residuals — boredom, depression, resentment, disillusionment, cynicism, and the mindless escapism of sports, shopping, and entire evenings lost in the blurred stupor of television. The family quarrels, divorces, financial failings, addictions, obesity, lunatic children to corral and support, stalled, failed careers, idiot bosses, and soul-killing jobs take their toll. The sexy cheerleaders, top jocks, and National Merit finalists are now a pitiable assortment of anorexics, potheads, AA-meeting stalwarts, and SSI-dependents. Those who have "made it big" are arrogant, condescending snobs; those who haven't are must-avoids, unless you happen to get off on large doses of envy, self-pity, and bitterness.

Need I mention the mandatory indulgence of necrology that always adds a boost to these happy shindigs? I feel I must. With this gathering of the weak, wizened, and withered, there is dutifully enacted a lugubrious ritual: the naming and lamenting of those unfortunate classmates who have passed to the other side — the dead — a depressing and completely unwelcome, needless reminder that the Grim Reaper, who once roved in faraway fields, lurks for you just around the next dark corner. Here's how the typical conversation goes with this:

"What ever happened to Chuck Percy? Didn't he end up making a killing in real estate?"

"Oh, you didn't know? The 'killing' he made was

himself."

"What?"

"Hung himself."

"Oh, God, that's terrible!"

"Yeah, didn't even leave a note."

"Yeah, it's terrible, no question. Not that I needed something else to be depressed about."

Yes, along with the painful contemplation of how time has ravaged that girl you lusted after a half century ago, you are forced to contemplate the grim "inevitables," one of which will soon be scribbled by someone who never knew or cared about you on your death certificate — "cancer," "heart disease," "stroke," "Alzheimer's," "blunt-force trauma," "suicide." That covers most of them, I hope.

No, I think I'm going to pass on this auspicious gathering and go ahead with the colonoscopy I was scheduled for on that date. I really couldn't get into the "spirit" of the celebration. Anyway, I doubt that I'll be missed.

Chapter Two

FDR in Terre Haute

In spite of all my Sunday learnin',
Toward the bad I kept on turnin'
                    Merle Haggard, "Momma Tried"

Yes, Reader, I know, and I'm sorry. You're picking up on some rancor and disillusionment. I couldn't help myself. This sounds massively bitter and deeply resentful to you, but I've got a good reason — a damn good reason. I have failed to mention that this reunion invitation was forwarded to my current residence, which is: Terre Haute, Indiana, at the Terre Haute Federal Correctional Complex — a high-security Federal prison. That's correct. I've been living here in fully-funded government retirement for about six years; my puny revenge on the American taxpayer.

Not that anyone should care, but my "retirement home" was authorized for construction in 1938 by Franklin Delano Roosevelt, the most acclaimed and idolized of all our former Presidents since George Washington or, maybe, Abe Lincoln. So, I sit and molder away in a 6 x 8 feet metal box in this crummy joint, a lesser-known old remnant of his highly touted "New Deal." So many cruel ironies to contemplate. For one, shortly after the prison opened, FDR's Stalin-loving

Vice President, Henry Wallace, solemnly declared the start of a new era, "the dawning of the Century of the Common Man." What could be a more fitting as a legacy for the President of "the Common Man" than a big fancy prison to make a home for some of the common men?

With not much to do, I can't help but think a lot about old Saint FDR. Mostly, I can't help but wonder why we continue to admire rather than despise this crypto-potentate who, along with his Ivy League "Brain Trust" cronies, turned the bad times good for themselves while worse for the little people. This prison captures, in a personal way, the spirit of the Great Depression he seemed determined to prolong. Yes, I know: He finally got us out of it. How? By plunging us into a World War, the granddaddy of them all, WWII. Out of the unemployment crapper and into the meat grinder, getting killed by and killing Germans, Italians, and Japanese — multi-culturalism at its finest, the way the good Lord intended.

What a genius! Don't forget, he was "against the war before he was for it" — a notorious bait-and-switch script dangled out more than once by conniving vote-chasers to fool the unsuspecting, trusting American electorate. Pre-election, 1940: "Vote for me, and I won't ship your sons off to fight in some Godforsaken place you never heard of — Guadalcanal, for example — a place you don't care about or have good reason to care about to get killed in service to a bunch of useless abstractions and vacuous exhortations like 'defending democracy,' 'self-determination,' and 'making the world a better place for one and all.'" Post-election, 1941: "Oh, wait, hold on a minute. I'm now safely reelected. Thank God for the Yellow Peril. We need this war to distract you saps that voted for me from grousing about the lousy economy. Let's hear it for 'democracy.'"

Well, by God, Franklin! You got the bloody WWII you

were pinning for, the one you connived behind our backs with Winston to us get into. After all, WWI, the one Woodrow What's-His-Name got us into after promising he wouldn't — just like you did — didn't exactly make the world "safe for democracy," did it? And on your glorious road to getting rid of *Der Fuhrer*, you snuggled up to and went palsy-walsy with his chief competitor in killing whomever-you-feel-like, Joseph Stalin. "Uncle Joe," you affectionately called him. Yeah. He played you, Dude, like a cheap kazoo. Then, you up and died and left Harry the Haberdasher at Potsdam to gift-wrap most of central and eastern Europe for old Joe as a great big "thanks a bundle" for colluding with Hitler in the carving up of Poland and swallowing the Baltic states, attacking neutral Finland, murdering 15,000 Polish officers at Katyn, and deporting several hundred thousand folks to do slave labor in the Gulag. That was the Uncle Joe you were so fond of. Yes, and how about those black American soldiers in racially segregated units you shipped across the pond to fight those "racist" Germans and liberate their internment camps?

Meanwhile, for all you FDR-worshipping saps, the man with "forked tongue" turned loose then-Governor of California Earl Warren to round up perfectly law-abiding, loyal Japanese-Americans from the West Coast and throw them into…that's right, you probably forgot, internment camps — in a desert, no less — with fewer amenities, like indoor toilets, than his new prison in Hoosier-land. Not to mention that he gave the green light to his minions like David Bazelon in the "Justice" Department to confiscate (steal) their hard-earned and valuable West Coast properties. And do exactly what with them? Auction them off — at bargain rates — to his buddies, with generous kickbacks.

Let's, however, linger with this edifying "lifestyles of the rich and rapacious." I must relate a sad story in the "How good things happen to bad people" category — Governor Warren, in this case. Ike rewarded Warren's state-sponsored criminality with a promotion: Chief Justice [sic] of the Supreme Court of the United States. From there, he dreamed up and handed down the wonderful "Miranda" decision — so that violent criminals whom the cops risked their lives pulling off the streets could have another "have-at-cha." "You have the right to an attorney." And from what clear blue sky did that "right" drop out of? Hey, sometimes you wake up feeling like God put you in charge of everything, and you just make shit up, hoping that no one notices, before everyone thinks it came directly from the Good Lord himself. Thank you, Uncle Earl. RIP, you douchebag. You always had the best interest of law-abiding citizens at heart, just like those Japanese American citizens in California before you had them rounded up and shipped them off to the desert.

While I am at it, there is more about this place that's eating away at me. The building of the Terre Haute facility was financed with Public Works Administration money — a gift that keeps on giving. Part of the Guantanamo Bay Detention Camps in Cuba that we heard so much about when "Compassionate Conservative" Bush II and "Hope and Change" Obama took turns lying to and screwing us was built using the "Terre Haute design." Best of all, Terre Haute is also where the Feds conduct their executions. Timothy McVeigh, the Oklahoma City bomber, was dispatched here in 2001. Oh, I almost forgot. The notorious former CIA counterintelligence agent, Aldrich Ames, is just a couple of cell-blocks over, serving a life-sentence for espionage. I was hoping for a quiet conversation with him to compare amenities, but he's in permanent solitary confinement.

Maybe you've guessed: I'm feeling the bad karma that hangs all over this place.

How I landed here to live out my golden years is a long story. I'll get into it shortly, for reasons I'll try to be upfront about. But, first: After a half century with no contact with my high school chums, how did these class reunion zealots know where to find me? Over much of this time, I had been in perpetual motion in sundry places, in many cases using aliases for my adventures that I've simply forgotten.

Well, they sent the invitation to my older sister. She lives near the little berg out in the sticks where I grew up in Michigan. My sister is my sole contact — other than my attorney — with the outside world. She passed it on to him, Bobby Griffin, a lazy, gin-soaked pettifogger whose sense of humor is even more feckless than his miniscule lawyering skills. He forwarded it to me with the quip attached: "Weren't you voted 'most likely to succeed'?"

One of my many personality defects is that, confronted with every choice and decision — big or small — I remain hopelessly conflicted. No contemplated course of action or its outcome gives me a moment's peace, satisfaction, or confidence. Whichever way I go, I shouldn't have.

Worse, though, is a second deformity. I obsessively need to conform to the desires and expectations of anyone and everyone I happen to be around. These are often people I don't particularly like or admire, which, as I think about it for a moment, combines with the first to make it impossible to function as a normal human being — whatever that might be. I haven't met enough "normals" to confidently generalize, and the few I did failed to impress me enough to ever want to imitate them. They tended to be the least interesting and the most predictable. There were some notable exceptions.

And so, here I am: always struggling, a completely disordered and anguished person, having spent too much of my life trying to please an array of mostly non-entities —

Anonymuncules, a nifty little Latin word for "nameless little men" — usually with radically conflicting and occasionally stupid takes on what my life should have been about. I give way easily, to those who threaten me more easily than to those I need a favor from. Sometimes, I even cave to those I barely know, for reasons that continue to escape me.

Why would I want to please anybody at this late stage of a completely failed life, moldering away in a prison cell, especially a bunch of aged stiffs I hadn't been around in fifty years? But…according to the invitation, if you couldn't attend (Ha ha!), then my classmates requested a current picture. How about my "Wanted by the FBI" mugshot? Also, a short bio — what you'd "been up to" for the last fifty years. How about "armed and dangerous"? Well, I was up to lots of capers that they would no doubt take a dim view of. I graduated from a tiny high school in rural Michigan — Hicksville, USA — where a "mortal sin" was "failing to come to a full stop" at any of the town's five stop signs or trying to feel a girl up on the first date.

Why couldn't I just throw this silly piece of paper away and continue to indulge my well-deserved self-pity? I felt obligated to respond. But, because I'm always conflicted, I resolved not to respond — but on and on, back and forth it went until the guard strolled by and growled at me: "Time for stand-up count."

Then, it came to me, known here as inmate number TH77666. This was my opportunity — to launch an overdue confession. I had a long, sordid career of "misbehavin'" that I should take a stab at getting off my chest. My life, from early on, had gone off the rails. There might be some redeeming value in rendering that sordid history as entertainment.

The old saw, "confession is good for the soul," I'm not sure of, particularly given my obdurate skepticism toward what the "soul" might be all about. Assuming there is such a thing, what might be good for it? But, good for my questionably existing soul or not, I resolved to get this mangy horse out of the barn and into a full gallop. My confession would be forthcoming. I would hold nothing back — well, mostly nothing.

But what kind of confession should it be? The competition is fierce. Lots of them compete for readers. Some are legit, a few of them are flat out masterpieces — Thomas De Quincey's *Confessions of an English Opium Eater*, the *Confessions* of St. Augustine, and J.J. Rousseau, for example. What should I say or confess to be the motivation that turned on the guilt spigot just now? Augustine, having attained Christian sainthood in his dotage, needed to come to terms with the prolific rogering during his youth. "Lord, make me chaste — but not yet!" I'm solidly behind him on the "not yet" part, and I'd want to make a powerful argument for an extended season of youth. Chastity, however, only makes sense to impose on young girls until they attain a solid grasp of what young boys are always after. That the Catholic Church for millennia turned chastity into celibacy and saddled that painful prohibition on their priests was an even greater mystery to me than the Holy Trinity or the transubstantiation of the Eucharist. But, then, theology was never my strong suit.

Rousseau remains a bit of a puzzle. His version is likely disingenuous. He opens with:

> *I have displayed myself as I was, as vile and despicable when my behavior was as such, as good, generous, and noble when I was so.*

There was, I think it is fair to say, a whole lot of "vile" and "despicable" and not much "generous" and "noble" with this fast-talking, neurotic jerk-off, and I'm not sure he had a solid grasp on the difference between any of them. My take on him is that he was a bright, self-infatuated, born manipulator trying to make the considerable perverted baggage he was toting around from day one come off like the harmless eccentricities of an unheralded genius.

> *I am made unlike anyone I have ever met: I will even venture that to say that I am like no one in the whole world* [not to mention missing the 'modesty' gene]. *I may be no better, but at least I am different.*
> Rosseau, "Confessions"

Oh, I'm not so sure, J.J., old chap. Rousseau strikes me in some respects as an eighteenth-century prototype of the preening, self-worshiping mental midgets who fill the sorry ranks of our virtue-signaling celebrity class. They're everywhere, the narcissists and egomaniacs from Hollywood cycling in and out of marriages and rehab programs. Don't forget the criminal cretins who populate the NBA and NFL and who regularly beat up their girlfriends. How about the late-night, foul-mouthed television comedians who pollute our living rooms? On the social media outlets, they drop chunks of cerebral offal that ooze out of their miniature minds. They confuse them with deep thought and pearls of wisdom. Rousseau, at least, was an original thinker and literarily gifted.

I am not suggesting that the confession you are about to read is a literary "masterpiece," anywhere on a par with Rousseau's or Saint Augustine's. However, beyond trying to keep myself occupied and looking to give people who once knew me a shocking but entertaining read, I have something serious in mind. I have an ax to grind. Quickly, I think, it will be obvious to any perceptive reader — already, perhaps — what I am up to.

I'll begin with a line from Merle Haggard's great song, "Momma Tried:"

> *In spite of all my Sunday learning,*
> *Toward the bad I kept on turning,*
> *Till Momma couldn't hold me anymore*

The chorus begins: "I turned twenty-one in prison, doing life without parole. No one could steer me right, but Momma tried." Mom, Dad, my dear sisters, a couple of preachers, and some schoolmarms steered hard with me, but, as you'll see, "toward the bad I kept on turning." Haggard, in the song, blamed no one but himself. Me, too. All my "bad" falls entirely on me, though there is a whole lot of it I've been involved with that's on other folks. It calls for serious attention. I'm painfully vexed by sinners in high places who make themselves into saints. My confession will be more like Haggard's than Augustine's spiritual meditation. It will be much less of an ego-massage and con job than J.J. Rousseau's literary masterpiece.

I'll begin with the most concise, accurate, indisputable owning up I can muster: I am a conman. I have been one reaching back to my early years. There it is. That's my story, and I'm sticking to it. That's why I ended up here. No excuses. The specifics, I'll get to shortly. For the reader, I do need to attach a "product warning label": This is the confession of a conman, so buyer beware.

But I do want to say with complete honesty at the beginning: I don't think that I was *born* that way or destined to be one. I am confident about this. My parents were perfectly good and decent, law-abiding people — honorable, even. My sisters turned out fine. They find it difficult to talk about their "black sheep" brother without considerable sadness. It wasn't genetic. As a young boy, I was perfectly —

well, mostly, I think — normal.

How did it happen? I know how and when it began.

CHAPTER THREE

How to "Lose Your Religion"

When the truth is discovered by someone else, it loses something of its attractiveness.

Alexander Solzhenitsyn

I was fourteen years old and with my father, who at the time was a lay minister and social worker. He was on one of his summer missionary trips to Latin America, supported by our church denomination. A sincere, devout, and humble Christian, he was without a devious or unkind bone in his gentle body. He was, as those whom I grew up around would say, "a Man of God." His entire life, he devoted to loving his neighbor as himself, doing good deeds, and spreading the hope of the Gospel, the "Good News" of Jesus Christ to those he believed most in need. In my still-innocent fourteen-year-old eyes, he was as perfect a human being as God would see fit to put on this earth. I had hoped to be like him.

This mission excursion took us to the Dominican Republic, our first time there, though not the first trip to Latin America — we usually went to Mexico or Honduras. Dad spoke passable, plebian Spanish he learned as a kid working on the fruit farms with the Mexican migrant laborers who made the long trek north to Michigan's western lake counties in the summers for the harvests. With the summers I had spent on these mission trips with Dad from a very young age, my Spanish was better than his.

Momma tried…tried very hard, that is, to discourage us from going to the DR. She'd been reading about bad things going on there. She pitched a fit when we decided to go. Momma tried. We should have listened to her. Over the years, Dad had traveled to many poor places — some of them not completely safe. Most of them were certainly not comfortable. He went wherever "the Lord called him." Wherever he went, he shared the poverty and material hardships of the people he ministered to, and with grace and dignity. We did not know it when we set out, but this journey would be the last of its kind for both of us.

At the time of this mission trip to the DR, the sadistic and venal Rafael Leónidas Trujillo Molina was President and Dictator-for-life of this Caribbean playground, where gambling and prostitution made up the biggest pieces of his revenue streams. I say "his" because he owned everything worth owning in the country and, as dictators are typically inclined, only cared to share his "stuff" with his family and his closest "friends." He ruled, as they say, with an iron fist. His enforcers were a cadre of loyal, ruthless yes-men who held nothing back when the serfs stepped out of line. That wasn't very far or very often, given the brutal proclivities of these gorillas who always had the green light for open-throttled beatings and a truncheon handy. To the casual, outside observer, the Dominican Republic was a safe, easygoing, and fun place: In a shocking, painful way, my father and I discovered the opposite.

One of the more remarkable and ingenious of President

Trujillo's "team building" exercises was, from one of his trusted consiglieres on the rise, to select a comely, pubescent daughter. The girl's father would then be "asked" to arrange an intimate little "party" — just the daughter and "El Jefe," as Trujillo was affectionately monikered. In his palace, El Jefe would then "deflower" the unfortunate and unsuspecting maiden, making her daddy into a knowing accomplice to the rape of his child. The monumental betrayal, terror, and depravity of Trujillo's sexual predations are captured rivetingly in an historical novel, *La fiesta del Chivo* (*Feast of the Goat*), by the great Peruvian writer Mario Vargas Llosa. The novel unravels itself, from the beginning, as a nightmarish flashback memory through the traumatized experience of one of his adolescent victims. The novel also recounts in brutal, graphic detail the assassination of the "Goat" in 1961 and the orgy of savage revenge-taking that followed in its wake. Not recommended reading for those with a weak stomach or a high estimation of human nature.

Call it "God moving in His mysterious ways" or the worst sort of luck imaginable for a well-intentioned gringo preacher-man and his tag-along, pimple-faced teenage son doing "the Lord's work," as we humbly imagined. Either way, Dad and I just happened to be in the DR spreading the Gospel when Trujillo got whacked. In his 1957 white Chevy, on the road from Santo Domingo, where Dad and I were staying, the Boss-Man was heading to San Cristobal, where he kept his regular mistress stashed. He was looking forward, no doubt, to a spirited session of "rumpy-pumpy."

A hit squad had set up an ambush just off the road. Four shooters took El Jefe and his driver out of this world with a sawed-off shotgun, pistols, and a couple of semi-automatic rifles. When the smoke cleared, he was quite a mess. It was a challenge for all the King's undertakers to gather Rumpy-

Pumper's pieces and put them back together again. The shooters were locals — home-grown Dominicans. Their weapons came courtesy of some guy named "Kennedy" from the American government. More on that item of interest and importance a bit later.

All hell broke loose on the island after the hit. Trujillo's son took charge, chasing down and killing his father's assassins — with one exception — in an especially…uh…"spectacular" way that was intended to make a deep, lasting impression on these unfortunate islanders. His hirelings occupied themselves rounding up a lot of other suspects — real and imagined — many of whom were subject to "enhanced" modes of interrogation.

Dad and I scrambled to hide out in the house of one of our host families. We feared that a major shit-storm was about to hit. It did. We had no way of knowing what exactly was going to go down, who to fear, who was in danger, and how bad things were going to get before we could get off the island. The chaos we thought was coming never happened — just sadistic retaliation and brutal repression, a piece of which clobbered the Man of God and his wide-eyed kid.

Trujillo Junior's goons were searching for and finally found Dad. Busting into the host house, they pushed me face-first down to the floor and pressed a pistol barrel against my forehead. There's nothing you can imagine like a gun pressed against your face to concentrate your mind and collapse your sphincter. They grabbed Dad, cuffed his hands behind his back, slapped a chunk of duct tape over his mouth, and yanked a black hood down over his head. Out of the house, they dragged him, stuffed him into the back-seat floor of a black Buick, and off they disappeared. They also did quite the number on our host family. They roughed them up badly, including breaking the jaw of the elderly grandfather, Don

Armando, when he tried to intercede on Dad's behalf. They also paused a bit before they left to paw over the beauteous sixteen-year-old daughter, Mariela, with whom, in just a few days, I'd fallen immediately and hopelessly in love.

The defunct Trujillo's equally sadistic little Junior was suspicious that Dad's mission-work was a cover and that he may have had Fidel-inspired Cuban or mainland involvement with the planning of the hit. His goons put him through an intensive three-day interrogation that you might say permanently changed his perspective, generally, on the world and, specifically, on the power of God's grace and the goodness of Christian love. I floated precariously through a nightmare of terror and fear that was far beyond the reach of what my undeveloped imagination had ever conceived. Those next seventy-two hours were sheer mental agony. I cried, pissed my pants, and agonized over what they were doing to Dad and wondering if I'd ever see him, Mom, and my sisters again. Terrible, recurring nightmares from this mission-gone-bad would come crashing in upon me in unrelenting waves for many years.

Finally, they turned him loose; filthy, soaked in his own urine, and covered with excrement. Our host family helped Dad clean up. We pulled ourselves together as best we could so that we could make it to an airplane and fly back to Michigan. Mom, my sisters, and our friends met us at the Detroit airport as we, zombie-like, emerged from the plane. They were beside themselves — completely traumatized and in shock. Our homecoming was bitter — an intense mix of relief and immeasurable sorrow.

It did not appear to me that the goons had done lasting physical damage to Dad, other than knocking out a couple of his teeth. After those three days, they decided that he was actually what he said he was, a simple Pastor on a religious mission. As an American citizen, there was no upside for them to maim or kill him, as that might not sit well with the folks in the U.S. State Department. But it was a month before he could eat much and utter more than ten words at a time. He never told me what exactly they did to him during those three days, and I was always loath to ask. We didn't talk about it. He was never the same. Neither was I.

His religion dropped away. Not immediately. It ebbed away slowly but perceptibly over several years. One day, there he was, a wholly different man than the one who had some years before left his safe, comfortable life to carry his faith to the people of the Dominican Republic: faithless, churchless, and restless. Over the following years, he switched jobs frequently. He'd been a social worker, but that sort of work requires something inside of you that he no longer had. He tried selling real estate, encyclopedias, and used cars, drove long-distance semi-trucks for a while and attempted, unsuccessfully, to learn to repair TVs. He wasn't much of a technical guy. Finally, he got a rural mail delivery route for the U.S. Post Office, which he did until he retired. He preferred, by then, to work by himself, driving the tree-lined country and township roads, putting the utility bills, postcards, and letters in the farmer's mailboxes. He became a voracious reader — of medieval European history, perhaps in an attempt to locate himself in a long-ago spiritual universe. He even retrieved and improved upon his High-School Latin so that he could read the Patristic Church Fathers in the original.

My mother suffered grievously for my father, watching the spiritual world of the man she had loved and admired so profoundly, gradually and finally completely collapse. He was no longer the "Man of God" I had idolized as a boy; he was a naive good guy who had haplessly stumbled into the wrong place and gotten raped by reality.

CHAPTER FOUR

Invidious Comparison

Moral certainty is always a sign of cultural inferiority. The more uncivilized the man, the surer he is that he knows precisely what is right and what is wrong.

H. L. Mencken

The fallout from the horror of the DR experience unfolded differently for me. For the effects to play out, it took a long time — a lifetime, maybe. The Michigan small town where I grew up was a solid, stable place. Without reservation or hesitation, you trusted those who had authority. My world had these "fixtures," I'll call them, that seemed to be good for everyone — the church and school I went to, benevolent organizations of various kinds, like the Lions Club and Rotary, run by decent people who helped to make life safe, predictable, and enjoyable. This world embraced and nourished me as a protected one of its own. I thought I would be able, someday, to be one of its respected guardians. It hadn't occurred to me that the guardians themselves might be a problem.

My former picture of the country and the government had been captured with a touch and flourish of conservative patriotism shaped by small-town attitudes, platitudes, and traditions. It gave me a confidence in the people running the show and a pride in the historical past that I learned about from my parents, ministers, and teachers. Those in charge were mostly good guys, I thought. I wanted to emulate them. They were what they said they were. I believed them. No reason not to. They knew who the bad guys were — clearly distinguishable from the good ones — and, to protect the rest of us, they dropped the hammer on them, whenever and wherever they appeared.

The DR fiasco and its terror opened my eyes — gradually but inevitably. I began to see behind the appearances. These "fixtures," not just in the Dominican Republic but everywhere, were facades of questionable, dubious authority. The guys who operated behind them were often not all that good. They were not to be completely trusted, particularly the ones who appeared to be better than the rest of us. I also became equally if not more suspicious of the journalists, the "court" historians like Arthur Schlesinger Jr., the professors, the professional myth-makers, who *said* that the lads running the show were better than the rest of us — FDR, case in point — which, of course, made me a pretty suspicious, cynical fellow. I kept my thoughts, as they migrated increasingly toward a dark-lensed view of the world, to myself, and my change went unnoticed by those around me. Except, I think, for my mother, who sensed it and was deeply troubled. Momma tried…to push it back. She couldn't. I wouldn't.

I became suspicious and utterly cynical about the goodness, ethics, spirituality, and morality "stuff," the staple of the educational and religious establishments. This stuff, I once took seriously and solemnly. Those of us who embrace it, I thought, would be virtuous, wholesome, and trustworthy. No. This *stuff*, I realized, is epiphenomenal, something analogous to what magicians do to distract their audiences and pull off the illusion of their tricks.

"Morality-talk" diverts us from the realities of what human society and human nature are about, how people act and how their actions and motives get represented or, more accurately, misrepresented. Taken seriously, "morality talk" creates the illusion that human beings can rise above and not be what they really are: easily corrupted, happily duped, frequently coerced, and hopelessly deluded actors in a perpetual struggle that usually comes down to take or get taken. *Homo Homini Lupus est* — "Man to man is a wolf," as the philosopher Thomas Hobbes succinctly put it. Hobbes nailed it. Some excel at the "taking" side of it, and the "morality" epiphenomenon is particularly useful for distracting the marks, the ones who "get taken." Not only does it distract; it also deliberately distorts the reality of the outcome with a confusing and misleading picture of the players, particularly the takers who don't want to look like takers and often successfully represent themselves as benefactors.

This denouement came to me in the form of an overwhelmingly simple confrontation with the hard choice I, as a young man entering adulthood, would have to make. The world that I confronted was populated with two kinds of players — predators and their prey. I resolved that I would not be "the prey," which, logically, meant that I would be a "predator" of some kind, yet never quite sure which kind it would be. Not that it was a good choice and not that I was happy about it; it was just a lesser "evil" than the alternative. Maybe there is a softer word for *predator* — *conman*, perhaps. This is what I opted for and that is what I now confess to being: a conman, but of a unique kind.

The world, I also concluded, is a vast playground for conmen. They descend in a variety of forms and in varying degrees of turpitude. Not all conmen are the same; some, of course, are worse than others. "Worse," of course, depends on where you're standing and in what direction you're facing. There are individuals on the make, just in it for themselves. They focus on not getting taken and less on taking.

Unfortunately, our institutions and organizations aggregate individual conmen into collectives. The biggest collective con artists are governments. It's in their nature; it's axiomatic. Governments *tend* to be predatory — preying on innocent marks is what conmen do — especially the ones with big armies and lots of police at their disposal — some of them secret, such as the KGB, CIA, Stasi, Mossad. They make rules, regulations, and expectations for the marks, exemptions for the bosses. Particularly, I want to stress, *big* governments. How many of its own or other people has the government of Liechtenstein or Switzerland killed or put into prisons or slave labor camps? Compared with, say, the Russian or the Chinese? The U.S. has the highest incarceration rate of all the so-called democratic countries in the world — housing for the common man, the little people.

These collectives get ugly in a hurry. In them, the distraction of "morality" works overtime. It puts the happy face of "public servant," or the "man of the people," or the "champion of the oppressed" on many of the predators. "Morally" ambitious, big projects are projected to distract the marks — "making the world safe for democracy," for example, a "war on poverty," or a "war on drugs." The planners bring out the worst in each other. Their projects churn calculatingly predatory quickly. They never hesitate to resort to lying and deceit to cover up their feasting on the spoils. There are countless examples. You can quickly insert your own. The lies and deceits are creative, convincing, and with long half-lives. I've spent most of my life *unconvincing* myself of the superior virtue of most people in charge of many of our "big projects" and doubting the intellectuals who suck up to the powerful and turn them into heroes and saints. Lord Acton put it this way: "The strong man with the dagger is followed by the weak man with the sponge."

My confession, then, targets the "big projects" that I was deeply involved in. Deludedly well-intentioned and usually criminal, some of them will be familiar to you. I hope that you are shocked when I tell you about them. Some of them were designed by government agents. Some were projects launched by unstable enemies of the status quo, hyperactive professional moralists who were convinced that they could create a far superior version of the governing order — a "moral" one, they promised. The specifics, I'll be getting into. But, first, I must put a broader, general perspective in place. This should help you understand why I came to embrace cynicism as the only "healthy" way to withstand — that is, to de-moralize — the experience of a long life and to make sense of what most people are about. Demoralizing your life experience doesn't make you happier — mostly, the contrary. It does, however, make you wiser.

The slicksters who rise to occupy the high perches in the big governments tend to score high on the predatory side of the personality profile as narcissistic and psychopathic. To provide cover for the criminal temptations they just can't seem to resist, they employ a variety of ruses and deceits — creative fiction: "rule of law," "Workers' State," "our democracy," "your vote counts," and invidious comparison.

"Invidious comparison" (IC) needs special, close attention. IC works via relentless propaganda. The goal is to make you believe that your government is vastly morally superior to a different one designated as hostile and menacing. That government becomes an appealing target — a vicious, threatening outsider used to create and stoke feelings of self-righteous superiority. IC generates the popular support for the ruling class and insulates it from criticism. Our protectors from the evil outsiders must be immune from criticism. Immunity from criticism is, to put it mildly, not the sort of state most likely to bring out the best in people, particularly ambitious, avaricious people.

IC often comes into play when the corruption and the incompetence of the oligarchs becomes more noticeable than usual. In some foreign place you never thought or cared about — like Afghanistan or Bosnia — a threat suddenly appears. The country must then mobilize, send the military to force people who "hate our way of life" and "our values" to take up our way of life and embrace our values. You might remember how well "winning hearts and minds" worked out for both us and the Vietnamese.

The Cold War is a great piece of history for showing how IC works. Growing up, I learned that the godless communist government of the Soviet Union had turned Russia into hell on earth, where every third person was thrown into a slave labor camp. Also, all the Russian leaders dreamed and schemed about, day and night, was how to take over America, kill all Christian ministers and Roman Catholic priests, and make the entire country into an extension of the Gulag. This storyline, our government used to justify CIA criminality, the Korean police action, and the war in Vietnam. From it followed countless destructive foreign interventions in many places most citizens didn't care about. Coups, political assassinations, and the propping up of vicious, corrupt puppet rulers all over the world became standard foreign policy. IC made possible the creation of a massive, perpetual, war-launching military-industrial complex — non-existent prior to WWII.

In Russia, the school kids learned that America was a

cruel, heartless, dog-eat-dog dump run by a few greedy, warmongering capitalists and their puppet politicians just itching to launch a full-scale attack on the Russian peace-loving people. The few fat cats here lived high off the hog while everyone else picked up the moldy crumbs and were told by the preachers that "heaven" would be a lot better place — "pie in the sky when you die." This picture was the excuse the Communist party chiefs used for sending nuclear missiles to Cuba, propping up vicious, corrupt puppet rulers all over the world, spying on us, building the Berlin Wall, and crushing the East Berlin workers revolt in 1953, the Hungarian uprising in 1956, and the Prague Spring of 1968.

Don't get me wrong. You have to grow up somewhere, and I'm not saying I wish I'd grown up in the Soviet Union — not for a second. For the average Boris and Natasha, I'm guessing, it was a crappy place run by badly dressed thugs. The predators there, all in all, were, most likely, a nastier crew than our own. Truman, no doubt, was a somewhat nicer guy than Stalin. J. Edgar Hoover was probably not as clinically deranged or wicked as Beria. Nixon, much as I hate to say it, was probably less sadistic and lethal than Lenin.

I propose a better way to grasp the "reality" of government than the "we're morally superior to you" approach. When your collective sense of moral superiority gets inflated, you quickly lose track of how dishonest the conmen in your own tribe are, which is, of course, what they most want you to do. That's the point. And when you believe what they say, you close ranks with the other lemmings. That makes the bosses deliriously happy, and it makes your own happiness and future uncertain and precarious.

The superior-inferior morality stuff, I can't stress enough, is a trap that you must avoid falling into.

CHAPTER FIVE

Attainting Alliteration

"Coercion" — Definition: the practice of persuading someone to do something by using force or threats

"Corruption" — Definition: moral perversion; depravity; perversion of integrity; dishonest proceedings; bribery; debasement or alteration, as of language

"Collusion" — Definition: secret or illegal cooperation or conspiracy, especially in order to cheat or deceive others

With this "better way" I'm modestly proposing, all you need is just three words in the English language to make your way through the distracting bullshit. They are easy to remember, and each begins with "C." Coercion, corruption, collusion — the 3-c's, as I'll refer to them. Yes, the 3-c's are all you'll ever need to draw an accurate and exhausting picture of most big governments and the politicians who run them. They also apply to other institutions, like labor unions, churches, and, most of all, universities, which I will have a lot to say about later on.

To begin: Don't fall for the chest-thumping bombast of superiority that government cheerleaders use to boast about their own operations. These guys are the worst, the biggest liars and the most obnoxious. Once you get past their mumbo jumbo, you begin to recognize that they are — all of them — fronts for coercion, corruption, and collusion. They just can't help it.

I know you're going to protest. "What about Hitler, Stalin, Donald Trump, and the assault on 'our democracy'? Some governments, some politicians are bad; some are good, and it's pretty obvious which ones are and which ones aren't." But, before you work yourself into a self-righteous lather, let me try to show you what I am getting at with this crucial admonition: Drop the Good-Evil dichotomy way of looking at the world — it's used by conniving sophisticates to manipulate simpletons. It makes for good entertainment — Hollywood does it magnificently and routinely — but it doesn't match up with reality.

To make this point as undeniable as I can, let me briefly compare two supposedly extremely different forms of government: Russia under Lenin and Stalin, and the USA, 21st century. I will apply the 3-c's, and they will reveal what is painfully real about each of these governments. They will also show how their false, feel-good fables encourage our indulgence in the need to feel superior and puff ourselves up with imaginary virtue.

Before that, however, a quick reality check: Coercion is the foundation of every government, from the kindest and benign to the vicious and brutal. Not even the most honest, honorable politician asks for less power. He never promises to make the government do *less*, does he? No government *asks* you to obey its rules. Remember that letter you've gotten to report for jury duty? It doesn't say "pretty please, if you have the time, it'll be fun, we'd like you to come and join us," the way invitations to parties or other social events are worded. It is a command with an implicit threat. Unpleasant things will happen to you if you choose to ignore it. The coercion-differential between nice and not-so-nice governments is just a matter of degree in the scope and nature of the rules and the consequences for disobeying them.

Stalinist regimes are heavy on the coercion side of the ledger. The Soviet Union came into power in a violent, hell-on-wheels fashion, launched by radicals who proceeded to kill off previous members of the ruling class, steal their property, and send lots of folks off to forced labor camps. They then proceeded to punish everyone not enthused about the "new sheriff" in town. Same thing in Mao's China.

That's one boatload of coercion that leaves a lot of corpses floating in the wake. The killings were intended to make a strong and lasting impression on those members of the hoi polloi who survived the initial shitstorm. They got the message and pretended to worship the new sheriff — that is, those who knew what was good for them. Initially, there was not as much corruption as compared with the old sheriff and his crew because the new ones who took over and did the killing did so because they truly believed that they were morally superior to the corrupt blood suckers they were shooting. Czar Nickolas' morally inferior hemophiliac son and teenage daughters deserved to be bayoneted, shot, and thrown down a well by the morally superior Bolsheviks.

Bolshevik reasoning went something like this: "The old order is completely corrupt; our new order must be morally pure. Otherwise, what's the point of all the coercion we're about to unleash? We gotta break a few eggs, Tovarich, to make that tasty omelet we've promised everyone. We don't want or need a lot of 'stuff' — that is, personal stuff like fancy cars or big harems — just the power to manage everyone's life and make them pure and virtuous like us or else kill them if they disappoint us, which many of them, of course, will. It will take some time and may require some rough stuff along the way, but the end result, somewhere down the road, makes all the killing, terror, misery, and repression a good return on the investment. Meanwhile, Viva la Revolution, and up against the wall mother-fucker."

The Stalinists initially went out of their way to avoid the usual temptations. Lenin and Stalin were relatively modest in their living habits. Mao, not so much, particularly when it came to teenaged girls. The corruption creeps in with an inevitable "quantitative easing." It becomes rampant because no one, not even the second-string mediocrities who step in to run the show, any longer believe the bullshit-myths that got those original guys in power, the morally pure ones who kept their boots on everyone's neck. You can only shoot and imprison so many people before the whole edifice begins to crumble, like Mao's Great Leap Forward. After Stalin, worn out from murdering millions of his subjects, croaked in 1953, Lavrenti Beria, who, with some pride, Stalin called "my Himmler," started emptying out the Gulag. He was aiming for a "kinder, gentler dictatorship of the proletariat," with, of course, him calling "the shots."

The Stalin-show started out "virtue-heavy," like Lenin believing everything was going to be sweetness and light somewhere down the road, once the evil capitalists were liquidated. Instead, a few decades later, the virtue-pretenders ended up with an alcoholic, decrepit, nepotistic mummy like Leonid Brezhnev running the show, staggering around in his general's uniform with forty pounds of fake medals stapled to his chest. All the while, the party suck-ups, elites, and their families were living it up. They were content to govern a cynicism-saturated land of besotted workers who couldn't make a toaster that worked. The ruling class needed to dial down on the coercion because it was now in it just for the goodies. The ruled-over moldered away in their crappy, tiny apartments, stood in long lines to buy sour milk and rancid butter, and shopped in empty-shelved stores. Soaking up cheap vodka helped them pretend their daily squalor was the workers' paradise.

Which takes us to the collusion side of the ledger. It abounded in the Stalinist paradise. Why? In spite of the ideological claptrap of "historical necessity," the real power was personal, informal, and highly concentrated, which meant that the hunt was always on for opportunities and colluding partners to outmaneuver the competitors. This was a must to avoid political and sometimes physical extinction. When Stalin kicked off, he left a government run mafia-style with no established political means of succession. None of the competitors were what you would call Boy Scouts. There were no rules in place for a transition. It got ugly. Nikita Khrushchev, in a power struggle, colluded with Malenkov and Zhukov, enabling them to outmaneuver Beria, whose approach to young women, it is reported by reliable sources, resembled that of Trujillo's, and eventually have him shot.

The workers, the lunch-bucket gang, colluded, as well. This might best be expressed as a subliminal pretending by everyone that this "wonderful" system they lived in was really swell. Certainly, it was far superior to one run by the evil, running-dog capitalists. Hence, the quip of the workers: "We pretend to work, and they pretend to pay us." Everyone went along to get along, all the while knowing the whole system sucked. This was late-Stalinism at its best — big-time coercion gave way to pervasive corruption with the creative pretending (collusion) that everyone was super happy with how crappy everything was. "What stage comes after socialism? Alcoholism." So said a standard late-Soviet joke. It took seventy years, but the system finally came crashing down.

Moving, now, to the U.S. government 21st century —
"post-democracy," as I prefer to call it. Jumping in, with both
feet, with our 3-c's should help us get a realistic picture of
what goes on in America the Beautiful.

Sure, there is less naked coercion than in the early Stalinist
version because we have this formal legal system that protects
the "rights" of the citizens. The government can't march in
and do whatever they want to you. Did you just fall off the
back of the turnip truck? Think again, Citizen!

Protecting and enforcing your rights — property rights,
for example — against government encroachment requires
lawyers. Lawyers bill by the hour, and there are more of them
in the United States than in the entire rest of the world. This
gives you a clue as to who's running the show and a glimpse
of the obvious: The legal system is a racket run by lawyers for
the benefit of lawyers, many of whom hang out in
Washington DC. Most of the asses parked in the seats of
Congress are bought-and-paid-for lawyers, not plumbers,
truck drivers, or dental assistants, people who actually do
honest, useful labor that makes ordinary peoples' lives better.
Doing what? Doing exactly what we don't need: passing more
laws, which make more work for more lawyers. Think of it as
corruption hardwired into a rigged system with a *collusion*-
multiplier mechanism. In D.C., they call what they do "public
service," a laughable euphemism for feeding off the public
trough. The government's pockets are much deeper than
yours. Its lawyers don't bill by the hour. Their paychecks
come as the result of coercion via the IRS, created, by the
way, in 1862 by President Lincoln to — are you ready? —
enforce (coerce) the raising of revenue to support the war he
was waging on his fellow Americans while locking up critics
of the war, minus habeas corpus.

Uncle Sam doesn't say: "Pretty please, pay your taxes."

Here's how the bosses put it: "Any person who willfully attempts in any manner to evade or defeat any tax imposed by this title or the payment thereof shall, in addition to other penalties provided by law, be guilty of a felony and, upon conviction thereof, shall be fined not more than $100,000 ($500,000 in the case of a corporation), or imprisoned not more than 5 years, or both, together with the costs of prosecution." (26 U.S.C. § 7201 - U.S. Code - Unannotated Title 26. Internal Revenue Code § 7201)

Sounds threatening (coercive) to me, and it should to you, but stay with the 3-c's to sort it out. The lobbyists for the rich pretend-taxpayer collude with the lawyers in Congress. They pass insanely complicated tax laws that rich tax lawyers use to help their rich pretend-taxpayer clients "evade and defeat any tax imposed." You, the middle-class little guy, pick up the slack, and you will be prosecuted if you try to do what the big guys routinely do. The law and the penalties for its violation fall upon the little people.

You pay the salaries — via your taxes — of the guys the government uses to come after you and make your life miserable. Its agencies can sic as many of its trained legal eagles on your lone sparrow of a defender and do their thing until you're bankrupt and throw in the towel and plead: "Guilty, please be gentle." It's called "unlimited power," which means that they *can* do whatever they want to you, which, the last time I checked, is the standard definition of "tyranny." It's not quite so obvious and just takes a bit more time than it did for the "public service" guys who ran the tyranny they called the "socialist workers paradise," but anyone who thinks he can win is delusional. Try getting cross-wise with the IRS, EEOC, or any government compliance or enforcement division, and you'll know personally what coercion, 21st century American-style feels like.

But let's move to an even more basic right — to the "pursuit of happiness." Since ways of pursuing happiness differ a lot from person to person, there is *supposed* to be copious room for many options. Different strokes for different folks, right? The "land of the free?" How about the "home of 'Do what we tell you, Asshole…Now!'"

Coercion in post-Democracy America comes in a tsunami of rules, regulations, and oversight. Your "options" diminish by the hour. Grab a copy of the *Federal Register* for light reading. Congress has passed approximately 4,300 laws, and the Federal Agencies, Departments, and Commissions have issued 89,000 rules and regulations in the last twenty years. The regulation-monster grows bigger by the hour, like the eggplant that ate Chicago. These humble public servants toil daily to put *your* "pursuit of happiness" in strict, coercive conformity with *theirs*. Theirs? Something like cigarette-smoking-cessation programs alternating with employer-mandated sensitivity training seminars.

Real coercion, post-democracy style? Try going off to mind your own business and exercise your right to get away from the rat race of modern America. Let's say in a place like Ruby Ridge, Idaho, like Randy Weaver, a former U.S. Army engineer, and his wife Vicki did in 1992. Randy and Vicki had taken up a fundamentalist-apocalyptic view of America's future. Not the sort of enlightened, right-thinking that they teach these days, or allow at Georgetown or Yale, or praise in the *New York Times*. But, then, the last I heard, the "pursuit of happiness" in following this kind of thinking was not supposed to be a government-sanctioned death sentence. For Weaver's wife, Vicki, and his fourteen-year-old son, it was.

On August 21st, six heavily armed, camouflaged U.S. Marshals invaded the Weaver property, supposedly for purposes of reconnaissance. They first killed Weaver's dog then shot his son Sammy in the back while he was running, just after yelling "I'm coming, dad." The Marshalls were just getting started. An FBI sniper was aiming for a kill shot on Randy. Weaver moved at the last minute. The shot entered his shoulder, exiting through his armpit. A second shot aimed at his friend, Kevin Harris, missed and hit Vicki in the head. She was holding their 10-month-old daughter in her arms. The same second shot hit Harris after exiting Vicki. An internal investigation found that the second shot was out of policy and that the failure to request surrender was "inexcusable."

George H.W. Bush's Attorney General, William Barr, authorized the government assault on Ruby Ridge. After leaving office in 1993, he worked behind the scenes to obtain immunity for Lon Horiuchi, the FBI sniper who had been charged with manslaughter for killing Vicki Weaver. Horiuchi went on to be promoted in the FBI. Not a day in jail. He never missed a day's pay. Barr? He's now Donald Trump's Attorney General.

For those who like to do feel-good "moral" comparisons, try this one: What is the difference, "morally" speaking, between the FBI agent, Horiuchi, who shot Vicky Weaver, and one of the East German border guards who shot an East Berliner trying to escape across the wall and become a West Berliner? And their bosses — Bush? How does he differ from DDR head claw, Erich Honecker? They seem, to me, to be, morally speaking, a lot alike, but I'm a prison inmate, and I'd be happy to have some moral philosopher explain the difference to me.

Corruption? Remember our co-Presidents of the 1990s, Bill and Hillary Clinton? They left the White House "broke" but went on to amass hundreds of millions of dollars influence-peddling in bastions of freedom and democracy like

Saudi Arabia and Kazakhstan. Laundering the money through their pay-to-play, fake charity, they had a fair resemblance, I'd say, to Ferdinand and Imelda Marcos. Again, I'd like a philosopher or some other moral expert to explain how they differ from other illustrious man-wife studies in political scamming and corruption: Juan and Eva Peron and, my favorite pair, Nicolae and Elena Ceauşescu, who plundered Rumania before they faced a firing squad composed of eager Rumanian volunteers. Late-Stalinism and late-democracy differ in some important essentials, but most of the players are remarkably interchangeable.

Why stop with the Clintons? How about the Teamsters union Frank Fitzsimmons slipping cash under the table to President Nixon to give Jimmy Hoffa a "get out of jail free card." Nixon's pal, Bebe Rebozo, was closely connected to Santo Trafficante, the big Florida-based mobster and "Big Al" Polizzi, who was a bagman for Mafia Chief, Myer Lansky. Mr. Rebozo's net worth was estimated to have increased from $673,000 in 1968, when he was still a registered Democrat — he switched that year to the Republicans — to $4 million a few years later. Bebe, I suspect, would justify his party-switch along the same lines as famous bank robber Willie Sutton. When asked why he robbed banks, he replied: "Because that's where the money is."

The third of the 3-c's, collusion, is pervasive in "our democracy." The people who pretend to represent you in Congress or the Executive branch, who do they work for? Lobbyists, special interest groups, corporations, and foreign governments. What do they get? Exemption from the rules and regulations that apply to the "little people." Do the congressmen you vote into office have Obamacare health insurance? Do they go through what you must when you want to fly somewhere on an airplane? You, an ordinary, law-abiding citizen forced (coerced) to act like a motely inmate on a county-jail work detail. You strip off your clothes — jackets, belts, shoes, jewelry — and thrust your wrist-clasped arms above your head, in symbolic surrender before the scanners of your naked body. You are ordered about by the legions of federal warders. You watch them paw through your personal belongings, pat down old women, people in wheelchairs, and young children. They jam their hands into your pants and feel your crotch.

The difference between these two systems is not that one is rife with coercion, corruption, and collusion while the other is not: The two systems differ only in the relative proportion of the 3-c's. The proportions shift over time. The Soviet Union, early days, was coercion on steroids; it eventually relaxed. The moral purity of revolutionaries gave way to establishment corruption. The pervasive coercion of post-democracy U.S. has ramped up so much in my lifetime that the country is unrecognizable. The coercion is softer than the Stalinist version; it's the decentralized kind that threatens your job, career, reputation, and social standing.

The change in your status in 21st century post-democracy America is imperceptible but profound — from a citizen, to whom the ruling class is accountable, to a subject, who does whatever the ruling class tells him to do. Stalin's dictatorship was "iron" — dissent got you a bullet in the back of the neck. Ours is mostly "velvet" — Vicky Weaver excepted. Stalinist tyranny was concentrated, radiating down from a single power center. Late post-democracy, the U.S. version, is faceless and decentralized, distributed through government agencies, corporations, educational institutions, the legal system, and the media syndicates.

The front men are the commissars of political correctness and their government enforcers. They create and reward the official victim classes and unleash the diversity scolds. Everywhere, the virtue-signaling social-justice warriors are lurking to torment you. They tell you what thoughts are permissible and what your vocabulary should consist of — down to the pronouns. This moral mafia enforces the speech codes, tells you what to teach your kids about sex, who to hire, who you can't fire, and what your "values" are. They take your tax-money and give it to foundations and NGOs engaged in projects designed to turn you, the wrong sort of person, into the "right sort." This coercion is largely invisible because Americans are predictably conformist, with a remarkable capacity to embrace the desires of the elites. They quickly learn the boundaries of public and private, what is taboo, what words, phrases, and expressions are "appropriate."

Governments are the muscular arms of coercion: the tax collectors, the regulators, the army, and the police. Corruption and collusion? The power and resources at government command make corruption and collusion inevitable, with other social institutions in imitative participation. The fourth-estate, the independent journalists who are supposed to shine the disinfecting light on the power-brokers, are in on the fix.

This is how my confession must begin. My discovery of the 3-c's explains how I got where I am today.

CHAPTER SIX

Camelot Crumbles

The Eastern world, it is explodin'
Violence flarin', bullets loadin'
You're old enough to kill but not for votin'
You don't believe in war, but what's that gun you're totin'?
And even the Jordan river has bodies floatin'
But you tell me over and over and over again, my friend,
Ah, you don't believe we're on the eve of destruction
Barry McGuire, "Eve of Destruction"

In the Spring of 1969, I graduated from college — the end of that tumultuous decade. Coincidentally, it was the last year of that catastrophic period: political assassinations, race-riots, social turmoil, and the sexual revolution. The center did not hold. The world seemed to be coming apart. The hallowed institutions that were supposed to be holding us together were suddenly mirages; their history was doctored and falsified. The lives of most of our "heroes" were creative works of fiction. Corruption had always been the norm; it was now becoming obvious, at least it was to me — the 3-c's coming into a sharp focus.

To make sense of my early adult life and why it unfolded the way it did, the decade of the '60s holds the answer. It was this slow dance of deviance and defiance that put its stamp of chaos and corruption on my own character. It set the stage for my descent into criminality. I carry that past as my eternal burden. As William Faulkner so perceptively put it in *Requiem for a Nun*: "The past is never dead. It's not even past."

I am asking you to think of how the 1960s were "bookmarked," what they seemed to promise at the beginning, and how agonizingly differently they appeared at the end. This, I assure you, will not be an edifying experience.

The 1960s began momentously, in the midst of the U.S. Cold War with Russia and the razor-close election of a Kennedy to the Presidency of the United States, John Fitzgerald, the first Roman Catholic to hold the office and a bona fide WWII war hero. It was the first Presidential election I really remember following. I did so with a passionate interest.

My parents voted for Richard Nixon. They feared that, if elected, Kennedy would take his orders directly from the Pope. I don't remember what these orders might have been and how they would have been transmitted. It's hard to understand now what leverage the Holy Father would have had with the new President. Maybe, it would have been something like this:

"Mr. President."

"Yes, Mrs. Lincoln?"

"The Pope is on the line for you, calling from the Vatican."

"The Pope, my God, are you joking?"

"No, Mr. President. It's his Holiness on line three."

"What does he want?"

"He won't say, Mr. President."

"Ok, I'll take it… Hello, this is President Kennedy speaking."

"Good afternoon, my son, Pope John the 23rd calling from Vatican City. How is the weather there?"

"Actually, it's morning here, your Holiness. It's sunny and cool here. How can I help you?"

"Oh, yes, of course, that annoying time difference thing. I'll get to the point of my phone call. The reason for it, my son and Mr. President, is to ask you to issue an executive order that will forbid marital divorce in the United States."

"I cannot do that, your Holiness."

"Why not, my son?"

"Well, you see, that would amount to being a law. Only Congress can pass laws. If I did this, I would be impeached and removed from office. Johnson would be President. My impression is that he is a Baptist, or one of those other backwoods Bible-thumper faith-types, your Holiness."

"Oh, my. No, that would be terrible. I'm so sorry. I didn't realize you face so many limitations. It must be so frustrating for you."

"Yes, your Holiness. I'd love to do this for you, but, of course, you understand. My hands are tied."

"Yes, of course. I won't bother you again, unless you want me to hear your confession."

"Certainly, I have a list, uh…a short one, and I'll get back to you on that. My best to the College of Cardinals. Goodbye, your Holiness."

"Goodbye, my son."

Click.

"If he calls again, Mrs. Lincoln, tell him I'm in an emergency Cabinet meeting."

"I will, Mr. President, but just so you know: You're asking me to lie to the Pope."

Difficult it is to imagine now, isn't it? JFK's Roman Catholicism was a big scary deal and perceived in many circles as an obstacle to his election. In retrospect, he appeared not to take many of its moral teachings too seriously. Mom and

Dad were Baptists, and Baptists in our little town were highly suspicious of Catholics. Why? Why not? Well, it was because they prayed to Mary, which, looking back, doesn't seem to me like a big thing, since I'm guessing that Mary would have wanted the best for everyone, even us Protestants. Pretty funny and preposterous to think of now. My mother forbade me to date Catholic girls, which made them even more alluring. They were supposed to be more, well, friendly than Baptist or Methodist girls.

Nixon's reputation as a staunch anti-Communist was, however, the clincher for my parents. Religion-wise, he was a Quaker, slightly ironic for a guy who incinerated a sizeable chunk of Indochina's peasant population. Mom was terrified by communists — me, too, at the time — and thought that Nixon was the best guy to drop a dime on them. Nixon had ousted Helen Gahagan Douglas, the spouse of Hollywood actor Melvyn Douglas, from her Senate seat in 1950. During the election campaign he made her into the "Pink Lady" — "Pink right down to her underwear," as he so delicately put it. Hollywood then, as now, was full of commies, so, maybe, Nixon was on to something. It was Nixon, too, as a California Congressman, who helped ex-Communist spy Whitaker Chambers — bad teeth, fat, and badly dressed — bring down the handsome East Coast patrician, Alger Hiss, then perched in the top circles of FDR's illustrious chosen ones. A Harvard man, who had clerked for Supreme Court Justice Oliver Wendell Holmes, he was also president of the Carnegie Endowment for Peace and seen as a likely future secretary of state. There are photographs of him with Roosevelt, Churchill, and Stalin at the 1945 Yalta conference. Though contested by his partisans for decades after, Hiss was, indeed, the Communist traitor Chambers accused him of being.

I revered Ike. He'd crushed the Nazis, wound down the

Korean War, and got the interstate highway system going. But, by 1960, he was showing some serious wear and tear. He was old, bald, and had a bad ticker. First Lady Mamie was nice but dowdy. JFK, with glamorous wife, the chic Jackie, in tow, was young, hip, and had lots of hair. Maybe, it was time for me to ditch the crew cut. Old "square" was moving over for new style. "Roll over Beethoven and tell Tchaikovsky the news," as the duck-walking Chuck Berry warbled it. Shortly after the election, Jimmy Dean released "The PT 109," a pop-nod to JFK's war heroics. Hokey as it was, I liked that song.

> *Smoke and fire upon the sea,*
> *Everywhere they looked was the enemy*
> *The heathen gods of old Japan,*
> *Yeah, they thought they had the best of a mighty good man*

Yeah, those "heathen gods of old Japan." Somehow, I don't think that chorus would get past the PC censors these days. "Heathen" no longer flies in polite company — too insensitive and judgmental.

Indeed, John Kennedy came riding in on a wave of youth and style, the reboot we were looking for to step out of the staid 1950s — urbane, energetic, coming in with a beautiful family that loved to play touch football — a great big bundle of wonderful! And not just style. Sophistication, smarts (Harvard), culture (bi-lingual; art-loving Jackie), and vigor. Even Mom, who worried about the Pope connection, thought he was something. And, of course, the younger brother Bobby, who launched his career as an aide to Senator Joe McCarthy. After having gone after union corruption in the person of Jimmy Hoffa from his Chief Council chair on the McClellan Committee, RFK became, at thirty-six years old, the country's chief law enforcement officer and his brother's closest confidant. Youth and vigor were now running the show. I was utterly fascinated. My worries about the Pope dropped away. "Let me, ahh, say this about that," in that Boston accent, was JFKs' standard lead in to questions posed by the White House press corps chasing him around. I would do JFK imitations for my friends.

Ok, the appearance; the truth behind it, however, was not so bright and shiny. This Presidency was launched by Papa Joe's money and his connections made from bootlegging, stock manipulation, and organized crime. Like the old man, JFK was a compulsive, almost pathological womanizer. His best-selling, Pulitzer Prize winning *Profiles in Courage*, much touted as proof of his superior, sophisticated intellect, was ghost written by his speech writer, Ted Sorenson. This was not a complete secret. I remember a television interview with Mike Wallace when columnist Drew Pearson repeated the quip reported to have come from Eleanor Roosevelt: "I wish Jack had a little less profile and more courage."

The athletic energy and youthful vitality that really appealed to us teenage guys? That was an additional piece of the glitzy façade covering over the not-so-pretty physical realities that later floated to the surface. Kennedy's alarmingly serious fragilities and disabilities were concealed. He was a sick man in racking pain from his deteriorating, debilitating back, and he was suffering from Addison's disease. His elderly mother, Rose, was in better shape. When in office, he fell into the clutches of Max Jacobson, "Dr. Feel Good," who fed him a hefty diet of amphetamines. "I don't care if it's horse piss; it works" was JFK's response when questioned about the FDA warnings. Elvis Presley and Elizabeth Taylor were two of Jacobson's many famous patients. He lost his medical license after his patient, Mark Shaw, a presidential photographer, died from an overdose. Much of this was common knowledge in the ranks of our much heralded fourth-estate. Like the rest of us, they were infatuated with the images. Happily, they looked the other way. We trusted these "guardians"…then. Big mistake.

JFK's arrival in Washington was the bright, optimistic face on the beginning of the decade that also launched my teenage years. In 1965, I turned eighteen and registered for the draft. By 1967, tens of thousands of guys my age were sucked into the maw of military conscription. Then, bam! Off to Vietnam — to fight communist aggression in the jungles.

> *There's something happening here*
> *What it is ain't exactly clear…*
> *I think it's time we stop, children, what's that sound*
> *Everybody look what's going down*
> Buffalo Springfield, "For What It's Worth"

From 1967, the trajectory was a sharp plummet to the end of the decade. It was July 1969. Another Kennedy, this one, Edward — Teddy, as that big Loveable Lunk came to be known to us — was in high gear. He was on one of his Johnny Walker-guzzling escapades that went, uh, down the drain, so to speak, ending at the bottom of a tidal pond. Murdered Jack and Bobby's baby brother crashed over the side of a bridge, leaving his mistress-of-the-moment to perish in the watery bowels of his mother's 1967 Delmont 88 Oldsmobile. He hiked off to sober up. Oh, and then to huddle with the Big Kahuna handlers, Robert McNamara and Ted Sorenson. Papa Joe had quickly summoned them to help him concoct a cover-up story. The most creative part was the fake neck brace Teddy donned at Mary Jo Kopechne's funeral to divert the reporters' attention away from the young woman in the casket, who got there as a result of his reckless carousing and instinctive criminality. By any measure of just desserts, a future in politics for this spineless wastrel with the lifestyle of

Caligula and the morals of a Bunko artist should have been kaputski. But he was, after all, "a Kennedy." There was still wind in the sails of "Camelot." Massachusetts voters, I guess, still had to have a Kennedy in Washington — perhaps, to keep the women in the Bay State safe.

In the years that followed, Teddy invented for himself a fashionable championing-the-underdog image that focused on...yes...women. Irony was never his strong suit. He appeared to experience no remorse for what, if the legal system had not been suborned and the autopsy tossed, was an act of manslaughter. Teddy's last dog before he died, he named "Splash," making one wonder what sort of malignancy was embedded in that poisoned soul enclosed in the body he had, with his long gluttonous and dissipated life, transformed into a massive, unwieldy mountain of corpulence.

Kennedy's abandonment of Mary Jo to die and his despicable ass-covering became mere peccadillos, just collateral damage of the sort happily overlooked so as to keep a playboy with a magic name and "progressive" politics in a high place.

Burned into my memory: The beginning of the 1960s saw a Kennedy launch himself to the top of the heap. Two Kennedys were murdered in the middle of it, the circumstances so loaded with sinister intrigue that people argue to this day over who the killers were, how high up they went, who was giving the orders. At the end, to get out of a jam, a Kennedy suborns the local heat, dodges a manslaughter rap, and presto: the Lecher went on to become "the Lion", the "Lion of the Senate," as his *New York Times* obituary read, "a champion of women's rights," dying as the Catholic Church puts it, "in the odor of sanctity."

Now, I don't believe in secret cosmic forces at work. I don't believe in much of anything, but something terrible seemed to be going on here. I still feel it. Its memory is still painful and profoundly sad. It's almost as if America was going through its own *Kali Yuga*, the Hindu fourth-stage cosmic cycle of decay and decadence.

Chapter Seven

Hey, Hey, LBJ...

False face must hide what the false heart doth know
Shakespeare, "Macbeth"

"A fish starts rotting from the head down" is an old Turkish adage. Richard Nixon, one of the most cynical, duplicitous, conniving politicians one could find in this country — and there was an abundance to choose from — had been elected President in that dark year of 1968. I had just turned voting age. That November, I cast my ballot for the druggist from Minneapolis, Hubert Horatio Humphrey — I'm a sucker for alliteration. That same year, assassins ended the lives of Martin Luther King Jr., in April, and Robert Kennedy, in June. That August, Mayor Richard Daley turned the cops lose to beat up the Hippies and anti-war protestors at the Democrat convention in Chicago's Grant Park. Vietnam had turned into a national nightmare.

Nixon had directly succeeded the most venal, corrupt, and vicious man ever to occupy the White House, Lyndon Baines Johnson. LBJ had sent half a million mostly conscripted American soldiers — speaking of coercion — off to the jungles of Southeast Asia, at a price tag of twenty-five billion dollars year. The purpose? To kill a million or so peasants who had never done anything mean to us. Yes, and completely wreck a country that no one in the U.S. before 1960 had ever heard of. JFK was the good Catholic lad who got this sorry business going. Vietnam, he imagined, was another "domino" falling to the commies, who were gobbling up Asian countries like popcorn. He needed to prove to the Barry Goldwater faction that he wasn't "soft on communism." There was some evidence to confirm this impression. A couple of months after taking office, he clutched and went on to bungle the Bay of Pigs invasion. The American-backed invasion force, the poor suckers who trusted their commander-in-chief to come through with air support, he stranded on Castro's beaches. They would face, unimpeded, Fidel's full fury and feel the effects of his revenge. JFK, I remember, was hammered hard in the press for this debacle at the very beginning of his watch.

Nixon later claimed that CIA Chief Allan Dulles had slipped Kennedy inside information on Eisenhower's plans for overthrowing Castro, thus giving him an advantage in the debates. Who knows? Who cares? But here was corruption in full swing in the sleazy reality of Camelot — not to mention collusion. Sam Giancana, who had, by the way, generously shared his girlfriend with the President, was murdered in his home in Oak Park, Illinois in 1975, shortly before he was scheduled to appear before Idaho Senator Frank Church's Committee. Church and his crew were investigating possible connections between CIA and Cosa Nostra collusion in JFK's assassination in Dallas. Giancana apparently hadn't read the memo from William Faulkner: "The past is not even the past."

President Kennedy must have forgotten what he said in his Inaugural Address just a few months before the Big of Pigs invasion. I clearly remember the handsome, hatless JFK on that cold January day and the inspirational words. I heard it just a few months before Dad and I went to the Dominican Republic, before I understood the cynical dishonesty behind this kind of oratory.

"Let every nation know, whether it wishes us well or ill, that we shall pay any price, bear any burden, meet any hardship, support any friend, oppose any foe, to assure the survival and the success of liberty. This much we pledge — and more."

Try to reconstruct in your imagination Ted Sorenson coaching JFK, pre-Inaugural, rehearsing this part:

Sorenson: "Jack, come on, you need to get serious for a while. When you get to this section, you've got to try to keep a straight face and put some solemnity in your diction."

Kennedy: "Yeah, ok, Ted. Liberty-schmiberty, burden-schmerden — thank God, I've got you here to crank out this crapola. I don't know how you do it. Ok, I'll deliver it straight. Nobody is going to hold me to this 'and more' part we're supposed to be pledging, are they?"

At work in this piece of soaring, inspirational oratory is the seeming innocuous little pronoun "we." Almost slipped that one past you, partner, didn't he? He did me, but I was only thirteen at the time, so I have an excuse. Who *exactly* is the "we" that will "pay any price" and "bear any burden"? The answer is: The "we" is "us," the ruled-over, who "pay" for and "bear" those burdens that "they," the rulers, want us to think are so important. "We," I repeat, "we" is the politician-magician's verbal wand of misdirection, like Houdini's gesture to distract the audience as he gets ready to saw his lady assistant in half. Few would imagine that something as mundane as pronouns could be so tricky and slippery. That is what makes them so useful. I don't know who wrote this, but this "pledge" should never have been made: Pretending to carry it out would bring the destruction of "liberty," not its success.

The Bay of Pigs was certainly an ominous beginning for JFK's "New Frontier" Presidency. But he recovered with considerable panache — shagging Chicago Mob boss Sam Giancana's moll, Judith Campbell Exner, diddling Hollywood hotties, Marylin Monroe and Angie Dickenson, and splashing around with hookers in the White House swimming pool. Oh, yes, and playing white-knuckle, nuclear-war chicken with Nikita Khrushchev. All the while, Fidel Castro was going flat-out ape-shit in Havana, jumping up and down, furious with Khrushchev's ("no cojones") retreat, hoping that Cuba was going to be ground-zero for WWIII. *Götterdämmerung*, Latin-style. Who could separate the cops from the robbers in this bizarre movie script?

I remember that October 1962 night. With Mom, Dad, and my little sister, I watched President Kennedy on our black-and-white TV as he showed us the aerial shots of nuclear missiles nestled in Cuba. Oh, God! Mom was beside herself; Dad didn't react. I was fifteen, wishing I'd lost my cursed virginity and wondering, with so few prospects immediately available, if there was time left before I went radioactive.

Overshadowed by the flashy President and mostly ignored by the media was the cornpone Vice President of the United States. His "style" was in stark contrast to the slick Hyannis Port crew. I remember how he set off a storm of protest from animal lovers, lifting his pet beagle up by his ears to pose for AP photographers. Senator Everett Dirksen gave him hell for that. Then, there's a great picture of him hoisting his shirt up and showing off his recent gallbladder incision to reporters on the White House lawn.

LBJ's enormous ego took a daily hammering as JFK's

Vice President. He felt the sting of their condescension — his humble west-Texas origins in contrast to JFK's Boston pedigree, his Pulitzer, and glamorous Hollywood entourage. In his self-pitying, lubricated cups, he was heard once complaining about JFK's pampered life: He got to go to Harvard, and "I had to go to a crappy little Texas college."

Late in 1963, LBJ's chaffing, humiliating submission to the Kennedy mystique was about to end. Bobby Baker, his trusted fixer, pimp, and general errand boy from his Senate days, was just two weeks away from spilling his guts about Johnson's boundless immersion in corruption before a House Committee hearing. This was, just coincidentally, at the time when President Kennedy was on a tour in Dallas, Texas. The trip was substantially planned by LBJ himself, by the way. The President ended up as target practice in his limousine convertible. The First Lady was captured gruesomely by Abe Zapruder's video camera recording as she climbed out on the trunk to retrieve a piece of his shattered skull. Her husband was laid low by — take your choice — a commie loser or right-wing nut, blazing away with a $19.95 mail order Italian rifle, who was — take your choice — alone or with help from — multiple choice here — the CIA, J. Edgar Hoover, LBJ, the Mafia, commies, right-wing anti-commies, the Russians, Fidel Castro, the Lone Ranger and Tonto, some combination of the above.

With "Landslide Lyndon" — sarcasm denoting the 87-vote margin from a cemetery in a little southwest town that put him in the Senate in 1948 — as POTUS, surprise, surprise, the House hearing with his gofer-pimp-fixer, Bobby, was scratched. I remember watching the Bobby Baker, Billie Sol Estes scandals hit the news shortly *before* the assassination, then wondering why it quickly disappeared *after* it. This was my earliest experience of the way "the memory hole" works for the folks who manipulate "the news" to please the powerbrokers. Draw your own conclusions on that highly relevant item of interest that continues to rile up the folks in the "who-killed-Kennedy" publishing houses, still in high-gear even though, for the general population, it is far down that particular memory hole. Just the fact that there are, still, so many seemingly plausible suspects who wanted the over-his-head JFK outfitted for wings and dispatched to the hereafter tells you something about how corrupt things had gotten and on the way to worse. JFK to LBJ to RMN — bad…real bad…sigh!

CHAPTER EIGHT

…What Really Happened with JFK?…

JFK's murder was a profoundly traumatic event for me. I'm deeply, permanently sorry that he got killed. His assassination profoundly changed the nation in ways that took decades to unfold. The history of that event still lingers in a strangely unresolved disturbing manner that casts dark shadows over so many places.

But forget "Camelot" and the loathsome, suck-up "journalist" Teddy White, who conceived and peddled this lame, smelly horseshit that still sticks to the soles of our shoes. Let's choke on the ugly truth for a change: The guy was a reckless, sex-addled, amphetamine junkie, who would never have been President if his dad hadn't connived with Dick Daley and the Chicago machine to get JFK the votes he needed to offset the downstate returns, carry Illinois, and edge out five-o'clock shadowed, jowly Nixon in the Electoral College.

Which leads to a little piece of advice I must pause to offer: Don't even scratch the surface of the interest you might have on the haloed lives of our so-called "betters" — the moral authorities, the heralded saints of political leadership, the goodie-two-shoes of philanthropy, the journalists, professors, and intellectuals — if rampant corruption, rank hypocrisy, betrayal, and shameless dishonesty bother you. None of them hold up for a long look: The longer you linger, the higher you go, and the greater the accolades, the uglier it gets.

Me? In 1969, I was focused on my favorite scoundrel of the moment, Richard Milhouse Nixon. For the soon-draft-eligible, he was the super scary guy, whose career went from: "I come before you tonight as a candidate for the Vice Presidency and as a man whose honesty — and integrity — has been questioned" (Checkers speech, 1952) to "You won't have Nixon to kick around anymore" (1962) to "I am not a crook" (1973). These, anecdotally, suggest his inevitable trajectory on a rail of corruption, and they capture some of the more intriguing sides of Nixon's career and personality. When he wasn't hastily back peddling away from scandals he'd touched off, he was feeling sorry for himself.

Nixon was a guy who had a lot to do with my future, specifically one that I hoped would involve staying alive a few more years — and with all my essential parts intact. He was trying to defuse the growing anti-war, anti-draft fury attached to the Vietnam War. It was the war launched by JFK, on the advice of the demented General Maxwell Taylor, expanded by LBJ, and completely fucked up and lied about by the highly touted genius "Whiz Kid," Secretary of Defense Robert McNamara.

Remember: The higher up you go, the uglier it gets. So, I'm going to here ask you to pause and gird yourself for a lethal dose of ugly. Begin by puzzling yourself about the "Defense" part of Secretary Bob's title. I remember how he looked — steely-eyed, with the round, steel-rimmed glasses, hair slicked back, with that precision part, and a chiseled face

— Mr. Rationality and Efficiency. Then, ask yourself how waging war in an agrarian country about the size of Arizona, on the other side of the world, had anything thing to do with defending the United States of America.

But, keep this in mind while you do. Maybe it's the most important thing I want to say in this entire, non-self-serving, humble confession. The one form of corruption that is pervasive and yet imperceptible is the worst corruption of all. It's the corruption of language, like those little, fake "we," "we," "we's" in JFK's inaugural pep-talk. Words are the vehicles of thought. Manipulating, perverting them (the words), twisting their original meanings into their opposites makes it easier to change and control the way people think and to manipulate them (the people).

Word corruption lets the lads in charge forego the cumbersome thumbscrews, the labor camps, the firing squads — in a word — the naked, physical coercion. Physically breaking people is messier, ugly, more expensive and challenging than a bit of creative wordsmithing behind a propaganda barrage. Think of it as *coercion* (expensive and wasteful) giving way to *corruption* (less expensive and more efficient) and *collusion* (the grease that makes the machinery of power operate for the benefit of the silent partners). Joe and JoAnn Sixpack have to earn a living, raise their kids, and pay their taxes. They don't have the time or the inclination to ponder the meaning of the favorite slippery words and phrases that get massaged and pretzel-twisted up by politicians, like "freedom," "democracy," "justice," "our values," and "worse than Hitler." The full-time job of the impresarios running our Opera buffa of a "government" is to prove Abe Lincoln wrong: We *can* "fool all the people we pretend to serve all of the time." They keep the bread-and-circus going. The snake oil pitches are professional. The show is entertaining enough to keep the little people distracted. The boys and girls at the top devote their time and energy to customizing their whoppers, polishing and streamlining their fictions, and making up bald-face lies that sound like the God's truth.

If people come to *think* that your devious, dishonest, schemes are wholesome, legitimate, and for the "public good," you don't need that cumbersome, expensive apparatus to force them to go along with the crooked, self-serving stuff you want them — they always say "we;" always watch out for that word — to pay for in blood and treasure. "The whole aim of practical politics," H. L. Mencken astutely noted, "is to keep the populace alarmed (and hence clamorous to be led to safety) by an endless series of hobgoblins, most of them imaginary."

Back to that weasel word, "Defense," as attached to "Secretary" in Bob's prestigious title to belabor this critical point. That word encourages you to *think* that it's just okey-dokey for Bob to conscript your kid, teach him to salute, hand him a rifle, and send him ten thousand miles away to get killed in a jungle because…? Well, because you've come to "think" that your son will be "defending" something very important. Mission accomplished: no threats or secret police needed. After all, someone perched high-up above, calling himself "the Secretary of Defense" and reporting to the President of the United States, wouldn't be about anything other than defense, would he? He wouldn't be putting your son in harm's way and asking him to kill perfect strangers, people he never had any beef with, for anything other than the noblest of reasons, would he? We know that these guys never lie to us, don't we? "Read my lips. No new taxes." "I never had sex with that woman." "If you like your doctor, you can keep your doctor." Sure.

CHAPTER NINE

...I Still Want to Know

C orruption is my specialty. I know it when I see it. I want to go on a bit more with this corruption of language business because there is a connecting thread moving through it related to our "Defense Secretary." The "Secretary of Defense" used to be the "Secretary of War." The title was changed by the National Security Act of 1947. What's the big deal with that?

"Defense" loads up with more positive connotations than "war," right?

> *War, huh, yeah*
> *What is it good for?*
> *Absolutely nothing*
> *War, huh, yeah*
> *What is it good for?*
> *Absolutely nothing*
> *Say it again...*
>> Edwin Starr, "War (What is it good for?)"

No, we don't need to say it again. Twice through with the "huh's" and "yeah's makes the overly obvious point. Can't say as I cared much for the grunting that launched this popular and thoroughly retarded piece of vulgarity wafting out of the radios in the early 1970s. But, yeah, huh, yeah, we're all against war, aren't we? Yet, no one could figure out why, even though "all we are saying is give peace a chance," somehow, Nixon never got the memo from John and dimwit Yoko until the damage was done.

But you can see what the conmen were doing with this change in nomenclature — something government apparats do a lot to throw us off the trail. It's just more of the magic show, misdirection to keep us from catching on to what they are up to. War is bad, but it's ok — righteous, even — when you are *defending* yourself and servicing slippery abstractions like "democracy," "our values," and the current go-to, "human rights."

But bear with me a little longer, sports fans. This thread of word-corruption continues in a blockbuster way. Nothing tops "Security" in the Orwellian "National Security Act" — legislation drafted by democracy-despising Allan Dulles himself — which, among other things, authorized — are you ready? — the creation of the CIA, a secret organization that has been in continuous mutiny against the American people since the day of its creation. This organization, created to strengthen "our democracy," is run by Brahmins nobody voted for, who despise the demos and tolerate annoyances like elections as long as they rubber stamp the secret boardroom plans of the smart set. From the beginning, the CIA has been accountable only to itself — planning and conducting assassinations and whimsically toppling foreign governments the bosses don't like and installing ones they do are shrouded forever in secrecy.

You might care to ask: How does secret spying power, wielded by mysterious guys in trench coats with the resources of a great big government, enhance my "security?" The answer is: Well, maybe it does, and maybe Santa Claus will drop down the chimney this Christmas. But, to believe that these guys with no accountability, oodles of power, limitless resources, massive egos, and their own personal agendas, have the humility, wisdom, and benevolence to look out for our — your — interest would be a bigger leap of faith.

Unless you are an utterly delusional optimist with no clue as to how human nature works, "secure" is not remotely how this event should make you feel. Even some of FDR's Brain Trusters were temporarily disturbed by the secrecy of the CIA, including Secretary of State Dean Acheson. Acheson was a chief architect of the post-WWII interventionist, bring-democracy-to-the-world foreign policy. He executed FDR's secret plan to maneuver the Japanese into attacking Pearl Harbor. The joint American-British-Dutch oil embargo cut off 95 percent of Japanese oil supplies. The aim was to escalate the crisis. It worked.

In 1944, Acheson was the State Department's head delegate to Breton Woods. Woods led us down road to the IMF, the World Bank, and what became the World Trade Organization, all transnational organizations concocted to give American politicians handles to meddle all over the world. Put this in the category of "do-gooder corruption." That's some of the worst. It's always lathered up with moralistic bombast and financed with money extracted from the little people. The CIA, apparently, was scary for even an eager make-everyone-like-me Acheson. He warned President Truman that neither he nor the President — nor anybody else — would have a clue as to what it, the CIA, was really doing. If a proposal to abolish the CIA were submitted to a national referendum, I'd wager that it was pass with an overwhelming majority. In post-democracy America, that will never happen.

I'm not quite finished yet with McNamara, one of the chief villains of my time — and probably beyond. It would be fitting to place a mummy of him in Madame Tussauds wax museum of famous blackguards.

Installed as Mr. Defense, he, apparently, thought that what had worked for him at the Ford Motor Company — "Systems Analysis" — would magically turn Vietnam, politics-wise, into Switzerland. Hey, big cars, little yellow people with funny, pointed hats tending to their rice paddies, what could be an important difference? For McNamara, people were not that much different than cars — just another slightly more complicated interchangeable "unit." You count them, analyze them, and manipulate them until you get everything to work out just the way you wanted it to be, including killing a lot of them off, if that's what your formulas dictate. He was a data-driven guy. What can possibly go wrong?

Secretary Bob did such a terrific job of saving Vietnam from the commies that they later on put him in charge of — what else? — The World Bank. This was the perfect next career move for Bob, a well-deserved promotion. The World Bank, like the IMF, is, as I said, one of those post-WWII, highly ambitious, "good intention" inventions — "end poverty," in this case — best administered by those highly skilled at pretending to be the latest, greatest humanitarian. You know the type. They're the oligarchs who think that their failures occurred because they didn't have quite enough power. They imagine themselves doing "the Lord's work" — by doing what? By wasting vast sums of somebody else's money, throwing oodles of it at third-world kleptocrats who pretend to use it for "the public good" while moving into Swiss banks whatever they don't spend on their mistresses and armored Mercedes. McNamara made it to age ninety-three, giving conclusive proof to that old adage: "Only the good die young."

"I have a plan" Nixon, once elected and busy building his

enemies list, began winding down the war. But, in his typical Tricky Dick, statesman-like fashion, the secret plan was to drag out for years what he knew from the beginning was a lost cause — for political purposes. More American soldiers, not to mention Vietnamese, would get killed. As Country Joe McDonald at Woodstock belted it out:

> Come on, mothers, throughout the land,
> Pack your boys off to Vietnam
> Come on, fathers, and don't hesitate
> To send your sons off before it's too late
> And you can be the first ones in your block
> To have your boy come home in a box

But, who cares, says Nixon, when you can brag about achieving "peace with honor" — almost on a par, joke-wise, with FDR's "Four Freedoms" speech in 1941 that lots of American soldiers were soon to be killed for. I'm still, here in the slammer, looking forward to experiencing my "freedom from fear" (the guards and the inmates) and freedom from want" (want to be out of here). Defending these sorts of "freedoms" meant that the U.S. military establishment could go almost anywhere anytime it pleased, which was the whole point.

With the exception of the White House Plumbers, Nixon had an eye for talent. He worked his magic with the help of that lying, devious, treacherous, pompous weasel, Henry Kissinger. Not content with wrecking Vietnam, Nixon and Kissinger bombed the bejesus out of Cambodia — more helpless peasants and their fields needed incinerating. After everything got out-of-control hopeless, they hightailed it out, clearing a path for one of the biggest psychopaths in the history of the planet, Brother Number One, Pol Pot, and his Khmer Rouge homicidal goons to move in and take over. In an amazingly short time, they turned the bombed-out remains of what was once beautiful country into a vast, grisly cemetery, decorated with mountains of skulls. In their romance with mass-murder, they managed to butcher about a quarter of their fellow countrymen before the Vietnamese intervened and ousted them.

Mr. Nobel "Peace Prize Laureate" — how is that for words coming to mean their opposite? — left government "service" and — this will shock you — launched a highly profitable government-access-peddling "business." "Kissinger Associates Inc.," the retired Secretary described as "an international geopolitical consulting firm that assists its clients in identifying strategic partners and investment opportunities and advising them on government relations" — perfect choice of weasel words that put "the odor of sanctity" on insider profiteering and influence peddling.

It would have been entertaining and edifying to be a fly on the wall and experience Henry with his Dr. Strangelove accent and robotic stamp in "consulting" action. Imagine him dispensing the fruits of his wisdom to some keffiyeh-bedecked Saudi billionaire prince, helping him steer his mountains of petrol dollars to useful "friends" in the U.S. government and the arms industry and to get his favorite worthless, playboy son into the Harvard business school.

In case you were ever able to indulge that fantasy, you'd still need a special lexicon to translate the mellifluous Kissinger-speak into standard, recognizable English. Being a career conman myself, with a trained ear, I can help with this: I developed the proprietary translation code — a complete manual, soon to be available for purchase on Amazon. Here are a few key phrases and lead-ins you can use to grasp how essential and useful such a lexicon might be for understanding the nuts and bolts of lucrative geopolitical consulting for retired diplomats.

Kissinger: "Let me be perfectly clear on this."

Translation: "What I am going to say will be couched in terms sufficiently flexible and ambiguous as to give me plausible deniability in the highly unlikely event that things go astray, in which case, you'll be on your own."

Kissinger: "Yes, potential strategic partners can sometimes be intractable in this challenging business. But I think with the right approach and a sufficient amount of *your* resources invested in *our* efforts, they can be persuaded to move in the direction *we* desire." [Follow the pronouns]

Translation: "I'm going to have to call in my markers from some very high rollers I know in order to set them up to receive the bribes you will need to pay to get you the kind of access you are asking for. Bottom line: It's going to be expensive."

Kissinger: "There will be some significant challenges we will have to deal with, but I have a great deal of experience in assisting my clients clear these hurdles. I can get you where you want to be while you remain confident and comfortable."

Translation: "What we are contemplating is totally unethical and illegal, but trust me: I know exactly what I am doing."

At the conclusion of one of his "consultations," you can then imagine the former Secretary of State leaning back in his Arper Aston Executive chair, relaxing that poker face a bit, and musing with some of his "associates." After a sip of Germain-Robin Select Barrel XO Brandy from his ARC Excalibur snifter: "You know, I really admired that old bag, what's her name, Leona Helmsley. My favorite line from her was: 'We don't pay taxes. Only the little people pay taxes.' Well, I can do better than that Leona, baby. We don't follow the rules. Laws and regulations are for the little people. What do you think, guys? Dick would like that. Teddy would love it, I'll bet. Uh, now that I think about it, so would most of the people over in Congress and the State Department I peddle influence, uh, I mean, I consult with."

I'm not sure what "little people" Mr. "investment opportunity," savvy Kissinger had in mind, but I occasionally think about the "little" South Vietnamese people in Saigon, loyal to their American occupiers over the years They were abandoned to face their revenge-minded neighbors and relatives from the north, who swept down in serious payback mode when we cut bait and bugged out of there after years of bombing and napalming. Probably, I'll bet, not many of their names ended up on Henry Kissinger's rolodex of "strategic partners" to match with his "investment strategies."

I could go on a long time with this, but it's a real downer, and I think you get the picture. Henry, last checking, is still kicking at ninety-five. The devil, I guess, has higher standards than Nixon did.

CHAPTER TEN

Philosophy Bakes No Bread

Philosophy consists very largely of one philosopher arguing that all others are jackasses. He usually proves it, and I should add that he also usually proves that he is one himself.

H. L. Mencken

"The reason why university politics are so vicious and treacherous is because so little is at stake." Henry Kissinger, among others, is sometimes credited with this. He would know.

College, for me, was over in 1969 — poof went my draft deferment. The bodies of American soldiers, however, were still coming back from Vietnam. I tried to get into the Navy. No interest. National Guard? *Nyet!* Long waiting list. No chance, even with the Coast Guard. Beat it, son!

Canada? Rumor was that the stolid Canadians were not all that thrilled about long-haired American draft dodgers lounging around Toronto, Montreal, and Vancouver, smoking dope and drawing welfare. Imagine them trying to make it through the first verse of "O Canada."

O Canada!

Our home and native land!
True patriot love in all of us command.
With glowing hearts we see thee rise,
The True North strong and free!
From far and wide.

No, I can't imagine it; no way. These guys were not exactly the sort of up-and-comers the Canucks would be eager to have marrying their daughters. Plus, Michigan was as cold a place as I ever wanted to live.

Sometimes, though, the planets align in your favor. Nixon was trying to move to an all-volunteer army and hoping to get the anti-war students, by then a considerable political force, off his case and give him time to pull of his "Vietnamization" of this idiotic war. This got another 20,000 American soldiers killed. But he still needed the draft to maintain the manpower level, with enough young men as cannon fodder to keep filling the body bags coming back from Vietnam until he could finagle his "Peace with honor" and put that ridiculous lipstick on his public relations pig. By then, most of the fighting-aged guys, like me, wanted no part of this slow-motion train wreck. The slogan "Girls say yes to boys who say no" was below the picture of a gorgeous, slinky, long-haired girl with a "come hither" look on a popular anti-war poster put out by the draft-resistance movement during that time. A lot of guys were in keeping with Phil Ochs' "The Draft Dodger Rag:

Oh, I'm just a typical American boy
From a typical American town
I believe in God and Senator Dodd
And a-keepin' ol' Castro down
And when it came my time to serve,
I knew "better dead than red"
But when I got to my old draft board, buddy,

This is what I said:
"Sarge, I'm only eighteen, I got a ruptured spleen
And I always carry a purse
I got eyes like a bat, and my feet are flat,
And my asthma's getting worse
Yes, think of my career, my sweetheart dear,
And my poor old invalid aunt
Besides, I ain't no fool, I'm a-goin' to school,
And I'm working in a DEE-fense plant"

Nixon, no doubt, caught the drift of that clever tune and moved to put a lottery in place to keep his military conscription machine churning way. But this one was based on a random drawing, using birth dates rather than the rich-kid-favoring deferment system that put the poor black kids and young coal miners in the rice paddies toting M16s. This made the draft less of an anti-war rallying cause. My number came up a magnificent 300. I was safely out of the reach of Selective Service, a "get out of jail free card" for the army and Vietnam.

How does it feel
To be without a home
With no direction home
Like a complete unknown
Like a rolling stone?
Bob Dylan, "Like a Rolling Stone"

The lyrics captured my state of mind and predicted my future.

I wasn't so much of a rolling stone, however, as a drifting canoe. Making my future questionable — less than promising, actually — was the fact that, in college, after drifting aimlessly and trying to find a suitable major to push me barely across the finish line to graduation, I proudly chose the most useless of majors, philosophy. Other possibilities, like petroleum engineering, accounting, or landscape architecture would have led to more certain, predictable employment and respectable professional advancement, not to mention worthwhile contributions to society. However, "useful," "worthwhile," and "respectable," I was convinced at the time, were for schmucks over thirty, one of the many categories of people for whom I had a deep and abiding distrust.

Philosophy, so splendidly impractical and pointless — that is what made it so appealing to me and so appalling for most people when I told them.

"Phul-lhaaas-ophee? What the hell kind of a job is *that* going to get you?"

"That depends," I would answer, "on how you define the word 'job.'"

Well, that gives you some sense of what a completely unserious person I had managed to turn myself into.

In the classroom, philosophy typically caught you up in intense but inconclusive — even better — wrangling about what the "Greats" like Aristotle, Thomas Aquinas, Immanuel Kant, and David Hume were actually trying to say about burning issues of the day such as the existence of God, the meaning life, and the basis of morality. Which, for me, as I reflect back upon it, was an inexcusably stupid waste of my limited brain power. I didn't give a rat's ass about God — an existing or non-existing one. I believed that life had no meaning beyond taking as much as you could possibly get and avoiding responsibility. "Morality," I concluded, was just an abracadabra word that kept those 3-C's away from public scrutiny, a word disguising the claptrap that shaped the anodyne, feel-good lingo of politicians, preachers, and educators always trying to slip us a rusty musket. It worked for Nixon — remember his morally superior "silent majority" — until Watergate snagged him, and it worked for the

Democrat "Champions of Women" like Teddy Kennedy and members of the so-called fourth-estate (journalists and media-types), the self-infatuated phonies who are always pretending to speak "truth to power."

After hundreds or even thousands of years of no one being able to nail down what these profound thinkers were trying to say, all this pretentious chatter, I now must confess, was just a highfalutin waste of valuable time. Philosophy was a hobby for navel gazers and nerds or for guys like me who went down that path because they thought that chicks dig dudes who can do a "real deep" shuck and jive and throw around fifty-cent words like "epistemology," "ontology," and "analytic-synthetic dichotomy." This sort of hamster-wheel cogitation seems to stimulate the brain of a certain kind of social misfit. I'm not opposed to it, just like I'm not opposed to greasy haired ne'er-do-wells who hang out on street corners and play hacky sack all day or women who decide to get breast implants. But nobody should get any encouragement for it, not to mention getting paid for teaching other people how to do it.

There was another even bigger problem with philosophy than just its impracticality. Many of the big-name contemporary philosophers were disreputable slugs and hypocrites — *Wasser predigen und Wein trinken*, as the Germans like to express their contempt for how their "moral" superiors operate: "Preach water; drink wine." My purpose in this confession is to uncover corruption, so I must bear down with ferocity on a couple of these fraudsters. They had enormous influence on impressionable young people. I foolishly took them and their ideas seriously. Here, you will detect some rancor and bitterness. I must be indulged. It is necessary to give you a clearer picture of how and why I went off the rails.

CHAPTER ELEVEN

Bought and Paid For...

Hell is other people.

Jean Paul Sarte, "No Exit"

The worst of the odious bunch was the Parisian, Jean Paul Sartre. Sartre was the intellectual's intellectual, ideal as a theorist for the cultural sewer that the 1960s turned into, the one that I marinated myself in. Sartre produced reams of unreadable bilge that aspiring sophisticates in college dorms and faculty lounges in the U.S. during the 1950s and 1960s would flaunt as deep thought. Sartre's magnum opus, *Being and Nothingness*, was a massive 700 pages in tiny print, so dense and impenetrable no one I met ever made his way completely through it. I got to page sixty. Yet, his Existentialist baloney was all the rage for wannabe intellectuals and aimless, louche malcontents like me.

At that time, JP was the hippest of hip counter-culture figures lounging about on Paris's Left-Bank with that affected pose of moral superiority so characteristic of effete French lefties. It was a pose copied by many American intellectuals whom I encountered. Some of them even took to wearing berets, hanging out in coffee shops, dispensing sonorously decorated warnings about the resurgence of fascism.

Sartre embodied everything that was wrong with 1960s-era intellectuals, an "everything" that included an enthusiastic embrace of sexual predators. JP, his girlfriend, feminist Simone de Beauvoir, together with the equally loathsome philosopher, Jacques Derrida signed a petition to decriminalize pedophilia. These moral philosophers apparently had decided that there was nothing wrong with adults seducing young children because such prohibitions were bourgeoise "hang ups," part of the traditional culture they were in the business of dismantling.

I called myself an Existentialist, then, because, in part, it seemed so anti-bourgeois and cool. Counter-culture was all the rage — goatees, black turtlenecks, and sandals as the standard costume in early and mid-1960s. I could make neither heads nor tails of what it took to be one, other than to act incurably bored and try to depress everyone you meet with your rehearsed, jargon-laden babble about how meaningless life is. No one needed Jean Paul Sartre or any of his silly impersonators to figure this out. For me, it was a juvenile act that I enjoyed putting on. Announcing breathlessly…roll the drums…"I'm an Existentialist." That would shock or at least irritate conservative Christians and button-down, country-club, corporate types, and/or get back at Mom and Dad for being too strict when growing up and making me go to Sunday School and Youth for Christ meetings. They had no idea what it was other than it was not a path to stable family life, religious devotion, and a steady job. I was trying to avoid all three of these things. One of Sartre's more memorable lines was "Hell is other people," which I thought captured one of his few genuine insights, one that I could fully embrace.

In the Spring of 1968, I was caught up in the heady student radicalism sweeping across the U.S. and Western

Europe. I borrowed some money, which, now that I mention it, I still need to repay. Off I went to Paris for a semester to get the nonsense straight from the horse's mouth.

Once again, I arrived in a foreign country when all hell was breaking loose; French students were in full insurrection-riot mode, trying to bring down the government. Why not? Knowing nothing about France, this seemed perfectly fine to me. It was great fun. The riots were epical and later inspired the Rolling Stones "Street Fighting Man."

> *Hey so my name is called Disturbance*
> *I'll shout and scream*
> *I'll kill the king; I'll rail at all his servants…*

Yeah, except the radicals had killed the King about a hundred and seventy-five years earlier. He reappeared a short time later, in a more sinister, lethal guise, as Napoleon Bonaparte. But, as Henry Ford put it so eloquently: "History is bunk." I did end up as "Disturbance," pitching chunks of street concrete at the French cops instead of reading. Also, I was at the Sorbonne when Sartre appeared to egg the students on to ramp up the vandalism. Not that he himself would go out and put himself at risk of arrest. Later, in a secure perch on Radio Luxembourg, he accused his own generation of "cowardice, sluggishness, and servility…Violence is the only thing remaining to the students who have not yet entered into their fathers' system and who do not want to enter into it." That was vintage JP. Violence is great fun, particularly when you can vicariously enjoy the show from safe, faraway digs and act morally superior to all the schmucks from "my generation." He had no kids himself but was eager to see other peoples' act like criminals.

> *Ev'rywhere I hear the sound*

Of marching, charging feet, boy
'Cause summer's here and the time is right
For fighting in the street, boy
　　　The Rolling Stones, "Street Fighting Man"

Having experienced him in person, I can say that Sartre himself was a real piece of work. An ugly little bastard with bad breath, a lousy haircut, bug eyes, and a pasty, pitted complexion. It's worth pausing in the description of this squirrely little eye-sore and lift this inspiring snippet from a *Playboy Magazine* interview he did in 1965.

Ok, it's *Playboy*, so the interviewer has to get the philosopher to expound on...what else?

"It's true that I have always tried to surround myself with women who are at least agreeable to look at. Feminine ugliness is offensive to me. I admit this, and I'm ashamed of it. But the reason is simple. Even at its most formal level, even when there's complete indifference, the association of a man with a woman always has sexual implications. An ugly woman evokes, like all women, that special pleasure we get from being in a woman's company, but she spoils it by her ugliness. Alas. When you have the man-woman relation interfered with by ugliness — provoked and denied, well, it's a very awkward business."

Ah, yes, very awkward, Mr. Philosopher, but, hey, you have to endure all of those ugly ladies who should know not to "evoke" that species of femininity that "spoils" your fun. I don't know if he said this in French or English, but, in either language, he comes off as a pretentious bullshitter. Remember, this was 1965. Mr. Existentialist hadn't experienced the molten volcanic lava eruption of feminist fury. Had he delivered that little soliloquy today, his existence would — to put it chichi philosophically — no longer precede his essence, or, in a more comprehensible argot: His ass would be grass.

"I'm ashamed"? No, the man was shameless. And, condescending. "Women who are at least agreeable to look at"? I'm guessing that, when the "agreeable" ones got up close, Mr. Existentialist suddenly became a lot more appealing at a safe, intellectual distance. And: "The association of a man with a woman always has sexual implications." Really? Deep thought and firm grasp of the obvious. Yes, but it was good for all those ugly women over there in the land of Gaul to know that an even uglier little philosopher found them offensive, spoiling whatever it was that gave him pleasure — some well-earned revenge. What happens when an ugly, irresistible force meets an uglier, unmovable object? I don't think he ever addressed that most profound of philosophical questions, which should have been at the top of his list. Did he ever look at himself in the mirror?

Throughout his long, miserable career, you could find him slobbering multi-syllabic hosannas over every mass-murdering communist dictator who was coming into vogue. It was Stalin for a while, Mao for a season, and then Castro. Being a wimp, he projected himself onto macho guys. Sartre's wannabes in U.S. universities were passing his leftist dictator worship rituals on to bumpkins like me, who idiotically imagined that someday we'd be doing the dictating.

JP preferred to live in France, where the bourgeois he professed to loath more or less ran the show. Why not? That was where he could find an assortment of intellectual groupies cute enough to keep him entertained. He developed his hip, anti-bourgeois put-on while sucking on his little pipe and parked his flabby ass in Paris cafes with Simone, even during the Nazi occupation. While their courageous buddies in the French Resistance were getting pummeled by the occupying Krauts, little Jean Paul and sassy Simone took it easy, enjoying the comforts of celebrity intellectuals, eating well, drinking, and partying. *Wasser predigen und Wein trinken.*

Post-war, Sartre peddled the fiction of his "Resistance" bravery. "Oooh, life was sooo hard, risky, and dangerous for us with those mean old schnapps-guzzling Herman's and Helmut's all around, and all of Paris smelling like wiener schnitzel instead of fresh croissants; we were soooo principled and brave."

Sartre's plays during the occupation? They easily passed the German censors, and German officers happily attended first-night performances and the post-performance parties. Too bad they didn't have cell phones back then. Perhaps, now we'd have a post-performance party selfie of JP yucking it up with Wehrmacht Colonel Max Müller.

Jean Paul got called on his little reputational shell game. He eventually "fessed" up with a heaping of nauseous, self-serving drivel that captures the hypocrisy and dishonesty of this "great" twentieth century thinker.

"In 1939, 1940, we were terrified of dying, suffering, for a cause that disgusted us. That is, for a disgusting France, corrupt, inefficient, racist, anti-Semite, run by the rich for the rich — no one wanted to die for that, until, well, until we understood that the Nazis were worse."

Well, thank God for those Nazis who loved his plays; otherwise, Sartre might have fallen in with racists and anti-Semites. The only "cause" that didn't disgust JP was himself. The "terrified" Sartre slips up with this chickenshit confession. Mr. Existentialist is nothing but a weak-sphincter scribbler, reduced to trashing his homeland. He happily crapped on the country and the people that made him rich and famous as if he and Simone were the last virtuous couple in awful "rich for the rich" France. Most hard to stomach is the cowardice — physical and intellectual — hiding behind this obscene outpouring of sniveling, ass-covering self-righteousness.

Why all this spleen on some long-dead, phony French intellectual? Yes, I realize that it seems over the top. But corruption is the heart of my confession, and Sartre, more than any 1960s thinker, embodies the intellectual corruption of the times and its horrible contagion. You can see the projection of self-hatred at work with this.

For a true picture of how corrupt the intellectual class had become, I must move from the 1960s and the loathsome Jean Paul Sartre decades forward to one of the brightest of our contemporary philosophers, Judith Butler. I met her in the mid-1990s, at a conference at Berkeley. By that time, "post-modernism" was the latest French import, having displaced Existentialism as fashionable left-wing bilge and also having spawned a new and hideous philosophical dialect that no one outside the initiated could comprehend. Butler, a radical lesbian, was one of the hottest "post-modern" academics, already with a long train of admirers and imitators.

Below, a sample of the post-modern dialect in its most lucid expression. In a few short years, Butler became one of the shining lights of contemporary philosophy, a full professor with a high salary and tenure at the University of California, Berkeley.

Thus:

"The move from a structuralist account in which capital is understood to structure social relations in relatively homologous ways to a view of hegemony in which power relations are subject to repetition, convergence, and rearticulation brought the question of temporality into the thinking of structure, and marked a shift from a form of Althusserian theory that takes structural totalities as theoretical objects to one in which the insights into the contingent possibility of structure inaugurate a renewed conception of hegemony as bound up with the contingent sites and strategies of the rearticulation of power."

I wish I could rearticulate the structural totality of social relations in this mountain of manure in a relatively homologous way. I can't. This kind of word salad is what gets one promotion and tenure — a free ticket to fuck off, if you like, for the rest of your life and get paid — at Berkeley. "Corruption" is the word that comes to mind when you think of this illustrious university where people get paid lots of someone else's money for doing a fake job. The German word for corruption, incidentally, is *Käuflichkeit* — literally, "buyable," — which I really like since it captures the transactional core of what goes on, what is the essence of corruption. Corrupt people are buyable, and what the likes of Sartre and the wannabes like Butler are, above all, is buyable.

But, if you insist on offering tenure to these poseurs, how about doing it this way?

Select three or four couples, moms and dads of kids soon to be going off to college, to be subjected to the likes of Judith, weighted down with Althusserian theory. Bring them in to review the tenure application of Professor Butler. Read to them some of the jewels like the one from above. Then, ask the moms and dads about to plunk down their hard-earned dough to send junior or juniorette off to the Ivy halls: Do you want your kid to come home and talk like this? Would they seem any smarter? Do you think that they would be more knowledgeable, more capable, more likeable, more employable than when you sent them off? No on every single count.

Now, to be fair to the good professor, she might want to step up and interject: "Wait a minute. You could read excerpts from a lot of specialized disciplines, like physics, chemistry, or engineering. To most non-specialists, they would sound like gibberish."

Nice try, fat-salaried, sinecure-squatting Jargon Queen. But that nattering negative, random-word-generating hound of yours won't hunt. Physics, chemistry, and engineering lead to things like bridges that don't collapse, safer cars with backup cameras and airbags, quieter washing machines, faster computers, hair dryers, and deodorants, all things you have no clue as to how they work and could not do without, particularly the last one. What, beyond paid-for junkets to conferences, grad students to sexually harass and fob off your grunt work on, no accountability and schmoozing with your like-minded gaseous charlatan pals, does your gibberish lead to? Anything useful? *Nein!* Entertaining or even mildly amusing? *Nyet!* Just what we thought! *Scher dich!* Beat it, Judith! Take your "question of temporality into the thinking of structure" and go do an honest day's work somewhere.

CHAPTER TWELVE

"I Might Take a Train, I Might Take a Plane"

Say what you will about the Ten Commandments, you must always come back to the pleasant fact that there are only ten of them.

H. L. Mencken

June 1969. I emerged from the intellectual wasteland and the self-indulgence swamps of university life. I was no better — probably a whole lot worse — than when I entered. From 1965 to 1969, anger was exploding through the entire country like a Kansas prairie fire. University students were angry. Drunken fraternity bashes were out; occupying and vandalizing university administration halls was in. Parents were angry at the students for protesting. The cops took their anger out on the protestors with tear gas and clubs. The protestors were angry at the cops. Who couldn't be angry about Vietnam? The civil rights movement turned into a hostile takeover by angry guys like Stokely Carmichael and the poetic H. Rap Brown — "if America don't come around, we're gonna burn it down."

And so, they did. It doesn't get much angrier than a race riot; they were erupting by the dozens in cities all across the country — and the political assassinations. Angry women moved the sexual revolution into high gear. "Men are afraid women will laugh at them: Women are afraid men will kill them." From Margret Atwood — a little angry, I'm guessing. You couldn't go anywhere without meeting angry people who made you even angrier. Righteous anger of the self-righteous species was the "in thing" and highly contagious. And everyone was righteous. That was one of the biggest problems.

Four years of subjection to the sputtering of professors of philosophy, as you can grasp from my ruminations on the likes of Jean Paul Sartre and Judith Butler, plus pretending to be a member of the first generation to perfect the planet, did nothing to equip me for operating in the real world. I had pissed away four years of youth, older but no wiser. The planet and its perfection were no longer high on my list of priorities. I confess they never had been. Attempting to shake off my shackles of self-prolonged, institutionally indulged adolescence and no longer subject to the draft, I realized that I was supposed to get a job, employment of some sort.

Doing what? My grades were lousy, so I couldn't get into law school and be enlisted "legally" to shake people down. But, after four years of esoteric philosophy, I arrived at two shattering un-esoteric truths: Philosophy bakes no bread; money *can* buy happiness, or at least some satisfying simulacrum.

> *The best things in life are free*
> *But you can give them to the birds and bees*
> *I want money*
> *That's what I want…*
>
> Barrett Strong, "Money (That's
> What I Want)"

There had to be a road for me to it — money, that is. Fortunately, I had developed my natural aptitude for fast talking and being able to tell people what they wanted to hear — remember, I always aimed to please. After some false starts and disappointments, I landed a position with an A-rated investment brokerage firm in Kansas City, Missouri. Given my useless college major, and a less than stellar transcript, I also need to mention — ok, confess — that I had taken some "liberties" in drafting the resume that secured my interview with the firm and ultimately the offer of a job with a big starting salary, a position for which I had zero of the required qualifications.

"Creative" resume writing was a highly useful "skill," about the only one I had acquired in college. And not from any of the mostly useless classes I had skated through or the goofy professors in their comfy sinecures whom I tried my best to ignore.

I had a friend, Phil Hart, I met my junior year in academic adolescence who had discovered how careless and sloppy many companies and employers were in vetting their newly hired employees. This provided openings for burgeoning hustlers like me, who weren't afraid to be bold in "inventing" ourselves. These were pre-Internet days, when it was easier to patent "the inventions" and work the three-card monte on the HR doofuses who were supposed to catch the fakers.

Phil looked older than he was. He had mastered a phony but highly effective sophistication that, along with fake-resume creation, would get him in the door of a prospective employer and launched into some well-paying jobs. With his skills, Phil had conned his way into various positions: He was in charge of quality control for a large supermarket chain, worked as an administrative assistant in the Governor's office, and was the director of personnel at the small local hospital, all before reaching the age of twenty-six, a "Great Imposter" sort of a guy. No doubt, he is now high up in education, the government, or a mainline religious denomination. Maybe, he's a Mormon Bishop, a university president, or head of a Federal regulatory agency chasing the female staff around the office and making the lives of the little people miserable.

He was amazing — gifted, even — and took me on as an understudy. He tutored me on how to fake transcripts, make up bogus credentials and professional licenses, and how to bullshit my way through an interview — even how to dress professionally. A real professor, he taught me skills that were useful throughout my entire life.

"Kansas City, here I come. They've got some crazy little women there, and I'm gonna…" Well, ok, I'll be getting to the gritty details on that shortly. A couple of months after my arrival, I started dating a woman I met at an Arts Gala fundraising event at the prestigious Nelson-Atkins Museum of Art. I say "prestigious" not because I have a clue about why that would be, or even if it was true. That's what I was told by a couple of the senior partners in the firm where I worked and affirmed by the eager-beaver staff of the Museum. I learned long ago that any fiction, no matter how far-fetched or preposterous, can transition itself to self-evidently "true" by constant repetition — universities are about the pursuit of knowledge and truth and "All men are created equal" are two spectacular examples of utter nonsense widely embraced.

> *I'm gonna be standing on the corner*
> *Of Twelfth Street and Vine*
> *With my Kansas City baby*
> *And a bottle of Kansas City wine.*
> Little Willie Littlefield, "K.C. Loving"

I must admit: I had no appreciation or knowledge of art and even less interest. When I was a university student, I had a gigantic velvet Elvis stapled to the wall in my bedroom. It cost me all of ten bucks at the Claire County fair. My hippie girlfriend at the time, Stormy — she'd changed her given name from Gwen — picked it out because it was so kitsch.

Conversations of "connoisseurs" of art, particularly so-called "contemporary art," made those of the soporific philosophy professors and fellow students from my university days seem, by comparison, almost lucid, coherent, and remotely stimulating. What could be a better setting for limp-wristed intellectuals, haughty dilettantes, pompous sophisticates, and phony, rich socialites to practice their tedious rituals of preening and self-promotion than an Arts Gala? Where else could one dumpster dive into a "serious" discussion of the wonders of something like a Jackson Pollack painting or an expensive pile of junk — sorry, I mean, a piece of contemporary sculpture?

For philistines like me, it was a challenge. I didn't grow up with sophisticates. Most of my non-Amish neighbors and friends lived on Four Roses and roadkill. Art, for them, was the preferred nickname for "Arthur" — stupid punchline in the joke: "Do you like art? Yes, but Bill's my best friend."

However, being myself an accomplished and agile phony from my philosophy days, I had picked up useful non-verbals to skate me through those tight situations where I had no clue about what anyone was saying. I'd mastered the slow chin stroke with the pursed lips, a slight quizzical, knowing smile, raising the eyebrows, nodding at just the right moment. Plus, under the pressure of that awkward silence when it's your turn to say something profound, you can always dispense a useful banality or filler phrase. "Well…I suppose that depends on your perspective" or "Hmm…good point; I need to consider all the implications." Or, if you are a hopeless suck-up: "That's a very insightful observation; I wouldn't have thought of *that*" — without missing a beat. Most of the pretentious poseurs you have to endure at these events enthuse only about hearing themselves talk. What they crave most is flattery. They are charmed if you just confirm their high self-regard and massage their bloated egos with an obliging nod and a subtle, knowing smile that pushes the fatuous ritual forward to its useless, meaningless conclusion.

The investment firm, my new employer, had been pressured by the persistent, obnoxious museum fundraisers to make a "generous" donation. The firm's president, Bill Bennett, had been scheduled for the formal appearance at the gala to present the donation check and make the obligatory remarks.

However, Bill was also "booked" for a tryst with one of his mistresses — I think, for that particular evening, it was the youngest one — and he was a serious man who knew how to keep his priorities properly aligned. So, he ordered me to go as the firm's junior representative in his place. "You go as my surrogate, Mike. This is something I occasionally ask my new associates to do for me as a...uh...personal favor. I can't drag the wife to these fucking shake-downs. Besides, it's good exposure for you." He told me this as I sat in his office. Then, after a thick blast of cigar smoke, he paused and jabbed his finger at me with my charge: "Be on time, but not early. Look serious, but not somber, for Christ-sake. Hand over the goddamn check and mumble something vague, superficial, and, most importantly, non-controversial — repeat, non-controversial — ok? Don't try to be funny, either — too risky. You might awake and offend one of the old humorless logs they roll into the premises on these snooze fests. The main thing is to satisfy the flunkies who have to promote the place.

Plus, it'll help stroke the egos of the well-heeled patrons — some of our best clients — the ones who write the real big checks to get their names on the donor walls in order to impress their friends and feel good about themselves. Yeah, right, I really do want them to feel good about themselves, of course, but, more importantly, feel *real* good about us." Big grin. "You understand. You don't need to stay to the end. Use your own judgment on that. Be sure to mention the name of the firm as often as you can without being too obvious."

I greatly admired Bill and his candid view of the whole philanthropy racket. I hoped someday to be sitting in his chair, making the happiness of my mistresses my highest priority.

Chapter Thirteen

An Enchanted Evening

Some enchanted evening,
You may see a stranger…
Across a crowded room

Rodgers and Hammerstein,
"Some Enchanted Evening"

Trussed up in an expensive dinner jacket — first time ever in one — I arrived on time, not early. I made my canned spiel — prepared by my secretary — and circulated for a respectable amount of time, making small talk with the stodgy aficionados and a wearying assortment of museum lounge lizards. As I was extracting myself from the clutches of the most tedious pair of habitués I'd ever met and getting ready to leave, my bored eyes suddenly zeroed in on a young woman.

So far, this evening was about as enchanting as a Wednesday evening prayer meeting in the Baptist church basement. But there she was, dead center in my field of vision — in one of the galleries — a blond in a tight, black, strapless dress adorned with a single strand of pearls. Standing alone, she was perched next to a painting and looking just slightly out of sorts, like she was as thrilled to be at this event as much I was, which meant she might be approachable.

I headed over, through that "crowded room." For effect, I paused a moment, glancing at a Henri Matisse, "Woman Seated Before a Black Background" — I repressed a grimace and feigned a studious, interested look — then pulled up in front of Blondie and smiled. She looked back at me somewhat disdainfully and gestured with a little thrust of her sexy chin at the canvas, a six-by-eight solid, black rectangle by Mark Rothko bearing the title "Untitled No. 11, 1963." Yeah, really! It wasn't the sort of anything that would benefit from a title. This was supposedly one of the Nelson-Atkins abstract-expressionist jewels.

"What do you think?" she asked, looking like she didn't much care what I thought.

To be honest, I couldn't tell a "Mark Rothko" from a used fish wrapper. What I was thinking at that moment was an especially unspeakable "guy" sort of thing that, as you can guess, had nothing to do with the painting or with anything remotely connected with the world of art. I paused, hoping I could slip a few slippery syllables of slightly coherent mumbo-jumbo past her and move on to a more rewarding topic like her phone number. Eyebrows lifted, spectacular face fixed in an intimidating question-mark pose — she was waiting… And, and…

Finally…"Very nuanced and expressive," with a lot of drawn-out stress on "expressive," I responded and put on my best "I'm a serious intellectual" pose. "Nuanced" is a fallback word pulled from the mental cheat-sheets of the fake — the only — intellectuals I've learned so much from. It's always a good one to throw in to make the pose halfway believable: "nuanced," a euphemism for what you might more honestly call inherently incomprehensible, "an incoherent, pretentious pile of shit."

"Expressive of what?" she immediately shot back,

wearing a smug little "gotcha" look.

This time a longer pause. Where, if anywhere, to go with this? I was biding for some time to blow out more verbal smog that I could hide behind.

"Well, [pause, uh, ahem] given the, uh, title, or rather the lack of it, I would say that is a subtle invitation to, I'd say [pause and little hesitating circular gesture with the left hand], perhaps, for the viewer entering in a purely phenomenologically way into a state of pre-judgement, to viscerally absorb a soft field of color with hard boundaries, how can I say this [pause, eyes roll upward], a forced movement within the contrasted shapes that turns abstract color into concrete emotion. [Pause, deep breath, exhale] It's amazing, isn't it, what a wide range of powerful emotions you can actually take out of this painting — nihilism, a self-righteous posturing, a cry for…"

"Stop," she groaned and put her hands over her ears, half bent over and laughing derisively. "Knock it off! You've blown the fucking fuse on my bullshit detector. Amazing! More creative and more fun than I get from most of the phonies that hang out in this place. But, come on, dude. Really, do I look stupid?"

No. "Stupid" did not remotely describe how she looked. So, I declined the easy opening for a cheap put down with a faint hope that I could get past the caustic hostility and to a point where I could make some sort of a move.

"I guess I'll take that as a complement of sorts. So, then, what do you think of it?"

"All I see is a slab of canvas with black paint — it doesn't "express" anything that I can imagine."

Well, that took me back a bit.

"Ok, then, uh, if I may ask, why are you standing here looking at it?"

She paused for a long moment and studied me as though she was about to tell me to get lost, and then responded: "My finance was supposed to meet me here about an hour ago. He's a Ph.D. candidate in art history at the University of Kansas — specialty, contemporary European painting and sculpture. He spent a year on a Fulbright at the Musée d'Art Moderne de la Ville in Paris. I was hoping that he might to be able to tell me what's supposed to be so monumentally profound about this "famous" hunk of canvas because I haven't a clue. Why someone — anyone — would put out the big bucks to put something this monumentally insipid on their living room wall rather than wallpaper or a Norman Rockwell knockoff is a mystery to me."

"Really?" I said, then thinking to myself: "You don't meet many hot chicks with such a hard, sarcastic edge very often, particularly at dull gigs like this, where everyone is supposed to act sophisticated fake-nice and slobber over some wonderful artwork, rattle off predictable clichés, and hope that someone with something to offer — sex, for starters — will be impressed."

What, I wondered, was up with the AWOL boyfriend? I was hoping that maybe he'd gotten into a car wreck or something.

"Well," she sighed, "looks like he has stood me up...again, the second time in a week."

"He must be insane or blind," I said.

She laughed again, but just a little, and then, with considerable irritation: "Hey, knock it off, already, whoever you are. Is there anyone around here that does straight lines rather than bullshit?"

What did I have to lose now? Probably strike three, but I thought: "What the hell, I'll swing for the fences."

"Ok," I said, "neither one of us seems to be enjoying

ourselves here, so why don't we get out now and grab a drink in a quiet place somewhere nearby? How's that for a straight, no-bullshit line? The right lounge atmosphere, quiet conversation, and a little Chivas Regal tend to bring out the more genuine, less phony side of me. What's your name, by the way? Mine's Pablo Picasso."

"Rachael."

I guess my company and brassy, smartass schtick was preferable to her than staring at splashes of paint, standing alone, and feeling nasty about getting serially stiffed by her stupid-ass, artsy boyfriend. So, Rachael and Pablo slipped off and away and settled into the corner booth of a quiet little bar down the street, mercifully removed from the grandiloquent babbling brook of KC's aesthetes. A couple glasses of Chardonnay made her a lot friendlier. After a couple of Scotches for me? She was even more beautiful. Thank you, Bill.

CHAPTER FOURTEEN

Enchanted Days

Who can explain it,
Who can tell you why?
Fools give you reasons,
Wise men never try

Rodgers and Hammerstein,
"Some Enchanted Evening"

For sure: Fools are always full of reasons, which is why you should always be suspicious of anyone who offers them.

Turns out that the beauteous Rachael was an up-and-coming civil rights lawyer not long out of the Stanford Law School. As in many other parts of the country, there was racial unrest galore in Kansas City in the late 1960s. "Civil rights" were all the rage with the morally enlightened. Not me. I was not paying close attention those days. Reaching moral enlightenment remained solidly at the bottom of my to-do list. To the plight of the oppressed, I was intentionally indifferent. I simply preferred to stay out of their ranks. My brief encounter with oppression in the DR was enough for a lifetime. Not that I cared about or liked the oppressors — the opposite. It's just that thinking about the oppressed is a downer, and helping them is a drain on your precious resources. Worse, your efforts are likely to turn around and bite you. "No good deed goes unpunished" was the golden rule I lived by. I was intensely interested in Rachael, so I pretended to care — for a bit.

Rachael was a "red diaper baby," the only daughter of communist parents. Country Joe McDonald, mentioned above, was a red diaper baby. Remember him? I saw him and his band, Country Joe and the Fish, at the Woodstock festival in 1969. He was a smash hit with the delicious anti-Vietnam War sarcasm in "I feel like I'm fixin' to die rag." Somewhere, I read that he complained that growing up in a communist family was pretty tough. I wouldn't know. I don't think I met a real, live communist until I went off to the university. There wasn't much for them to do in Podunkville, Michigan, where I grew up, and a communist there would have been as popular as the Grand Kleagle at an NAACP fundraiser.

The first communist I recall knowing was my English Professor, Sander Levin, who taught a Shakespeare class I was required to take my second year at the university. Professor Levin was a slovenly, chain-smoking, foul-tempered Jew from somewhere originally on the east coast. He was rumored to have been married three or four times, the latest to a gorgeous legal secretary who dumped him for a named-senior partner in the firm where she worked — twenty years her senior, he was a tax-litigating shark with a villa outside of Wimereux, Pas-de-Calais. Supposedly, it took the cuckolded Professor Levin a year and an expensive, Betty Ford-type detox program to recover from the blow to his masculinity, such as it was.

A brilliant Princeton Ph.D., he could reel off from memory entire acts of the old Bard's plays. Stuck temporarily in the Midwest and having to teach literature to a bunch of hicks off the farms and out of small towns, like me, was a cruel exile for Professor Levin. He compensated by turning his teaching into a form of raging psychological projection. Educational, it was not; entertaining, absolutely. You could smoke anywhere in those days, even in the classrooms. He spent the entire semester pacing back and forth across the front of the room self-engaged in a non-stop furious monologue aimed at McCarthyites, paranoid right-wingers, Vietnam War criminals, and the stupidity of traditional Christians like Dad. All the while, he would puff away, blow out billows of cigarette smoke, and flip ashes carelessly all over the front of his rumpled suit and soup-stained tie onto the floor. Occasionally, he would pause, take a deep drag on his Kool, and hold it for a moment. His deep-set eyes would then dart about the classroom almost snake-like, with two columns of smoke pouring out of his nostrils. For an instant, he looked like a tumbledown dragon. He would slowly amble toward the back of the classroom, then pounce upon and interrogate one of the male lummoxes slouched in his chair, reducing him syllogistically to a pathetic state of stammering mental incontinence. Word was that the girls he successfully hit on after class always got "A's."

Rachael grew up with mommy and daddy as pinkos, and I'm not sure it was all that tough for her. Her parents were communist Jewish activists in their youth who, no doubt, went to Pete Seeger concerts, campaigned for Henry Wallace instead of Harry Truman in 1948, thought Alger Hiss got railroaded, and protested the execution of Julius and Ethel Rosenberg for espionage and treason, of which, by the way, they were stone-cold guilty. Her older brother, Murray, was one of the organizers of the Student Nonviolent Coordinating Committee (SNCC) before Stokely Carmichael took it over. He was involved with organizing the student-conducted sit-ins to protest the racially segregated lunch counters in the

South in the early 1960s.

Rachael's mom was a professor at the University of Kansas. She wrote poetry, taught feminist literature, and was a charter member of the American Association of University Professors (AAUP). Also, she was a leading organizer for the pro-choice movement and was on the Kansas City board of Planned Parenthood.

Rachael's dad was a labor union attorney in Kansas City. He did pro bono work on death penalty appeals with the ACLU. He'd been involved in the unsuccessful execution appeals of Perry Smith and Richard Hickock, the pair of degenerates who had brutally murdered four members of the Clutter family in their farmhouse outside of Holcomb, Kansas in 1959. It was the first mass-murder I remember reading about in the papers as a kid — back when they made the front page. The state of Kansas finally put Perry and Richard where they belonged, at the end of a rope, in 1965. This was one year before Charles Whitman climbed up the Texas Tower in Austin and shot thirteen people, barely missing my Uncle Bob, who was coming out of a restaurant. He was visiting his daughter, Beth, a student at the university's engineering college. Perry Smith was interviewed on death row and eventually befriended by Truman Capote while he was working on his famous book dealing with the murders, *In Cold Blood*, one of the few books I had managed to read in college.

Rachel's dad had also, in the late 1950s, spent time in California on a clemency appeals team of lawyers attempting — unsuccessfully — to prevent the execution of convicted rapist Caryl Chessman. He was a long time on San Quentin Prison's Death Row — twelve years. His case had become an international *cause célèbre* for the anti-death penalty bleeding hearts. Eleanor Roosevelt and Norman Mailer, among others, had made clemency appeals on Chessman's behalf. Why? I haven't a clue.

No, actually, I do. It's the do-gooder side of the moralistic egomania that attaches itself to the likes of Mailer and his ilk, turning them "sweet" on violent criminals — Allen Alda, by the way, played Chessman, sympathetically, of course, in a television replay of his final days before execution. I remember the day they put him in "the chair" and the reaction of Mom when it hit the national news: "He was an awful man: About time they put an end to him."

Mailer, some years later, developed a man crush on a thug whose prison writings enthralled him — Jack Henry Abbot. We are now rummaging about in the ugly history of celebrity-intellectual corruption, and it doesn't get much worse than Norman Mailer's terrible venture.

Abbott was a career criminal, just like Chessman, violent like Chessman, and a writer, just like Chessman. He'd been locked away for forgery, bank robbery, and manslaughter. Abbott was just too literarily "gifted," Mailer decided, to be locked up merely to keep the rest of us safe. So, why not help secure the release of this dangerous felon so that he could write books that thrilled the intellectual class — or maybe kill innocent working-class people, some little people? This, he did — the latter, that is. Six weeks after his release, Abbott stabbed a waiter, Richard Adan, to death in a restaurant because he thought Adan had been rude to him — advice: Don't be rude to a celebrity's pet-criminal. Other celebrities at the time joined into the lovefest over a thug who murdered a poor guy for looking at him crossways. After killing Adan and fleeing the police, another anti-death penalty virtue-princess, actress Susan Sarandon, went gaga over the gifted author. When he went on trial, she named her baby boy "Jack Henry" after him. Mailer, the famous author, post-Abbott affair, went on to complete eighty-four years; Adan, the waiter, thanks to Mailer, made it to twenty-two.

The Arts Gala was the beginning of a torrid romance. Four or five dates later, Rachael unceremoniously ditched the art history Bozo named "Kenneth," not "Ken." Yes, "Kenneth," who weighed in at around 140 pounds. He was a supercilious black-turtleneck-sweater-wearing "expert" on abstract expressionism. Not to mention that he was a salon socialist, so practically and pathetically helpless that he couldn't change a spare tire or survive twenty minutes of light manual labor. He looked like Don Knots with a suntan.

Rachael finally, I guess, concluded that Kenneth's future would be making a peanut-salary teaching in some no-name college in a sedate "Nowheresville" hamlet in the dreary Midwest. A few years hence, he would be a bored old professor doing the horizontal Mambo with the coeds from his classes. She'd be deep in therapy and Chardonnay, contemplating a divorce, wondering why she had had the two brats who were driving her crazy on an hourly basis.

I met Kenneth once, shortly before she dumped him — for me. This is a confession I'm writing, so I offer a bit of our conversation at that encounter just to show how a nasty I could be. Kenneth, at the time we met, probably knew he was losing Rachael — to me.

"Great to meet you, Ken. I've heard a lot about you."

"It's Kenneth. Yeah, nice to meet you, Michael."

"It's Mike, Kenneth. I try to avoid multiple syllables when I can. They're too advanced for me to get the hang of, you know, like "modern sculpture' and 'French impressionism'. I go for the simple one-syllable standbys like 'sex,' 'chicks,' and 'cash'."

I was being a prick instead of a generous winner.

I took Rachael to Michigan to meet my parents. Dad was deeply impressed with her brains and her beauty, but not sure in that order and in what proportions. When we were getting ready to leave, Mom pulled me aside.

"Yeah, Mom, what do you think? She's a knockout, no?"

She looked at me for a what seemed like a long time, and then, in a very sad, quiet voice: "Yes, she's quite the knockout. That girl is going to eat you alive, Sweetie."

Four months later, we were married, a development that Rachael's parents were, to put it mildly, not overjoyed about, as you can probably understand. Two of my unemployed college friends from Big Rapids, Michigan drove over in a rusty pickup truck festooned with an old George Wallace for President bumper sticker and a gunrack holding a pump twelve gauge. They crashed the wedding reception, during which they got obnoxiously drunk and insulted half the guests. They didn't even bring gifts. This might have been an omen.

You might wonder why a Jewish, social justice, lefty chick with a Stanford pedigree would want to wed a button-down, corporate goy, graduate of a crappy university no one had ever heard of and whose view of the world was largely social Darwinian — focused entirely on money, status, and himself. What can I say? Opposites attract, maybe. Plus, she probably got off on pushing back on daddy and mommy, not an uncommon move for the kids in my generation, particularly for those who came from the "upper echelons" and felt the need to "rebel" against parental authority. Let's be honest: Parental authority, by the end of the hierarchy-smashing 1960s, had less fire power than the French army at Dien Bien Phu.

And, not to put too cynical a twist on it, I think she was looking for a potentially well-heeled guy who could afford to cover the lease on her BMW convertible, plus be able to channel some Benjamins toward her pet causes. Civil rights lawyers, at least at that time, were not making the big bucks. I was the right guy at the right time…for a time.

CHAPTER FIFTEEN

Then, What?

Then what?
Where you gonna turn,
When you can't turn back for the bridges you've burned,
And fate can't wait to kick you in the butt:
Then what?"

Clay Walker, "Then What?"

At the firm, I was rising fast and soon making more money than I could have imagined. My parents never had two nickels to rub together. Their house was old, small, and modest. The used cars they bought and drove started occasionally and broke down regularly. They shopped at K-Mart, ate TV dinners on the weekends instead of going to restaurants, and purchased the expensive stuff on layaway. Entertainment was Lawrence Welk on Saturday evenings on the black-and-white tube — Cissy and Bobby dancing up a storm, "Wunnerful, wunnerful." The big city, for us, was Big Rapids and the Friday evening fish-fry at the American Legion. The only family vacation I can remember was one summer crossing the Mackinac Bridge to Michigan's Upper Peninsula and spending a week at the rustic Tahquamenon Falls State Park.

I had arrived: crass nouveau riche, with a flashy, well-curved wife, driving a silver Bentley, wearing Italian custom-made suits, and relishing the envy of my peers, even the senior partners in the firm — a triumph of style over substance. I was also checking all the right boxes: joined the Rotary Club, found a "progressive" church to attend, schmoozed with up-and-coming local politicians, tried to be seen at the important charity events and fundraisers I cared nothing about. I was pushing toward the top — too fast — and, unfortunately, developing an arrogant "attitude" and reckless ways that would soon culminate in a colossal crash landing.

That attitude and the recklessness that followed carried big-time into my work, and crash, I did. I had finally stepped across "that line" into a legally murky region in which one day I found myself under arrest and escorted out of the office building by two federal marshals. I couldn't believe it. Well, to be honest, I could. I had sort of been engaged in insider trading and securities fraud, for which, if I was convicted, I would go to prison for up to ten years. I was smart enough to figure out how to do it; dumb enough to get caught.

Then, what? To my rescue came Renaldo Ricci, my attorney, an Italian-American rumored to be a mob-lawyer. Kansas City, thank God, I discovered, was one of the most corrupt municipalities in the country, so there were a lot of crooked lawyers to choose from, some of them very good.

The corruption reached back to at least the days of the Tom Pendergast machine. Harry Truman had been Tom's boy. In his early political days, HT looked the other way at TP's criminal shenanigans as a quid pro quo for the backing of the elected judgeship that launched his political career. "Give 'em Hell, Harry" was then later tapped and promoted for his U.S. Senate seat in order to protect Boss Pendergast from the backlash over the recent local murder of four federal agents. They had been poking into the corruption of the KC police force run by the ex-Capone mobster installed by the Boss. Remember, Reader: I cautioned you about digging into the lives of our purported "greats." It's never edifying.

Renaldo was the younger brother of one of my well-healed clients who had benefited generously from the insider info I had been slipping him. He was rightly concerned about what I, being quite the talker, might say about him if and when I really got started talking. Renaldo's biggest client was the KC Teamster's Local, run by none other than Roy Lee Williams, a good buddy of Jimmy Hoffa, whose life and career probably embodied as much as anyone I can think of all three of the 3-C's operating in overdrive, particularly collusion but no slouch on corruption and coercion either. Hoffa was pardoned by President Nixon in a secret deal he made with Frank Fitzsimmons for Teamster re-election support.

Williams, a big heavy-set galoot with a hatchet face — I met him once at a KC political fundraiser — was a hoodlum extraordinaire who had done some heavy lifting for Hoffa. He moved Teamster union pension funds into cost overrun construction projects with built-in kickbacks to the mob bosses and the construction companies' owners. It was a win-win for everyone but the guys who drove the trucks and paid the dues — the little guys. Williams eventually became President of the Teamsters after Hoffa was disappeared by some of his gangster associates who were guessing that he was about to sell them out to the Federales. Williams ended up in the Federal slammer for conspiring with Teamster pension fund manager and Chicago-based mobster Allen Dorfman to bribe Nevada Senator Howard Cannon. Cannon was being "encouraged" to defeat a trucking industry deregulation bill. Dorfman was murdered gangland-style to prevent him from testifying. Renaldo's brother, Angelo, my rich, former client, owned one of the biggest trucking firms that operated mostly in Missouri and Kansas. It employed a ton of Teamster members. I was in good hands.

The prosecutor offered me a plea bargain. I was sorely tempted, but Renaldo convinced me to roll the dice and take my chances with a jury trial. Good advice and good decision. With Renaldo as my counselor and a wee bit of jury tampering — a Teamster-lawyer specialty — I beat the charge, infuriating the judge, and, I am now sort of ashamed to say, laughed my way out of the courtroom. Laughing, but not for long.

Unfortunately, the bribes and legal fees left me broke. The firm kicked me out. I had damaged its reputation. The few friends I had were shunning me. The pastor of the church I had been going to, however, did offer to pray with me to help me seek humility, find forgiveness, and atone for my shortcomings. I politely took a rain check on that. Rachael concluded, correctly, that I was hopelessly damaged goods. She left me for Rocko Rollo — yes, that was his real name — a Kansas City Chiefs second-string linebacker I had been hanging around and partying with. He had been a sixth-round draft choice for the Chiefs several years back out of Clemson University, if you can believe that. She took my Bentley with her. Her departure reminded me of a line in a Country and Western song I heard a while before: "My wife ran off with my best friend, and I'm sure going to miss him."

CHAPTER SIXTEEN

Incarceration

I fought the law, and the law won
Bobby Fuller Ford, "I Fought the Law"

I came to Kansas City with fire and ambition. I left angry and bitter, but unrepentant and headed for the West Coast. For a few months, I drifted around Oregon and California, working temporary jobs, trying to find myself. Unfortunately, "myself" was an elusive, maybe non-existent, entity and, likely, unrecognizable for me. It wasn't in Portland, San Jose, or Los Angeles, or in any of the bars and night clubs where I was busy conducting "the search."

I spent four lonely days
In a brown L.A. haze…
Jimmy Buffett, "Come Monday"

That period remains "hazy," since I was, as they say it now so understandingly and compassionately, "self-medicating." But, for reasons I cannot recall, I headed back toward the east on a southern route. I ended up in, of all God-awful places, Mississippi — Tupelo, to be cruelly precise. Tupelo is the birthplace of Elvis Presley and, at one time, in the poorest county of the poorest state in the country — symbolic, I guess, of where my life was heading. There, I got a job selling used pickup trucks during the day and one as a bartender in the evenings.

My "myself" wasn't anywhere to be found in the birthplace of Elvis, either, and at this point, I had no firm grasp of "what condition my condition was in." I was ready to move on and get a firm hold of it — maybe in Atlanta, where an old college girlfriend, Brenda Leigh, recently divorced and temporarily lonely, was living and was offering some comfort. She had been married to a friend of mine from college, Jim Traficent. A year after the nuptials, Jim had taken up with her younger sister, Sarah. That was after briefly dating her mother, Peggy. I had tried to warn her that thinking that Jim was going to be faithfully monogamous was like believing in Nixon's "peace with honor." But she was "looking through the eyes of love." Maybe, that's why she reached out to me, which shows how reliable "love" is.

I stayed two days too long in the Magnolia State, and never got the chance to disappoint Brenda. Late one evening, after a high infusion of cocaine and a several of beakers of Jack Daniels, I hooked up with a couple of the locals — wild-man palookas I met at a party. They talked me into helping them hold up a local liquor store. The plan was to knock off the place, drive to Mexico, and hang out at a timeshare that belonged to an uncle somebody. It was supposed to be a cake walk. It wasn't my idea, of course, and I never imagined I could go down that road. But, after the coke and the booze, I was feeling, well, downright invincible and up for a hefty challenge. I've always been too easily influenced by those around me, which, I suppose, goes a long way to explain why I am where I am today.

My memory on this is alcohol-hazy, but with these two screwballs leading the charge, it was inevitable that we would bungle everything. And we did…in spectacular style. I was the designated wheelman for this heist. After the getaway, we holed ourselves up in an empty little Pentecostal church on the edge of town, where our getaway car had run out of gas. That car, a crummy, old 1970 Plymouth Duster that hit on five of its six cylinders could not have outrun a riding lawnmower. I had somehow neglected to notice that the needle for the gas gauge was firmly on empty. In this humble sanctuary, we took on the local cops and the FBI — the two idiots had kidnapped one of store clerks — in a ten-hour standoff. Fortunately, no one was hurt. I negotiated, and we surrendered.

The Feds handed me over to the state. After pleading guilty before a judge — no slick lawyer for me, this time — I was penitentiary bound to the Mississippi State Prison known as "Parchman Farm."

> *Let the Midnight Special shine a light on me*
> Creedance Clearwater Revival,
> "The Midnight Special"

About a hundred miles south of Memphis, on the Delta, "Farm" did not exactly capture the essence of this august institution of correction and reform. One of William Faulkner's characters in *The Mansion* called Parchman "destination doom," and it was featured in the movies "Cool Hand Luke" and "O Brother Where Art Thou." Elvis's dad, Vernon Presley, had been a guest there for writing bad checks.

The first few weeks at the Farm, I spent at the foot-end of the guards — the "black aspirin," as they called it — a full-body "boot massage" whenever they got bored with just screaming at me. On the other side were the inmates, most of whom didn't much care for the few Yankees who had stopped in to share their misery and misfortune.

I made a fateful decision to pull out all the stops the first time one of the Bubbas tried to break some of my bones. In the exercise yard one afternoon, I was tipped off that one of the crazies was planning to stomp all over my sombrero. I was waiting for him. When he got in range, I did a pivot-kick that drove my shin hard into the side of his left knee. He buckled half over, and with a piece of rebar from the machine shop in my right hand for heft, I landed a haymaker to the side of his head and got a hard kick into his ribs when he was going down. I had wrecked the ligaments in his knee and broken his jaw and a couple of ribs. It happened so fast that the guards — always bored and inattentive in the yard — didn't see it or pretended not to see. With that, I figured that I was sending the right message to improve my odds for survival.

In my cell block was another Yankee, Dick Durbin, from Cleveland. Dick had just gotten back from a tour in Vietnam — freshly discharged, full of rage. He was visiting Biloxi to hang out with one of his army buddies who was from there. Dick was nothing if not predictable. Imagine. A fight in a bar over, what else? A chick. Dick carved up one of the locals with a hunting knife he happened to be carrying in his boot.

> *I said: "Jailer, hey, what y'all got me charged with?"*
> *He looked at me, and he halfway closed one eye,*
> *He said: "You mean to say you don't remember*
> *Cuttin' up some honky with that bone-handled knife?"*
>   Delbert McClinton, "Victim of
>   Life's Circumstances"

Dick and I became friends. We formed a protection coalition with a couple of other Yankee inmates that kept us both from slipping on the soap in the showers.

I began to imagine what I would look like, feel like, and be like after a few years of the Farm's aggressive version of "rehabilitation." And, since I was looking at fifteen of them, my plan for an earlier way out took shape — specifically, an escape route. Difficult, dangerous, and improbable as it was, I figured that I had little to lose. I pulled it off after a year by crawling through the prison sewer system — actually, swimming through a river of…well, I think you get the picture.

I had help with this from Belinda Kay Conklin, a woman who had been writing to me early after my arrival at the Farm. Belinda Kay was a "prison-inmate-groupie" who worked in Jackson for the State Bureau of Corrections. She had access to the prison schematics that detailed the physical infrastructure — showed duct work, plumbing, etc. For reasons that remain mysterious to me, after a few letters and a couple of visits, she conceived a huge crush on me, along with a daring plan for my freedom so that we could "be together." I confess, I gave her ample encouragement. She proceeded to smuggle the relevant drawings to me in a Bible — King James translation, of course — that I used to map my escape.

Belinda Kay was waiting for me. I stuffed myself into the trunk of her old Buick La Sabre a few miles from the prison. After my quick clean up in a gas station john, she drove straight through to South Florida. A few weeks there of battling the heat, humidity, and mosquitos brought Belinda Kay to a realization of the painfully obvious: She had been temporarily insane. No argument there. What can I say? "Love is a many-splendored thing." It expresses itself in so many strange and unpredictable ways, but, as you may have already guessed, in that mystical region of human experience, I was not always at my finest.

I was certainly appreciative of all her efforts on my behalf. She was a jewel, and I remember her with the greatest affection. But, somehow, lounging about in the swamps, broke, with a surly fugitive, turned out to be less exciting than whatever bizarre fantasies she had entertained at her desk back in Jackson. We amicably split, and she headed for West Virginia with a handsome second baseman she'd met named Tony Dow. Tony had just been rejected by the Detroit Tigers during his spring training tryout. She'd been "looking for love in all the wrong places." Maybe, Tony was the right place. I hope so.

CHAPTER SEVENTEEN

Government Criminality

Every decent man is ashamed of the government he lives under.

H. L. Mencken

I hid out in the Everglades for several months, making due by poaching alligators, petty burglaries, and occasional shop-lifting. I snagged a part-time job as an extra in a film being shot near where I was hanging out. The movie was a horror-thriller, "Impulse." It starred one of my favorite actors, William Shatner — Capitan Kirk from "Star Trek." He played a serial killer who preyed on wealthy widows.

Off the set, however, Shatner was a great guy. The ego attached to a swaggering, vainglorious asshole — the kind you expect from the typical movie star — he didn't have. In the mid-1950s, as a twenty-something, he played Ranger Bob on the Canadian "Howdy Dowdy Show." Shatner also had a small role as an American Army Captain in "Judgement at Nuremburg" years earlier in his career.

He took a shine to me, and we would occasionally knock down a couple of beers together after a shooting session. He recalled the stir created when he kissed Nichelle Nichols, the sultry black actress who played Lt. Uhura in the "Star Trek" episode "Plato's Stepchildren" — the first kiss between a white man and a black woman on scripted U.S. television. When he aged out of acting, as I later recalled, Shatner turned spokesman for Priceline.com. He produced scripted ads in exchange for stock in the company. Allegedly, he sold it just before the burst of the dot-com bubble, making a $600 million profit.

Shatner would reminisce about his native Montreal and some of the stars he had worked with like Yul Brynner, Carol Channing, and Walter Matthau. The "Capitan" was a graduate of McGill University — the best university in Canada, he claimed. He was a student there the same time as Leonard Cohen. Cohen's "Everybody Knows" captures my philosophy in the first verse.

> *Everybody knows that the dice are loaded*
> *Everybody rolls with their fingers crossed*
> *Everybody knows the war is over*
> *Everybody knows the good guys lost*
> *Everybody knows the fight was fixed*
> *The poor stay poor, the rich get rich*
> *That's how it goes*
> *Everybody knows*

I'm not sure everybody knows; but that's how it goes, and that's why it's better to be rich and not too attached to being a "good guy." Shatner thought I had acting potential. He said that he would look for another gig for me when the shooting ended. It did not work out. Because?

Shortly after the filming, I ran out of luck, so to speak. The local heat grabbed me coming out of the back of a drug store with merchandise I "forgot" to pay for. The State of Mississippi wanted me back at Parchment Farm to spend the next twenty or thirty years and probably undergo some prolonged payback for my unapproved departure while working on adjusting my attitude.

The Federal agents, however, who showed up at the Collier County jail to interrogate me seemed to have something different in mind. They took a lot of time over several days questioning me. I had greatly impressed them with the escape I had pulled off from the Farm — no easy feat. After a heated debate, the agents decided to subject me to an extensive and excruciating psychological-psychometric evaluation that included IQ, HEXACO Model of Personality Structure, NEO-PI-O, the Eysenck Personality Inventory, among others.

I don't know to this day exactly what the evaluation revealed other than that I was exceptionally smart plus missing many of the essential "moral parameters" that were firmly in place with most people. That, combined with a very low register of risk-aversion, which explains the crazy Tupelo business, I guess, put me in a category, to put it clinically, as an amoral daredevil well-suited for dangerous style operations. This meant I had maximum potential for success with a special kind of government work, one for bright individuals trusted to operate with the absence of ethical, legal constraints. That I was an escaped, convicted, dangerous criminal did not seem to weigh negatively on their deliberations about the future employment they were contemplating for me. This, of course, makes sense when you think about it, since there is a very large and murky region of criminality within most governmental operations. Our government, as you know, emerged out of a revolution, and, as you also know, revolutions are not exactly models of procedural "legality."

However, what matters most to the self-infatuated, amoral, Rottweiler-personalities who conduct the dark-side (the real) business of the state is not the unseemly and fundamentally criminal features — murder, extortion, kidnapping, narcotics trafficking — but (a) how to devise the sort of criminality most likely to advance the nefarious, power-enhancing ambitions of the boss while preserving the caring, virtuous, conscientious public-servant pose he's fashioned to fool the rubes, (b) how best to keep the messy, smelly, embarrassing stuff under wraps and away from public scrutiny, and (c) taking pride and satisfaction in a line of work that most people would recoil from in visceral disgust.

Having a conscience does not work well for big government work. Don't get me wrong. I'm not saying that everyone who works for government is a lowlife crook. Scruples and principles will just quickly put a hard ceiling on your efforts to rise high in government employment.

The CIA stepped into the act and into my future. Dr. Ari supervised the psych evaluation and analyzed the data. He was a Mossad agent on loan to the Company from the Israeli government. Dr. Ari was "prisoner psychologist" who evaluated prospects for potentially dangerous undercover operations. The Mossad was the best in the world at them. Straight out of the *Talmud*: "If someone comes to kill you, rise up and kill him first," which puts you in the business of designing lots of lethal, secret operations. Dr. Ari screened potential operatives to determine their potential for resisting enhanced interrogation techniques if captured in mission.

The Doc was highly impressed with mine. So were the CIA operatives. I got an offer I couldn't refuse. They tore up the Mississippi Parchman Farm paperwork, and — Bingo! — I got full immunity from extradition and prosecution. In exchange, I spent four arduous but exhilarating months with the alligators in the Louisiana swamps at a clandestine training camp.

Remember what I said at the beginning of my confession: "I obsessively need to conform to the desires and expectations of anyone and everyone I happen to be around, often people I don't particularly like or admire." Dr. Ari zeroed in on this with my psych evaluation: "The subject has a high compensatory dependency. He responds positively to in-group reward incentives, which would make him an ideal subject for participation in special high-risk projects that require unquestioning group loyalty and target selected hostile outgroups for aggressive confrontation."

I was the "ideal subject," someone to help them pull off an "aggressive confrontation." Any "selected hostile outgroup" was fine with me. Those days, I was not particular in such matters, just eager and willing to confront them — aggressively.

I quickly bonded with the other guys in the unit, many of whom had successful aggression-experience. These guys were "likable" enough, not, however, what you would call highly "admirable." But I was eager to fit in and go the distance. My training included enhanced interrogation methods and close-up, silent-kill techniques. As well, I acquired proficiency with the latest weaponry, Uzis and Heckler & Koch G3 assault rifles, 7.62 mm, used by NATO military forces and the Green Berets in Vietnam. Best of all, I was in the company and tutelage of high-skilled, brutal ass-kickers as they prepared to launch a top-level, secret mission that involved considerable "wet work," if you catch my drift.

Training and preparation completed, with these "torpedoes," I flew secretly to Chile. There, we would have "a few days to kill" — that is, to do some serious U.S. government business. That "business" just happened to be "regime change," meaning that a U.S. designated client and his henchmen were going be installed. And the predecessors?

Use your imagination. Hint: not a retirement that included golf or tennis. This sort of business, American voters are not supposed to know or care about. Believe me. It's better not to know.

In Chile, we set up "black sites" — secret CIA prisons. In these, we trained local, Chilean army personnel how to interrogate local prisoners using waterboarding, stress positions, and "sleep management." Prior to arrival, our mission had acquired a study by the American Medical Association on interrogation methods used in the Soviet Union. It went back to the early Stalin days, when NKVD interrogators used "the conveyor belt" for sleep deprivation to break down prisoners and obtain false confessions. The interrogators would work round the clock, in eight-hour shifts, keeping the prisoner awake, usually standing. The prisoner's feet would swell. He would experience terrifying psychotic attacks. A maximum of seventy-two hours was all it took to break the toughest guy. After two or three twenty-four-hour shifts, a prisoner would say or do anything requested without having to lay a hand on him. "Look, Ma, no bruises." I can tell you, from first-hand experience, it works better than you can imagine.

CIA Director Richard Helms, who I always thought could double as Count Dracula, had the green light for this "special op" directly from Nixon. Helms put a scary cat named Everette Howard Hunt, better known as E. Howard Hunt in charge. Hunt was a man of action, especially the kind that involved the breaking of laws and the disposing of "problems" — of a human sort.

One "problem" that Hunt had solved was the "Arbenz problem" in Guatemala in 1954. More on that shortly. With G. Gordon Liddy, he had also masterminded the Watergate burglary of the Democratic National Committee headquarters at the behest of Mr. "Law and Order," President Nixon. The White House had also ordered Hunt to invade the office of Daniel Ellsberg's psychiatrist, Lewis Fielding. Ellsberg was a high-level military analyst at the Rand Corporation. Given what they were about, how many of these high-ranking military analysts, I wonder, were under the care of psychiatrists?

Daniel Ellsberg: "I don't understand, Doctor Fielding. Why am I feeling so depressed and guilty these days? Christ, I'm a Harvard grad, have a posh house in Georgetown, a hot wife, three nice kids, and a high-paying job. And I keep having these nightmares. What's going on?"

Dr. Fielding: "Let's see. What have you been working on these days, Daniel?"

Ellsberg: "Vietnam."

Dr. Fielding: "We might be getting to something important here, Daniel. Let's talk more about Vietnam."

Ellsberg: "Just to be sure, now. Doctor-patient confidentiality is inviable, right?"

Dr. Fielding: "Absolutely. You don't have to worry about anything you tell me going outside this office."

Ellsberg was in the crosshairs of the gangsters who ran the White House. They were hot after dirt to discredit him because he had leaked the Pentagon papers to the *New York Times*, spotlighting the mendacity and criminality of the U.S. Government in its conduct of the Vietnam War. E. Howard ended up serving thirty-three months in prison for planning and carrying out the Watergate burglary. His long career as a professional, high-ranking spook personified the mobster-like features of the intelligence community. Some people believe he was closely involved in planning the hit on JFK. Having spent too much time with him, I'd say it's highly likely.

CHAPTER EIGHTEEN

Lansky or Dulles

You have to have a few martyrs. Some people have to get killed.

Allan Dulles

I n Chile, we hooked up with that ornery cuss, General Augusto José Ramón Pinochet Ugarte, and his right-wing officer buddies to help them overthrow President Salvador Guillermo Allende Gossens. Dr. Allende, the co-founder of Chile's Socialist political party, was also a crypto-Marxist. He had gotten himself crosswise with Nixon and the State Department because he had "expropriated" (commie-speak for "stolen") the big U.S.-owned copper companies in Chile without compensation, making him look like he was on the way to being the next Fidel Castro south of the border.

Well, he was. Allende was, in fact, under Fidel's "tutelage." Worse, he was scheming to turn Chile into yet another Marxist-inspired third-world slum, where the party overlords live it up while the humble "workers" learn to love the bosses, work for nothing, and celebrate the "Revolution" on calorie-restricted diets. Not much action for Weight Watchers or Jenny Craig in Cuba. Nixon must have been thinking: One of these fucking guys is more than we need.

After JFK's botched Bay of Pigs invasion, the CIA spooks became obsessed with Castro — with killing him, that is. Three American Presidents gave the nod for his murder: Eisenhower, Kennedy, and Johnson. The Company plotters had devised some bizarre but unsuccessful schemes to try to kill him — some, Hunt was involved with. Poison pills, a toxic cigar, exploding mollusks, a chemically tainted diving suit, and powder to make his beard fall out so as to undermine his popularity were a few of the more innovative ones. These schemes were financed with drug and gambling dollars funneled through Caribbean banks.

When you want to bump someone off, you hire a professional to do it. At the top of that professional assassin heap was the notorious Jewish gangster, Myer Lansky. Myer, a little guy at about five feet tall, had a big resume in the murder business, including some of his former associates like Bugsy Siegel and Arnold Rothstein. A guy who will murder his business partners is obviously someone you can trust — at least, that's how the CIA seemed to look at the relationship.

Lansky, though, was the guy because Fidel Castro was at the top of his hit list. Lansky had conceived a massive hatred of *El Lider Maximo* because the Cuban had shut down his lucrative gambling and prostitution empire in Havana after he took power. It wasn't as if the Cuban people were getting a lot out of the arrangement that was filling the coffers of the American mobster. Lansky had long been in cahoots with Fulgencio Batista. So embedded was Lansky in American-Cuban relations, his connection to Batista became common knowledge and was later fictionalized in a Havana scene in *The Godfather Part II* — Lee Strasberg played a Lansky-character who teamed up with Al Pacino as Michael Corleone to negotiate a Cuban business deal involving a number of American business partners.

Sustained in large part by his phenomenal entrepreneurial skills, Lansky's criminal career ran almost fifty years. The Rockefeller of the gangster world, he built the National Crime Syndicate, a vast operation in lock step with corrupted law enforcement. So extensive and powerful was it that Lansky once boasted: "We're bigger than General Motors." He became known as "the Mob's Accountant." But he did take a "sabbatical" from full-time "mobstering" during WWII to partner with the Office of Naval Intelligence's Operation. The "accountant" was well "connected" and recruited some of the finest criminal talent anywhere to compose this unique government-private enterprise relationship. The Feds and the Mafia colluded on a project that managed to get something for everyone involved.

They busied themselves detecting German infiltrators and submarine-borne saboteurs. Lansky's expertise came with a quid pro quo: his "business partner," Lucky Luciano, who, early on, had helped him murder his major competitor, the notorious Arnold Rothstein mentioned above. Rothstein himself was no minor league criminal. He had created an international drug-smuggling empire on top of liquor bootlegging during Prohibition — one of the early entrepreneurs in organized crime, assisted by corrupt law enforcement. As part of the government deal with Lansky, Luciano got a release from the slammer. In exchange, the Mafia provided security for the warships that were being built along the docks in New York Harbor.

This seamy little piece of high-government corruption would make one of today's "Diversity" consultants burst with pride: Jews, Italians, and government WASPs working together to stick it to the evil Germans. Not quite, but a promising beginning.

Recall my earlier comment on Stalinist-style regimes, how

they come out of the gate lower on the corruption side. Fidel followed that script. Once he'd chased Batista off the island, he cleaned out the American-run gambling casino-stables, along with the prostitution. Early communism must always be a virtuous affair. That is the allure and moral drama that grabs so many intellectuals, celebrity socialists, and faculty-lounge lizards. Marxist revolutions make for considerable irony, if nothing else.

Fidel, like Lenin and Mao, believed that you could coerce your way to the perfect society: Shoot the rich, bad people, take their stuff, and give it to the good, poor people. Somehow, the poor people still stayed poor — some even get poorer. Nobody, except for a few select, got rich. Cuba became a terror-command state, with a cult of personality to fool the inmates. A sinister cabal of American gangsters, politicians, government spies, and professional assassins wanted to get the casinos and the whores back in business in Havana.

How do you get more corrupt than that, and where are the good guys in any of this? I gave up trying to figure it out a long time ago, suspecting that "good guys" exist only in two places: the movies and the imaginations of the "triumphalist" historians who write about the great and virtuous "winners."

The CIA would never pull off the Fidel wet job. They — I mean, we — did give the heave-ho to his Chilean wannabe, which gave something to stick in Castro's eye. Mission completed. That was the entire point. The fact that Allende won his Presidency in a legitimate election in his country didn't matter to Nixon and Kissinger, who were behind the coup. They were big on "democracy" when it put their flunkies in place — no commies allowed. Not that "legality" for them was a high priority: They were comfortable operating in that "murky region."

Allende wasn't the first democratically elected head of state to be toppled by the CIA, operating behind the scenes. There were many. In 1953, the CIA staged the overthrow of Iranian Prime Minister Mohammad Mosaddeq after he seized British Petroleum (BP). He had the audacity to think that Iranian oil belonged to Iranians. Just to rub salt in Iranian wounds, twenty-five years later, President Nixon sent former CIA Chief Richard Helms to Iran as American Ambassador.

Guatemala 1954 was an equally — if not more — egregious CIA piece of state criminality. Ike's Secretary of State, John Foster Dulles, and his younger brother, Allan, the CIA Chief, project-managed the coup that brought down Colonel Jacobo Arbenz Guzmán, who was the democratically elected President.

By coincidence, Che Guevara was in Guatemala during the staged coup. These events stimulated the birth of his hatred for the U.S. The Dulles brothers did not work for the American people; they did not care about the citizens of Guatemala. They worked for executives at the United Fruit Company, who looked upon this Central American banana republic as their private, exclusive domain. Arbenz's plans for agrarian reform threatened to shake up the status-quo. The United Fruit Company had been a client of the Wall Street law firm of Sullivan & Cromwell where John Foster had been a senior partner before running Ike's foreign policy, along with his secret partner in regime destabilization and change, Allen. This U.S. intervention, in the long run, was pretty hard on the little people of Guatemala, setting off a civil war several years later that lasted three and a half decades, killing an estimated 200,000 Guatemalans. The ubiquitous E. Howard Hunt had helped design the political-warfare portfolio for that operation, as well.

Oh, and I almost forget about the CIA-backed coup that

toppled and assassinated Ngo Dinh Diệm, President of South Vietnam, and his advisor and younger brother. It happened just three weeks before JFK was gunned down in Dallas. Diệm was installed in Saigon by Detroit-born Edward Lansdale and the CIA. Lansdale was fictionalized by Graham Greene in his novel *The Quiet American* as Alden Pyle. He had done some earlier assassination and torture work for the CIA in the Philippines. Diệm was a corrupt U.S. fixture in the mess of what the U.S. was making of his country. He wasn't working out, so he had to go. Making "problems" go away via murder in countries whose politics we manipulate is a CIA specialty. The CIA's Lucien Conein, nicknamed "Black Luigi," had been assigned by JFK to spy on Diệm. He colluded with the South Vietnamese Generals in Diệm's betrayal and murder, serving as the U.S. bagman and handing over $40,000 to the Generals carrying out the coup, with the promise that the U.S. government would not protect Diệm.

You might begin to suspect that, sometimes, it's worse for someone to be our friend than our enemy. Word was that President Kennedy was pretty torn up when he got the news. He was thinking that Diệm, a fellow Roman Catholic, who was highly esteemed and supported in his U.S. puppet role by Cardinal John Spellman, was just going to get a pink slip from the job and retirement somewhere. He was not supposed to get one of the special, final exit-interviews the CIA conducts with its dictators in-progress with an "expired shelf-life." The Pres — probably distracted with one of his bimbos — was not expecting a mafia-style execution. Maybe, he was beginning to get a glimpse of who really runs the show.

Back to Allende. Shortly after we got to Chile, Pinochet put his rebel officer crew in place and was ready to move against the President. We followed a well-worn script used by the CIA when called upon to overthrow duly elected foreign leaders perceived to be "uncooperative." Disgruntled traitors in the officer-corps are identified then loaded up with weapons and covert U.S. assistance. American personnel and propaganda expertise make the engineered coup appear to be the outcome of popular discontent.

I was assigned to a unit that rounded up and interrogated suspected communist activists who were suspected to organize and resist the coup. Post-interrogation, we then handed what was left of them over to Pinochet's people. Don't ask me to elaborate on that.

During the coup, Allende shot himself in the Presidential Palace with an AK-47 rifle given to him by Fidel Castro. I watched a unit of soldiers and firefighters carry his body out of the *Palacio de La Moneda* wrapped in a Bolivian poncho.

Pinochet took over as scripted — unofficially, one of "our son of a bitches," a firm anti-Communist in place in the southern cone, those "troubled waters" where Castro had long been "fishing." This was part of the rationale for the U.S. supported coup.

Six years earlier, Ernesto "Che" Guevara had convinced Fidel to send him to Bolivia. He was to duplicate the Cuban guerrilla revolution there, hoping to create "another Vietnam" in which to mire the U.S. Empire. Che's efforts were a bust. The Bolivian army, with the help of Felix Rodriguez, a CIA operative and Cuban exile, captured him and let the Bolivians put an end to him. They chopped off his hands, and the rumor was that they sent them to Castro to confirm his killing. This worked out well for Fidel, who had been happy to get his old comrade-in-arms off the island. Che had been getting too full of himself: now, gone and conveniently dead was Fidel's charismatic, ruthless competitor. Dead, he got bigger and better and a less of a threat to Fidel than alive — and so much more useful. Cuban photographer Alberto Korda's photo of Che may be the world's most popular poster image. A martyred symbol of Fidel's revolution, Che came to be worshiped in Cuba, a haunting, romantic image that fit nicely on tee-shirts, posters, and coffee mugs — a way to thrill the college kids in the capitalist world. Fidel understood better than anyone else the value of branding and image-making for making ideology come alive and remain enticing.

Pinochet was not exactly a Boy Scout, to put it politely. Don't say too many nice things about him around many folks from Chile — even now. Imagine that: getting resentful when big bully outsiders sneak in under cover and overthrow your leaders. Then, they pretend it was all your idea and doing. But at least this piece of criminality on the part of Nixon and Kissinger didn't end up, like in Cambodia and Vietnam, destroying the country and killing thousands of American soldiers.

Chile, probably, did end up being better off long-term than it would have been under a Cuban-style regime — not because Pinochet was any kind of saint. He was a nasty SOB, to be sure. You did not want to get on his bad side. The next time you visit Washington D.C., head to the Dupont Circle area. Check out the "Letelier and Moffitt Memorial," at the roundabout at R Street NW and 23rd Street. The memorial is placed where Orlando Letelier, an exiled Chilean diplomat, and Ronnie Moffitt, an American friend and colleague, in 1976 were blown to bits by a car bomb right in front of the Romanian embassy. It was detonated, as it is now firmly established, by thugs at the behest of Pinochet. Letelier had been stoking foreign government and business opposition to the Chilean General's regime. The investigation into a foreign-engineered assassination in the American capitol, you may be astonished to learn, never got much traction: Henry Kissinger was Secretary of State at that time and on friendly terms with Pinochet.

All that said, Pinochet, by twentieth-century dictator standards of mass-murder, forced labor, torture, and corruption, was in the minor leagues. He was your run-of-the-mill, corrupt Latin American Caudillo, concerned mainly to take care of his friends, shaft his enemies, and keep the commies at bay, less brutal and a bit less corrupt than some of Latin Lords the U.S. had propped up over the years, like Trujillo. He had the good sense to import free-market whiz kids from the University of Chicago to Santiago, including George Schultz, U.S. Secretary of Labor under Nixon. By the late 1990s, Chile was the economic powerhouse of South America and one its most politically stable countries with free elections. Unlike Cuba, lots of folks weren't literally dying while trying to leave, and unlike Castro, Pinochet eventually stood for an open election and voluntarily stood down when he lost.

CHAPTER NINETEEN

Relocation

The '60s are gone, dope will never be as cheap, sex never as free, and the rock and roll never as great.

Abbie Hoffman

Mission accomplished, I came home to the US of A through New Orleans — happily, not on a return trip to Parchman Farm. The "Company" cut me loose in the San Francisco Bay area. I was a free man, so to speak, set up with a new identity that included a fake Ph.D. degree in — you guessed it — philosophy. This got me an instructor job at a local community college; plus, I was able to teach some adjunct courses at U.C. Berkeley.

The early 1970s Frisco counterculture was racing forward in mindless, full-throttle self-indulgence. The young, the confused, and the overindulged were traveling two different roads in quest of the real "self," flower-child Hippie — "Turn on, tune in, drop out," as Timothy Leary so eloquently put it, passing your time with casual-acquaintance copulating, frying your brain with pharmaceuticals, and avoiding regular showers. "If you're going to San Francisco, be sure to wear some flowers in your hair."

To put your gag reflex to the ultimate test, listen to Scott

McKensie warbling a few bars from that tune that made it to the top of the charts in 1967. The lyrics capture the mindless appeal of a zeitgeist that found its ground-zero location in the City by the Bay. "There's a whole generation, with a new explanation." But it was not "new" or even an "explanation," for that matter, which is why there is no clue in the song about what the explanation was that was making this generation so special. My favorite line in the song: "You're gonna meet some gentle people there." Yeah, like the Zodiac killer, the Zebra Murderers, who shot the future Mayor of San Francisco, Art Agnos, the Black Panthers, or the Reverend Jim Jones. Stray a bit south toward LA, and you might bump into some of the gentle people from the Manson Family.

If flowers in your hair and meeting gentle people were not your highest priorities, there was another way to go: the radical route — "Off the Pigs," "Revolution for the hell of it" politics, Abbie Hoffman, Yippie style — Karl Marx meets the joyful Nihilists. With few of the "moral parameters in place," I paused momentarily then jumped quickly, with both feet, into the latter, going, going, going…gone — far, lunatic left.

I read the right books: Herbert Marcuse's *One Dimensional Man* — Marcuse was Communist Angela Davis's mentor — and Luis Althusser — the infamous, wife-strangling Parisian Marxist — and Frantz Fanon's *Wretched of the Earth*, one of President Obama's favorite books from his college days. Convinced that the U.S. proletariat, aligned with radical blacks, Chicanos, and women oppressed by their husbands was about to arise up and throw off its chains, I went full-delusional. I imagined that I could be in the vanguard, calling the shots — you know, sort of an American Leon Trotsky, in charge of a Red Brigade. As Mao said: "Revolution comes out of the barrel of a gun." If there is going to be a revolution, make sure you are not on the barrel end of the guns. At least,

I was being consistent. Marcuse, the ex-pat German-Jewish philosopher who was all the rage with the Berkeley radicals, worked, by the way, for the OSS, precursor to the CIA, in the Allied denazification program in Germany, post WWII — a Marxist CIA agent, the contradictions abound! This was not widely known. He wasn't the only commie involved in trying to make bad Germans into nice Germans.

For someone harboring these kinds of megalomaniacal hallucinations, I could not have been better placed than in the early 1970s Lotus Land. Reality and fantasy were here indistinguishable and interchangeable. About the time I arrived in the Bay Area, the New World Liberation Front (NWLF) had begun a four-year Bay Area campaign of bombing government and corporate targets.

Such a place was fertile ground for conmen, particularly the "spiritual" guru yahoos. I started looking for action in my new relocation with radical ambitions, and the Reverend Jim Jones caught my attention. His sermons struck me as so bizarre that I thought he must be hiding some rare kind of genius. Soon, it became obvious to even me that the guy was completely unhinged. One Sunday morning, I sat in the front pew listening to one of his stemwinders. Worked up more than usual, he revealed that God had empowered him to raise people from the dead. I was starting to get nervous. "Ok," I'm thinking, "he's not the first man sent by God to claim such powers; calm yourself down." But, then…he said that he could do it as long as the deceased had not been embalmed. Whoa, Nellie! His resurrection powers had come with some weird limitations. I knew I was listening to a full-blown psychotic.

Jones' base of operations was his People's Temple. I should have known from the beginning: "People's," as in "People's Temple," was the give-away. "People's" is one of the mid-twentieth-century triumphs of word corruption. "The People's Temple" was as much a "temple" of the poor people in San Francisco as the "People's Republic of China" or the "Democratic People's Republic of Korea," are governed by the people who live in those places. "People's" was a lynchpin of Marxist, alternative-reality mumbo-jumbo. Same thing for "Democratic." "Democratic" demonstrates how communist logic and wordplay works, which is like this:

"Communism is wonderful because we communists say it is. Democracy is wonderful because everyone says it is. Therefore, communism must be democratic, the real kind, not the phony capitalist version that stomps all over 'the people,' which is why we have to add 'People's' to the name to distinguish it from the fake ones." That makes perfect sense.

Before "real" democrats snicker away at this obvious commie subterfuge, hold on a second. Our own wordplay is a mirror. Thus:

"Our limited system of government is wonderful, even though the few 'limitations' get fewer by the hour. Democracy is wonderful because everyone, even the commies, says it is. Therefore, our government is a democracy and far superior to the so-called 'Peoples Democracies,' which we know are a sorry joke."

This should be a clue: Talking about governments of any kind, "democracy" is a useless, one-upmanship, feel-good word. Ditch it: No government today says that it is not "democratic." The word doesn't describe anything. It is an example of language that the philosopher J.L. Austin called "perlocutionary," language that praises and self-affirms — as I said, "feel good." Better to fall back on coercion, corruption, and collusion to grasp how a political system operates. With these, you zero in on the crucial features: Who gets screwed, who does it, how it's done, and, most importantly, how the screwing is made to look fair and reasonable with words like "that's who we are," which make everybody feel ok about it.

There were stunningly obvious signs that the People's Temple — previously, a cobbled together sect of Pentecostalism and Marxism that Jones originally called the "Wings of Deliverance" — was a corrupt, criminal enterprise. Jim Jones was a highly lethal, psychotic timebomb, ticking away. But, pointing out the "obvious" had become a social and professional hazard. In a sane world, a conman like the "People's" Reverend would have been locked up far away in a psych-ward, loaded up and heavily sedated with schedule-II classed drugs. But this was the San Francisco I had come to embrace, and, given the state of the *Weltgeist* at the time, Jones was handed the keys to the city by the elite, who clearly didn't know shit from Shinola.

Reverend Jim had two huge things going for him. First, his crude, Marxist-ministerial malarkey — fashionable, at that time, for sophisticates and unsophisticated, alike. "I call capitalism the devil…and socialism is God" — from one of his sermons. Until the 1970s and outside of California, you would only find someone talking like this perched out on a sidewalk somewhere, shunned by passersby, a street-corner prophet howling out imprecations announcing the end-of-the-world.

Instead, Jones was the toast of the town, amassing a huge following, lauded by the city fathers as the greatest spiritual leader since Moses. This was because, second of all, and clinching the deal, he was terrific at posturing as a savior for the poor and oppressed, specifically for "people of color."

The leading lights of community and the ace reporters were slobbering over this fake man of the cloth. If there was ever compelling evidence that you should never trust the judgement of politicians and community leaders or believe a word they say, the rapture over Jim Jones that came from this bunch makes it case closed. Jim Jones's operation sucked them in by the worshipping drove. He was visited and anointed by Roselyn Carter and two vice presidents, Nelson Rockefeller and Walter Mondale. Governor Jerry Brown and Lieutenant Governor Mervyn Dymally of California paid him effusive tribute. Willie Brown, who became speaker of the California assembly and mayor of San Francisco, compared Jim Jones to Martin Luther King, Jr. and Mahatma Gandhi. Dianne Feinstein, now one of our illustrious Senators from the Golden State, joined the rest of the San Francisco board of supervisors in honoring Jones "in recognition of his guidance and inspiration" in furthering "humanitarian programs." Perhaps, she had met some of the un-embalmed dead people he had resurrected. Big-named journalists like Herb Caen and Paul Avery couldn't find enough superhuman attributes in Jones. Here was an extraordinary array of powerful and influential leaders in politics, religion, and journalism, all in enthrallment to a vicious psychopath.

Jones' congregation was made up of poor black people. About 900 of them packed up and decamped to the paradise he promised to build for them in a fetid jungle in Guyana, South America. The preacher turned out to be "the devil." At his planning and instigation, his loyal followers drank the poison Kool-Aid and made history as a mass suicide that stunned the outside world. "Drink the Kool-Aid" soon became well-worn slang for mindlessly following the crazies or embracing the absurd. Abruptly, the hosannas for Jones and his Temple that rained down from the powerful and enlightened came to a halt. It was time for some corrective amnesia.

CHAPTER TWENTY

Radicalization

He's a real Weatherman
Ripping up the motherland
Making all his Weatherplans
For everyone.
Knows just what he's fighting for
Victory for people's war
Trashes, bombs, kills pigs, and more,
The Weatherman

Weatherman song; parody of
the Beatles, "Nowhere Man"

Being done with Jones and his "Peoples Temple," here is where I must confess to the beginning of one of the most shameful and regrettable parts of my life. Teaching philosophy at Berkeley put me up to my ears in radical politics. I was looking for a way to make that leap from thinking and talking into action. High-profile radical movements in the U.S. and Western Europe were raging. And, of course, Latin America, where Fidel was constantly stirring the pot. The universities in Germany, France, and Italy were disgorging university students, encouraged by intellectuals the likes of Jean Paul Sartre, who turned themselves into terrorists, killing policemen, kidnapping businessmen, taking hostages, and bombing government buildings.

The Red Army Faction (RAF) in West Germany — aka the Baader-Meinhoff Gang — made world headlines kidnapping and assassinating politicians in between bombing government buildings and department stores. They were fueled mainly by hatred of U.S. conduct in Vietnam. In Italy, the Red Brigade founded by Renato Curcio, throughout the 1970s, kidnapped, murdered, and sabotaged industries — the goal, to overthrow the government and install a Marxist dictatorship.

Naturally prone to delusion, I wanted to be part of the "solution" that the Marxists I regularly associated with constantly talked about. At Berkeley, I had radicalized myself to the point where I wanted to do more than just think about how wonderful taking power would be.

The Weather Underground was the best choice to pull it off — fanatical and violence-prone. A breakoff faction from the Students for a Democratic Society, once launched, it dove deeply into criminality and domestic terrorism — bank robberies, jail breaks, and blowing up stuff. Targets that symbolized American power and oppression topped their list. They blew up an old statue in Haymarket Square, Chicago because it commemorated the policemen killed in the vicinity during the anarchist riot in 1886. The symbolism rubbed at them. The Weathermen hated cops and enthused about killing them — "offing the Pigs," as they poetically put it. In retrospect, the irony in this stuck home. Pampered rich-kid graduates from elite universities imagined that killing working-class guys, who worked dangerous jobs and supported families on modest paychecks, was somehow "revolutionary." "Killing a Pig" turned a blue-collar housewife into a widow left to raise her kids by herself.

The San Francisco Bay Area, where I was living, was the

hub of Weatherman activity. Their combination of audacity and operational success made them appealing to me. In 1970, they pulled off the jailbreak of Timothy Leary — smuggled him out of his prison cell in a pickup truck. Leary had been doing "a dime" (ten-year sentence) for drug possession in Men's Colony West, a minimum-security prison outside of San Louis Obispo. Once out, they got him to a service station two miles south of the prison, where he ditched his prison garb, then to a safehouse. He and his wife eventually made their way to Algeria, where Leary hooked up with "Soul on Ice" Black Panther Eldridge Cleaver, who was presiding over his "Government in Exile."

Through a friend I had made while teaching at Berkeley, I met Annette Lunacelo, who was then around thirty years old. She had studied sociology at UCLA and Berkeley off and on for ten years and was part of the Free Speech Movement (SPM) on the UC campus, headed and led by graduate student Mario Savio. His "put your bodies upon the gears" was his best line from a rousing speech in front of Sproul Hall that got the protest going. The SPM was the ignition spark that set off much of the later 1960s campus protests and disruptions.

Annette, a seasoned veteran of mass protests, sit-down strikes, and political organizing, was working in a record store in Berkeley. When not working, she devoted her efforts to managing the safehouse in Oakland and moving the Weatherman fugitives in and out. Country-wide, they gathered in cells — typically, three to five men and women who lived together in a house like the one in Oakland. The cells were linked to the Weathermen leadership, "the Weather Bureau," by active members like Annette, who provided the above-ground support.

Annette set me up to meet with Bill Ayers and his wife Bernardine Dohrn. They were the two Big Enchiladas of the operation. "Bomber Bill," I called Ayers, as he was into blowing up stuff — between 1970-1974, twelve bombings — like the Headquarters of the New York City Police Department, the U.S. Capitol, and the Pentagon, striking, as he put it, blows against U.S. Imperialism.

By 1974, Ayers was hard to get to, even for people on the inside of the movement. He lived in the Bay Area, but he was reluctant to meet me there. I'm not sure why. With Dohrn, he was touring the Midwest, meeting with operatives in the cells. I had to find him there if I wanted to join his revolution-in-progress — a test, I suppose, of how serious I was.

Annette arranged it. I would meet him in front of the Art Museum in Forest Park, St. Louis, Missouri, wearing a black Alice Cooper tee-shirt and an Oakland A's baseball cap. Annette gave me coded answers to what would be his questions. If I checked out for him, from there, we would go to a safehouse in the central west end to conduct an interview. If all went well, I'd get "an assignment."

I flew to St. Louis. It was mid-afternoon when I met him in front of the museum in Forest Park. We made the initial signals to confirm the meet. Let me say here that we didn't hit it off at our first encounter. I led the way. We walked into the museum and entered the men's room off the lobby, where we would exchange the codes that completed our introduction. When I turned around, he lunged and pushed me up against the wall, his forearm rammed hard under my jaw, half-choking off my breath. "The code words, fucker," he hissed. If I wasn't fast enough with them, he threatened to punch my lights out.

Just before walking into the men's room with him close behind, I was already picking up some bad vibes from the guy and had jammed my hand into my right jacket pocket and slipped on the brass knuckles I always carry. When Ayers pinned me against the wall, I yanked them out of my pocket and popped him low, somewhere in his groin. With him on me, my leverage for the punch wasn't that good, but good enough that, when I connected, his arm dropped from my throat, and he reeled away. I stepped forward, loaded up with the arm and shoulder, torqued thirty-five degrees, and nailed him hard with a straight shot to the diaphragm. If you've never used brass knuckles in a fight, I highly recommend them. They conceal easily and give you an additional element of shock and surprise. Also, they negate your size disadvantage and add power to a punch by about a factor of ten — a slight exaggeration. You can kill someone with them if you need to. In most states, they are considered a deadly weapon and possession of them is illegal.

With that blow, Ayers folded up, went wobbly. I then took him down, landing on top, with my knee on his chest. I drew back like I was going to let him have another blast of knuckles, this one in the chops — I wasn't really going to. Getting his breath, he gasped: "Whoa, whoa, whoa, comrade… Truce, truce. I was pushing you too hard. I'm never sure what I'm going to get from a new guy, so I've got to come on heavy with the unknowns I meet. Really… Truce."

"I didn't come all the way from California to get bounced off the walls and a fucking neck massage. I'm up for a gig with the Weather, but if this is your MO, I'm out of here."

Ayers talked me off him — he was an accomplished talker — and I finally went for a truce. Ayers was a strong, physical guy, not huge, but he was quite athletic in high school and college. He made physical intimidation one more piece of his romantic outlaw persona with the macho touch. With about twenty pounds on me and several inches, when he first looked me over, no doubt, he probably figured that, with a surprise move, he'd get little resistance and easily scare the shit out of me.

He read that one wrong — dead wrong — and he was lucky I didn't rupture his spleen, or worse. One of my fondest memories; not his favorite, I am certain. Later, I learned that, inside the sandbox he played in, Ayers had a reputation for pushing the guys in the gang around, physically as well as verbally, both of which he excelled at. No testosterone deficit for him: He eagerly acted out the Alpha-male role, partly, I suspect, to signal to the cute girl-radicals in the pack that he was the top dog.

We ended up in Tom's Bar & Grill, one of the better hangouts in St. Louis's central west end. We didn't go to the safehouse. If and when I got caught, I wouldn't be able to reveal its location. Ayers was vain, arrogant, and full of himself, but he was the smartest and most savvy of the bunch. My pushback worked to my advantage in dealing with him. I was tough, aggressive, and adventurous. He recognized the same thing the Feds had in my detention cell in Florida — that I was low-risk averse, criminally inclined, and up for doing what it takes to make the guys in my gang happy with me. As Dr. Ari from my CIA days said: I was "high compensatory dependent." The only question for him was whether I was on board, ideologically speaking.

I told Ayers about the wet work I did for E. Howard and the Company in Chile and my "on the road to Damascus" Marxist epiphany once they kicked me loose. He was blown away with my recounting the ousting of Allende and the inside machinations of the CIA and Helm's fingerprints on the coup. Being a total-immersion personality himself, he completely identified with my "conversion" to Marxism, along with the fanaticism I was seized with. I told him that I could be very useful: He agreed. I have to say here, Ayer's "new-left," antinomian enhancements — copious sex and lots of drugs — made the radical life so much more of a hedonistic adventure to be a part of than the grim, puritanical 1930s version. I was all in.

CHAPTER TWENTY-ONE

Decimation

Kill all the rich people. Break up their cars and apartments.
Bring the revolution home, kill your parents, that's where
it's really at.

Bill Ayers

From the bar, we jumped into his beat-up Ford and drove south out of the city, to a truck-stop diner outside of the little town of Festus, not far from the Mississippi River. There, we met up with Bernardine Dohrn, a most stunning, wild-ass piece of radical work. She was as sex-exuding, good-looking, and maniacal as a woman can possibly be. She was also Bill's current squeeze and future wife. She and Ayers were the brains of the Weatherman operation.

Old J. Edgar Hoover had dubbed Dohrn as "La Pasionaria of the Lunatic Left." The reference was to Isidora Dolores Ibárruri Gómez, a Spanish communist, unquestionably the most famous woman of the Spanish Civil War. She was acclaimed for her cry "*No Pasarán!*" ("They will not pass") in a rousing speech that moved the embattled Republican troops to halt Franco's ferocious assault on Madrid in November 1936. La Pasionaria was also a conniving, murdering Stalinist. Following many years of exile in the Soviet Union after the defeat of the Republicans, she returned to Spain upon Franco's death. Soon after, she took an elected seat in the Spanish Cortez and became a high-profile feminist, leading many rallies. Hoover's comparison was perfectly drawn. Dohrn, a treacherous Stalinist personality from the get-go, was a braless La Pasionaria in a mini-skirt. She even followed a similar career trajectory that took her from the life of fugitive terrorist to a feminist law professor.

While Bill was into bombs, Bernardine, who had, incidentally, graduated from one of the top schools in the country, University of Chicago, was turned on by mass-murder. Some years before I met her, I heard of a pep-talk she had given to the SDS "National War Council," before the Weathermen eventually broke from it. It was in 1969, not long after the Charles Manson family murder of actress Sharon Tate — eight and a half months pregnant, at the time — and four of her friends. Bernardine was in a pique because some of her SDS colleagues were too shy to "go the distance" killing-wise. The Manson family, she enthused, set the style of murder that makes a statement of maximum impact. "Dig it," she said. "First, they killed those pigs, then they ate dinner in the same room with them, then they even shoved a fork into a victim's stomach! Wild!'" Then, she put up three fingers in a Manson fork salute.

Ayers came from money. His dad, Tom Ayers, was chairman of the energy company Commonwealth Edison in Chicago. When I met him, Bomber Bill was acting out his wildest fantasy as a daring-doo, Robin Hood Revolutionary with the Sheriff of Nottingham, bungling cops chasing him around. He was having a blast as a national center of attention. Finally, both the cops and the robbers decided the fantasy wasn't all that interesting anymore. The cops figured out that the robbers were grandstanding knuckleheads — big into demolition vandalism, not a serious threat to overthrow the government. And the robbers? The "Revolution" they endlessly talked about and were so devoted to was a laughable parody. It was cheap theater, staged with attacks on the "symbols of U.S. Imperialism," gimmickry reduced to the blowing up of restrooms in government buildings. They imagined themselves as the Lenin's, Castro's, and Ho Chi Minh's of America but were locked in a state of delayed adolescence made possible by "the system" they wanted to bring down. Their parody got stale, and they never got their own joke. The paradox that their cartoon careers embodied was to end up being indulged, forgiven, and ultimately rewarded by the society they professed to hate and wanted to destroy. Life on the lam eventually got old, not so much fun anymore. Adulthood called. They wanted to live unmolested in nice houses in good neighborhoods, fine dining and top-shelf wine, kids, professional trappings — you know, that bourgeois existence, part of the "Fascist Amerika" upon which Ayers and his pals — like me, for a time — poured out the boilerplate Marxist diatribes and kept threatening to overthrow. There was never the slightest chance. I think that they knew it.

The most intriguing part was how it all turned out for Ayers, which was amazingly well. No other society in the world would shower its avowed enemy with such amenities. Ayers managed to grab the best at both ends of life, plus a comfortable middle — acting up in youth; security, comfort, respectability, even admiration, as a grownup. Bomber Bill got to do it all — everything, and at no personal cost — in his youth to be the complete antinomian, making it with tons of chicks, doing lots of dope, wild, crazy, lawless. In his prime, bomber Bill grabbed all the perks of professional respectability. He landed the sweetest of sinecures, a tenured professorship at the University of Illinois, Chicago, impressionable young people at his disposal. He retired to the tony Hyde Park neighborhood in Chicago. There, he got social access to a future President of the United States, schmoozing with the up-and-coming Senator Barack Obama via an Annenberg Foundation gig, and, some say, ghost wrote his two books for him. In Ayers, all right pieces of "loco" came together at the right time, making him *the* model mentality of late '60s, early '70s student radicalism turning lethal and going completely off the rails. But he was "crazy like a fox." A consummate opportunist and conman — it takes one to know one — Bill Ayers lived the life that many lesser talents, like me, could only look upon with the greatest envy.

Wife Bernardine pulled off the same act. After "retirement" from her career as a murder-inciting criminal, the logical next step would be…? No less than a law degree from the University of Chicago — then, to teach. Instill future lawyers with respect for…what is it now? The law. Give interviews to admiring, suck-up young "journalists" and gush about your youthful, idealistic days of speaking "truth-to-power" and poking your finger in the eye of the rotten establishment — the one that has forgiven your law-breaking and now rewards you. Hot in youth, she aged well, so there were flattering fashion asides galore coming out of the published interviews. As much as possible, she sought to keep the embarrassing sorts of "Sharon Tate, Dig it" talk under wraps. Nobody important to the advancement of her post-criminal career ever held it against her.

The "establishment" that Bill and Bernardine professed to hate so much and wanted so much to destroy turned out to be more than forgiving. It conferred on them that chic-radical celebrity status that opened all the right doors and made post-revolutionary America for them a very comfortable place.

His 2001 Memoir, *Fugitive Days*, Ayers begins: "Memory is a motherfucker." Who can say what that means? I don't know. I do know that it didn't come from Marx, Marcuse, or Oliver Wendell Holmes.

Here is my best guess. He was signaling to his readers that they should not expect his memory to be particularly reliable — wink-wink. He was not even going to make a serious effort at honest recollection. Nor should he have to. Whatever he did back then, no matter how stupid, flagrantly criminal, or despicable, well…for all his fans and admirers out there, "motherfucker" signals that the past is all cool now. It's fine because he had always arranged his world in a perfect symmetry of the forces of Good versus Evil. And, unquestionably, he was and still is always on the side of the angels. What matters is not what you do. Who, *really*, cares about "memory"? After all, the thing's not that reliable, anyway. Rather, it's about how good (virtuous) you felt — and still feel — about doing it. So, yes, in your inimitable 1960s counter-culture patois, you relegate memory to that hip, "whatever" region of "Motherfuckerness." That is the fantasy realm where what counts is not what happened but how your imagination and fantasies played out for you in all the right ways. All the roads taken turn out to be avenues of vindication, self-satisfaction, and self-promotion.

But, to return to my adventures. I spent the afternoon and evening with Bill and Bernardine — B & B, as I came to call them — getting myself inducted into the ranks of these trend-setting social justice warriors. It was 1974. Never have I met a more self-infatuated duo drowning in delusions of moral-perfection surrounded by an evil world.

Weather Underground was coming off a two-year period of semi-dormancy, in part because the Vietnam war, a chief source of its moralizing energy, was winding down. In 1973 and early 1974, Ayers had been bouncing his manuscript *Prairie Fire: The Politics of Anti-Imperialism* off the rest of the Weather leadership. Fancying themselves as high-powered intellectuals, they believed that a radical manifesto would boast the Weather Underground's revolutionary creds. They were "thinkers" — in their own minds — as well as doers. So, out it finally came, a 156-page screed covering the entire universe of "injustices" ranging U.S. imperialism, ubiquitous racism, destruction of the environment, the exploitation of women, and the oppression of Native Americans. I've probably left something out.

From me, Bill and Bernardine wanted two things. First, I was to become one of the "mules" they commandeered to distribute their books nationally, to radical and counter-culture bookstores, where it would make its way out to enlighten potential new bomber-wannabes. To give the book, literally speaking, an explosive launching, a series of actual bombings was also in the pipeline. This made good sense, in a way. When you're blowing up restrooms in government and corporate offices all over the country, sophisticated-sounding, morally-charged lingo informs the yet-initiated that what might appear to the casual onlooker as what-the-hell spasms of vandalism are, actually, revolutionary blows that signal the destruction of the corrupt establishment. Juiced up "revolutionary" moral imperatives are essential. These books would rile up their readers, who they hoped would enlist in the "cause." Weather Underground folks had to prove it was not all-talk-and-no-action, and that the organization was still committed to "the Revolution." *Prairie Fire* was also an invitation for other radical groups to take up "armed struggle" against the establishment.

Second, I would launch one of the bombings, an opportunity I had hoped for. I was ordered back to San Francisco, to blow up the office of the California Attorney General as a response to the police killing of six Symbionese Liberation Army (SLA) members. Earlier in 1974, the SLA kidnapped publishing heiress Patty Hearst in spectacular fashion. The country was riveted by its sheer brazenness. The day of the kidnapping, the country was focused on the impeachment proceedings against Richard Nixon. Nixon's Presidential ass was now in a vice grip: Special Prosecutor Leon Jaworsky was demanding that Nixon turn over the White House tapes.

The Hearst kidnapping had a personal dimension for me. I was teaching a philosophy class at Berkeley at the time. Patty was a sophomore there and a student in my class — an especially good one. She was living in an apartment off-campus with her fiancé, Steven Weed. Steve was a graduate philosophy student. I had gotten to know him when we team-taught a class at the community college, a class on ethics — yes, I know what you are thinking. We were friendly, based on our mutual engagement with philosophy. He was engaged and serious about it; I had become good at pretending to be.

I had been to their apartment several times and met Patty, unaware that she was an heiress from a famous family. I didn't then pay much attention to last names, and neither one of them, understandably, mentioned it. Steve had encouraged her to enroll in my class, which she had done not long before she was snatched away by the SLA crazies. Patty was a lovely, serious, down-to-earth young woman.

The SLA had burst into the apartment that Patty and Steve shared and dragged her out. Off she went into a captivity that played itself out in a wild, national, attention-grabbing drama. Patty joined in on the bank robberies and was finally captured a year and a half after the police had killed the six SLA leaders, including head guy, Donald DeFreeze, in a wild shootout. She got a prison sentence she didn't deserve. Her conversion to "Tanya" during her abduction was clearly a Stockholm Syndrome event. The SLA had kept her blindfolded for more than fifty days, closed in a safehouse with a non-stop harangue of radical rhetoric. She was repeatedly raped. Bill Clinton eventually pardoned her — one of the few he didn't get something from, like the infamous Marc Rich.

In Pittsburgh, one of my new colleagues blew up most of the 29th floor of Gulf Oil headquarters. *Prairie Fire* had the impact Ayers and his crew were hoping for. It inspired a wave of terror by a fringe, Puerto Rican radical sect on the East Coast. Its members set off a series of bombings that hit U.S. skyscrapers, landmarks, and presidential campaign offices, killing dozens of innocent people. This was second generation Puerto Rican terrorism. Terrorists from an earlier one had tried to assassinate President Truman in 1950 and launched a machine-gun attack on the floor of Congress in 1954. To help Hillary pander to the Puerto Rican voters when she was running for the U.S. Senate in New York, you may have forgotten that Bill Clinton, in 1999, offered clemency to sixteen of the bomber-assassins who were still in prison.

Bill and Bernardine had given me contact information for one of the Weather Underground bomb-makers in the Bay Area. Three days after I flew back to California, I was in the basement of a safehouse in San Jose with Nick Sacco, nom de guerre of the guy who was building the bomb I was going to place in one of the restrooms of the California Attorney General's office. The real Sacco was the sidekick of Bartolomeo Vanzetti. The two were American-born Italian anarchists — Sacco and Vanzetti, that is — executed for murdering a guard and a paymaster during the April 15, 1920 armed robbery of the Slater and Morrill Shoe Company in Braintree, Massachusetts. They were supposedly framed and unjustly convicted, and their trial and subsequent execution made them international martyrs of the Left.

I knew only Sacco's real first name, Kevin, who, unlike most of the hard-science and technology challenged Weatherman — Ayer's college degree was in education — appeared to be, by education and inclination, a chemist-physicist. He was a very smart guy. Unlike Ayers and Dohrn, Kevin came from a real blue-collar background. He gave me a three-day crash course on dynamite: how to fuse it, how to transport it without blowing yourself up, how to denote it, and where to place it to give it the maximum explosive effect.

On May 31, 1974, twenty minutes before the office-listed closing hours at 5:00 p.m., on a Friday, I took a Yellow Cab to 455 Golden Gate Ave in San Francisco. With short hair, a clean shave, and dressed in a three-piece, Bill Blass, pinstriped grey business suit, I couldn't have looked more corporate. I carried my bomb in a briefcase into the Attorney General's Office building and placed it in a waste container in the men's room on the third floor. It was timed to go off at 5:25 p.m., just after the building closed its offices — after the patrons and staff vacated and before the custodial staff began their early evening shift.

I left the building, stepped into a payphone booth a block away, and dialed the San Francisco City police station. The following conversation with the sergeant on the other end of the line ensued.

"San Francisco Police Department. Sergeant Peterson, speaking. How can I help you?"

"Good afternoon, Sergeant Peterson. I am calling to tell

you that in twenty-three minutes a bomb will be blowing holes in the Fascist headquarters of the California Attorney General's Office. Be assured, this is not a prank call. I speak on behalf of the People's revolutionary struggle against United States imperialism, racism, militarism, its methodical destruction of indigenous populations, and its devastation of the environment. This is just one of many blows to come that will strike against an Empire that conducts genocidal wars, subjugates people of color, and pollutes the planet. Again, this is not a prank call." Click.

Kevin waited for me two blocks down the street and drove me to the safehouse. The bomb went off as planned, destroying most of the third floor. Fortunately, no one was killed or injured from the blast. I laid low for a couple of weeks inside the house, living on take-out Pizza and *Anchor Steam* beer.

Ayers and the Weatherman leadership were hot to get *Prairie Fire* distributed nationally. With a van loaded with cases of the book, I set out on a route down the California coast then headed east through Arizona and New Mexico, making stops and deliveries at left-wing bookstores, many of them adjacent to university campuses.

When I got to Santa Fe, I was hoping for some R&R and then another assignment. Instead, a rude surprise was waiting for me. In a phone call to Kevin in the safehouse in San Jose, I learned that an FBI informer had penetrated the cell. My name and photograph were now featured on the FBI's wanted list. I was on my own: the high-profile target of a nationwide manhunt.

CHAPTER TWENTY-TWO

My Friend, Fidel

Cynicism is something which has become symbolic of imperial policy.

Fidel Castro

Before I wound up fitted for another orange jump suit, I decided to blow Dodge. From Santa Fe, I made my way south, across the border. In Mexico City, I found the Cuban embassy and made my pitch for political asylum. Thirteen years earlier, Lee Harvey Oswald had appeared there. He tried to defect just a couple of months before his November rendezvous with destiny in the Book Depository building above Dealey Plaza in Dallas. The Cubans nixed on Lee Harvey. He came off as a weirdo and a loser — supposedly.

But Fidel Castro, always pleased to show Uncle Sam the middle finger, decided to roll out the welcome wagon for me. The difference, maybe, was that Oswald, at that time, was an unstable nobody while I was "high profile" — a radical wanted by the reactionaries for "political" reasons. That made me a useful and somewhat stable somebody — finally.

I wasn't the first radical fugitive from the U.S. to get the welcome mat from Fidel. That honor belonged to Robert F. Williams, a black labor organizer in the early 1960s from

Detroit. Williams was a talented fellow, a big player early on in the civil rights movement, with an unusual twist on self-defense. In the early 1960s, he'd obtained a charter from the National Rifle Association to set up a rifle club to help blacks in Monroe, South Carolina defend themselves against the Klan. He followed this up with his book *Negroes with Guns*, which had a big influence on the Black Panthers. During the Cuban Missile Crisis in 1962, Williams used Radio Free Dixie, a radio network that Fidel had let him set up, to urge black soldiers in the U.S. armed forces, who were then preparing for a possible invasion of Cuba, to engage in insurrection against the United States. Williams eventually returned to the States and died in Baldwin, Michigan. My Uncle Bill's funeral home there handled the funeral arrangements.

I made it to Cuba. There, I set up shop in Fidel's socialist workers paradise, where everyone worked as little as possible. Well, except for the sadistic state security goons, who put in a lot of overtime torturing the serfs insufficiently enthused about the equality of poverty Fidel and Raúl had lovingly made for them.

I've met some infamous people in my adventures. Fidel was one of the most cunning, intriguing, and impressive. He did political theater like no other — a consummate performer. Like a lot of other politicos at the top of the heap, he was a self-infatuated megalomaniac and a charmer, a master manipulator.

The Lefties from the U.S. over the decades trooped down on que, eager to pay him homage. They departed in a hypnotic trance. The Hollywood celebs, particularly, turned themselves inside out slobbering about his unparalleled endowments. Robert Redford, Jack Nicholson, Spike Lee, Oliver Stone, Woody Harrelson, Danny Glover, Ed Asner, Shirley MacLaine, Leonardo DiCaprio, and Kevin Costner all made the journey to Havana to bow and genuflect before *El Maximo Lider*. Paul Hollander called them "political pilgrims" — rich and famous ones. Cayo Piedra was Fidel's island retreat, ten miles off the coast. Only special guests were allowed to visit him there. You had to be a high-up "somebody." Gabriel García Márquez, the Columbian novelist, Ted Turner, founder of CNN, and DDR's Erich Honecker got to see the luxurious setting where Fidel would go to relax, snorkel, and enjoy fine dining.

Steven Spielberg, too, was wined and dined by *El Maximo Lider*. They chatted through the night. Spielberg emerged at dawn to yammer about his "close encounter of the best kind." "This," he breathlessly announced, "was the eight most important hours of my life." Okay. I can imagine Fidel at hearing this, thinking to himself: "What a hopeless suckup!"

No one could amass celebrities and play them as starstruck stooges better than Fidel. Setting him apart from so many other cult-creators was his wily ability to overcome nearly impossible odds stacked against his success. He thrived on adversity. In the late 1950s, Fidel, brother Raúl, Che Guevara, and a small collection of rag-tag revolutionaries sailed from Mexico on the rickety "Granma" to Cuba, where they got ambushed by Batista's troops near the shoreline. The small band of guerillas survived and made it to the remote Sierra Maestra mountains in southeastern Cuba, where they staged their makeshift, highly improbable revolution. Conditions were primitive, but they persisted, and, thanks to local peasant support, turned their long-odds gamble into a stunning success.

Fidel's determination and smarts against staggering odds put him in the driver seat. He also had a big boost from *New York Times* reporter Herbert Mathews, who smuggled himself into Fidel's Sierra Maestra camp, interviewed him, and returned home to write glowing, worshipful *NYT* reports about the rebels. Charismatic Fidel, he gushed, was leading a youth movement that would bring free elections and democracy to Cuba. Here was a masterpiece in the finest tradition of *NYT* alternative-reality fantasy-journalism. Matthews' Grey Lady articles also served to push away U.S. support for Batista's corrupt, crumbling regime.

On New Year's Day, 1959, on a captured tank, the thirty-two-year-old revolutionary rolled triumphantly into Havana. The imperialist puppet had fled the island with 300 million hard-earned dollars and headed for Salazar's Portugal. The former army sergeant had served faithfully as a corrupt, but mostly reliable dictator who had worked very hard to make Cuba a hospitable destination for American tourists and a profitable place for American gangsters and U.S. investors. Many of the latter were the clients of John Foster Dulles's law firm. Puff! Gone was the American-owned Cuban yes-man; in his place, an implacable American enemy — a wild-man Marxist, just ninety miles away. Never did they dream he'd rule the island for the next fifty-five years and arise — exalted worldwide — as a personal symbol of virtuous anti-Americanism.

A cautionary note: The long-term future for American-installed puppets can be dicey because Patron Uncle Sam always turns out to be a fickle partner. He looks at these relationships in a strictly "what have you done for me lately" sort of way. The puppets? A highly disposable commodity. Many of them don't seem to grasp just how far down this downside can take them. When it's clear skies for Uncle Sam, it's "we." When the dark clouds roll in, it's "at the sound of the tone, you're on your own, Amigo." Batista — later, South Vietnam's President Ngo Dinh Diem and the Shah of Iran — learned the hard way that promise-keeping is not Uncle Sam's strong suit. The puppets end up between a rock and a hard place because Uncle Sam's happiness often does not match up with the well-being of the little people, the ones the puppets are supposed to be looking out for.

Castro's skill and moxie turned his revolution and Cuba, a former U.S. vassal state and American tourist playground, into symbols of triumph in a never-ending faceoff against U.S Imperialism. Scruffy beard and military fatigues, strutting and posturing, he was always a frustrating, fury-arousing step ahead of the button-down stiffs from Foggy Bottom and the cloak-and-dagger suits out of Langley. For him, it was a win-win; for the Cubans under his heel, not so much. Still, he became a mythical hero in many parts of the world where the U.S. was seen as a bully, but especially in Latin America. Particularly impressive for me was his perfectly played role of David taking on the U.S. Goliath, constantly poking his finger in Uncle Sam's eye. Love him or hate him, Fidel played the high-stakes game of geopolitical brinksmanship with perfection, manipulating and playing the world's two superpowers — the U.S. and the USSR — against each other, nearly causing WWIII in 1962, a mere three years after he ran Batista off the island.

Fidel was enduring enchantment for the Left, not only the Hollywood idiots, but also many of the college kids in the land of his archenemy, the U.S. His expertly choreographed romantic revolutionary politics was compelling — the young, rugged revolutionary courageously confronting a corrupt system topped out with decadent, Brooks Brothers-suited elders. He created the "Che Guevara martyrdom brand" that thrives worldwide fifty plus years after the death of his psychopath assistant. He built a huge military machine in a small country and sent his armies to support communist guerilla movements all over the world, including Africa. A

U.S. attempt to overthrow him — the Bay of Pigs — he turned into a massive propaganda victory and humiliation for the U.S. government. Also, he fended off U.S. attempts to assassinate and depose him, rode out the crushing decades-long U.S. embargo, and got his ultimate revenge against Uncle Sam by frustrating and outlasting an astounding one-quarter of all the U.S. Presidents — count them, eleven — from Eisenhower to George W. Bush and into the Obama administration. From his modest perch on the Caribbean island, Fidel Castro was a larger-than-life player on the 20th century world historical stage.

CHAPTER TWENTY-THREE

Assassination Destination

The best government is a benevolent tyranny tempered by an occasional assassination.

Voltaire

Ensconced in Cuba with the exalted status of a U.S. political fugitive, I hesitated to tell Fidel about my CIA involvement in toppling his Chilean protégé, Salvador Allende. I feared that I could end up in one of his penal camps, or worse. However, Fidel seemed to know everything about the U.S.'s intelligence community, and I wasn't confident that, somehow, via one of his moles, my role in the Chile coup might eventually come to the surface — better to chance it, get out in front, and put my own spin on it. Plus, I thought he would be keen to learn more about the specific details of the operation and the CIA-hired assassins. E. Howard Hunt connived with mobsters like Chicago's Sam Giancana and Santo Trafficante, Jr., the top Miami crime boss and chief hood in pre-Revolutionary Cuba. They did their damnedest to assassinate him during the JFK years. Castro was forgiving. Like all the treacherous types who connive their way into top positions of power, consistency and high principle are lower priorities than, as Barack Obama in one of his Caudillo-sounding, un-self-censored moments put it during his Presidency: "Punishing your enemies and rewarding your friends."

One of the "enemies" long fixed in Fidel's crosshairs was Anastasio Somoza DeBayle, known affectionately to his friends as "Tachito." Somoza, a run-of-the-mill banana republic Caudillo, knew to respond, when Uncle Same asked him to jump: "How high, *Patrón?*" He had "inherited" the country from his daddy, Anastasio Somoza García. They both ran Nicaragua in Central America as their personal piggybank and "family" enterprise until Daniel Ortega and the Sandinista Gang, with a lot of help from Fidel, Raúl, and, it may surprise you, Jimmy Carter, chased Junior out of the country and into exile, in the 1970s. Fidel nurtured a huge, festering grudge against Tachito for offering Nicaragua to the U.S. Government as a launching pad for the 1961 botched Bay of Pigs invasion.

Given my success with the CIA-staged coup in Chile, Fidel assigned me the role of "El jefe de Proyecto," "Project Manager" for "Operation Reptile," a plot he had hatched with his Sandinista amigos to assassinate the hated Somoza, whom they had recently overthrown. The ex-dictator had fled Nicaragua and was ensconced in exile in President Alfredo Stroessner's creepy Paraguay, reputed to have been a retirement community for high-up, post-WWII Nazis looking hither and yon for a soft landing. The notorious Nazi chief and private secretary to Hitler, Martin Bormann, for years was rumored to be hiding there, until DNA evidence in the late 1990s confirmed his death in 1945 in Berlin. Bumping off Tachito in Stroessner's backyard would be the icing on the cake for Fidel and the Sandinistas, a delicious twofer.

Stroessner, sartorially speaking, was inclined toward sash-resplendent, garish General's uniforms. A big sinister-looking dude with a broad impassive face, he decorated his upper lip with one those closely-cropped fussy mustaches popular with South American dictators. Son of a German immigrant and a spooky, far-right anti-communist, he ruled Paraguay with an iron fist for thirty-four years with an aura of dark, sinister cruelty. With him was the usual stuff you get from these second-tier, corrupt strongmen — cult of personality, kinky, sadistic, pedophilia quirks, public-asset plundering, torturing and "disappearing" critics and opponents. He survived in power those long years in part because he was very tight with the U.S. government, for which, during his years in power, anti-communism was the sole criterion for being a favored destination for American largesse. All else was forgiven or ignored. As nasty and repressive as he was, the U.S. loaded him up with military weaponry and trained his officers at the Army School of the Americas at Fort Benning, Georgia. For Marxist, Yankee haters like Fidel and Daniel Ortega, few U.S. lackeys were more odious than Stroessner.

With the plans for Operation Reptile in place, Fidel sent me to Asuncion to carry out the preliminary reconnaissance and the get the lay of Somoza's compound and the surrounding neighborhood. I was to study his daily routines and plan for the execution of the hit. I entered Paraguay with a forged Canadian passport by way of Mexico City, posing as a bespectacled professor of urban anthropology from the University of Alberta on sabbatical tour doing research for a book on the culture of South American cities. My first stop was the anthropology department at the *Universidad Nacional de Asunción* to make some professional contacts in order to bolster my cover as a researcher and writer. Besides being flat-out weird, like most of Paraguay, the place was an excruciatingly uninspired imitation of an institution of higher learning — staffed by glowering government toadies, the inert, time-serving professors camped out in their gloomy, rundown offices and classrooms, hazy-blue with cigarette smoke. Unlike the university students in the U.S. and Western Europe, those in Paraguay appeared to be uniformly docile, seemingly content to scurry unmolested to their scheduled classes and endure the dullness and tedium that awaited them.

Being a clean-shaven, rugged but professorial-appearing gringo looking a bit like Harrison Ford in the *Indiana Jones* movies gave me perfect cover. I raised no suspicion with the ever-vigilant knuckle crushers who staffed Stroessner's secret police force. These shiny-black-suited gorillas, for obvious reasons, I wanted at all costs to avoid. Around the district in Asuncion near where Somoza lived as well as other neighborhoods, I rummaged so as not to arouse suspicion. I occasionally snacked on the delicious *chipá manduvi* I bought on the street and busied myself acting professorial, interviewing people, openly taking notes — staying out of the bars — all the time gathering the necessary intelligence and preparing for the hit.

For several weeks, I carefully logged Somoza's daily routines. They turned out to be surprisingly regular and predictable. Stupid of him, but he had deluded himself into imagining that he was safe. Most days, he emerged midday, chauffeured in an unarmored white Mercedes-Benz S-Class sedan.

At last, I signaled Fidel: The operation was ready to launch. The Sandinistas came to town big as bear shit and ready to rock-n-roll. A team of eight — four men and four women, including myself — it was time to move in for the kill. We were loaded up with Soviet-made firepower: machine guns, AK-47s, assault rifles, automatic pistols, and, best of all, an RPG-7 rocket launcher with four anti-tank grenades and two anti-tanks rockets. All of this to knock off some out-to-pasture, fat-ass, ex-dictator moldering away in a country that

American wise-cracker P. J. O'Rourke once quipped "was nowhere and famous for nothing." No matter. Abandoned by Uncle Sam, he was in for it, soon to be "toast," literally, even though tucked away — safely, he believed — in Stroessner's out-of-the-way Dark Kingdom.

No one could nurse a grudge like Fidel, particularly for someone connected in any way with the U.S. imperialists. Leading the charge was a wild man, Enrique Gorriarán Merlo (code named "Ramon"), who had been a *Ejército Revolucionario del Pueblo* (ERP) leader before he got chased out of his native Argentina by the right-wing generals. Our hit job would go down as one of the most spectacular and gruesome in the annals of modern-day political assassinations.

With my intel, our team set up for a side-street ambush, a short distance outside of Somoza's residence. His limo emerged midday. We hit it with one helluva firestorm.

The first anti-tank rocket, aimed head on, missed. But Hugo Irurzún, known as Capitan Santiago, charged the limo and gunned down the chauffeur. We began blasting away with grenades — then, a second rocket launched from the side. It sealed the deal, ripping off the top, turning Somoza and his two passengers in the Mercedes into unrecognizable charcoal briquettes. Tachito's charred remains had to be forensically identified with his feet. With the international press announcement of the assassination, the Sandinista government declared a "national day of celebration." *Sic semper tyrannis!*

The gruesome killing of Somoza had some eerie connections and resemblances with the assassination of Rafael Trujillo — both taken out in their cars in ambush attacks — in the Dominican Republic in 1961. The eeriest connection of all, I suppose, was me. I was involved in both. The first, indirectly; I was collateral damage — lifelong. The second? Well, obviously, I had near complete ownership of this one, and as I reflect on it now, assassinating Somoza was a deeply subliminal act of filial revenge for my father, a way somehow to balance the "moral" ledger for his violation and suffering — perhaps, a tiny piece of "cosmic" justice.

The two assassinations also had a curious, complicated, and indirect "Fidel" nexus that takes a bit of unraveling to get at — one that goes back to FDR. Though nineteen years apart, both assassinations — Trujillo's and Somoza's — pivoted around Uncle Sam's Fidel Castro obsession and the decades-long feud that it propelled.

Here's what I learned years after Trujillo's killing: From the beginning, he was a U.S. stooge. Once in place, he was supported by the U.S. government for almost thirty years. By the late 1950s, Trujillo's reign had become so brutal, disgusting, and corrupt that the U.S. decided to oust him. Eisenhower wanted him gone, but he went down early under Kennedy's watch. JFK had signed off — secretly — on the hit and approved the weapons handoff to the Dominican assassins — but no U.S. fingerprints on the operation. "We don't care if the Dominicans assassinate Trujillo; that is all right. But we don't want anything to pin this on us," JFK said. That's not the sort of "transparent decision-making" you might expect from a democratically elected head of state. His language, rather, has a gangland ring — picked up, perhaps, from his father. Trujillo's brutality and corruption didn't much bother the American government — not there; not much anywhere else. It was just that El Jefe was at the saturation point of decadence and corruption that threatened the stability of his regime and, more importantly, U.S.-connected interests.

The Somozas — father and son — were always U.S. puppets. FDR, in the 1930s, was supposed to have said of

Somoza senior: "He might be a son of a bitch, but he's our son of a bitch." Takes one to know one, as they say. But he and junior remained "our son of a bitch" for a long time, until Jimmy Carter's improbable and unfortunate assent to the White House. James Earl, among other things, considered himself to be the World's Chief Moral Policeman, meaning, in a practical way, that there were in place too many U.S.-supported SOBs in his holier-than-thou estimation of who should be left to their own devices. This translated into stripping away their U.S support and turning loose on them the dogs, the radical opposition in their own backyards to have at them, as he did with the Shah of Iran. All of that played out, as we so happily recall, so much the better for the Iranians and the Americans. President Carter hadn't grasped the basic lesson of Dictatorship 101: One SOB strongman deposed usually gives way to one who is worse, often a lot worse. The big-bearded lads who chased out the Shah became, as we all know, our closest ally in the Middle East, and Iran emerged as a model of the kind of modern, secular "progressive" sort of polity that Carter so much admired. Just two years before Carter bailed on the Shah, at a state dinner, he toasted the Shah's Monarchy as "an island of stability in a sea of turmoil." Did he really believe that? Who knows? The Shah must have stupidly believed Jimmy, though, when he said: "I will never tell a lie; I will never betray a trust."

Jimmy, the Parson Scold, decided that the Sandinistas would be a vast improvement over Somoza, just the kind of humanitarians to install "democracy" in Nicaragua and make "human rights" their highest priority. The "rule of law" and "limited government" would arise there just as it did in Castro's Cuba.

Like many self-appointed arbiters of the just and the righteous, Carter's vocabulary favored those nebulous abstractions that appeal to the high-minded busy-bodies and make them feel virtuous and superior. You've seen these earnest folks in action, toting their water bottles, hoisting their signs at protest rallies, and posting on Facebook and Twitter, always struggling to demonstrate how virtuous they are.

Virtue-words. They make you feel good, but they get limp and soggy as you try to make them into something that's not incurably vague or meaningless. "Human rights," for example, sounds swell. It tugs at the heartstrings, but what, exactly, are "human rights"? Where did they come from? How do they differ from regular "rights"? It gets complicated. Is the "right to an abortion" a "human right"? And how does whatever you chose to call the "aborted-one" figure in? Not human, so no rights? There is heated disagreement on that, as I recall. So, who gets to say? "Right to healthcare" — a "human right"? Didn't used to be. When did it become one? In a country like Somalia, with one doctor per 8,000 people, how does that "right" work — that is, get enforced? Polygamy? Is a guy having more than one wife violating "women's rights," and are "women's rights" "human rights?" And, if so, then shouldn't we be trying to overthrow all the governments in the Muslim world to promote human rights? Is the "right" of a religiously motivated parent refusing a vaccination for his kid a "human right," or does the kid have a "human rights" claim on the vaccination he believes will keep him safe from disease?

When "rights" compete, as they often do, who gets to decide? Those with the power, or the helpless — which ones do you think? It gets messy quickly. Down it goes, down the slippery slide from high-minded moralizing to moralistic masturbation to amoral hypocrisy. The lofty morality of "human rights" churns its way into muddy politics; politics degenerates into ideology. From the sperm of ideologies, ideologues are hatched. Ideologues can't help turning into fanatics. Fanatics want people to be just like them and are hot to kill the ones who refuse. We've seen how that scenario unfolds all around the world.

Instead of one of "our son of a bitches," happy to do Uncle Sam's bidding, like Fulgencio Batista in Cuba in the 1950s and Somoza in the 1970s, the U.S. could have ended up with a contrary son of a bitch like Castro running the Dominican Republic — another populist Marxist raising hell and threatening American enterprises, like gambling interests in Cuba and the banana imports from Guatemala to enrich the United Fruit executives and stockholders. Plus, Castro was chomping at the bit to have a go at doing to Trujillo what he had done to Batista and would eventually do to Somoza. The U.S. needed a more predictable, reliable puppet than the Caligula-like Trujillo. He had to go, but in a way "not apparent to unauthorized persons."

The brutal interrogation that Dad experienced, I came bitterly to realize, was a consequence of the criminalized way the U.S. regularly conducts its foreign policy under the pretenses of whatever moralistic claptrap is currently in vogue — anti-communism, human rights, upholding "our values," promoting "democracy." It's conducted secretively, cloak-and-dagger style, by guys nobody knows or voted for, nameless rogues who should be behind bars or in psychiatric hospitals.

Thus, the irony of how this all played out, corruption and collusion-wise. Castro wanted to kill Somoza because he, as well as his father, had been a U.S. stooge and had connived with secret U.S. operatives to overthrow him. Castro rightfully hated the U.S. and the corrupt puppets they had installed throughout the Caribbean. The U.S. government wanted Trujillo dead because it rightly feared the DR was on the way to having another Castro near our shores making even more trouble. Jimmy Carter wanted Somoza gone, thinking, apparently, that a Castro-style Marxist dictatorship would stabilize the region. Both assassinations were, in a sense, complicated Castro-affairs, but with completely different ideological twists and turns. Anti-communism and Castro-phobia was behind Trujillo's messy exit; communist, Castro-fueled, anti-Uncle Sam revenge blew up Somoza.

CHAPTER TWENTY-FOUR

Ennui on the Island

If I'm a fool for leaving,
I'd be twice the fool to stay
      Gene Watson, "If I'm a Fool for Leaving"

Fidel was ecstatic with the spectacular way we had taken out Somoza. Through safehouses and an underground network, I made my escape from Paraguay. In Havana, I got a hero's welcome and settled in for what I thought would be the long haul.

Raúl was impressed, as well. He functioned as Fidel's chief enforcer (Defense Minister), running the secret police and his military intelligence. Fidel and Raúl quickly concluded that I would be a good fit for further undercover operations under Raúl's supervision. I got to spend some time with Raúl and must confess that I came to like him better than his *hermano mayor*. Physically, the clean-shaven Raúl was much smaller than the 6'3" Fidel, with none of his charisma, but the guy was one tough hombre, a special someone you did not want to fuck with. In their early days of the Revolution, in the harsh rigors of the Sierra Maestra mountains, Raúl excelled as a guerrilla fighter taking on Batista's troops, getting shot at, taking hostages and executing them. Fidel himself had fostered a "good cop-bad cop" picture of their respective "styles." Sometimes, he'd intimidate people with the prospects of his possible demise. He would point to Raúl — "He will be much worse than I am," he would threaten. He may have been right.

Unlike Fidel, as well, Raúl avoided the spotlight and disliked public attention. Also, unlike Fidel, a "big picture" guy, Raúl focused himself on the specifics and details of translating whatever schemes Fidel would come up with into reality.

Raúl's "Achilles heel," however, was alcohol: The guy consumed vast quantities of Vodka with seemingly no effect on his work. More than once, he drank me under the table, and I was no slouch in those competitions. He could set 'em up and knock 'em over like no one I've ever seen. Late in the 1980s, it came up to bite him. That was when Fidel leaned hard on him to frame up the Bay of Pigs veteran, military general Arnoldo Ochoa, for drug smuggling and treason. Ochoa had been awarded the "Hero of the Revolution" title by Fidel himself in 1984, and he was personally very close — like family — to Raúl. Ochoa was tapped to take the fall for the international drug-smuggling scandals — the shit coming out of them was beginning to stick to the Castros themselves. They had to shanghai someone high up to frame, throw under the bus and show the international community that the Cuban government was all about "the workers," not a front for just another Caribbean drug cartel. Raúl staged the show trial and gave the order for the execution. Ochoa, I later learned, went out with courageous, spectacular class: He requested not to be blindfolded, and he gave the command to the firing squad himself.

The whole ugly business was to tear up Raúl. Imagine having to throw your best friend off a cliff. He began to hit the sauce with a vengeance. He was falling apart. The visible breakdown and screw-ups were putting Fidel in a fix. Word was, Fidel finally went to Raúl with an ultimatum, as only Fidel could deliver them: "Get sober, and pull your act together, Bro, else I'm going to have to put you down like the arthritic, old, family-favorite pooch that's taken to pooping on the carpet." Raúl got the message.

Shortly after I returned from Paraguay, I was introduced to an East German woman I'll call Elsa. Elsa worked as a Stasi agent in Leipzig in the 1960s and 1970s. Her daddy, Egon, was a big player in the communist resistance in the 1930s, during the run up to the Third Reich. Egon spent his WWII years in exile in the Soviet Union. He was dispatched by Stalin at the end of the war back to Germany, where he rose high up in the Stasi ranks, one of its most productive interrogators. He preached water and drank wine with Walter Ulbricht, who ruled the DDR early on, one of his most trusted capos. During the late 1930s, he was number two to Ernst Thälmann, leader of the German Communist Party, KPD. The German commies turned Thälmann into a martyr-saint. He was shot in Buchenwald in 1944, on personal orders from Hitler himself. On a street in Weimar, Germany, just a few miles from the camp where he was executed, is a big statue of the German communist martyr. Elsa's younger brother, Jürgen, rose to the top of East German intelligence. Jürgen, in the 1980s, headed up the palace guard for the Marxist Haile Mengistu, the Ethiopian strongman, one of the most odious of the many dictators in the region.

Though in her 40s when I met her, she was still a knockout commie broad — dark brown hair, green eyes, tall, and a stunning physique. The Stasi used her back in *die Deutsche Demokratische Republik* (DDR) as "honey trap" bait. *Die schöne Frau* had reeled in some pretty big fish, in the form of high-ranking diplomatic personnel from the UK and

France, including a cabinet minister. She'd also done some wet work in Italy — could break a man's neck without making a sound, had a chemist's command of poisons — and was fluent in at least five languages.

Elsa arrived in Havana on a long-term assignment. She came to train some of Fidel's young counter-espionage personnel in his intelligence service, the infamous *Dirección General de Intligencia (DGI)*. Fidel's intelligence-espionage was top-notch, world-class. The *DGI* ran circles around their keystone-cop counterparts in the U.S. One of his great successes — there were many in the contest of spooks that he played so well against the U.S. — was the placing of Ana Belen Montes — trained by Elsa — as a mole in the Pentagon's Intelligence Defense Agency. Ana spent sixteen highly productive years at the Pentagon. That's correct, big ones, undetected. She reached top-secret clearance, keeping Fidel "in the D.C. loop," before she was finally busted in 2001. This was four years after getting a "Certificate of Distinction," personally awarded by CIA Director George Tenet — what a pathetic patsy. There's a great photo-op of the award ceremony with the not-a-clue CIA Director wearing a shit-eating grin while standing beside a sphinxlike, smiling Cuban spy, Ana. No American spook got anywhere near that close to Fidel's spying operations.

Elsa had had a fling with Fidel, but the Big Guy, always looking for new action, had moved on to greener pastures. He tended to stick with the Cubanas. I ended up working in a counter-intelligence unit under Elsa's direction, and we got to be, how shall I say this, very close. We lived together for three years. From Elsa, I learned to speak passable German, a bit of conversational Russian, and how quietly to break someone's neck. Elsa also taught me how to listen to and appreciate Beethoven's String Quartets.

I enjoyed my off-hours with my *hübsche Freundin Spion,* but Fidel's speeches had become excruciatingly long and increasingly boring. He claims the *Guinness Book of Records* title for the longest speech ever delivered at the United Nations: four hours and twenty-nine minutes. Worse even, he bested that at the Third Communist Party Congress in Havana. There, he delivered a mind-numbing seven-hour-ten-minute stemwinder. I was in the audience for that eternity of inspiration. It only seemed like *half* a lifetime. You didn't dare fall asleep or look bored, and you clapped enthusiastically on cue. Fidel may have had the biggest ego in the entire solar system. So, it was never a healthy move to have him think you thought that he was a mere mortal.

By 1981, life in Cuba had become, as we used to say, "a bummer." There wasn't much to offer beyond the vast volumes of Fidel's increasingly stale hot air to listen to, beans and rice to eat, and posters of *"Che por siempre"* everywhere to look at. After a while, the rah-rah "Revolution" rhetoric just doesn't get you going like it used to. The country was running short on toilet paper. It was time to leave.

An opportunity suddenly presented itself in Argentina. The CIA was there, helping the right-wing government crush the increasingly violent insurgent leftist movements. Many of them were factions of the Peronist coalition that had taken turns ruling and ruining the country. Fidel, too, was fixated on Argentina, looking for opportunities to upend the ruling class there. Making life miserable for U.S.-supported right-wing generals, especially in the southern cone, was always a high priority for him. Hatred for Uncle Sam got Fidel out of bed and up and going in the morning — maybe, the fact that several U.S. Presidents tried to kill him had something to do with it.

Bored and secretly tired of Cuba, I was itching for some

action far away from the island. Argentina held some fascination for me, particularly the post-Peronist period. The ruling class there was careening out of control, with each government giving way to one even more corrupt, murderous, and incompetent. Fidel gave me the green light to go there and try to stir up some trouble on his behalf. Gringos drew less attention from the security forces than Latins, and it was easier to come up with a plausible cover to gain entry.

After a sad adios to Elsa, I left for Buenos Aires, there to initiate contact with the insurgency movement leaders and set up channels of Cuban support. They were getting hammered by the right-wing generals who had taken over after ousting Juan Perón's widow, Isabel, a fifth-grade drop-out and ex-nightclub dancer, from the Presidency in 1976.

CHAPTER TWENTY-FIVE

Agonistes in Argentina

One cannot accomplish anything without fanaticism.
                                        Evita Perón

I entered Argentina with a forged West German passport as Klaus Tschesh. My German was passable enough to get me by the few times I needed it. Posing as a freelance West Berlin journalist, I was supposed to be covering developments in the Argentine cultural and educational sphere for German readers. Germans very typically, unlike many Americans, have an insatiable curiosity about the world outside their own country. They love to travel, and South America is a popular destination for them.

Argentina, you will probably recall, had achieved notoriety for the extensive "hospitality" she extended in the late 1940s and early 1950s to some bigwig Nazi fugitives fleeing via the "ratlines" from the collapsed Third Reich. Perón's government provided them soft landing spots a safe, long way from *Der Vaterland* and the Simon Wiesenthal-type Nazi hunters. The notorious Croatian Ante Pavelić found comfortable safe haven in Buenos Aires, courtesy of Perón. Pavelić founded and headed the fascist Ustaše that ran Croatia as a puppet government for the Axis powers during WWII. He had presided over the mass-murder of tens of thousands of Serbs, Jews, and Roma. Eluding capture by the Allies, he hid out for a time in Rome, where he was able to get transit to Argentina.

The most notorious of the bunch and the most sought after, however, was *SS-Obersturmbannführer* Adolph Eichmann, one of the so-called "final solution" (*die Endlösung*) architects. Colonel Eichmann arrived there in 1950 and lived quietly as Ricardo Klement, a factory technician. In 1960, a Mossad — Israel's version of the CIA — commando unit tracked him down and kidnapped him in a Buenos Aires suburb. They then smuggled him out of the country in a pilot's uniform and whisked him off to Jerusalem. There, they staged a show trial — the guilty verdict and sentence were obviously predetermined — thereafter hanging him and scattering his ashes in the Mediterranean.

The trial was world sensational. The Israelis encased Eichmann in a glass booth — the movie "The Man in the Glass Booth" with Maximillian Schell was based on the trial — in the courtroom throughout the course of the proceedings, supposedly to protect him from assassination. I'm more inclined to believe that it was part of the Israeli government's efforts to turn the fake trial into "theater," having Eichmann resemble something more like an insect specimen under glass than just some ordinary old defendant on trial — symbolic revenge. When on the hunt for Eichmann, the Israelis had given him the codename "*Dybbuk,*" from the Hebrew word for an evil spirit that takes hold of a living person. You wouldn't have gathered that from looking at him.

Hannah Arendt, a German-born, Jewish-American philosopher covered the trial for the *New Yorker* and published her reflections on it in the highly controversial book *Eichmann in Jerusalem*. It was another one of the few books I read during my university days. In it, she reduced Eichmann to an intellectual pigmy. His personality was that of a stunted amoral bureaucrat, not the unfathomable monster demanded by the theodicy of Nazism — the "banality of evil," as she called what she saw in him during the trial. Evil in the form of banality? Well, that, you might conclude, didn't sit so well with some of the interested parties, and not a few of her Jewish friends unfriended her. Eichmann's forcible abduction by agents of the Israeli government on Argentinian territory, without the consent of Argentina, constituted a violation of Argentine sovereignty, an international tort. They pulled it off, however, without serious international repercussions and got their revenge.

The Argentina I discovered in the 1980s was a creepy place. It was all there: the ubiquitous sadomasochistic Tango, the ghosts of Juan and Eva Perón, and even then, ex-Nazis in the local bierstubes, hoisting their foamy steins and bellowing out *Horst Wessel Lied*.

I didn't last long there, either. Argentina was being whipsawed with urban terrorism reigning down from two directions: the government-sponsored version, with the right-wing Generals, intent on wiping out the increasingly radicalized leftist urban guerillas. They had launched "Operation Condor." The U.S. provided technical support. The CIA was knee-deep in the action. Its operations personnel used the *Human Resources Exploitation Manual* to train Argentine military officers — the title, a deliberately insipid circumlocution. A more descriptive and appropriate title would have been: "Interrogation Techniques of Physical and Mental Torture." These had been refined in Vietnam, in the infamous Phoenix Program run by CIA Director William Colby.

The Phoenix Program was said to have killed twenty

thousand Vietnamese suspected of being communists: It was one of the most notorious pieces of U.S Vietnam-era criminality. Called to testify before Congress and asked about Phoenix, Colby did a plausible impression of *Mad Magazine*'s gap-toothed, freckled mascot, Alfred E. Newman — "What, me worry?" He responded: "I would not want to testify that nobody was killed or executed in this kind of program. I think it probably happened, unfortunately." Unfortunately? Well, only when you're caught doing the killing. Mr. Chief-of-Secret-Operations had mastered the shoulder-shrugging, passive voice of the verb. "Probably happened?" — CIA-ese for "shit happens; time to move on." With Colby's testimony, you struggle to decide which is more contemptible, his staggering arrogance or the "give-him-a-pass" of the congressional committee. Colby, incidentally, died alone in a boating "accident," the circumstances of which, to this day, remain suspicious.

Continuing in that fine, Phoenix Operation tradition, American-trained Argentine-government agents conducted covert, illegal arrests and detentions. They carried out assassinations and kidnappings, tortured detainees, and unleashed independently operating death squads that "disappeared" terrorist suspects and collaborators.

The Left, too, was busy assassinating its opposition. Peronist guerrillas, Montoneros, and various splinter factions engaged in bombings directed at European and American-based companies — Goodyear and Firestone, Riker and Eli pharmaceutical labs, Xerox Corporation, and Pepsi-Cola bottling companies. European and American business executives were targets of kidnapping and assassination attempts, including the Director-general of the Fiat Concord Company-Argentina Office, kidnapped and murdered by the communist ERP guerrillas (*Ejército Revolucionario del Pueblo*) in

Buenos Aires. John Swint, the American general manager of a Ford Motor Company was killed by FAP (*Fuerzas Armadas Peronistas)* guerrillas.

My destination, I discovered, was a killing field, a non-stop scene of violence and terror. It was one of the many places in the world where the Cold War tensions between the U.S. and the USSR were dramatically playing themselves out in a limited sort of hot warfare by their ideologically driven proxies. I was hoping to be able to stir the pot a bit more, with some Cuban flavoring courtesy of Fidel.

I had discreetly installed myself in a hotel in downtown Buenos Aires, a stone's throw from the Recoleta Cemetery. The Recoleta is surreal: an opulent, afterlife piece of real estate occupied for the most part by Argentine's rich and famous, although Napoleon's granddaughter somehow found her final resting place there.

In the Recoleta, the mortal remains of Eva Duarte de Perón — expertly embalmed by the distinguished pathologist, Spaniard Pedro Ara, at the bidding of hubby Juan — had been deposited. This was after a twenty-year post-mortem world tour that took her from Argentina to Italy to Spain and finally back home to the land of the Gauchos. Ara had been summoned by Perón to employ his macabre skills and arrived just before Eva — in the final stage of cervical cancer and down to 79 pounds — died, in order to get a jump on the…uh…well, you get the picture. After her long, arduous journey, depicted by Tomas Eloy Martinez in his *Santa Evita* in all its richly bizarre twists and turns, as you might expect, her travel-worn corpus needed a bit of repair work. Fortunately, Domingo Tellechea, who had a worldwide reputation for the restoration of art, antiquities, and human remains was available and decidedly up for this pressing task. Evita wasn't just any ordinary, garden-variety stiff long overdue for a traditional burial underneath six good feet of Buenos Aires soil.

Argentina's recent history is incomprehensible without knowing something about her. She was an incredible, contradictory myth of sainthood and sexuality. A slightly educated actress of questionable "virtue" from poor, rural origins, she rose to become a highly personal symbol of the populist Peronist identity with the "*descamisados*," shirtless ones, the downtrodden working class. The Argentine Congress awarded her the title *Jefe Espiritual de la Nacion* (Spiritual Leader of the Nation). In a collective spasm of grief, two million Argentinians had filed past her coffin when she died in 1952. She was given a state funeral, an honor usually reserved for Heads of State. Her embalmed body became a big "tug" in the long, ongoing, and often brutal tug-of-war between the Peronists and anti-Peronists. The legacy of Peronism was always playing out in one crazy way or another — a soap opera sort of craziness that you could only find in Argentina, its people still chasing and busting the ghosts of Juan and Evita. The Generals, in 1976, decided to terminate Eva's afterlife peregrinations and adventures. They put her in the family's mausoleum, far out of the reach of any would-be body snatchers, where, now, as the BBC put it: "She lies five metres underground, in a crypt fortified like a nuclear bunker, so that no one should ever again be able to disturb the remains of Argentina's most controversial First Lady."

> *Don't cry for me Argentina*
> *The truth is I never left you*
> *All through my wild days*
> *My mad existence*
> *I kept my promise*
> *Don't keep your distance.*
>
> Andrew Lloyd Webber, "Evita"

Both living and dead, there were many "wild days" for her. There remains something perennially mysterious about Evita Perón.

CHAPTER TWENTY-SIX

Fake Cristina

Drunkenness is nothing but voluntary madness

Seneca

Evita and her crazy romance with Argentina aside, inside of a month, it was all over for me in Buenos Aires. This was due to a first-rate fuck up on my part.

As part of my journalist cover, I had arranged to meet and interview an Argentine woman. The meeting had been set up by a third party, Alejandro, who worked as a reporter at *Clarín* ("Bugle," in English), the largest tabloid newspaper in Argentina. Loitering about the *Clarín* offices, I'd been schmoozing with the reporters there, keeping up "the appearance" as a journalist. My hope was to make connections with some of the serious players in the underground anti-government apparatus.

The woman I was to meet, I was told, was a professor of Politics at the *Universidad Nacional de Mar del Plata*. Her name was Cristina de Fernández — not to be confused with de Cristina de Fernández Kirchner, the future kleptocrat *Presidenta* of Argentina, the wife of Néstor Kirchner. Néstor preceded his wife in office. He was the Argentine President when he did the best thing imaginable in his entire political career: He up and died. Cristina and Néstor were the Bill and Hillary of the Pampas. Like the Clintons, they discovered each other in law school. With their mutual lust for power and money, like the Clintons, they set their sights on the country's Presidency — first Nestor, then Cristina. They were, also like the Clintons, with little shame and had no aversion to the unseemly methods for getting whatever they were after. The Kirchners launched their careers as members of the *Juventud Peronista*, the Peronist Youth. They took up the left-wing Peronist tradition of promising free-stuff to the public-sector union members: With their coalition-building talents, some wheeling-dealing, and luck, they both made it to the President's office on a high-speed train of rampant corruption. Shortly after she left office in 2015, Cristina found herself facing dozens of criminal charges, reaching back to her Presidency and that of her husband, including bribery, embezzlement, and money laundering.

The other Cristina and I met at a restaurant downtown in the early evening. My plan was to interview her over dinner and collect ideas for an article that I was supposed to be writing — my reason for being in Argentina. It would appear in the popular German weekly, *Der Spiegel*. This was my cover story. It was all part of my attempt to appear legit and remain free to pursue contacts with clandestine opposition groups. I was nervous about who might be watching me and what they might be thinking I was up to. My instincts were on the mark, but on this occasion, they failed me.

Because she was a university professor specializing in politics, I would tell her that I wanted to learn more about the efforts of Argentine students at coping with the political unrest, radicalism, and government repression as source material for the *Der Spiegel* piece. West Germany, at this time, was plagued with bombings, kidnappings, and assassinations by radical students coming out of the universities. There would be huge German interest in knowing more about radicalized South America, a geographical source of inspiration for their own "home-grown" left-wing student-terrorists who were blowing up buildings, murdering policemen, and kidnapping politicians.

The RAF havoc-makers in the Federal Republic, Andreas Baader, Ulrike Meinhof, and Horst Mahler, had been carefully reading the *Minimanual of the Urban Guerrilla*, written by Carlos Marighella, a Brazilian theorist and practitioner of urban terrorism. Unlike Fidel, who began his revolution in the remote rural mountains of Cuba, Marighella, in the 1970s, had developed the strategy and tactics for launching the overthrow of authoritarian regimes in urban settings. Big cities were highly vulnerable places for small numbers of skilled terrorists to operate with great impact. I was familiar with Marighella's work from my days with the Weather Underground. The first English translation of the *Minimanual* appeared in the radical underground weekly *Berkeley Tribe*, a breakaway from the more famous *Berkeley Barb*.

Cristina and I met in the lobby of the restaurant and hit it off nicely straight away. We conversed in Spanish — she couldn't speak German — and, remember, I was supposed to be a German, so it was good that she couldn't. The evening unfolded, very long — enjoyably long, that is — with the consumption of several bottles of Malbec. She was very easy on the eyes: dark-haired, dark eyes, flirtatious and friendly, sending not so subtle signals with her hand on my knee that a post-interview "wrap up" might be in the offing later. With too much to drink — ah, yes, *in vino veritas* — I stupidly slipped into English several times with some careless remarks about life and politics in the U.S. that must have confirmed her suspicions that I was not really the "Klaus" I was pretending to be, more likely an American lefty and up to some serious mischief connected with the local terrorists. But, fortunately, before I fell completely into her clutches, I realized that (a) Cristina, like me, was not who she was pretending to be and (b) I had stupidly blown my "journalist" cover.

She was on to me. To my dismay, I realized that she was probably an undercover federal policewoman or an Argentine military intelligence officer trolling for outside, left-field players operating in support of the guerillas. I had been warned about undercover, Argentine women cops on the prowl and should have been more careful — good-looking women and alcohol, a potentially fatal combination in this dangerous setting where no one should be trusted. I began to notice that she was doing an expert job of pretending to be drinking while attentively refilling my wine vase. She excused herself to make a run to the ladies' room and was gone, it seemed, a bit too long. She must have been making a phone call. I was being set up, my ticket soon to be punched and my remains definitely *not* to be deposited in the Recoleta.

With the ruse of my own need for a men's room dash, I excused myself and made my way out the back of the restaurant. What to do? Going back to my hotel was not an option since I had let it slip where I was staying rather than giving her a fake address — another inexcusably stupid slip up.

This was likely what was in store for me if I had left the restaurant with her, half in the bag: When she and I arrived at my hotel room, instead of the hanky-panky I was thinking might be in the offing, there would be a surprise "meet and greet" with her pals from a death squad, some "enhanced" interrogation, and poof! Off I would go on a one-way, twenty-mile excursion via an army helicopter, bound and drugged, to be pitched out from high up somewhere above the Atlantic Ocean — a "Phoenix" sort of operation, Argentinian style. One less left-wing terrorist for the Generals to worry about.

First order of business was to get the hell out of the country posthaste, if I didn't want to be turned into shark food. The rest of the night, I spent in a nightclub I found near the central bus station. Morning came. I bought a ticket on a tour bus for Chile. Fortunately, no one seemed to notice or care that I had no luggage. The tour was for Americans, so I fit in language-wise and made it safely out of Argentina. On the way, I sat next to a middle-aged woman who was a sociology professor from the University of Wisconsin. She seemed to be more impressed with her theoretical wisdom and moral virtue than most of the other sociologists I've encountered, which takes quite a leap. She had recently spent a couple of weeks in Cuba and couldn't have been more enthralled with life in Fidel's Magic Kingdom: non-stop about its wonders — universal healthcare and high rate of literacy, over and over. Why, I couldn't bring myself to ask her, was it that so many of the young people were desperate to leave this paradise? It was entertaining for me to observe her enthusiasm for the dictatorship. It set me to wondering about *El maximo lider's* propaganda skills, his ability to make a huge chunk of the American vaunted intellectual class, as well as the college kids it inflicted itself on, into true believers. It then hit me: Intellectuals are natural marks for ideologue conmen like Fidel. They *want* to believe. Wanting to believe, I could see, is a big problem. But how to escape from it?

CHAPTER TWENTY-SEVEN

Conception
in Concepción

A revolution is not a bed of roses

Fidel Castro

Arriving midday in Santiago, there came flooding back those memories from the heady days when my CIA *compañeros* and I gave old Doc Salvador the heave-ho from the Presidential Palace. There, I mounted a regional bus and made my way a couple of hundred miles south to Concepción, the second largest city in Chile. Fidel himself had visited there in 1971, where he gave one of his typical long, blustering speeches to an adoring throng at the university — eager believers. Given the political climate in the country, it was the safest place for me to take temporary refuge until I could figure out what next. Home of *Universidad de Concepción*, it was the most left-wing locale in all of Chile, with serious underground opposition to the government of Pinochet, most of it associated with the university and the radicalized professors. Many of the Chilenos there were filled with hatred of him. Richly ironic — and fortunately — for me, no one there had a clue as to how instrumental I had been in putting the odious Generalissimo in place. At the university, I connected with a radical student group that put me up and helped me establish a communication channel with Fidel back in Havana.

It was decision time: I couldn't go back to Buenos Aires and did not want to return to Cuba. But I needed a good reason to convince Fidel that he should continue to funnel me the resources and let me roam around South America on the fake German passport he had entrusted to me. He liked his emissaries to be task-oriented, productive, and on a short leash.

Fidel's massive ego, however, was heavily charged with his need to be perceived by friend and foe alike as *the* inspiration and guide, *El Supremo* of all the Marxist-inspired revolutionary movements throughout Latin America. The overweening jealousy of every "great" successful revolutionary is to hold the undisputed title "Most profound and perfect Interpreter of the Master himself, Karl Marx." Marx's wisdom remains inerrant. Since the Master's demise, charismatic psychopaths compete for this title. Predictably, they hate each other — "Marx-Master envy," I call it. Stalin and Mao famously loathed and antagonized each other. Once Stalin died, Mao shifted his massive hatred over to Khrushchev.

Understanding this and knowing that up north in Peru there was a major revolutionary movement underway, led by an upstart interpreter of the Master, I was confident that Fidel would like to get a "close-up and personal" report on the guy. I would try hard to persuade him to let me head for Peru to try to meet with Manuel Rubén Abimael Guzmán Reynoso, who was beginning to make quite the name for himself under the nom de guerre "Chairman Gonzalo."

Guzmán was the founder and leader of *Sendero Luminoso* (the Shining Path), a revolutionary Marxist movement that was threatening the violent overthrow of the Peruvian military government. Guzmán began his revolutionary career as a professor of philosophy. This, I suspect, goes a long way to explain a deeply warped personality that had turned homicide-in-service-to-humanity into his life's sacred mission. He had gone underground in the mid-1970s to live out his dream, which, for the government and many of the peasant farmers, was a continuing nightmare. Like Fidel, Guzmán's secondary schooling was private, Roman Catholic. Stalin's education was in an Orthodox seminary: just an observation hinting at a connection you might want to draw — Marxism and religion? As in Argentina and Chile, in Peru, the U.S. government had been giving the right-wing military government money and military support to wipe out Marxist guerilla movements like the Shining Path.

In 1965, Guzmán traveled to China. There, he got for himself a first-hand, up-close glimpse of communism in its wildest, tumultuous, pathological contortions. Mao's Cultural Revolution was moving along in high gear. With the Chairman himself egging them on, the boys and girls of the Red Guard were roaming the country, clutching Mao's *Little Red Book* for inspiration while they terrorized Mao's Senior Partners — the very ones who had helped him usher in the Revolution in 1949. The youth were on an unfettered, frenzied warpath against the "Four Olds": Old Customs, Old Culture, Old Habits, and Old Ideas. All this seemed a little like a bizarre plot out of a Stephen King novel — thousands of adolescents turned loose and set upon their elders, wrecking anything "old" they could get their hands on. Kids all over China had decided that centuries of cultural real estate were disposable debris, along with the old people who had maintained it. America's 1960s youth-culture expressed itself in the decadence of Rock-n-Roll; China's was dunce-caps for the elders, the burning of old books, and the smashing of old statutes.

The distinguished elders found themselves wearing dunce caps, subjected to — sometimes fatal — "struggle sessions" and shipped off to remote locations of hard labor. This was Mao's not so subtle way of signaling his old comrades-in-arms that he was not ready to be put out to pasture. China was descending into chaos, a lesson for the outside world of what happens when you take teenagers seriously and encourage them to think they are in charge.

Guzmán gathered his impressions and took them back to Peru. He put them into his little Marxist theoretical crockpot, added some Peruvian spices, stirred, and let them simmer for a bit. His recipe would produce a more potent brew. He decided to out-Mao Mao, meaning that he thought Mao was a little too ho-hum and easygoing with how he was clearing away all that "old" debris, which gives you some sense of the depths of the Peruvian's pathological brain. Gonzalo was convinced that he needed to raise the bar for the level of violence and brutality it would take to wipe out the "corrupt order" he had put in his crosshairs. In the mid-1970s, he began the planning of an extremely violent guerilla operation, the goal being to overthrow a right-wing government supported by the U.S. and erect his Andean utopia. No "olds" of any kind for this guy.

As I thought, Fidel was pleased to let me head for Peru and take a run at Guzmán, but he warned me: "Be careful. Don't trust him. This guy is an unpredictable, fucking wild man." He wasn't kidding. Hiding out at the university in Concepcion was a Peruvian dude, Carmelo Gomez, from Guzmán's movement who had barely escaped arrest in Lima and needed an exile hideout for a time. It took a bit of cajoling, but I was able to get from him the address of a safehouse in Lima, the name of a contact there, and pass codes for when I arrived. Off I went on one more bus ride. I entered Peru with my fake passport then made my way to the safehouse. There, with some persistence with one of his lieutenants, I negotiated a clandestine meeting with Chairman Gonzalo with the promise of greetings from Fidel. Guzmán, I was told, was reluctant to see me. The fact that I was an emissary from Cuba, I think, sealed the deal.

Guzmán lived secluded and undercover in the Andes highlands, in a small town, as far as I could surmise, near Cusco. A guide was arranged to drive me there. It took about twenty, bone-jarring hours on the primitive unpaved Peruvian mountain roads by jeep to arrive at the meeting place. The last three hours or so of the ride, I had to wear a black hood over my head so as not to know exactly where I was going and where I would meet him.

CHAPTER TWENTY-EIGHT

Kant's Crazy Disciple

The baddest man in the whole damned town
Badder than old King Kong
And meaner than a junkyard dog
        Jim Croce, "Bad, Bad LeRoy Brown"

My encounter with Guzmán was one of the more terrifying, nightmarish experiences of a life filled with many memorable ones. He was living in the back of a tienda, a large room with some sparse, simple furniture and piles of books and papers everywhere. When I entered, he was sitting completely motionless in a straight back wooden chair in front of a table with nothing on it but a dimly lit lamp and a pistol upon which he was resting his right hand. Jet black hair wildly swept back high and away from a round face framed with big, black-rimmed glasses, he was fixed on me with the most smoldering, searing eyes I'd ever experienced. Next to this guy, Charles Manson would come off like that Elder you'd find at a Quaker Friends meeting leading a silent prayer session. Remaining seated, he slowly gestured, left to right, with one finger at a chair on the other side of the room. I moved slowly — oh so slowly — and sat down. Wisely, I remained silent. He stared at me for a couple of infinitely long minutes before speaking. I was beginning to think: "Holy shit. I'm going to be lucky to get out of this place alive." His first words came at me in a blast like out of a megaphone: *"¿Quién coño eres tú? y ¿Quién te mandó?"* ("Who the fuck are you, and who sent you?")

A real charmer, this Guzmán fellow. Not unlike a lot of his ilk, he exhibited the classic symptoms of schizophrenic paranoia. Having hung out with lots of frothing-at-the mouth radicals, I had learned to appreciate how scary and deranged these guys can be. His symptoms, I must confess, were completely off the charts. For starters, he did not offer me a beer after my long, arduous journey. No, we went in a different direction. He was thinking that I was a mole or a government spy. Being a gringo did not help matters. I had to go through some extraordinary, sphincter-challenging contortions to convince him otherwise, including, at his insistence, playing a round of Russian roulette — one bullet in a seven-round chamber of a .357 Magnum, Smith & Wesson revolver, the one that was on his table. Nice guy that he was, he only made me do it once, and proudly, I need to add, my underwear remained mostly unsoiled. His paranoia was exceeded only by the highest order of psychopathic delusions of revolutionary aspirations and grandeur. By his pristine standards, the revolutions of Lenin, Mao, and Castro were lackluster homicidal affairs, meaning that the mayhem and destruction unleashed was administered too lightheartedly for "real" peace and prosperity to pop out magically in the end. A careful, detailed examination of this man's personality would likely have broken significant new ground in the field of forensic psychiatry, with a specific entry in the next edition of the *DSM* describing the "Guzmán Disorder."

At this time, Chairman Gonzalo was just warming up

with the holy war that he believed would rain down on the ruling-class schmucks of Peru. It wasn't to be: His revolutionary perfection was just a little too perfect — that is, savagely brutal. Even the Indian campesinos he was supposed to be the savior of eventually turned against him and went over to the military to find relief from the terror on steroids. His "cure" was far worse than their disease. According to the *New York Times* reporting I read some years later, Shining Path guerillas were using machetes to hack their captives to death in order to save on their bullets. In 1992, Guzmán was finally captured, and his movement eventually crushed.

I should pause with my encounter with Guzmán and note here: After it had dispatched the Shining Path, the Peruvian government, in 2004, created a "Truth and Reconciliation Commission," supposedly to investigate the decades of terror. If you know even a little about the history of Peru's governments, this should give you a couple of hearty guffaws. From past experience, government commissions of most kinds are bad news for anyone even casually interested in the truth. This should be obvious. Governments of almost every stripe, as I mentioned earlier, tend to be predatory. They are about — and only about — power. Truth is an obstacle; reconciliation an impossibility. Under oath and with the threat of perjury, Dr. Kissinger might confirm this with some entertaining anecdotes to illustrate this truism. As he once, in his more candid, relaxed moments, quipped: "Corrupt politicians make the other ten percent look bad."

The Warren Commission on the Assassination of President Kennedy is the best illustration imaginable of this unpalatable truth: *Government commissions are to governments as getaway cars are to bank robbers.* Yes, this "Warren" of the so-named "Commission" was the very same Earl "Fuck-over-the-Japanese-Americans" Warren who was put in charge of the highest-profile murder investigation in history.

It's old history now, but a fascinating take on this is that Warren was installed to investigate a murder by the guy who just happened to step into the murder victim's job on the very day of his unfortunate demise. It gets better. Appointed to this Commission was Allen Dulles. JFK had fired him from his job as head of the CIA for steering him down the disastrous Bay of Pigs road — no possibility that he might have had a grudge against his former, now murdered, boss. Better yet: Prior to his forced retirement, Mr. Dulles's professional portfolio included targeting foreign leaders for assassination, those his brother, John Foster, had decided were "a problem." So, on this blue-ribbon Assassination-Investigation Commission, appointed by a plausible suspect, was placed a man who planned assassinations for a living and who likely bore rancorous ill-will toward the victim

All this struck some people at the time as a bit fishy. Just maybe, the Warren Commission was a put-up job, staffed and signed off on by the right mix of perps and stooges. They thought that having the guy with a plausible and powerful motive to commit the crime in charge of the investigation might not be the best way to get to the bottom. Sure, but this was around the time that "conspiracy-theorist" was getting major traction with the smart set in charge of the propaganda mills. The corrupted guardians of the established order would attach it as a stigma to anyone inclined to ask annoying questions of the boys in charge when they say: "Move on, folks; nothing to see here." It worked. "You're a conspiracy theorist" is the adult adaptation of the child's "Ooh, you've got cooties." Now, after decades of regular use, "conspiracy theorist" means "mentally unbalanced," "kook," a "disagreeable person." In the old Soviet Union, conspiracy theorists got locked up in psychiatric hospitals. In post-

Democracy America, they're just banished from polite society. You'll never find one in a faculty lounge, a Georgetown cocktail party, or in front of a CNN camera.

Hint: When a government-created body attaches "truth" to its title, that's a sure sign that a cover-up is in the making. I'm sorry, but "Government Commission" is code for a hapless collection of government-appointed leak-pluggers, naive do-gooders, corrupted bureaucrats, cynical opportunists, and hell-bent revenge takers.

In its report, the stooges from the Peruvian Commission stated that the "human rights violations of the Shining Path had evolved into generalized and systemic practice." "Evolved"? "Generalized and systemic practice"? How is that for the perfection of insipid, mealy-mouthed, government-commissioned lingo, cranked out "in committee" by wheedling, faceless nonentities? To call getting chopped up by a machete-wielding homicidal fanatic a "human rights violation" doesn't quite capture the sounds, colors, smells, screams, and a visceral reaction that anyone could imagine.

"What happened to Papa, Juanito? Why are you crying hysterically?"

"Oh, Momma. It was so awful! Papa was just minding his own business, working in the fields, when some mean men with big rusty machetes came and systemically violated his human rights in a horrible, generalized way. And then" — sob — "they evolved him into little bloody pieces."

All the while, I thought a typical "human rights" violation was having to pay out of your own pocket to fill your Viagra prescription or for gender reassignment surgery. I'm thinking that Jimmy Carter supervised this bunch of "truth-seekers." This would be the same ex-President who sent a letter of condolence to the Democratic People's Republic of North Korea's Kim Jong Un on the passing of his "Dear Leader" daddy, Kim Jong Il, who, in the "human rights" violation business, had "evolved" quite the impressive "generalized and systemic practice" of his own. I'm guessing Jimmy must have said to himself: "Hey, they're "Democratic" there, aren't they? What's not to like?"

Truth and Reconciliation Commissions were all the rage for the high-minded apparatchiks, beginning in the 1990s. The governments of South Africa, Canada, and Liberia — yeah, Liberia — assembled these "commissions" to conduct their politically correct voodoo ceremonies and Kabuki dances, and, as you might guess, no truth and little reconciliation came of them.

I spent the next two, terror-stricken hours kibitzing with this Prince of Darkness while he instructed me as to how a *real* revolution should be made, all the time boring through me with those laser-beam eyes.

I knew that he had been a philosophy professor before taking up the profession of overthrowing governments and killing the reactionaries, both real and imagined. Maybe I could divert him to a less volatile topic of conversation and calm him down a bit. So, I asked him how his current plans of revolution tied in with the philosophical thought of Immanuel Kant, the German philosopher who was reputed to be his moral guide and intellectual inspiration. Maybe that would take some of the murderous edge off and nudge him toward a more contemplative — at least temporarily — state of mind, until I could slip away.

Well, no. This was like poking a surly bear. That question sent him into a frenzied spiral, with the furious outpouring of a "short course" on the history and ontology of evil and its purification through the appropriate rituals of revolutionary violence — real "tear-their-guts-out, poke-their-eyes-out" violence, mind you, not the watered down, chickenshit version that you see in most revolutions. How Kant figured into all this, I knew no more after his frothing-at-the-mouth fulmination mercifully ceased than before it irrupted. All the while, I was thinking: "God, I hope I can get the fuck out of here before I end up lathered all over with berry juice and buried up to my neck in a mound swarming with killer ants." Memories of Parchman Farm didn't seem quite so horrifying by comparison.

When the pleasantries were finally over, Guzmán, for the first time, smiled, just for a flickering moment, and then broke out into a sneer. He stood up and dictated the message he wanted me to take to Castro. Here's how I translate it: "Ok, bootlicking, Gringo worm (*gusano*), haul your sorry ass (*lamentablo culo*) back to Cuba. Tell that little fucker Fidel (*hijo de puta Fidelito*) and pecker-head Raúl (*la cabeza de pavo Raúl*) that what I need are guns, bombs, money, and intelligence. I won't tolerate their worthless advice or interference. I know Peru. I live with its oppressed people, and I know how to make the revolution here succeed."

Wow! With that heart-warming send-off, I couldn't help but feel a reluctant surge of genuine awe and admiration for this lunatic. What kind of cojones he had to flip off the Castro brothers, the Maestros of Latin American-style Marxist revolution, regarded by most radical thrill-seekers throughout the region as Gods.

Twenty hours later, I was back in Lima, safely attached to a bar stool. One hand was wrapped around a Pisco Sour glass, the other a bottle of *Cusqueña*, Peru's strongest beer. Once again, I was facing decision-time. Even less was I thrilled about going back to Cuba than before. I certainly wasn't looking forward to Fidel's reaction to Chairman Gonzalo's friendly message of revolutionary comradeship and the possibility that he might take out his frustration on the messenger.

> *Take me home, country roads,*
> *To the place I belong*
>> John Denver, "Take Me Home,
>> Country Roads"

It was time, yes, time to go home — that is, back to my native land, where I remained on the FBI's "Wanted Fugitives" list. Even so, it was the only place I could go. I was homesick. Having recently been nearly abducted by an Argentine military goon squad and pitched into the Atlantic, then nearly having my tongue cut out by a Peruvian philosopher gone kill-em-all apeshit had finally taken a toll on me. I was flirting with a psychotic breakdown. Life was beginning to feel like Bill Murray in his memory-loop — "Groundhog Day."

"Fuck Fidel," I said to myself, "and the Revolutionary white stallion he rode in on." I decided to take my chances as a fugitive back in the U.S. In Lima, I bought an old, used Kawasaki motorcycle, and from Peru, I made the long journey, with frequent stops to compose my nerves, drink the local hooch, and reflect on what a goddamn mess I had made of my life. I made it into and across Mexico and, from there, to the U.S. border, slipping over from Juárez into El Paso, Texas.

In El Paso, I spent a week of emotional decompression, "feelin' the love" of home. I sold the motorcycle and mounted an Amtrak train, which took me to Little Rock, Arkansas. My cousin Curtis — named for General Curtis LeMay — from Dad's side of the family, I hoped, was still living there. We'd been close as kids growing up in Michigan — like brothers — but we'd lost touch when we went off to different universities. It had been years since I had seen him, but I thought I could trust him not to turn me in. I was right.

CHAPTER TWENTY-NINE

"Slippery" Little Rock

Immorality: the morality of those who are having a better time

H. L. Mencken

I arrived in Little Rock and found my cousin Curtis…three months before he died — end-stage pancreatic cancer, which usually knocks down much older people. He was a statistical outlier. Cancer of various varieties had mercilessly descended on most of his family. His father died from its attack on his liver; his mom, a heavy smoker, a slow, agonizing death from lung cancer; his older brother, Gus, a Vietnam vet, was killed by mesothelioma caused by Agent Orange; his older sister, Brenda, at forty-seven, breast cancer. Curtis was divorced, with no children. His wife, Fiona, a stunningly beautiful — from her photographs, anyway — massage therapist originally from Dublin, Ireland, left him for a woman. He joked about it, pulling out a couple of lines from that old Jerry Lee Lewis ballad "She Even Woke Me Up to Say Goodbye:"

> *It's not her heart, Lord, it's her mind*
> *She didn't mean to be unkind, why*
> *She even woke me up to say goodbye.*

I remember, as a kid, hearing the reassuring words from the preachers: "God will never give you more than you can bear." Perhaps, but I think God was using Curtis as an experimental testcase to find the upper limits.

With no family around, he was facing his final days on his own. He was overjoyed to see me, and I had not felt such a depth of emotion since Dad's release from his torturers when we were in the Dominican Republic. I stayed with him for the last months of his life — everyday. We reminisced about what it was like growing up in northern Michigan, the bountiful starry night skies, fishing for large-mouth bass from our rickety rowboat on the remote inland lakes. We recalled hiking the rugged Lake Superior shoreline, racing our dads' cars on county roads, high-school football games, and the thrill of a high-school cheerleader in the back seat of a Chevy. He had known that I was a fugitive and had been interviewed a few years before by the FBI. There was no way he was going to rat me out.

Curtis had worked for the Social Security administration and ran the Little Rock office before the cancer finally laid him down. His gift to me shortly before he died was to show me how I could forge paperwork that would create a new name with a SS number. He was also able to help me get a passport. This gave me a solid new identity and international mobility, if I needed it. I became John Davis, with no middle initial, about as close as I could get to "John Doe," which made background checks on me a bit more challenging. Curtis also made me the beneficiary of his life insurance policy, which was $30,000. The day of his burial was one of the saddest of my life.

With a new identity and some money to grease the skids, my re-entry to American life was underway. I had been out of the States long enough that I was not a high priority for apprehension and arrest by the Feds. Bill Ayers and Bernardine Dohrn had begun their no-pain, big-gain transition into high society. They were soon to be rewarded with the celebrity status of well-connected ex-radicals with cushy jobs. They would be bathing in the warm attention of the younger generation of lefty-infatuated ass-kissers who fronted as journalists pumping out the puff-pieces featuring the youthful "idealism" of the 1960s radicals. Speaking truth to power got turned on its head: Now, it was power messaging truth.

With my new ID, I was able to get an apartment, a job, and reestablish myself, with no particular agenda other than trying to stay out of trouble, which always seemed to be a challenge for me. Little Rock, I concluded, was a sufficiently backwater place that, at least for the time, I could feel confident in avoiding exposure and arrest.

Even with the good ID, however, I couldn't risk trying for a line of work that required an extensive background check. Bartenders don't get much of a look, so I started tending bar in downtown Little Rock, not that far from the Governor's Office. The Duck in Waddle out Tavern was on 12th Street, only a few blocks from Central High School, where President Eisenhower had sent Federal Troops in 1957 to enforce the court's school desegregation order resisted by then-Governor Orval Faubus. The photographs of the nicely dressed, scared black kids menaced by angry whites really stirs your sympathy. I like to think that, if I had been there as a teenage white boy, I wouldn't have acted that way. But I'm a realist and a cynic, so I can't delude myself.

Orval Faubus's younger brother, Darrow, was an occasional customer at the Duck In when I was behind the bar, a quiet, sort of thoughtful guy. After a couple of Pabst Blue Ribbons, he could be encouraged to talk a bit about his famous brother. The Faubus kids had a real-hard scrabble start in life. Their dad was a poor tenant farmer in Northwest Arkansas. Orval was a Democrat populist with Socialist leanings. After he was elected Governor in 1954, he appointed six blacks to the Democratic State Committee. That tagged him soft on race and made his reelection bid in 1956 a tough one — which is why, in 1957, for reasons of political survival, he grandstanded in resisting the Federal desegregation order. Faubus's resistance to the Feds was more political calculation and election expediency rather than pure racial bigotry.

Faubus went on to serve six consecutive two-year terms as Governor of Arkansas, from 1955 to 1967. Darrow wasn't much interested in talking about the 1957 desegregation convulsion, but he passed on an interesting story of vintage Arkansas political corruption attached to his big brother. Orval Faubus's annual Governor's salary in the early 1960s topped out at around $10,000. The typical voter in Arkansas was poor and wouldn't stand for an elected politician to make a big salary. So, the puny salaries had to be — wink-wink — enlarged from other sources. During that time, on a beautiful mountain top at the northwest end of the state, just outside of Huntsville, Faubus had a house built that was designed by Faye Jones. Jones, who taught at the University of Arkansas in nearby Fayetteville, was a student of Frank Lloyd Wright and one of the most sought-after architects in the region. The house was a spectacular piece of design. Huge, built completely out of native Arkansas stone, it perched high on the top of a mountain, facing west, with a beautiful view of the valley below. I drove up one weekend to admire it. Rumored to cost hundreds of thousands of dollars, it even had a bomb shelter, reminiscent of the early 1960s fear of a nuclear conflagration with the Bolshevik gang from Moscow.

I couldn't resist asking Darrow how a guy from a dirt-poor family with a ten-grand-a-year salary could afford a such mansion. Darrow just grinned, took a long pull on his beer bottle, and said: "Well, Orv had some very good friends who helped him out, and that's all I care to say about it." Orval's last shot at a comeback to the Governors' mansion, in 1986, fell short. He was dispatched in the Democrat primary by a guy from Hope, Arkansas, someone who would continue the tradition of squeaky-clean Arkansas politics.

CHAPTER THIRTY

The Man from Hope

Hope, in reality, is the worst of all evils because it prolongs the torments of man.
                Nietzsche, "Human, All Too Human"

State government workers were among the many regulars who attended this cozy, little bar, and they went for Singapore Slings — which loosened their tongues, and out spilled interesting "secrets" surrounding the "public servants" who ran the State. With Little Rock being a smallish capital city in a relatively — population-wise — small state, gossip was rife, and with every hour on the job, I was in a rich harvest mode, storing it away, confirming my view of the world. I soon learned how the machinery of state government of Arkansas was regularly lubricated: sex for employment, raises, and promotions; kickbacks for state contract awards; state regulators who, via green-interior, plain brown envelopes, smoothed the way for building permits and commercial licenses; state police officers who served as "collection" agents, enforcing the pay-to-play rules for dealings with the state legislators. Arkansas State Government was a model organism of corruption and collusion — top to bottom. I was impressed. How could I get in on the action?

One of my regular customers turned out to be Roger

Clinton, half-brother of you-know-who. Roger was quite the original piece of work. Always struggling under the shadow of his high-achieving *frère aîné,* still, some pluses were in store for him, a big one being able to snag himself a Presidential pardon for drug trafficking later, when Bill was on his way out of the White House. Never underestimate the value of "friends in high places."

It was no secret: Roger was a compulsive gambler, a serious alcoholic, and a cokehead, much of the time out of control. When Bill was campaigning for President, the Secret Service gave him the codename "Headache" because he was such a predictably unpredictable mess. No matter, God damn it, even drunk, he was greatly likeable. Roger and I struck up a "friendship" of sorts. I liked him enough that I loaned him a chunk of money he used, temporarily, to get an aggressive loan shark off his case and keep his kneecaps intact. Not that this was entirely a gesture of pure altruism on my part. It put me in a good place with him. He was appreciative, and the appreciation of the brother of a powerful man in the State could turn out to be useful. Not many people would have loaned this pudgy-faced dipsomaniac a dime, except for the sharks.

Much of the time when I was around him, he was three sheets to the wind and not exactly discreet when it came to tattling on his big brother. Most intriguing was the kinky hokey-pokey with the ladies Bill was consistently up for in his spare time. That was when he could occasionally slip out of the iron cuffs of Hillary's ball and chain. Well, "ladies" is not quite the right word. Roger did a kind of "escort" duty (*chulo,* in Spanish) for the Governor. Roger's specialty? Wild and willing teenage girls from various locales in Little Rock. He escorted them to the mansion for "parties" when Hillary was away. The Clinton brothers' little secret was confirmed by the gossip mill that I tended to in the bar. Post-Presidency, Bill found a *chulo* with a more sophisticated, extensive reach. That was billionaire Jeffery Epstein, who came with his own plane, private island, and an assortment of teenage girls.

Through my big-heartedness for Roger, I was able to finagle an invitation to an informal Governor's bash at the mansion. This "reception" included an assortment of political groupies, government job seekers, and a select few of the high-octane local party animals. These latter sorts seemed to be overflowing in Little Rock at that time. Little Rock, back then, had a superficial veneer of gentile Southern propriety. Barely underneath was a wild and antinomian jungle, with lots of "lookin' away" from the rampant bribery, sex-trafficking, and ubiquitous nepotism. Hillary appeared at the event, so none of Bill's teenage admirers were able to make an appearance. It was, at this festivity, that I was finally introduced to Arkansas' Deceit, Inc., Brother-Bill and his charming consort, an introduction that would ultimately culminate in a temporary "business relationship."

Bill was the governor of one of our less-than-up-and-coming states in the Union. Arkansas was the butt of not a few jokes that feasted on its backwardness and political corruption. Unfortunately, the man from Hope wasn't doing much in the way of turning those impressions around. Still, an occasional topic of humor in Little Rock was the spectacular crash down from the heights of national power of Arkansas' Wilbur Mills, the long-time chairman of the U.S. Houses of Representatives Ways and Means Committee from 1956-1974, undone by the busty Argentine stripper, Fannie Fox and her "Tidal Basin Romp."

In the 1930s, the acerbic H. L. Mencken returned from a tour of the south. To the *Baltimore Sun*, he posted these kind words about the state:

"[Arkansas] has some good soil, but in the main it is poor and worked out, and two-thirds of its people are benighted and miserable. Two gangs of grafters prey upon them, the one made up of professional politicians of a peculiarly vicious and unconscionable type, and the other composed of cross-roads ecclesiastics even worse."

Parts of the first sentence are debatable, but "grafters" on the "prey" describes what I saw decades later. There were a lot of them, and we know to which gang of "grafters" the Clintons belonged — the words "vicious and unconscionable" cannot be surpassed in a search to capture succinctly the character of these 1960s "I feel your pain" "idealists." Still, the Gods were smiling on them — tells you something about the Gods — and they had already set their sights high, on the loftiest perches in Washington D.C.

So, what did a bartender on the FBI's fugitive list have to offer an up-and-coming Governor? Well, with my involvement in the CIA's takedown of Allende and the years I spent in Cuba with my proximity to the Castros, I had become intimately familiar with the operations of money laundering through Caribbean banks. Fidel and Raúl got into the drug-smuggling business, the proceeds of which they used to launch and subsidize their extensive subversion efforts of right-wing governments throughout the southern hemisphere. The proceeds had to be laundered. On numerous occasions, I had served as one of Fidel's "mules" for cash delivery. Being a visible gringo, I was less likely to raise suspicions as a Cuban operator. I got to know the "islands" quite well. The U.S. government intelligence community, primarily through the CIA-linked Bank of Credit and Commerce International (BCCI), also used laundered Caribbean dollars to finance sting operations, political assassinations, foreign political campaigns, and government destabilization schemes. Drug smuggling and money laundering in that region are vast and complex businesses. They comprise the financial lifeblood and backbone of much of the underworld — the government side and the mafia.

From my conversations with Roger when he was sloshed, which was much of the time, I learned that the Clintons were heavy on the prowl for funds to amass a campaign war chest that would launch their anticipated entry into politics at the national level. Coming from a hick state, they needed mountains of cash to get attention outside of the region and compete with better-known contenders from more upscale and respectable regions of the country. Some of their sources, as you would be shocked to discover, were not completely on the up-and-up. These dollars coming in had to be moved out of sight for a time — "cleaned up" a bit and ready for reentry at a later time, when needed.

Roger introduced me to his brother shortly after we arrived at the party. Right away, I could tell that Bill was appreciative for my help with Roger's loan-shark problem. I also sensed that he rightly suspected that, given his brother's alcohol suppressed filters and my close proximity, I may have learned things from Roger about him that, maybe, I shouldn't have. That, plus being new to Little Rock, intrigued the Governor as to what kind of character was so generous in helping out his little, big-problem brother. He was also probably thinking that I might, sometime down the road, become "a problem" for him.

Roger drifted off in search of a George Dickel refill, and in my casual conversation with Bill, as expected, he probed a bit on my history. I purposely let it "slip" that I had extensive business-banking experience in the Caribbean. That piqued his interest. I was trying as much as possible to come off as a little "mysterious" and carrying some suspicious baggage that had pushed me temporarily "on hold" into the bartending business while looking for a "breakout" opportunity. He pressed a bit, and I pushed back, acting nervously. That further piqued his interest.

We arranged to meet for coffee later that week, ostensibly to talk about Roger's drinking problem. I promised to let him know if Roger was getting "more rambunctious than usual." In my conversation about Roger with Bill at the Governor's mansion, I had dropped into "therapy-babble" for a bit — some of which I picked up from watching Oprah Winfrey on television. That helped to connect me more closely to Bill. It was one of his favorite argots and got him a lot of millage on the campaign trail. He would do that fake empathy pose with a bite on his lower lip. I'm guessing he'd practiced "Ah feel yore pain" numerous times before the mirror.

At coffee, I still played it cagey, but let out some more line, hoping to set the hook. I was vague about who I had actually worked for, and being the very smart guy that he is, Bill figured right away that I was just the right kind of operator he preferred to do business with. No further questions about my background. Confirmed: I was sleazy and unethical, someone who could help him pull off a little ethical-legal bob-and-weave of his own that he had in mind for his national campaign while keeping it between just the two of us. Well, the three of us. He didn't want to know any more about me personally; just who I knew and what they could do for him. What I was doing, I realized, was high-risk, and he may very well have had me checked out, but I gambled that he wouldn't care, as long as I could deliver. He could always blackmail me if he wanted to. As that battery of psych-tests I took in Florida showed, high risk is what keeps me going, and I bend to people around me. I knew the banks, protocols, and the right personnel. The contacts I gave him checked out. Bill was up for a "mutually beneficial" relationship. He had to get Hillary on board. A week later, I met with them both, and we worked out the details. They would get contacts, protocols, the modus operandi, and access to the appropriate bank personnel. I would get a one-time "broker's" fee.

I've rubbed elbows with a medley of psychopaths in my time, but as a conniving, grifting duo, Bill and Hill were Hall of Fame achievers. Their twisted, pathological relationship was sustained and enriched by their complementary talents and inclinations. Bill was the consummate Slickster. Some LBJ, a little Billie Sol Estes, and part Oral Roberts, he could sell a broken-down air-conditioner to a Bemidji ice fisherman while diddling his daughter. Calculating, empty-souled, and cobra-like, Hillary's stratospheric avarice was exceeded only by her overweening ambition and ruthless, take-no-prisoners approach to dealing with people. Bill was the poetry; Hillary was the prose. Bill was lead guitar; Hillary was rhythm.

I went forward with my end of the deal, but Hillary stiffed me out of my "brokerage" fee. She knew I had no recourse. Thick glasses, at that time, in front of those limp blue eyes, I never liked or trusted her from the moment I laid eyes on her — not a visual treat. "Politics is showbusiness for the ugly," someone said. She most resembled, in style and substance, Erich Honecker, the East German Stalinist stooge who ran the DDR as his personal commie fiefdom before it collapsed — a nasty, cold-blooded prick, who believed he was entitled to manage every detail of everyone else's life and live like a Pasha while everyone else sucked eggs.

My relationship with Arkansas Elvis and the future Our Lady of Chappaqua convinced me that American politics was, to take a line from Bruce Springsteen, "going down, down, down." I began to fear that I might end up in a pair of cement overshoes at the bottom of the Arkansas river, if I didn't put

Little Rock in my rearview mirror.

Ferdinand and Imelda were heading north to Washington D.C. You can take the Clintons out of Arkansas, but you can't take Arkansas out of Bill and Hillary. In a few years, a new scandal a week and blowjobs in the Oval Office would be the hot topics of day. Post-Presidency, they were making "Kissinger Associates" look like a bunch of schlemiels, sucking up $500,000 per speech from the likes of Saudi princes and Goldman Sachs execs — the little people, right?

That said, being close to the Clintons was often not good for your future and, sometimes, your health. "Dead men tell no tales," I suspect was one of the Clintons' favorite private mantras, not to mention a chapter heading in their secret diaries. Jail for Clinton's Assistant Attorney General Web Hubbell for wire and tax fraud, widely rumored to be the father of Chelsea Clinton. At your next séance, ask Ron Brown, Vince Foster, or James McDougal, Bill's convicted Whitewater partner who died of an apparent heart attack while in solitary confinement, a key witness in Ken Starr's investigation. Had Monica Lewinsky not taken her friend Linda Tripp's sage advice to save the Gap blue dress with…uh…the incriminating stains, she would now, likely, as they put it in *The Godfather*, "sleep with the fishes."

CHAPTER THIRTY-ONE

Selling Heaven

It's love, Brother Love say
Brother Love's Travelling Salvation Show
Pack up the babies
And grab the old ladies
And everyone goes
'Cause everyone knows
'Bout Brother Love's show

Neil Diamond, "Brother Love's
Travelling Salvation Show"

Little Rock was no longer a safe, comfortable place. Time to move, but where? After all these years spent flinging myself about in helter-skelter directions, I was still looking to find that ever elusive "myself." Now, maybe, that "myself" was a "spiritual" entity — spiritual in an Elmer Gantry, Americana sort of way — that might also provide some entrepreneurial avenues to explore with some improvements at the material end of the human spectrum. I spent my spare hours watching the "masters" of television evangelism — Oral Roberts, Jimmy Swaggart, and Jim Bakker — and taking notes. Each one had a unique style. Each, through their television ministries, had amassed huge numbers of faithful followers who sent along their money — lots of it. I could do this.

No one could top Roberts for pure chutzpah. In 1987, pushing nearly seventy, the crafty old traveling tent-faith health healer pulled an ace out of his sleeve, one that hauled in a winner's jackpot in the excess of eight million dollars. He needed, he said, the eight million bucks to complete some mission work he had in mind. Oral was exceedingly oral, never at a loss for words, particularly for things to do with someone else's money. To his devoted followers, he then let it "slip" that he had developed a slight hitch in his earthly-future giddyup. "I know with all sincerity that God will move you to give generously, but there is the greatest urgency for our ministry to complete the goal in three months. From my daily prayers, I also know that if I fail to meet this crucial deadline, my work on this earth will be done and the Lord will call me home."

Hey, *no problema* for the "faith-partners." They came through under the deadline with almost nine million — the gold-standard, I'd say, for peak-credulity and proof positive that the bigger the Whopper, the higher the payout. The Lord had to give his homecoming planners a different three-month assignment.

That same Lord was not nearly so easy on Praise-the-Lord Minister, baby-faced Jim Bakker. In North Carolina, Bakker had built himself quite the entertainment empire, a mega-operation that catered to the millions of Americans with evangelical inclinations. Jim was down-home slick, and his makeup plastered wife, Tammy Faye, who seemed to blubber on cue, made them an appealing, cornpone couple.

Below the surface, we dive in search of "corruption." Not just in politics: Its tendrils reach everywhere. Reverend Jimbo was paying hush money to the church secretary and after-hours playmate, a Ms. Jessica Hahn. The Lord, apparently and understandably, didn't want the Bakker-Man "home" right yet, just locked up for a while in a comfortable, earthly calaboose until he had a little better handle on "zipper management" and how television evangelists ought to behave themselves off-camera. Jim did a stint in the slammer for mail fraud. Tammy dumped him, remarried, and eventually died of cancer.

My sentimental favorite, though, was a yokel from Akron, Ohio, Ernest Angley, who called the church he founded the "Temple of Healing Stripes." I did a double-take hearing that the first time. It might take a bit of decoding from a shrink with expertise in S&M. Ernest was a chubby little rascal who stuffed himself into garish — mostly white — suits and sported a cheap-looking toupee. He seemed to come off as the opposite of "earnest." But he could pack a hall and watch the money roll in.

Reverend Angley's schtick was his comic-vaudevillian, slapstick-style faith-healing performance on those "lesser among us." His "patients" did not appear to be drawn from a demographic that included many from the Mensa set. From an assortment of woebegone, dilapidated folks lined up in front of his pulpit during his televised sermons, two of his burly ushers would yank a poor, decrepit guy out of a wheelchair, push him in front of the Reverend, whereupon, after a terse interrogation as to the nature of the affliction, Angley would arch his back and thrust his arms straight above his head then yell "Heeeyaal." He would then whack the guy on the forehead with the palm of his hand and watch him collapse into the arms of the ushers in a miraculous swoon, healed and now able to walk, or throw away his insulin, or cast off his knee brace. Up would be wheeled another impromptu performance artist for a healing cuff on the noggin.

Watching these spiritual hustlers gave me enormous hope

and consolation. They confirmed my long-held conviction about the rule of corruption. There might, I was thinking, be an opening in the spiritual arena for me to use my talents.

I was thinking of Bakker, Roberts, and Angley as possible models. I grasped that these guys were selling themselves as consumables in the marketplace of ideas and beliefs — not so different, in the *essentials*, than the Clintons, the Kennedys, or the Bushes. Bakker and Roberts were "bottom-shelf" products — Walmart, Dollar General, so to speak. The Kennedys and Bushes were, by comparison, top-shelf, name brands — "Grey Goose," "Chanel," "Gucci," and "Tiffany" — better packaging, more sophisticated, superior marketing. The medium of exchange for what Roberts and Jim Bakker were peddling was your money. You believed what they were telling you about Jesus, God, your spiritual condition, and future in the afterlife. You sent them your dollars so that they could wear custom tailored suits, drive fancy cars. For you? Continued nourishment of your spiritual life, a cure for your diabetes, alcoholism, bankruptcy, or whatever affliction you were trying to cast off.

With the Clintons and George W, the medium of exchange was your vote. Their takeaway was power. They were peddling — depending, I guess, on your perspective — a more potent brand of snake oil: their plans for the economy, about which they knew little; a more safe, peaceful world, brought about by starting senseless wars; and a better future for your kids, about whom they cared nothing. Still, they had to pull off a highly challenging balancing act: promise lots of free stuff to get the votes of the young and poor on the one side; on the other, promise the middle class to be tougher on deadbeat poor people, with better prospects for the kids of the middle class. Oh, yes, and to be tougher on crime. All the time, they were banking on the assumption of very short voter memories. You believed them, and you gave them your vote so that you could live in your own Big Rock Candy Mountain, with few demands and enough perks to make you willing to keep the same rascals in charge.

> *In the Big Rock Candy Mountains,*
> *You never change your socks,*
> *And the little streams of alcohol*
> *Come trickling down the rocks*
>
> Harry McClintock, "The Big
> Rock Candy Mountains"

Once Clinton and Bush got your votes, what did they do? Clinton bombed the Balkans to smithereens. Bush launched a trillion-dollar war that continues to this day. Both unleashed the regulators for more control over your daily lives. Every day, the level of "sensitivity" you must exhibit to keep your job and advance your career creeps up. The rules pile up; you ignore them at your peril. Which of the two groups were the bigger conmen?

Skeptical? Ask yourself: What did they get out of it? As your elected "servants," did Nixon, Reagan, Bush I, Clinton, Bush II, or Obama leave office with fewer benefits, amenities, and net worth than when they entered? Did they make any material sacrifice from their "public service?" And how did *their* personal success work out for us, the little people?

Nixon was going to establish "law and order." Been to Detroit, Baltimore, or St. Louis lately? Reagan was going to "reduce the growth of government." He couldn't even get rid of the mother of all useless government agencies, the Department of Education, Jimmy Carter's pay-out to get the support of the teacher unions. Bush I: "Read my lips, no new taxes." Then, of course, our genius "W." Vietnam was a smashing success for the Vietnamese and the Americans.

Why not go for a replay in Iraq? Jungles, deserts — what's the big difference? Both regions were hot, dangerous for everyone involved, particularly the natives. However, they were profit centers for the likes of Brown & Root Haliburton. History was repeating itself — body bags, "light at the end of the tunnel," "mission accomplished." LBJ slipped the Gulf of Tonkin-card off the bottom of the deck to make Vietnam a military playground; Bush's WMD was his bottom card for expanding the cemeteries of Iraq and a trillion dollar blow out. Nixon's "Peace with honor" morphed into Bush-Obama's "Continual war for unobtainable peace." Obama was going to "heal the planet," and Trump was going to "drain the swamp."

I wanted in on the action. It had to be peddling the bottom-shelf product. Ohio had been good to Ernest Angley. It had also been the home of Rex Humbard Ministries, with its "Cathedral of Tomorrow" church that sat 5,400 in Cuyahoga Falls. Humbard was the man of the cloth who officiated at Elvis Presley's funeral. The Buckeye State, I decided, a long way from Arkansas, would be most suitable for a start-up in television spirituality. Plus, thinking of my favorite 3-C's — the 3-C alliteration of its three biggest cities, Columbus, Cleveland, and Cincinnati — I took as a kind of cabalistic sign pointing me in the right direction.

Ohio, crumbling into a rust-belt region, was beckoning. Misery makes mischief easier for the mischief-maker. Television religion became my new calling. With some creative forgery that enabled me to intercept some stray social security checks and income tax refunds, I assembled enough funds to purchase access to a cable TV station. I ginned up myself as "Reverend John," an "aw shucks," straight-talking reformed sinner who had slipped out of the Devil's grasp. In a divine spiritual trance, I had glimpsed directly into heaven.

The "sinner" part was indisputable. In that trance, I observed that the real estate business up there was not so different than in any upscale suburban market right down here. My cable network was called "Celestial Real Estate" — "Why buy a house on earth when you can own a home in Heaven, and at a fraction of the cost?" Who would have guessed that buyers by the droves would line up to plunk down for a notarized plot in the afterlife? I couldn't print the deeds fast enough. You cannot go broke underestimating human gullibility. If I hadn't been taking advantage of it, someone else would have.

The FCC, however, took a dim view of my business model, and a couple U.S. Attorneys out of the Cincinnati office were chomping at the bit to prosecute me for violation of the RICO statutes. These guys had no sense of humor — atheists, probably. I had, however, made some rather generous campaign donations to a certain Ohio U.S. Senator. They say that money can't buy friendship. I beg to differ. My good "friend" in D.C. pulled in the chain on those two enemies of religious freedom, and I was able to keep the coffers filling for a while longer. Eventually, my spirituality waned — the "myself" remained out of reach. I closed down my operation, disappointing a lot of people looking for that special post-retirement home.

For a number of years after that, I ran a Dunkin Donuts franchise in Wapakoneta, Ohio and built a nice little marijuana farm out in the country. Marijuana — oh, yes, I should mention: I never smoked the stuff myself. Well, just once, but I never inhaled.

CHAPTER THIRTY-TWO

Holy Toledo

That it should still be necessary, at this late stage in the senility of the human race, to argue that women have a fine and fluent intelligence is surely an eloquent proof of the defective observation, incurable prejudice, and general imbecility of their lords and masters.

H. L. Mencken

Now began the longest period of what you might say for me was a "normal" life — no criminality, second marriage, and a "regular" job.

My marijuana farm had been highly profitable. There was little overhead — other than the bribes I had to pay to the county sheriff to have him look the other way. Enough, though, was enough. I shut it down. Setting my sights on life in the bigger city, I no longer needed a rural spread to grow my product. The Dunkin Donuts franchise in Wapakoneta, I sold to a nice extended family from Kolkata, India (formerly called "Calcutta," when the Brits ruled there — renamed as a little poke at Western Imperialism).

Happily out of both the donut and marijuana business, I planned my next move — somewhere in Ohio. A long-distance relocation did not appeal. The dart I threw at the state map hit closest to Toledo, one of the many Ohio towns named after a nicer, famous European city — Versailles, London, Dublin, Athens, Lisbon, Berlin. What a relief! It could have been worse. I could be headed for Akron or Youngstown.

> *Just two lonely truckers from Great Falls, Montana,*
> *And a salesman from places unknown…*
> *All huddled together in downtown Toledo*
> *To spend their big night all alone*
> *You ask how I know of Toledo, Ohio?*
> *Well, I spent a week there one day*
>
> John Denver, "Toledo"

I made the two-hour trek north on Interstate 75 in my new black GLE Mercedes coupe, in the company of my two faithful Rottweilers, Leopold and Loeb. Ohio and the, at the time, Michigan Territory fought a war — the "Toledo War," as it was called — in 1835-36 over a small strip of land near Lake Erie. Long forgotten, it was the best kind of war, unlike Vietnam or Afghanistan — over quickly, one casualty, a Michigan deputy sheriff stabbed in the leg by Two Stickney using his pen knife. Mr. Two was trying to prevent the arrest of his brother, One Stickney. In the settlement, Ohio ended up with the land on Lake Erie; Michigan got to snatch the entire Upper Peninsula, which probably should have gone to Wisconsin, receiving statehood the next year. Who was the winner in that minor dust up, and who really cares? Maybe, Wisconsin.

I paid cash for a small, modest house outside of Toledo. It had a bit of acreage, and I spent my days beekeeping, gardening, and reading books about the American Civil War. My great, great grandfather was a cavalry soldier on the Union side — for four years, he fought on the Western front.

In Wapakoneta, my best friend was a local attorney, Herman Gering. He claimed to be a direct descendant of George Armstrong Custer on his father's side, from his alleged "morganatic" marriage to the daughter of a Cheyenne Indian Chief. Herm, who had a law degree from the University of Michigan, was a peculiar but brilliant guy. He possessed a photographic memory and had amassed an incredible range of knowledge about American Indian culture. I spent many happy hours with him, drinking gin rickeys and listening to his richly detailed stories about Cherokees, Navajos, and Apaches, especially the latter and what they did to captives garnered from their raids, which was pretty much their full-time pursuit — extraordinarily creative stuff, sadism-wise. In my next life, I think I want to come back as an Apache chief.

Lawyering in a small town — DUIs, divorces, probate, and wills — had become for him a huge drag. He had long aspired to get himself certified as a cultural anthropologist and do…I am not exactly sure what. First, he closed his office and sold his law practice. He then shed his third wife, Jasminka, a sultry, dark-haired beauty he'd met on a long vacation in Macedonia. Jasminka, he had to his sorrow discovered, was an incurable kleptomaniac whom he had to regularly bail out of jail. He'd spent a lot of money on her, trying to fix both her and things — fines, counseling programs, and psychologists. The last straw was her arrest for stealing a pair of designer jeans from an outlet store outside of Dayton. They were a size eight; she wore size four. Herm was a very tolerant guy, but he could not endure stupidity.

Sans business and wife, off he went, back to Ann Arbor and the University of Michigan. This time, he was in quest of a Ph.D. There, he enrolled and, I am certain, deeply impressed the folks who handed them out — the exalted, tenured know-it-alls who quite likely knew less than he did.

Soon after I got settled on the outskirts of Toledo with Leopold and Loeb, I summoned a small gathering, a little housewarming party, actually, including a few of my old friends from Wapakoneta. Herm was now in the process of finishing his dissertation, "Prisoner Torture Practices and Techniques by the Lakota, Oglala Sioux." He drove down from Ann Arbor, about an hour away, in his 1963 Lincoln Town Car, painted with various Indian art motifs. With him, he brought three quarts of Diplomatico, top-shelf rum, a case of Heinekens Dark, a box of Cuban Cohiba cigars — Fidel's favorite, I recalled — and several of his more intriguing colleague-friends from this highly distinguished credential factory.

Herm's bizarre personality was a magnet for extremely unusual, fascinating people. One was a Miami Cuban, Tony Gómez, son of a Bay of Pigs soldier who had lost a couple of years and his health in one of Fidel's dungeons. Tony was getting an MBA at Michigan's Business school. In addition to being bright, he was an accomplished jazz trumpet player and a spectacularly handsome guy who constantly had to fight off the broads. Tony was hoping to get into the business side of music and make a financial killing as an agent and a producer.

One of Tony's idols was the legendary jazz trumpeter Dizzy Gillespie, whose cheeks bulged out like giant balloons when he blew on his horn. When we strayed off into the topic of politics, Gillespie, Tony told me, had, in 1964, run a hilarious spoof campaign for U.S. President as a write-in candidate. I didn't remember any of this. Gillespie had promised, if elected, he would appoint Duke Ellington as Secretary of State, Miles Davis as head of the CIA, and Ray Charles as Librarian of Congress. Phyllis Diller was to be his VP. None of them could have been any worse than what we ended up with.

Another of Herm's friends was a defrocked Orthodox priest, Father Dragan Stojanović, a Serbian with connections to the ultranationalist far-right Serbian Radical Party. A huge, physically intimidating hulk of man, Father D was also a polymath of staggering dimensions: two Ph.Ds, mathematics and psycho-linguistics; fluency in six languages, including Farsi and Hindi; and a concert-level mastery of the violin. Father D had left Yugoslavia in the early 1990s, with the onset of the civil wars and the political upheavals. He was team-teaching a course on linguistics and the law with fellow guest-lecturer Noam Chomsky at the University of Michigan Law School. A far-right Serb team teaching with the old leftist radical Chomsky — that must have been a spectacle to behold.

The one guest, though, who made the biggest impression on me, was a Korean lassie named Kim Sun Ah. Herm thought I'd like her. I did — right away and very much. She was a Ph.D. candidate in "Women's Studies." This was a relatively new "research" discipline that devoted itself to the discovery and elaboration of reasons why women should resent and reproach many things in their lives that they used to sort of like — such as, and especially, men. Doesn't sound good so far, does it?

Like poison mushrooms sprouting exponentially in shaded, soggy soil, these "New Frontiers of Knowledge" were ripe for exploration and expansion in the 1970s. The "Studies" thing at American universities was metastasizing to accommodate prospective students from the expanding victim classes: Gay/Lesbian Studies, including Queer Theory, African American Studies, Latino Studies, Post-Colonial Studies. So much to be bitter about; so little time.

These nouveau victims were riding the wave of an

exploding demand for sophisticated vocabularies and tortured "narratives" to express their smoldering anger, animosity, and resentment, which, previously, had been non-existent or in lesser quantities. The forced march toward competitive, universal victimhood was underway. University credentials were in high demand. The non-negotiable-demand table-pounders needed credibility — more umpf, so to speak. The cascade of grievances was spilling all over. All the degrees came with a heavy load of self-righteous certitude invincible against counter-arguments. With an easily mastered vocabulary of handy accusations, eviscerating invective, insults and slurs, and an in-your-face attitude, you could intimidate most people and send them running for the exits.

Sun just happened to be the grandniece of Syngman Rhee — speaking of men who richly deserve to be deeply resented. Sun's father, Kim Jihoon, was the son of Rhee's younger sister, Kim Minsun. Rhee had been a long-standing Big Cheese in the early politics of post-WWII South Korea. He was tapped to run what eventually became the Republic of South Korea after Japan surrendered unconditionally to the U.S. following the incineration of Hiroshima and Nagasaki in 1945. Rhee brandished an MA from Harvard and a Ph.D. from Princeton. He lived like a Pasha in Washington D.C. during WWII — a good indication that he was a guy who could be easily bought. He also was a well-known entity to the U.S. government and a staunch anti-communist, which, at that time, was actually considered by most Americans to be good thing. It didn't seem to matter to the post-war schemers in the intelligence community, however, that he was corrupt beyond normal standards, which is saying something, considering how low they were. Even the State Department didn't want much to do with him, but…the OSS (precursor to the CIA) got into the action — are you beginning to see a certain pattern here, gentle Reader? — and one of its agents, Preston Goodfellow, finagled a passport for Rhee that allowed him to fly to Korea and meet secretly with General Douglass MacArthur.

Oh, good, you know that things are going to unfold wonderfully from here on out with the two Koreas, which, of course, they did, with gobs of American soldiers getting killed for exactly what? What else? Some useless abstraction no one now seems able to remember. Not to mention all the Koreans who died. No one now seems to remember much about that Korean "police action," as it was called. Just another distraction conjured up by the connivers here at home to divert our attention from the corruption and abuse of power.

Sig, as we'll call him, was installed in Seoul U.S. puppet-style because our betters wanted "our democracy" replicated worldwide in both form (pretended legality) and substance (grifting and corruption). Sig was the perfect choice. He reigned there as you might predict a man with well-established corruption-credentials, hand-picked by nameless, unaccountable spies would. Well, his performance surpassed all expectations. He ruled until having fucked things up so badly with his fellow Koreans in that wonderful "democracy" we'd installed him in, the CIA snatched him up and flew him out of the country, in 1960, to Hawaii. The CIA giveth; the CIA taketh away. Blessed be the name of…

At least they didn't kill the poor bastard. That crew must have been on tranquilizers. Where could you retire more comfortably than Honolulu? Better than creepy Paraguay, and no hit-team of disgruntled, revenge-fueled commies to sweep in and blow him to smithereens from out of retirement, like the Sandinistas and I did to Somoza. The passport deal that helped get him installed, it was rumored, was a quid pro quo with Goodfellow for him to get concessions for commercial operations he was setting up for the Korean peninsula. Don't forget, the CIA — working to protect you from non-existing foreign threats — courtesy of the "National Security [sic] Act, was created by our "wise" legislators to make America a safer, more secure place for you, my fellow citizens. You can see how their foresight and wisdom played out for your benefit, and, as always, the bottom line is some form of corruption, paid for by the little people.

I spent most of the evening and into the morning of that party drinking Herman's rum, puffing on a Cohiba, and talking with Sun. We were instantly, mutually smitten. For the next few months, I would go to Ann Arbor to spend time with her. She would visit me on weekends in Toledo.

Now, all this might strike you as a bit strange. Yes, I know what you're thinking. How does a professional conman, loathing intellectuals — a confirmed, jaded cynic who tends to admire heavy-handed patriarchs — manage to impress an intellectual lady fully devoted to theoretically-inspired resentments of deep, male shortcomings, utopian delusions of equality, and the demolition of patriarchy? Well, for starters, she seemed to be quite fascinated — impressed in a sexy sort of way — with the extensive inventory of all my shortcomings, which spilled out over time. Uncharacteristically for a grievance specialist, she was extraordinarily lighthearted and imperturbable, with the most wicked sense of humor I've ever encountered. In short, she didn't take herself — or me, or much of anything else, including her "theories" — *too* seriously. She was a happy "warrior," a meta-intellectual who was amused by contradictions and paradoxes in her own theorizing — not an angry, true-believer. Plus, it wasn't just men for whom she had low expectations: Women, in her view, surpassed them in avarice, duplicity, and treachery, and she had never even met

Hillary Clinton. We were a perfect theory-and-practice complement of unfettered, glorious, radiant cynicism — unique in its weird ironic expressions — the Bonnie and Clyde of intellectual fraud and outlawry. Finally, I had found my true soul-mate. She was devastatingly cute, fantastically smart, and, of course, exotically Asian.

CHAPTER THIRTY-THREE

Dandelion State University

It's not enough to succeed. Others must fail.

Gore Vidal

Ms. Kim and I threw our mutual cynicism-fueled romance into overdrive. She finished the Ph.D. and got herself hired at Bowling Green State University (BGSU), twenty miles outside of Toledo, in Bowling Green, Ohio, host of the annual National Tractor Pulling Championship. There, she taught courses in Gender Studies, which we joked endlessly about. We got married — Buddhist wedding in Seoul — where we spent a summer, then a brief judge-officiated ceremony in Lucas County, Ohio. Sun moved into my house, a short commute from BGSU, and threw herself into her teaching, rose quickly through the professorial ranks with tenure, and became department chair.

I became a house-husband, tended to my bees, had dinner ready every evening for Sun, and read. I devoured all the books on the American Civil War that were worth the effort. Bruce Catton's were the best. He'd written a ton of them. Born in Petoskey, Michigan — not far from where I grew up — Catton became a researcher at the Library of Congress. *A Stillness at Appomattox* was magnificent. It got him a Pulitzer, but the snooty academic historians, of course, looked down on him because he wasn't an Ivy Leaguer with a Ph.D. He had never even finished college. Good for him: To his eternal credit, he had dropped out of Oberlin College, probably the best decision he ever made.

For those unacquainted with BGSU, its academic prowess and reputation is in the field of "popular culture." No, I am not joking. It boasts that "it is the only institution in the nation to have a Department of Popular Culture." No kidding. Maybe, BGSU's remarkably unique distinction is unique because it's unimpressive in an all-too-obvious way. Did it occur to whoever developed that bragging point that there were good reasons why everyone else decided to pass? Otherwise, BGSU is one of those third-rate regional state universities that had sprung up all over the country after WWII, many of them from teacher training normal schools or trade schools, in part to accommodate the returning veterans on the GI bill and, a bit later, the baby boomers like me.

Prior to WWII, only about five percent of Americans went to college. You didn't need a college degree, then, to be "a success" — Harry Truman, for example. But, in the post-WWII economy, the vast expansion of universities was connived at in order to keep all those young boomers like me out of the work force for as long as possible. They were to distract us from adult preoccupations and responsibilities — depressingly easy to do — fill us with delusions about our importance in the world — highly successful in that regard — and give teaching jobs to people otherwise not suitable for more productive lines of work. Tenure made it impossible to fire them from their jobs, no matter how badly they did them.

They morphed into a dandified social class, you might say, of professional grievance mongers. Where else could you find, all decked out with uselessly sophisticated vocabularies, such a collection of overpaid oafs who could make a "pig's ear" of complaining and posturing into a "silk purse" of self-serving, self-importance? Somewhere down the line, someone taught me not to confuse correlation with causality. With that in mind, I would cautiously add that the massive cultural rot that set in during the 1960s strongly correlates with the explosive expansion of the universities. Corruption and collusion, anyone?

The BGSUs, WSUs, WKSUs, and EMUs began popping up like dandelions on your lawn in the sunny month of June. And in the most godforsaken, improbable of places — like Warrensburg, Missouri and Marquette, Michigan. Once in place, they were handing out degrees left and right, like weekly grocery coupons from the Saturday newspapers. These "degrees" certified middling pursuits that needed no certification, such as "Fashion Merchandising," "Recreation, Parks, and Leisure Services," "Casino Management," "Leadership," "Organizational Leadership," "Educational Leadership," and "Library Science" — "Science"? What's scientific about checking out John Grisham and Stephen King novels to unambitious readers? How did Ike whip the Germans without a B.S. in Leadership? How did Bugsy Siegal build the famous Flamingo Casino in Vegas without a "Casino Management" degree?

"College educated" came to wield the same clout as "Have a nice day." The only thing "a college-educated person" could legitimately claim to be is a bloke who paid a sum of — often borrowed — money to a dubious enterprise run by sanctimonious pretenders who cater to whomever signs their paychecks. For what? In order to prolong his adolescence, stunt his critical capacities, and be certified to do something that, in many cases, could easily be done with an apprenticeship and a few months of on-the-job training. Or, perhaps, to warm a chair in an office doing "a something or other" that, if not done, would make no difference to anyone anywhere.

At BGSU and the like, standard English turned into "Edubabble," an engine for group-think. Edubabble turns banal, clichéd, everyday chitchat into incomprehensible gibberish, resembling the output of a random word generator. Curious young people subjected to it become shallow-minded, conformist knows-it-alls who believe whatever the talking heads from CNN or Fox News or MSNBC tell them and buy the useless junk pushed by their sponsors. Thus, idiotic memes such as "inclusive learning environments," "outcome-centered learning," "student-centered learning," "partnerships for collaborative learning." This last one made me think of two guys casing the route of a Brinks truck, trying to figure out how to pull off the heist.

Learning, learning everywhere, but no one taught to think. The savants turned loose on your kid have "developed career-ready metrics to ensure academic preparation that aligns with employability and professional expectations." It likely took a committee of twelve people with thirty-six advanced degrees three hours of posturing and bickering to produce a single sentence of fourteen words that makes sense to nobody. Thousands of young people go into debt to be subjected to people who talk like this? A herd of penguins would be taken more seriously. My favorite, though, is "preparing our global citizens for the future," apparently conjured up by some dimwit hellbent on expanding the far-reaching boundaries of contemporary banality and the propagation of gibberish.

Being done with the Civil War and tired of keeping my bees, I decided that I should be regularly employed. Sun, who had been reading the multi-cultural tea leaves at BGSU, suggested that I might shoot for an opening in the burgeoning "diversity" division of the university. I was skeptical. However, she convinced me that I would be a perfect fit for the position of "Associate Director for Diversity and Equality." "Come on, Johnny! You'll be able to employ the same skillset that made your cable network selling Celestial real estate so successful. You're a natural for it." This was terra incognita for me, but I was intrigued.

Now, you might wonder what the "Director of Diversity and Equality" does and why she would need an "Associate Director." These turn out to be rather complicated questions. So, before I can dive into them and explain — I mean, confess — how I finagled my way into this position and my new career, I must pause here and ask for some patience. This all goes to my obsession with corruption. A few pages are, unfortunately, necessary to lay the groundwork and history for any of my readers who aren't familiar with how what is now called "diversity" has come to be an overriding obsession with strong religious overtones at even the most secular of American universities.

Paying tribute to "diversity" is now mandatory, with the narrowest margin for error that will imperil your career advancement prospects and professional reputation at any university. I'm subtlety moving toward the subject of "thought crimes." "Diversity" is a euphemism attached to a booming industry that trades in "moral" goods — the "diversity industry." People who sell "morality" products are shysters. Applying de-moralizing cynicism to their work is like turning on the overhead light and watching the cockroaches flee. I was an insider for a number of years and came to understand how it functioned and why it has become so powerful and so quickly. The 3-C's, you will see, are an integral part of the story.

CHAPTER THIRTY-FOUR

Superiority Ain't
What It Used to Be

Aus Opertum erwächst Macht
(From Victimhood grows power)

Anonymous

My ongoing confession is that of a conman, and what I am about to confess here is one of the most despicable periods of my life — it's difficult, as you can see, sometimes for me to determine which one has that distinction. I became a part of what you'll see to be an ongoing, highly organized, sophisticated, phony "morality" business that shakes down the institutions to which it attaches itself, adding yet one more layer of corruption.

"Diversity" is something of a "Johnny Come Lately" piece of con artistry. Back in the 1960s, when I was wasting some of my precious young years at a typical American university, "diversity" had not yet become a code word that was reverently whispered and bore those sacred connotations that eventually made it the centerpiece in the "mission statement" of every college and university in the country. Though, I must confess, as a quick aside, I don't remember exactly when "mission statements" became the "in thing." I think it was in the 1980s that they hit the corporate world big and then became de rigueur for human endeavors of all kinds, even those as inconsequential as scratching your ass. Here's my ass-scratching mission statement: "My personal mission is to positively impact the impact of every scratch, especially where it itches, and to encourage others to aspire to scratch only when and where necessary and in complete privacy."

At the university, in the mid-1960s, there were no "Vice-Presidents for Diversity and Inclusion," no "diversity conferences" to go to, no mandatory "diversity" workshops and seminars you were forced to attend, no entertaining spectacles of desperate, frantic university administrators climbing up over one another's backs to vehemently express their "commitment to diversity."

"Diversity," then, was just the opposite of "sameness" or "uniformity." In some cases, diversity was a good thing, as in a "diversity of options;" in other cases, sameness and uniformity was the desideratum, as in "same high quality," or a "uniform" approach. What happened?

Here is where we dive into the deep end of the "morality" swimming pool — where they keep the hungry sharks. To see how "diversity" has emerged as the centerpiece of the multi-cultural faith, the starting point is to understand how deep and pervasive is a person's need to feel superior to others.

> *I'm in with the in crowd*
> *I go where the in crowd goes*
> *I'm in with the in crowd*
> *And I know what the in crowd knows*
> Dobie Grey, "The In Crowd"

Diversity is an "in crowd" sort of thing, and it definitely works through crowds. Knowing what the "in crowd" knows is the ticket. The great French polymath Gustave Le Bon observed in crowds what he called a "contagion," where individual reflection and behavior gets sacrificed for an illusive collective interest. Contagion is the vehicle of motion in the "diversity" in crowd.

To begin: There are boundless ways in which someone can feel superior to someone else — some obvious and basic, such as intelligence, looks, talent; some trivial, like your marathon finishing time or your kid's ACT scores. However, the best way, the one that will trump any other form of superiority, is to feel *morally* superior. Some folks have more of a natural knack for it than others. You've met the type. Their oily moral superiority oozes out of their pores. Their word selection, body language, posture, facial expressions, fashion statements, and even their cuisine choices evince their superiority. Just to be in their presence — they'll have you to understand — makes you a better person.

The feeling of moral superiority fueled the collective, contagious fanaticism of the Weathermen. It justified, in our minds, the damage we inflicted on people and property. It excused our rampant criminality and the ritualized, obscene celebration of it. "Dig it," as Bernardine enthused over the gruesome murder of Sharon Tate and her unborn baby.

Of course, logically speaking, morally superior people need morally inferior people to feel superior to. Like they used to sing: "love and marriage; you can't have one without the other" — well, that's not true of love and marriage, anymore.

The tricky part: Being morally inferior to someone else is not the sort of permanent deformity that the inferior party in this most invidious of all invidious comparisons is likely to happily or easily embrace. Doing so has seriously unpleasant practical outcomes. I have no choice and cannot argue: I must concede my inferior looks to George Clooney, my inferior intellect to Stephen Hawking, my inferior athletic ability to Johnny Unitas — well, when he was still alive. But I won't concede my "moral inferiority" to any of them, even though I've confessed to being a conman. Most people, I think you'll concur, will strenuously resist wearing the mantle of moral inferiority. Except…I'll get into that shortly.

Thus, the big question: How does someone come to admit that he is morally inferior to someone else and, more importantly, submit to playing the role of a defective? You already know the answer. It took me a while to figure it out. The quick answer: guilt — guilt that is collective in nature; guilt that can be leveraged. But it's a somewhat complicated business. I did pay attention in a couple of my philosophy classes, and some years later, it hit me how collective guilt and its leveraging works in the quest for moral superiority.

The British philosopher and notorious rake Bertrand Russell was on to it in the early decades of the twentieth century. Compared to Sartre, Russell was a veritable choir boy. He observed that a con game was being run by the intellectual class, especially the Sartre types, who tended to be commie-inclined hypocrites. They pretended to be about "truth," but it was really about the possession of power. Bossing everyone around and grabbing all the goodies was the goal. But you can't be upfront about it, which is how the game comes in. This game worked by getting people to buy into what he called "the doctrine of the superior virtue of the oppressed."

To be "oppressed" in a virtuous way, you claimed membership in a group with shared grievances. You then leveraged the grievances against members of another group who were responsible for those grievances — basic social physics. To simplify, call these two groups the "oppressor" and "oppressed" classes. Being in the "oppressed" class gives you "superior virtue" — what I call "moral superiority." Being in the "oppressor" class, using simple logic, means that you are morally inferior.

Russell was certainly aware that Karl Marx, a lifelong unemployed philosopher who mooched off his pal, Friedrich Engels, had dreamt up this clever piece of schnookery. Marx divided society into the two classes: the oppressed working class, whom he called "the proletariat," and the capitalists, who exploited and oppressed them. Simply put, with Marx, you had the good guys — morally superior-wise — who did all the hard work, and the bad guys who were bad — morally inferior-wise — because of how they treated the good guys — stealing the profits from their hard work and, worse, fooling them into thinking that this was normal and appropriate. The fooling part used by the oppressor class, most interestingly for Marx, was "morality" — that is, "bourgeoisie morality." Bourgeoisie morality produced what Marx called "false consciousness" — that is, believing in the con run by the oppressor class. Remember the onslaught of "consciousness raising" from the 1960s? That was a euphemism for ditching your burdensome, repressive bourgeoisie upbringing.

Once this sort of ultra-morally-superior/inferiority thinking gets serious traction resentment-wise, it can really crank out some serious fireworks, which it did… Big Time! Within sixty years after Marx croaked, in 1883, in London, the good guys — well, the guys who claimed to be representing the proletariat, the good guys — had stomped down the bad guys and were exclusively running the show in the two largest, most populous countries on the planet, Russia and China. You couldn't find a wall anywhere in these two countries without the mug of the hirsute, bearded prophet plastered on it. As self-proclaimed ultra-good-guys, my associates from my Weatherman days, of course, were hyper-active Marx-poster people, settling any and every dispute with a quote from him.

The best part of being a member of the good-guy camp is that, as mentioned, you have pretty much a carte blanche to do whatever you like to the members of the bad-guy camp. The euphemism for this carte blanche was "Revolution," my central calling when I was running with the Bill and Bernardine Gang.

Revolutionary thinking, planning, action — anything revolutionary, in fact — was good, as I recall, not to mention exciting, because it always aimed at the getting rid of the morally bad guys. Revolution, theorized by Marx and carried out by Lenin, Mao, and Castro, was unabashedly messy and violent — executing some of the bad guys and taking their possessions while putting some of the others into labor camps for reeducation, laboring against their will without pay. This was known as slavery, but only when done by the bad guys. As Marx technically put it: "expropriating the expropriators." Get it? Marx was quite the wordsmith. This nicely captures the moral asymmetry of the equation — the good guys use the methods of the bad guys to even things up. Think of it as morally justified revenge acted out on the world historical stage, a gripping drama that helps to sell it to the sophisticates and the high-minded, who are always hoping to be even "higher-minded" — that is, more moral superiority to be puffed up about. And who doesn't like revenge, even though we're not supposed to admit it?

Because everything the good guys did was revolutionary, it was morally acceptable. It was good, even, because getting rid of the bad guys, by any means necessary, was the only way to build the perfect society — bombing the California State Attorney General's Office, for example, or killing a lowly

Brinks Truck guard. I'm sorry, but you can't have a morally perfect society with morally contaminated knuckleheads hanging around to poison the wells — you gotta break-the-eggs-to-make-the-omelet deal.

Now, when the bad guys did stuff like this — plotting, lying, stealing, and killing — it was in the moral atrocity category — mass murder, slavery, exploitation. Unlike the heroic revolutionaries, they were arch-criminals, bloodsuckers, warmongers, scum to be thrown on the trash heap of history — "*auf dem Müllhaufen der Geschichte*," as Trotsky put it.

Such a dual system of morality is clearly a good deal for the oppressed, with many more options than for the bad guys. And there is no downside; it's win-win for you, the good guy. If you succeed in overthrowing the bad guys, you've gotten rid of the immoral parasites; if you fail, you're a martyr for a noble cause — Joe Hill, Patrice Lumumba, Che Guevara, the Spanish Republicans squashed by Franco — making the bad guys look even more cruel and despicable. Better yet, it puts the bad guys in a hell of a bind since they have some very seriously pissed-off folks, fueled with a self-righteous fury, gearing up to kill them or throw them into labor camps and take all their stuff.

That's how it turned out for the bad guys in Russia, China, big chunks of Central and Eastern Europe, and Cuba, where I got an up-close look. The capitalist and the bourgeois scum were…uh…"expropriated." As we all know, most of the good guys running the show turned out to be not all that good, worse, actually, than a lot of the bad guys they exterminated. This was a shock to some of their biggest fans in the West, who were rooting for them, many of whom were in the ranks of the professoriate and the editorial boards of the big newspapers like the *New York Times* and *Washington*

Post. The East German good guys had to build a wall in Berlin to keep their people from leaving for the bad-guy camp, and they shot them when they tried — not exactly a ringing endorsement for the workers' paradise that they had built and never stopped bragging about.

At some point, however, many folks began to realize that the "proletariat-capitalist" way of separating the good guys from the bad ones was absurd. Who actually were members of the proletariat? Are the lowly government clerks who process applications and forms and push paper around in the Ohio DMV members of the proletariat? Are the unionized college professors on strike at Central Michigan University — average annual salary of $90,000 a year, with summers off — members of the proletariat? In fact, the whole "good-guy worker, bad-guy factory owner" division of society became a tired, muddled, useless anachronism that no one paid attention to anymore.

However, Marx's seductive appeal of viewing society as a perpetual struggle of morally superior and inferior beings was firmly in place — locked in, actually. Post-WWII, this template needed a major overhaul, if you will, with two different sets of superiors and inferiors. It took some time. By the time Sun was encouraging me to get into the "diversity" business, it was well underway.

CHAPTER THIRTY-FIVE

"Racism," I Hardly Knew You

I maintain that every civil rights bill in this country was passed for white people, not for black people.
Stokely Carmichael

My morally-good and morally-bad understanding of the way society worked was based on economic class — initially. The theory behind it, however, was hopelessly muddled; no way for people to get worked up with feelings of moral superiority since nobody is sure which class they belong to. A bolder view, with more clarity, was in order. But based on what? Well…race.

Race, then, would be the fulcrum upon which moral distinctions were pivoted. "Racism" would be the key to unlock the dark history that revealed the deep divide between the morally good guys and the morally bad ones. Racism was more far-reaching than economic-social class. It would have a much longer shelf life than the puny proletariat-capitalist version.

"Racism" had to be "morally" re-engineered — its load-bearing walls expanded to bear the massive weight of the grievances it would soon have to bear. The good-guy group was no longer the downtrodden proletariat, the lunch-bucket gang. White workers, now, were the bad guys. The wickedness of white America ranged across four hundred years of slavery, segregation, and discrimination. Guilt-leveraged "racism" was on its way to becoming a "moral" stain that never washes away — ever.

It's hard to remember, I know, but you just didn't hear much about "racism" in the 1950s, the time I was growing up. Nothing remotely like you do today, where it is centerstage of American politics, where there is no escape from the agonizing over it. It is a much different creature now — its guilt-leveraging career had not, then, been fully launched.

Ironically, there was a lot more of it in play when I was a kid. The "it" being open, unabashed racial discrimination like separate drinking fountains, restrooms, and lunch counters for white and black people. Jim Crow was still in place, with segregated schools, public facilities, and businesses. Double standards of expectations and accountability for blacks and whites, all premised on a widespread white perception that blacks were…well, generally, less capable, less reliable, less intelligent than whites. Segregation was well entrenched — de jure in the South; de facto in the North. Blacks in America were significantly poorer, less healthy, less educated, less regarded than whites, as well. They felt the daily sting of the indignities, along with suffering the hostilities, mistreatment, and condescension of whites. However, outside of some academics and radicals, the racism did not get much attention.

Not by coincidence, the American conquerors, about this time, were just finishing their occupation of the defeated Third Reich. Their soldier boys in racially segregated units were sent across the ocean to dispose of the racist Fuhrer and stay and teach the *Die Frauen und die Herren* to love democracy and recite Thomas Jefferson's "self-evident" truth: "*dass alle Menschen gleich geschaffen sind*" — "that all men are created equal." President Truman's desegregation order for the Armed Services didn't come until 1948. Black American soldiers fighting oversees for equality and against racism came home to segregated public facilities, lunch counters, and schools.

This now brings us to address the critical question of how collective guilt works toward getting folks willing to wear the mantle of "morally inferior person." Having put the Germans in their proper place, it was painfully evident that it was time to get serious and put our own house in order, racial-equality wise.

There was a lot to feel guilty about: slavery, segregation, and all — I certainly did — and it was past time for a serious correction or, if you prefer, a theological slant, "atonement" — "healing," if you lean toward psychobabble. And not just black people were pointing it out, lots of white people were, too. Clearly, lots of white Americans were feeling pretty damn guilty about the current arrangements, and rightly so. Guilt is a nasty thing to have to cope with; most people prefer not to be burdened by it because getting past it requires having to do things most people don't enjoy doing, certainly not on an ongoing, regular basis. This collective guilt was mounting. It moved the majority-white American people in an effort to reduce and someday end racial prejudice and discrimination against black Americans, move past color in judging people's worth and on to the "content of their character." Doing would relieve the guilt. Everyone — black and white — would be feeling a whole lot better. No one, however, seems to be feeling better…just yet.

The 1950s began a legal dismantling of racial segregation and the criminalization of racial discrimination. With "Brown versus the Board of Education" the Federal government then acted to desegregate the public schools. In 1957, President Eisenhower federalized the National Guard and ordered a thousand soldiers from the 101st Airborne, along with a multitude of FBI agents, to Little Rock, Arkansas, to force the integration of Central High School. The University of Alabama and the University of Mississippi were, a few years later, forcibly integrated by the Federal government. This was clearly a huge step.

The 1960s, my coming of age, began a moral crusade, and the conscience of white America was convicted of its racial iniquities. In the summer of 1964, I was riveted by and followed the news of the murder of three young civil rights workers in Neshoba County, Mississippi — Andrew Goodman, Michael Schwerner, both northern Jews, and James Chaney, a Delta black man.

There, of course, was resistance, but the correction then began to move at top speed — the Civil Rights Act, 1964; Voting Rights Act, 1965. The civil rights movement led the way. Today, its history possesses a hallowed moral status that requires the most reverential deference. Martin Luther King, Jr. — sainted — is the only individual American who merits a dedicated national holiday. In the five decades that followed the equalizing of black and white, America became "mission central" with the legislatures creating and the courts enforcing anti-discrimination laws in the areas of housing, employment, government contracting, and education, including the forced busing of school children to achieve "equality of education."

Massive federal aid flowed to the heavily black-populated cities like Detroit, Watts, and Washington D.C., burned down by black rioters in the middle-late 1960s. Affirmative Action and EEOC came into being, with strict compliance requirements for universities and employers to make room for members of "underrepresented" groups. Schools and universities nearly everywhere focused their pedagogy on the evils of racism, the history of slavery and segregation, and the moral imperative of "equality." Blacks moved into prominent positions in every region of American culture and life, including big-city mayors, governorships, the U.S. Congress, the American presidency, Secretary of State, Attorney General, and the U.S. Supreme Court. Utterance of the "n-word" for whites became a career-killer and a ticket to social ostracism.

"Racism", at least as it was understood and practiced up into the 1960s, was under sustained assault by every institution — government, the legal system, schools, churches, universities, the entertainment industry, and college and professional athletics. Yet, in spite of this frontal assault and the breaking down of the long-existing barriers of segregation and the efforts of white America to right the wrongs, "racism," it seemed, was not diminishing but expanding exponentially. From this decades-long, massive, concerted "corrective action," racism had, apparently, emerged ubiquitous and pervasive.

After the decades of the throttle to floor in the pursuit of racial equality, as I sat in my comfortable house in Toledo, I realized that America was still deeply locked in racial hostility. When I watched the eruption of black celebration at the announcement of O.J. Simpson's not-guilty verdict in 1995 — thirty-one years after the Civil Rights act — I knew race relations in America were heading down. Black Americans were still angry; white Americans were still guilty. Both conditions bore the deeply disturbing feature of permanence.

How did this happen? There are different theories, but, as you have already noticed, I am a very cynical sort of fellow, and my take on it is, well, quite cynical. Not all is as it appears on the surface: Corruption pustulates underneath the surface, beneath the posturing of the professional moralizers.

To deny that what I am about to argue is the reason is impossible without climbing aboard your own Starship Enterprise and taking an extended flight from reality. The reality can be simply stated: Society, as a morally superior-inferior arrangement, is too sweet a deal to let go of for those who occupy the ranks of the superior. Why relinquish the driver's seat? I certainly wouldn't, and I would strenuously resist every effort to dislodge me.

Back, then, to Russell's doctrine of the superior virtue of the oppressed. The vehicle of oppression of black Americans — what makes them the good guys, endowing them with superior virtue (moral superiority) — is, above all else, their victimhood, the burden of racism laid upon them by white Americans. Without "racism," black Americans could no longer be, *collectively*, victims, and they would have to relinquish the collective prize of "superior virtue." White Americans, *collectively*, would no longer be "on the hook" and could finally cast away their guilt, free of the "moral inferiority" shackles that bound them in the long unfolding, never-to-end morality play of American history. Free at last; free at last. God Almighty, free at last!

Now, of course, I know how this is going to go over: Some readers are going to call me a Nazi, a Fascist, a racist bigot, and a hate-monger. That's fine: I'm happy to be any or all of these because, well, because those words have now become just *Schimpfworten* (swear-words), all evil connotation and emotional sputter, no denotation. We now are in "a night in which all cows are black," as the philosopher Hegel might say. And, if swearing makes someone feel pleased with himself or like a morally superior person for it, then I'm happy for him and for myself for making him happy and helping him feel superior.

But, just for the record: I've never been a Nazi and never wanted to be part of *die Herrenvolk*. I've never admired them. I don't plan on becoming one. Brown is not my color. And it's hard to pick up a woman these days, sporting a toothbrush mustache, goose-stepping around, and bellowing out "Sieg Heil!"

Fascist? I'm not exactly sure what one is. There are so many of them around that I can't keep them all straight. That said, I've never been a member of a club bearing that name. And, since no one in his right mind these days would admit to being "a Fascist," there is no way to separate the real ones — if any actually exist — from the exploding numbers of the accused.

A racist? Find me a white person who isn't. If you deny it, you're confirming it, so don't bother. No matter what you say to dispute the accusation, "racist" is "who you are." Calling me one doesn't hurt my feelings. I am happy to oblige and wear the scarlet letter, since it bolsters someone else's feeling of moral superiority to make the accusation.

I was a communist for a while, but, after being up close and personal with some of the biggies, I realized that communism was just one more "ism" that attracted the true-believers who rush-advertise their superior moral virtue and shame their inferiors. The name-callers are the foot soldiers for the ideologues, the professional "moralists" who shape the propaganda, coin the slogans, and hype the fictions that are most useful for expanding their power through affirming their moral superiority.

Taking a huge breath: All of this takes us to the birth and expansion of what is called the "diversity industry" that I, out of sheer opportunism, became a part of. Once you grasp the dynamics of "racism' and collective guilt, the emergence and explosive growth of the diversity industry will make perfect sense to you — even though, over the last fifty years, the barriers of race to social, economic, and political participation in American life, by all objective measures, have drastically fallen.

So, finally, I am ready to say what "diversity" is all about. It's a code word. When uttered, it signals that what follows will, in some way, critically reflect upon and expose the continuing, deep-structured unfairness of the status quo. It is worse, in a way, than before, even during the Jim Crow period, since the unfairness perpetuated by the oppressors is glossed over or hidden by a false cover of "progress." "Diversity" (usually introduced by the words "lack of") is the trigger that "diversity professionals" rely on to keep the doctrine of the superior virtue of the oppressed front and center and further leverage the guilt by exposing new and recondite forms of oppression. Jim Crow, back of the bus, segregated drinking fountains and restrooms, etc. are gone. No more Bull Connors, "whites only" signs, anti-miscegenation laws. One might be tempted to conclude that things, race-wise, are getting a bit better. Not so fast, Kemosabe! Getting "better," however, means losing that leverage, and who, rationally speaking, will voluntarily give up leverage of any kind?

Leverage comes from more rather than less "racism." Those looking for leverage will always find more rather than less of it. Logically, there is no other way to make sense of what is happening. Leveraging creates the multiplier effect, with a constantly updated industry manual of operation: generic "racism" expands and reveals the existence of covert and insidious forms of "racism" — institutional racism, systemic racism, structural racism, covert racism, overt racism, environmental racism, economic racism, legacy racism. The social pathology of "racism"? Well, it's endemic, systemic, systematic, institutional. It's entrenched in every crevice of American society — top to bottom. Which means that there is a lot of heavy lifting to do and endless opportunities for those to carve out new niches in the diversity industry.

These pathologies rage in and out of control — mostly, the latter. Containment requires pathologists, specialists trained to detect racism's permutations, label them, and call out its practitioners. Specialized personnel tend to the wounded. They focus on promoting their threatened interests. They guard their tender feelings, help them grasp and appreciate their moral superiority, and polish and upgrade their grievances.

The most challenging and intractable element is the racists — the morally inferior thought criminals — themselves. Many or most fail to understand that they are morally defective. At best, they are insensitive to the continuing victimization they are responsible for; at worst, hostile and resistant to efforts to reeducate them. Hence, "diversity training," a euphemism for the "shaming" and "struggle sessions," as they were called during the Cultural Revolution in China. Diversity training — ironically, for "whites only." They discover "white privilege," learn about microaggressions, and are encouraged to "celebrate diversity." Most importantly, they are ordered to internalize their guilt, self-censor constantly, grovel, and apologize when called upon.

I arrived on the diversity scene in the late 1980s, with the shift from economically determined oppressed to the race model. It was an opportunity to move into a growth industry that was taking off at the universities. The "diversity" office — or divisions, if I may simplify a bit — were tasked with what I would call "the racism watch." As I've noted, there were no incentives for anyone who wanted to be successful in this industry to report that racism was in decline. A decline would mean fewer staff members, smaller offices, smaller paychecks, fewer perks, and fewer conferences to attend, less visibility. If whites were behaving themselves, there would be no need for an office of diversity at all. You had to pretend you wanted racism to be eliminated because it's the ultimate evil, but if that happened, you'd be working your way out of a job. You never heard Jesse Jackson or Al Sharpton talking about racism on the decline. The material, self-interested incentives are entirely perverse to the moral ideal, and when those two come into conflict, everybody knows which one is going to win.

CHAPTER THIRTY-SIX

Sunny Cynicism

All men are frauds. The only difference between them is that some admit it. I myself deny it.

H. L. Mencken

With Sun's encouragement, I decided to join the diversity industry. Not only did I want to *be* morally superior, I wanted the perks that came with it. The industry was booming because the "ism" piece of "racism" was its foundation and engine. Even better, it could be franchised with spinoffs — more "isms" and "obias," like "sexism" and "homophobia." The menacing abstractions were multiplying. All of them fit into the morally superior-inferior template invented by Marx. The ranks of the "superiors" were growing. Of course. You don't argue with success, and you can never defeat an abstraction. Once born, an "ism" lives forever. The virtuous victim classes — the good guys and gals — were multiplying so fast it was a challenge to follow the course: Latinos, women, gays, and the disabled — sexism, homophobia, ableism, even non-humans, animals. To comprehend the subtle nuances of victimhood in this expanding clientele of morally superior people, you need more professional staff — lots of them — in specialized capacities to understand and serve their specialized needs.

This was an industry tailormade for a conman like me, experienced in pretending to be something I wasn't. And let me just pause to make this extremely critical point: Enterprises and industries that are built by professional moralists to advance hyped-up, lofty moral ideals are ripe for takeover by cynical opportunists, folks like me who move in, take advantage, and move to the top or as close as we can get. Faking moral outrage takes some unique talent. Quantity, however, can go a long way to make up for the lack of quality.

"Diversity" was not only a growth industry. It had insidiously morphed itself into a newish religion, with its own scriptures, rites, saints, and banishment rituals for heretics. Religion, with its mission of high morals, as you know, is fertile ground for fakers and fanatics. What we also know is that religion, in its early, expansionist stage — early Christianity and Islam, for example — is heavily focused on the heresy-banishment side of the ledger — no toleration for "deviation" from the established "truth." Healthy skepticism gets punished as blasphemy. Heretics are not just misguided, wrong, or mistaken: They are evil, morally defective, and have no place in the community of believers. The pursuit of heretics and their ex-communication is the business of true believers, not for timid personalities. Fanatics excel at it; conmen also make it happen, if there are advantages in it.

That said, the challenge for me was how to break in and become a lowly priest in this new expansionist religion with industrial strength. As a white male, I was a bone-fide member of the oppressor class; no entry, not even into the lowest rungs of the victim ladder. Ha! So, at least, I thought. Sun, however, stepped into the role of my spiritual advisor and professional coach. "Hey, Dummy. The best diversity offices employ enforcers from the widest possible range of official victim groups. The BGSU diversity office needs a "gay" diversity officer." Wink-wink.

"But, Sun, I'm not gay," was my horrified response when I realized where she was going with this.

"Ah, Johnny, you're a sweetie, but, clearly, you don't know shit about how this stuff actually works. Gender and sexual orientation, like race, are 'socially constructed,' love. You know, Michel Foucault, "deconstruction," and all. Think of it as an extension of 'the Revolution,' this piece of it being a revolution against the tyranny of biology."

"Well, good. I never liked biology that much. I'm up for a revolution against that oppressor. But Foucault? Come on. I read his stuff years ago. He was worse than Sartre. I couldn't make any sense of him. Didn't he die of AIDs he contracted in the San Francisco bathhouses? What does 'socially constructed' mean, exactly, Sun? It sounds like the 'philosophy' doubletalk from my college days."

"Well, probably, but here is how it works, Johnny: race, sexual preferences, gender — none of these are fixed in nature or objective reality. 'Objective reality' itself is a tool of white-male hegemony — not you, of course. They use it to keep themselves in charge and make the rest of us think it's normal and proper. Believing in 'objective reality' merely perpetuates and disguises the unjust practices of subjugation of 'The Other.' These 'natural' categories are actually 'socially constructed,' made up by people who use them to support and perpetuate existing oppressive, power structures. They are created by hegemonic social forces, not naturally or physically fixed. They are fluid. That's the party line."

"The party line? Which party? So, then, let me see if I understand this: Race-wise, I'm a white guy *because* I say I'm a white guy, which gives me undeserved privilege, not because I actually *am* one, biologically. Then, gay-wise, I'm…"

"Stop. Yes, you're on the right track; it can be a little bit confusing, I know, but that's a plus that's definitely going to work to your advantage. You see, if you can act like the seemingly confusing, incoherent, and contradictory message that you are peddling is clear, obvious, and necessary for people to be onboard with, you'll get a ninety percent buy in. The other ten percent will be indifferent or too intimidated to say anything. Throw in a few references to the "Heavies" like Foucault or Derrida and add some Oprah-style therapy-babble like "the need for healing," "the power of now," and "it will be ok," and it will be a walk in the park for you. You will be good at it. This is how group-think works. Brassy self-confidence — your strong suit — is a huge part of the success of group-think leaders and visionaries. You'll be a hit."

I was starting to feel her confidence as she was making the case. On she went to close the sale.

"That's the huge irony, Johnny. The cultivated university image as the bastion of independent free-thinking and quest-for-the-truth is a laughable crock. Universities are the biggest, cravenly conformist, suck-up-to-the-powerful-to-get-ahead fetid swamps in the country. They are now run by low-testosterone, careerist, ass-kissing pseudo-males, militant feminists, and nutzo lesbians. Group-think is easiest to pull off at universities because 'right thinking' is prized above anything else. It is what gets you the recognition and promotions. Believe me. I know how this system works. No one dares to say that the post-modern Gods are phonies and crackpots, except for a few grumpy, old, out-of-it white guys, whom everyone else ignores. They will soon be extinct. Fuck them!

"Now, go off. Give this serious thought, and think how you can pitch the "evolution" of your sexuality and its implications for your moral convictions. Most importantly, think of your career. Think 'nuance.'"

With expansion, these inspirational words from Sun could be written up as a modern and updated replacement for Cardinal John Henry Newman's classic, "The Idea of the University." Serious thought, however, was never my strong suit. And of my sexuality? "No evolution," just a gradual, inevitable slackening. "Moral convictions?" Well, by now, I think you should have a good grasp of how well I hold up for scrutiny in that sorry arena. Sun, of course, was being ironic or comedic about this whole business. She was firing at her meta-theoretical best on all cylinders. But, to myself, I kept repeating "nuance" until it sounded a bit like "romance."

So, about forty minutes later, a jar of Jack Daniels in hand and a big Honduran cigar clamped between my teeth, I dropped into a chair next to Sun and slide my hand up her skirt. She was working on a paper — "Dead Women Speaking: Images of Injustice in Asian Literature" — she hoped to publish in the *Asian Journal of Women's Studies*.

"Ok, Babe, I'm up for a challenge. How is this "gay" thing going get me in the door?"

CHAPTER THIRTY-SEVEN

A Gay Confession-Profession

In diversity, there is beauty and there is strength.
Maya Angelou

I was angling for the job "Associate Director of Diversity and Equality," as I noted, not the Director position — no possibility for that. Sun was running the Women's Studies department, and she was well-connected with the Diversity office. She knew the people who were going to be on the search committee and how "diversity" politics worked. And, best, she was a master of the lingo. With my college-era skills still intact, I ginned up a resume with some "relevant" experience — in Europe, where it would be more difficult to check up on. I bought a fake doctorate in "Higher Education," along with a transcript, from a Brussels diploma mill. "Higher Education" is a relatively recent "academic discipline." Its absence of intellectual content and scholarly quality means that the fake degrees are indistinguishable from the real ones.

In my application materials, I appended my "real" personal "mission statement." "My personal mission is to make every waking moment of my daily life a sacred ceremony dedicated to the advancement of human equality and the erasure of every trace of hatred, racism, and bigotry." I know, Reader, this puts your gag-reflex to the ultimate test. You will have to admit, though: It pushes many of the right buttons. I was very proud of it; it got rave reviews.

With Sun's expert coaching, I was a smash hit at the interview. Shortly thereafter, I was installed as the new Associate Director for Diversity and Equality. None of the BGSU enlightened gave the slightest indication that gay-me, married to non-gay Sun, was in any way out of the norm in their sophisticated, nuanced worlds.

Dr. Chiku Shakur, née Jenny-Wanda Barkmann, was the director and my new boss. Originally from Benton Harbor, Michigan, she had a Ph.D. in Afro-American Studies from Syracuse University and a dissertation with one of the catchier titles I've seen: "Black Female Sexuality (un)Hinged: Depictions of Racially-defined Derangement of Detroit's Strip Club Dancers." I confess, I haven't read it yet: I'm hoping to get to it soon. Maybe, the prison librarian can get me a copy.

"Chiku" was Swahili for "The one who talks a lot." She was perfectly renamed, and it was fortunate for me, as a rookie in this profession, to have her as a mentor. I listened a lot and imitated. Quickly, I learned the grammar, phrasing, and intonation to signal how diversity-office personnel dominate the agendas, shape university policies, and occupy the institutional driver seat. For example: "In this meeting, we will be *leading the conversation*…" Or: "Our objective is to help *shape the narrative*…" And we were constantly about "*changing the culture*." "Conversation," "the narrative," and "changing the culture" are loosely interchangeable code words for "control" and "domination." Taking control and bossing people around are what we were all about. Like politicians, we use the first-person plural pronouns — *we, us, our* — and the "we're-all-in-it-together" head fake, which downplays the heavy-handed propaganda that we hit them with. They signal that deviation from the "diversity way of thinking, the approved narrative" is not allowed in the "conservation" you are leading on the way to "changing the culture." "The urge to save humanity is almost always only a false-face for the urge to rule it," as Mencken put it. I was now not only in with the in crowd, but with the false-faced crowd, as well. I was in full stride.

Do-gooder bromides were overworked but useful. They had come into popular currency and were always good to fall back upon to bolster a false front. I was partial to "I want to make a difference." It had to be the mother of all banalities. Whatever you do or not do "makes a difference" of some kind — like holding up a liquor store, for example. You've made quite "a difference" with that bit of self-assertion, especially if you've gunned down the store clerk. That cliché was a hit in my interview. "I want to come to BGSU because I believe in this institution. I think that this is the perfect place, where I will be able to make a difference." Fortunately, no one at my talk followed up and asked me two stupidly obvious questions: Why did I "believe" in BGSU? And: What sort of "difference" would I be able to make? Group-think conditions you not to ask pesky questions like these.

I quickly learned four words, ending with a question mark, that, sternly posed, throw any university administrator, from the President on down, into a state of fecal incontinence. They are: "Your commitment to diversity?" "Diversity" had become so vaguely, numbingly ritualized, with no precise meaning, that no one could prove or demonstrate his "commitment" to it. Which is perfect, you see, because this always put me, the diversity inquisitor, firmly in the driver seat. I was the one paid to peer into the crystal ball, abracadabra-like, and find the illusive "commitment." What I saw was never good news for the poor sap on the receiving end of the question. I was good at "mau-mauing the flack catcher," as the inimitable Tom Wolfe put it. Mr. Administrator was permanently deficient in "commitment" — the more he babbled, the worse it got for him, which meant that I got to be in the "collection" mode, resource and power-wise.

Quickly, I figured out that "Your commitment to diversity?" was the combination that unlocked the university safe for our division. The seriousness of the university's "commitment to diversity" was directly proportional to a combination of factors in the diversity division: how many staff, the size of their salaries, the prestige of the titles, the size and prime location of the offices, and resources available for professional development and programming. The more expansive these, the more evident it was that "diversity" placed high in the university's firmament of priorities…but never quite high enough. The "smart" administrators quickly grasped that these metrics were the best evidence of their commitment and snapped to.

CHAPTER THIRTY-EIGHT

Pyramid Diversity

When we make the case for the importance of DEI, we can do so in two crucial ways: the moral case and the business case.

Claremont Lincoln University

As the new "Associate Director for Diversity and Equality," my first priority was the creation of a new position for the Division, an "Assistant Director for Diversity and Equality," who would report directly to me. You, no doubt, are going to ask: What different things does an Assistant Director do than an Associate Director? A more basic question, however, should be occurring to your inquisitive mind: What does the Associate Director do that the Director *can't* do? Don't stop now, Reader. You are almost there. What exactly does the "Director" do?

Ok, now we are getting somewhere. The light bulbs — bing-bing-bing — are beginning to go on. "Director," "Associate Director," "Assistant Director." Exactly! These titles are meaningless misdirections used to move the con forward, and I know all about cons. The number of people reporting to you signals how important you are. Slowly, this thing should be coming into a clearer focus. You have just stumbled into a pyramid scheme — a uniquely clever one.

Here is the classic definition: A "pyramid scheme" is a way of making money that cannot continue for very long. It involves promising people payment, services, or ideals, primarily for enrolling other people into the scheme or training them to take part. It does not supply any real investment or sale of products or services to the public.

Tweak this and discover how the diversity industry works as a pyramid scheme. Rather than "making money," this version is about "ideals" — "moral currency," so to speak — the making of racial harmony by promising people payments in the form of "fairness and equality" and the banishment of racism, bigotry, and discrimination. The lion will soon be lying with the lamb; universal peace is on the horizon. This scheme moves with the continuous enrollment of the professional proselytizers into the operation to convert non-believers into believers. The proselytizers and the converts, however, do not "supply any real investment or services" to the university. Racism is never extinguished. The promised fairness and equality — ever illusive — is never within reach: It's always somewhere down the road — often, less achievable than earlier. Only more staff and more sensitivity training will bring us closer. Yet, the goal posts are always moving farther away. As the diversity staff and initiatives expand, racism, bigotry, and hatred expand. The diversity pyramid is programmed for continuous expansion.

In order to combat the entrenched unfairness and move toward the equality that never materializes, you need more warm bodies underneath you, which pushes you higher up in the pyramid — the more staff added, the more inequalities they discover. This illustrates a variant known as Parkinson's Law: "Work expands to fill the time available for its completion." Thus, the Diversity Parkinson's Law: "Diversity work expands to fill the time of the staff added to the diversity payroll."

Diversity professionals' *talk* about how important diversity is, and, since there is never enough diversity and no one can tell you exactly what it is, much less when you've reached "peak diversity," you can never have enough people to remind everyone how important it is. The more the staff, the more the diversity-talk. The more diversity-talk there is, ergo, the more important it is. Are you beginning to grasp the circularity in play? Since the language of "diversity" is so nebulous, abstract, and expansive, the work of "diversity" is simply the expansion of talking about it — the praising of diversity or, as they put it, "celebrating diversity."

That was how I spent my workdays. All day long, I talked about the importance of diversity. I hoped that no one would notice how my job differed from those of most of the other university employees. Take a math professor, for example. A math professor isn't paid to talk about how important mathematics is; he doesn't have to. He just teaches people how to do mathematics because it is obvious how important mathematics is. You only hire as many math professors as you have students who want or need to learn mathematics; any additional math profs would have nothing to do. Or, take the custodian who cleans the classrooms and how quickly things get nasty without him: Think what would happen to him if all he did was talk about how important it is to have tidy buildings but never emptied the trashcans. I don't think the university would be adding more custodial staff to talk about the importance of custodial work.

My new Assistant Director for Diversity and Equality, I put in charge of Gay-Lesbian consciousness raising. The position had been advertised internationally. I got over one hundred and fifty applications, some from as far away as

England, Germany, and India. One applicant had four advanced degrees, including a law degree and an Ed.D. in Educational Diversity.

The new hire was Jenny Granholm, a lesbian, originally from Florida, who had a bachelor's degree from Oberlin College in "Gender and Sexuality." She was a Ph.D. candidate at UC Berkeley in "Women & Gender" with a concentration in Queer Studies. Just in case you're not *au courant* on the contemporary, cutting-edge "research" of Queer Studies, here is how Jenny described it on her thirty-page CV:

"My work in QS encompasses theories and thinkers from many fields, including cultural studies, gay and lesbian studies, transgender studies, race studies, women's and gender studies, film, media, postmodernism, post-colonialism, and more. I focus on issues surrounding sexuality and gender (and other axes of marginalized identity) and the way(s) that the questions raised in these other arenas might be modulated through that central lens. I attempt to explore the ways that culture defines and regulates sexuality and gender (and, more broadly, normativity) as well as the reverse, the ways that sexuality and gender structure and shape social institutions and power structures."

Yes, I realize that there's a lot there to digest slowly, like a giant boa constrictor that has just swallowed a baby water buffalo. The clincher for me was her "central lens." I keep misplacing mine. With "other axes of marginalized identity" and with the culture busy defining and regulating "sexuality and "other arenas that might be modulated," I knew that Jenny was my gal. She was hands down the best choice to belch out the sort of verbal smog that (a) would energize and impress the victims hoping to polish their grievance narratives, and (b) would utterly intimate the yet uninitiated on campus who would believe that their confusion and skepticism relating to "normativity" and "gender structure" is a cognitive, moral shortcoming, and (c) would be so opaque and incomprehensible that no one on the entire campus could ever figure out what the hell an Assistant Director for Gay-Lesbian Affairs was supposed to accomplish. Which meant that the purpose and justification for my position would be even further insulated from external inspection and, therefore, safe.

With her purple-dyed, 50s-retro flattop haircut, dressed in ratty bib overalls, weighing in at around 240 pounds, an Andrea Dworkin wannabe, she came in like gangbusters and hit the ground running — well, not real fast. She launched a campus-wide conscious-raising program on homophobia, including training sessions for resident hall RAs that focused on sensitivity and inclusion for Gay students living on campus. Everyone on campus was scared of her, including me.

Years went by. They were well spent — or not, depending on how enthused you are about celebrating diversity. Most of my working hours at BGSU were occupied with warming the chairs in meetings — meetings with administrators, faculty, and staff, meetings that focused on the need for more "diversity" at BGSU, more commitment, more resources. The commitment? Well, always in question, but the resources-spigot stayed on.

I finagled a generous budget to fund a "Diversity Speaker" series that let me to bring in expensive outside talent like Jesse Jackson, Angela Davis, and various well-known "activists" in regions such as "feminism," "animal rights," and "prisoner's rights." These hustlers were remarkably non-diverse in their requirements for high speaker fees, first-class airfare, top-floor, luxury hotel accommodations, and other perks, like beauty shop and massage services and, in good weather, a round of golf at the local country club. After a visit from one of these inspirational leaders, usually the first thought that came to my mind echoed the words of my spiritual mentor, H. L. Mencken: "Every normal man must be tempted, at times, to spit on his hands, hoist the black flag, and begin slitting throats."

It was surprisingly easy to keep "racism" front and center on the campus, so as to not lose the leverage it gave us for expanding our operations and asserting our continuing moral preeminence — I mean, superiority. Occasionally, we'd get a huge, unexpected boost from a local troglodyte or two who would scratch a swastika on the sidewalk near a dorm or scribble some obnoxious, "racist" graffiti on a restroom wall. With any fortunate occurrence of this sort of random stupidity, which anyone with better things to do would laugh at or ignore, we would be locked and loaded, primed to get the campus worked up into a pandemonium. Perfect! The Klan, we warned, would soon be in charge of student services, with racially segregated facilities, and the campus police would be about to don brown shirts and jack boots, beat up the Jewish students, and give the stiff-armed "Heil Hitler" salute to each other, a mini-Third Reich right here in little old Bowling Green, Ohio. Who could have imagined how useful a few dimwit wingnuts could be for us?

Sometimes, these "hate-events" would turn out to be a hoax, staged by a "victim." Real or fake — no matter. When these sorts of things happened, we would hold candlelight processions against hatred and bigotry and conduct even more mandatory sensitivity training sessions. We would also squeeze the President. He would fold like a cheap suitcase and give us almost whatever we asked for — usually, a new position that would be seen as a signal of his firm resolve to make the campus "fully inclusive and hate-free."

The job turned out to be not terribly challenging, but, for someone who enjoyed fooling people and getting well-paid for it, at times, it was a lot of fun. At other times, not so much. My attention and energy had finally flagged. I needed to take my leave and reflect on what I had been about.

The phenomenal success of the "diversity" industry, after years on the inside, I concluded, is not due to the logical rigor and empirical support for any arguments that might justify its existence. Nor can any serious historical reasons be given for tolerating what it has become. The kinds of practical techniques of psychological intimidation and coercion we used are what brought this monster into existence and continue to feed it. The invulnerability and growth come from what I was describing at the outset — the moral superiority of guilt-leveraged victimhood. It should be obvious, though, that "moral superiority," stripped of its bolstering rhetoric, is nothing more than a naked power relation. Power corrupts. The "diversity" ideologues who collude with the careerists and the trimmers who run the institutions are walking vectors of corruption. Power leveraged by moral superiority to extort (coerce) material advantage from the inferiors. For the careerist administrators? Career advancement. The diversity industry: a choir with the 3-C's singing in three-part harmony.

CHAPTER THIRTY-NINE

Diversity'd Up

It's a proprietary strategy. I can't go into it in great detail.
Bernie Madoff

Sun was a prolific writer, speaker, and administratively, kick-ass gifted. No way she would remain permanently potted in a backwater like Bowling Green, Ohio. By the mid-1990s, her professional star had risen. She was sought after by several top-dog universities. Vanderbilt wanted to hire her. So did Emory and Duke.

Northwestern University, however, was the next step. Sun was offered a job as a dean of the college of the School of Education and Social Policy. This was a big, well-deserved advance for her. The timing was also perfect for both of us. I had milked the "diversity" cow at BGSU for all it was worth. I was feeling sullied by the incessant wallowing in grievances, complaining, and contrived victimhood. A conman eventually wearies of his marks and projects his contempt for them back on to himself. My self-loathing was mounting; it was too much to cope with. I was depressed and eating mountains of junk food — Doritos, mostly. I also liked those waxy little chocolate covered donuts you'd find at a 7-Eleven; I'd wash down a box of six with a couple cans of Budweiser.

Frankly, I was longing to move to some greener and more nutritional pastures and do — how shall I say this? — a bit more "muscular" kind of work. Northwestern called, and off we went. We settled into a tiny apartment near the NU campus in uppity Evanston, Illinois. We discovered a place where everyone was convinced that they were well above average. At least, they acted like they thought others should think they were. I was, of course, always obliging, hoping some of that superiority would rub off on me.

I took time off to read military history — Sun Tzu, Clausewitz, B.H. Lidell Hart — upgrade my martial arts skills, and think about what my next career move should look like. It would be nothing — mercifully — connected with a university. I yearned to be as far away from the "morality" industry as I could get. My career planning was toward the physical. It moved along the lines of security services, the kind that catered to wealthy enterprises and prestigious institutions. From my Havana days, I always liked being close to — and ingratiating myself with — important, powerful people.

For the first eleven months or so in Evanston, all I did was obsessively workout, lift weights, and train intensively at the gym, where I was finally bench-pressing 350 pounds — one rep. I found a martial arts guru who was originally from the Philippines, Manny Pacquiao. He was an Eskrima Master — Eskrima being the traditional Philippine martial art. Chuck Norris was one of his more famous students. At a training session, I had the opportunity for a short sparing round with Chuck, who kindly pulled many of his punches.

Manny Pacquiao — same name as the Philippine national hero boxer — taught me how to fashion and wield improvised weapons. He trained me to execute deadly strikes with a knife. Best of all, from him, I learned weaponless "open hand" fighting techniques, both offensive and defensive. In sparring sessions, I'd seen the sixty-one-year-old Manny, at 5'6" and 150 pounds, quickly demolish opponents almost twice his size and more than half his age. I was in utter awe of this man, a walking dangerous weapon. He told me that his unfailing youth and high energy came from a secret cocktail that he ingested on a monthly basis. One of its ingredients was the urine of a virgin. I didn't ask him for the recipe or where he found the virgins.

I took what I learned from Manny, adding it to the silent strangling techniques Elsa taught me during my sojourn in Havana and my CIA stealth-training in the Louisiana swamp. At 5'8" and now chiseled and bulked up at a rock hard 180 pounds, I had become the steely-eyed, formidable bloke no one in his right mind would be advised to fuck with. My acquired formidable, physical, martial prowess, as I'll explain shortly, would come into play in shaping the events surrounding my life in the next several years.

With yet another one of my "creative" resumes — also with Manny's connections — I landed a job working for a Los Angeles based firm that offered security planning and protection services for host organizers of big-crowd events like rock concerts, political rallies, and high-end motivational speakers like Tony Robbins. I scored high on the personality and psych assessments and was assigned to a security detail covering the Midwest. We provided personal, individualized protection for event speakers, performers, etc., particularly whatever big, well-known "Name" who, without a watchful, protective assistant, would likely to be on the receiving end of unwanted "attention."

For this line of work, I turned out to be the perfect match. Not huge or too physically imposing and bruiser-looking so as to draw undo notice as a conspicuous piece of hired-muscle, I blended nicely into the background. Strategically stationed and dressed unobtrusively in a sport jacket — no tie; "business casual," as they say — on a moment's notice, I could easily, quietly, and quickly incapacitate undesirables, move them away from my clients and out of the picture. In extremis, I had a 9mm Glock tucked in the inside of my belt and a Ka-Bar spring knife in my pocket, just in case any John Hinkley or Mark David Chapman-types might drop by uninvited for a friendly visit. I enjoyed this work more than anything I'd ever done. It was a refreshing change from the endless, boring, butt-flattening meetings I had to endure at BSGU. Plus, I got to rub shoulders with some top-drawer celebrities, like Barry Manilow, Suze Orman, and Stephen Covey, and flirt with their cute, young personal assistants.

Most memorable of the motivational speakers I was assigned to was Leo Buscaglia, a psychology professor at USC who had become known as "Dr. Love." My introduction to him was one of the more unique encounters in my life. A big, bearded disheveled Paisano, when I stuck out my hand for the customary shake at our initial introduction, he broke into a huge grin, grabbed me with both arms, and gave me a big bearhug, with his exclamation: "You look like a guy who could use a 'love hug'." "This guy's a fucking lunatic" was my immediate thought. But "hugs" were what Dr. Love was all about — "5 to survive, 8 to maintain and 12 to thrive" was one of his favorite lines. Leo was my most challenging assignment, from a security angle. After his lectures, people would line up by the hundreds to get one of his signature "hugs." Dr. Love was a 180 from my worldview, which operated on the H. L. Mencken principle that I had long embraced: "The only cure for contempt is counter-contempt." I tried not to, but I couldn't help but come to admire the Love Doctor for his daily massive determination to defy reality. I don't think he was a con man.

CHAPTER FORTY

Diversity'd Out

Summertime and the livin' is easy
Fish are jumpin', and the cotton is high.
Ella Fitzgerald, "Summertime"

Yes, indeed, living was as easy as I'd ever had it. Sun and I were rolling happily around and frolicking in some very thick clover — looking up at the "tall cotton." Sun was shaking up academic departments at NU and getting noticed. I was protecting VIPs, working for the jet set, and getting an occasional "love hug." Both of us were pretending to contribute to the betterment of a society that was in a steady, inevitable decline. We were members of the orchestra, earning our wages playing light waltzes for the passengers who were dancing away on the top deck of the Titanic.

Suddenly, however, Sun's career took an unexpected turn that would eventually move me toward a grim place where the only fish I saw were breaded, greasy fish sticks on a plastic plate. The only cotton would be in the fabric of my prison uniform, blended with cheap polyester — my current residence at Terre Haute.

Sun had dual — American and South Korean — citizenship. She also had family members who were politically well-connected and operated at high levels in South Korean politics. One of her cousins was on a meteoric rise in the New Korea Party (*Shin Hanguk-dang*). NKP had recently been founded by the merging of three older parties: Roh Tae-woo's Democratic Justice Party, Kim Young Sam's Reunification Democratic Party, and Kim Jong-pil's Democratic Republican Party. The Koreans had long ago turned "democratic" into a happy, praise-word that didn't describe anything — just like it was now in the U.S. South Korean "democratic" politics was a wild, tumultuous business, with corruption and collusion as only Koreans are capable of. It had the twists and turns you'd expect from an industrious, ambitious folk in an up-and-coming U.S. vassal state hosting American troops on a permanent basis.

Three years after Sun's grand uncle, Syngman Rhee, was hauled off to Hawaii in 1960 by the CIA, the iron-fisted General Chung Hee Park launched a military coup. Park was reputed never to have smiled after the age of five. He ruled the country in good, American-supported, anti-communist style, with his own Korean Central Intelligence Agency (KCIA) modeled after...I think you can guess. For those unfortunates who weren't quick enough to get with the program: innovative, Korean-style knuckle crushing. No habeas corpus, Miranda, or unwarranted search protection bullshit allowed. Park ruled for sixteen years, until he was assassinated in 1979 by one of his own KCIA agents. Does this have a familiar ring? During the ensuing decades, there was the push-pull of repression and mass-protest, with alternating military and civilian governments. Periodic constitutional changes would rock the established political elites. The powerbrokers would rearrange their deck chairs, thus imitating their American masters. South Korea, along with Japan, remained a U.S. Asian pawn during the decades of U.S.-Soviet, Cold War chess. It was deemed a critical region because of its close proximity to China, where Chairman Mao was churning up his own corrupt establishment in three-ring circus mode and occasionally rattling his sabers to make the comedians running the show in Washington nervous.

Sun's uncle, Kim Shi Keng, wanted her in the worst way to come to South Korea — now in the Sixth Republic version of its Constitution — join the NKP, and take an active leadership role with his Party's attempt to take power. He needed to enlist smart professional women to help energize and create a more contemporary, western-oriented party and appeal to a broader spectrum of South Korean voters. The party was moving toward corruption with a softer, feminine face. "A spoonful of sugar makes the medicine go down," one of the basic elements of successful propaganda.

Sun was a perfect fit: U.S.-educated, accultured, refined manners, and good-looking, she could work her considerable charm with western diplomats, businesspeople, and policymakers in America. She knew who and who not to trust, who was dangerous, and who she could roll over and kick into the corner. All that, combined with her family connections to the political elites in South Korea, makes it easy to understand why Keng so desperately wanted her as part of his political movement and his party structure.

Sun was torn. We both loved life in Evanston and its proximity to the Cubs, the Bears, and the Windy City. Even better, our favorite pastime was following the topsy-turvy local politics of what was probably, outside of D.C., the most corrupt metropolis in the country.

D.C., however, deserves a brief comment. The capitol city of the Empire resembled a dangerous African post-colonialist urban warzone. D.C. was licensed to and operated by drug lords. The mayor at the time, Marion Barry, modeled the highest standards of the ruling class in that city. His arrest for possession and the use of crack cocaine caused quite the sensation and made national news. When the FBI and the D.C. cops busted him and a woman companion in a sting operation, he was the perfection of chivalry...well, expressed in Washington D.C gangland vernacular. "The bitch set me up," he snarled as they slapped him in cuffs. Not exactly Churchillian or Lincolnesque, but, Hey! You gotta play the cards God dealt you, right? It was a keeper — perhaps, the most memorable of any of his quotes. It captured the edgier side of his personality, his command of the language, and how wonderfully he met the demanding expectations of leadership. Perhaps, it should have been engraved on the eight-foot bronze statue that they later put up in front of City Hall, at a cost to the taxpayers of $300,000.

The city of Chicago, during our time there, had turned into the personal ATM of Richard M. Daley, another exemplary big-city mayor. He finessed his way through five scandal-ridden terms. The worst? Probably, it was the $40 million-a-year Hired Truck program. Do-nothing-for-pay companies enrolled in the city program kicked back more than $800,000, in the form of campaign contributions to various politicians, including Daley, State House Speaker Michael Madigan, and Rod Blagojevich. Daley himself collected at least $108,575. His brother John and his ward organization came away with more than $47,500. Daley's son, Patrick, also had his own ATM card.

One of his Honor's more notable and memorable pronouncements was in response to a question about Chicago's rising rate of homicides. He was getting a bit of nationwide heat that, apparently, made him a bit irritable: "The more killing and homicides you have, the more havoc it prevents." To be fair, maybe this was one of those astute observations that suffers a bit when taken out of context. Perhaps, our post-modern philosopher Judith Butler, lounging around at Berkeley, should have been summoned to tease out of the Mayor's structural totality a theoretical object that would reveal his renewed conception of hegemony. That, I think, helps us better understand the challenges faced by Mayor Daley.

Chicago was also home to Jesse Jackson, another talented wordsmith with a more practical bent. The race-hustling, extortionist business model he developed for shaking down big corporations made him quite the dashing, well-dressed man of the hour. No one in the country had a surer instinct for self-serving publicity. Jackson's son, Jesse Jr., a U.S. Congressman, was an apple who fell rather close to the tree. He reached a bit too far, however, and his career culminated in prison for fraud, conspiracy, making false statements, mail fraud, wire fraud, and criminal forfeiture. He had used about $750,000 in campaign money for over three thousand personal purchases. During our time in Chicago, Jesse Sr. had served as a "spiritual" advisor for President Clinton during the Lewinsky crises. Jackson's pregnant mistress joined him at the White House to counsel the beleaguered President. Imagine God eavesdropping on their private conversation off in the corner. He would need to consult a post-modern philosopher to help him figure out this pair of world-class slicksters.

If Sun were to stay at NU for a few years as a dean, she would be ready for a provost slot at USC, Stanford, or even Berkeley, the Mecca for Diversity-Worshippers. But Sun was Asian and dutiful. She couldn't say no to her uncle and her family. With regret, she resigned her dean's position at NU and planned to decamp for Seoul. Soon, she would jump into the life of treacherous South Korean politics.

A sudden bad turn on the road for me: I didn't want to live in Korea, North or South. We'd been married years before in Seoul. For visiting, it was a happy place for me, but it was not the sandbox where I wanted to sit and build my castles for my remaining days. At my age, there was no way I could learn a language as foreign and difficult as Korean anywhere close to fluency; the food, I thought, was awful, and it would be impossible to make friends and find work suitable for a conman. Koreans were harder to fool than Americans; fewer marks for the taking and more…uh…pain if you got caught.

Sun persisted. I agreed to move with her and give the Republic of South Korea a shot. After a couple of months, I knew it was not going to be for me for the long term. Sun was so immersed in her party's political work that I rarely saw her. Her lightheartedness, humor, and warmth were eroding from the daily grind and the vicious cycles of political infighting. Her wonderful cynicism and creative nihilism were being eclipsed by a sense of self-important seriousness. Worse, Koreans don't warm to occidental guys who marry their women. The word "hamburger," I came to realize, when used by Koreans was not about food: It was an ethnic slur reserved for white American men. South Koreans hadn't been sipping the "diversity" Kool-Aid that had been spiked in all the U.S. watercoolers. In the Korean deck of social cards, "diversity" didn't trump anything. It was not even a face card. I would be the perpetual outsider, not even able to understand what they were saying about me and guessing that most of it was not flattering.

CHAPTER FORTY-ONE

Hitlerization

We have no quarrel with America. We all know NATO is the strongest military machine in the world. We simply want them to stop being so busy with our country and worry about their own problems.

Slobodan Milošević

Some people are larger than life. Hitler is larger than death.
Don DeLillo, "White Noise"

I t was a painful split.

Ain't no sunshine when she's gone
Only darkness everyday
Bill Withers, "Ain't No Sunshine"

It tore me up, but there was no other way I could go. It was back to the States. Back, but where? Before I had left Chicago for Seoul, I had tracked down the whereabouts of Herman Gering, my American Indian-obsessed amigo from the Wapakoneta days. He'd finished the Ph.D. at Michigan and was teaching cultural anthropology at DePaul University in Chicago. He had season tickets for the home Bulls games. I would often go with him to watch Michael Jordan play. Herm had married for the fourth time. Number four was a Russian woman, Maiya, who was teaching urology courses at the DePaul University College of Medicine. The marriage was already in the struggling stage. A doctor friend of mine once told me that urologists were the weirdest of the medical specialists. The ones I've had poking into me confirm that professional assessment. The colorectal folks, come to think of it, might also have a shot at that distinction.

I called Herm from Seoul. He was delighted that I was coming back and arranged an apartment for me in a complex in Norwood Park, a Chicago near-northside community. Living nearby in a small house was Herm's mother, who, it turned out, was an elderly Serbian originally from Krajina. She was a WWII war bride.

Norwood Park was heavily ethnic Serb. The future governor of Illinois and eventual ward of the Federal retirement system that has been so generous to me, Rod Blagojevich, hailed from Norwood. I met him at a local restaurant and would occasionally see him circulating around the neighborhood. He was on his way up, then — a very impressive guy, even athletically. From his early years, he had amateur boxed in the 160-pound middleweight division and notched some victories in Golden Gloves bouts. A second-generation Serb, both his parents were immigrants from that long-troubled region of southeastern Europe. Papa Radislav came from a village near Kragujevac. He spent four years during WWII locked away in a Nazi POW camp. Rod's mama, Mila Govedarica, was a Bosnian from Gacko.

I got a job as a bouncer in a local club and settled into an apartment complex filled with ex-pat Serbs, many recently exiled from the early-1990s war in Bosnia. Living there, in fact, was none other than Father Dragan Stojanović ("Jano," as I came to call him), the defrocked Serbian priest, the hulking savant Herm brought to my party in Toledo some years before, along with Sun. He had left Ann Arbor and was teaching at the University of Chicago. He was also busy with an ethnic network in the U.S. that was closely connected with political affairs in Yugoslavia. The network was made up mostly of Serbians aligned with the President of Yugoslavia, Slobodan Milošević.

Living in the complex with Jano was Petra, his younger sister. Petra, a widow, was a victim of the Croatian ethnic cleansing that had hit Bosnia in the early 1990s. She got one of the few refugee-status visas given to Serbians. The U.S. government oligarchs, conniving at foreign policy at the time, for complicated and typically corrupt reasons had decided that the Serbs were the principal bad guys in the unfolding Balkan's mess of the 1990s. The propaganda campaign of demonization was picked up and driven hard by the mainstream media. The reporting turned selectively, intentionally, and vehemently anti-Serb. More on that shortly.

A Croat militia had murdered Petra's husband, an agronomist who had been living and working in Sarajevo. Her brother, Father Dragan, was able to extract her from Yugoslavia and to Chicago shortly before NATO forces began dropping bombs on Bosnia-Herzegovina, where she was working, in 1995.

Petra was a university graduate with an advanced degree in international law from the *Univerzitet u Beogradu*. In the U.S., she had recently certified herself as a paramedic, working at the Rush University Medical Center, which enabled her to earn a living and to try to rebuild her shattered life in a foreign country whose leadership was intensely hostile to her people. Before coming to the U.S., she had been in a refugee camp for over a year.

Petra was grieving for her husband; I was in deep melancholy over the split with Sun. She lived in the apartment next to me. We began playing a lot of chess, which she dominated, then spent long hours over Serbian-Turkish coffee and conversations that reached deep into Balkan history as well as the current conflicts in the region. It was history about which I knew little — fascinating, though, with its complex features of ethnic and religious conflict. I was able to follow the extrication of the Serbs from the Ottoman empire during its death spasms in the runup to WWI when it finally collapsed. The Serbian-Croatian historical chapter during WWII was particularly dark and violent.

In each other, we found mutual consolation, which turned into affection and, finally, romance. After a year, we got married, her defrocked brother officiating an Orthodox wedding — after I had converted. Sun had initiated a Korean divorce. I had not completed divorce proceedings to terminate our civil marriage in Toledo. So, technically, perhaps, my marriage to Petra was bigamous. I'm not sure, and, eventually, it would not matter.

Living with Petra and warmly welcomed into the Serbian ex-pat community, I immersed myself in the recent history of the Balkan wars, as well as the Serbo-Croatian language. I also came to share the community's obsession with the plight of the Serbs in the breakaway Yugoslavian republics, Bosnia and Kosovo.

Slobodan Milošević, I came to realize, had been christened as the latest "Hitler" by the propaganda organs of Western powers — die Lügenpresse ("the lying press"), as the German right-wingers say it. "Hitlerization" of foreign leaders by U.S. policymakers has long been a favorite tactic of the War Lobby to generate public support to bomb faraway countries that pose no threat to American citizens. Because Hitler is Evil to the *nth-power*, having a fresh one who is rising to the occasion means that it's mandatory for the "Good Guys" to "take action" — a euphemism for attacking people the average American has no beef with. The moral superiority that automatically accrues to anyone who takes a Hitler justifies an attack pretty much anywhere.

War propaganda's overt moralizing intent is to arouse war hysteria in folks normally inclined to be mind-their-own-business peaceful. It works best when the target is thoroughly demonized — it turns the manufactured enemy into a beast. With enemies, there are still constraints — civilian populations to consider. With beasts, however, anything goes. The Brits were the masters at this. My grandfather told me about how they went about raising fear and anger to a high pitch against German-Americans during WWI. The British press ginned up horror-stories about German soldiers in Belgium raping nuns, cutting off their breasts, and bayonetting babies — "atrocity" headlines that turned out to be false but served to bolster the image of the "evil, barbaric Huns." The lies were manufactured to stoke American public outrage and get American soldiers across the pond and into the killing fields against the evil Jerries. It worked.

For his Iraq invasion, G.H.W. Bush needed to rouse some righteous anger. He contrived for Americans an "evil-Hun-like" version, seventy-six years later. It must have made the Brits proud. Bush enlisted a PR firm working for the Kuwait Government. It found "Nayirah," a fifteen-year-old Kuwaiti girl, who was put in front of a U.S. Congressional Caucus. Miss Nayirah breathlessly, tearfully reported that invading Iraqi soldiers pulled newborn babies out of incubators in hospitals and left them to die on floors. Beastly doesn't get more "beastly" than that. Nayirah was only known by her first name at the time of her testimony, supposedly to protect her privacy. That was the cover story. Later, someone discovered that she was the daughter of the Kuwaiti Ambassador to the U.S. At the time, I was suspicious about this story. She was a good actress, but it was all horror-show fiction. It was widely disseminated and repeated. It achieved its propaganda purpose: Bush got his war.

Modern communication technology is creative with the atrocity accounts it churns out. They are quickly, easily launched and reach out to grab worldwide attention almost overnight — horrifying and with maximum emotional impact, often exaggerated or in error. The formula the War Party uses to maneuver itself into the driver's seat is the following: Atrocities + new "Hitler" + Indifference = Holocaust Redux. Only Nazi's want things like that. No decent human being wants to be thought reluctant in stopping it and have your family, friends, and colleagues shun you as a closet Nazi, shrugging your shoulders as innocents perish.

With Hitlers appearing on the horizon, morality and the dictates of humanity demand harsh and decisive military action, even if it involves imitating Winston Churchill's WWII firebombing of cities like Dresden, Hamburg, and Cologne to terrorize civilians — women, kids, and old people, killing who-knows and who-cares how many. You don't "negotiate" with Hitler, neither the original nor any of his so-called wannabees, and, sometimes…well…you have "collateral damage."

Given how it ended up for the Austrian corporal and his band of merry miscreants, it's hard to understand why anyone would want to follow in their footsteps these days. War propagandists, however, are about collapsing complexity and striking differences into a simple-minded equation of moral revulsion with unmitigated evil. No time or room for any pesky folks with questions or reservations. When do you achieve that coveted moral superiority? Well, you "adjust" reality so that it squares with the current propaganda pitch, no matter how fantastical.

When NATO began its Kosovo bombing, Slobodan Milošević, a communist lawyer-politician who proved to be a formidable competitor for power in the tumultuous Balkans, almost overnight was christened by the West as the new Hitler. Vice President Al Gore, a recognized and celebrated expert on Hitler taxonomies, described him as a "junior-league Hitler-type," which must have pained Milošević to think he might be only an inferior imitation of the original.

I circle back to the beginning of this confession and repeat my warning about getting sucked into the vortex of good-versus-evil narratives peddled by politicians and their press lackeys. Think about the unintended consequences — like the war in Iraq and the never-ending war in Afghanistan, not to mention Vietnam. Take it from a conman. You are the mark. You are being set up. Activate your skeptical, suspicious antennas. Look for those efforts of manipulation and tools of deception that are present in every powerful government and the mind-manipulation weapons used by its propaganda organs. Be attentive to the language used to shape the propaganda: The most powerful and effective is the kind that manufactures a target of supreme evil. Once in place, you, in righteous opposition, can feel supremely good, and, as we know, feeling morally good means you get to do whatever you think will enhance that feeling.

CHAPTER FORTY-TWO

Bully Boys
in the Balkans

The whole of the Balkans is not worth the bones of a single Pomeranian grenadier.

Otto von Bismarck

I wasn't paying that much attention at the time the multi-ethnic state of Yugoslavia started to unravel in 1991, after the collapse of the Soviet Union. What was not obvious to me — likely, to many Americans — is that, for the U.S. and its NATO allies, Yugoslavia's dissolution as a country into smaller, manageable pieces was the strategic goal, not the wellbeing of its people. With the Soviet Union kaput, Yugoslavia was no longer useful as a socialist, non-aligned, Cold War counterweight. This is the point where corruption as an explanation of what is really going on is essential. Cynical suspicions are usually the right ones. Yugoslavia broken into smaller states would make the region easier to dominate, exploit, and serve U.S geopolitical and business interests.

The first civil war broke out in Bosnia in 1992. Croatia and Slovenia were pushed toward secession by the U.S. and the European Union. Both the U.S. and the EU were looking for an opportunity for a military intervention in the region that would give them leverage against the Russians — collusion at the highest international levels.

Skeptical? Ask yourself: What is an easy way to turn an internal, civil-war conflict in a multi-ethnic region into a "humanitarian catastrophe" requiring massive international military intervention? Invent another Hitler. Blame him for the conflict and the killing of innocents from a designated victim class.

And so it came to pass, at just the right moment for the Americans and NATO looking for some muscle-flexing challenges. Behold…Hitler…of Serbian lineage. Into the skies arose American bombers to rain down punishment. Large chunks of the Federal Republic of Yugoslavia were torn asunder. Yugoslavian old pieces were being turned into U.S. puppet states. There had to be a cover story, a moralistic, humanitarian one.

The destruction and the chaotic dismantlement of the region was done under the humanitarian guise of corralling the "genocidal" Serbs. Petra helped me understand that Yugoslav President Slobodan Milošević had tried to protect Serb minorities in the breakaway republics like Bosnia. For that, he was converted into a monster. "Atrocity"-inflated language mounted, and, quickly, "genocide" *(Völkermord)* and "Holocaust" dominated the press coverage. Instead of a regional conflict with many ethnic, culturally diverse antagonists losing control of their extremists, who give way to occasional sprees of violence and killing, media patrons in the West were served up a replay of WWII, with "Nazi-style extermination" underway. This time, it was a Serbian diabolical master-planer guided by a "Master-Race," *Lebensraum* ideology. Milošević as Hitler was the perfect cover story to justify military intervention.

As I dove into the detailed recent history of the region, I discovered that none of Milošević's history as a politician matched the hyperventilating and demonization. Many of the reports and victim counts of the atrocities turned out to be false or exaggerated, but the back-page retractions purposefully failed to alter public attitudes and perceptions, condemn the excessive force applied, and bring the real rogues to centerstage. The Serbs were not Nazis. The real Nazis in the region had set up a puppet government in Croatia run by Ante Pavelić during WWII. It murdered hundreds of thousands of Serbs. The country of Yugoslavia, in the 1990s, was neither threatening nor attacking its neighbors; it was certainly not even a remote threat to the United States. So, why, I was trying desperately to understand, was the U.S. military leading the charge with NATO and bombing that country?

Using Occam's razor (*Entia non-sunt multiplicanda praeter necessitatem*: "Entities must not be multiplied beyond necessity") *corruption* on an international scale involving NATO was, for me, the key to get to the most plausible, simplest explanation. NATO's long-declared purpose was to protect Western Europe from Soviet aggression and domination. With the collapse of the Soviet Union and the end of the Cold War, what, actually, was the purpose of NATO? Perhaps, to protect the reunified Germans and their cushy lifestyle. From what or who, you might wonder? And the rest of Western Europe, they were to be protected from who or what?

Most Americans were probably not paying much attention to Europe. They did not seem to be inclined to ask why *their* taxes paid to *their* government went to heavily subsidize the military establishments of rich, powerful countries perfectly capable of defending themselves from non-existent threats. Enter corruption and collusion.

On the European colluding side, these countries were the recipients of lavish U.S. custodial assistance, in the form of foreign aid and economic partnerships, that chiefly benefited the elites of both sides. Not having to bear the burden and assume the full cost for their own military protection meant that the U.S. taxpayer was subsidizing the Western European comfy lifestyle — its social services, pensions, healthcare, vacations, and education, services many of which he could only envy.

On the U.S. side, the military-industrial complex — as Ike warned about decades ago — was originally expanded to protect the West from Soviet communism. With its demise, the new purpose would be to take on the muscular role as the World's "moral police" and the chief exporter of "democracy." To be the world's Chief Morality Enforcer, you need the biggest and best weapons, constantly upgraded, sold at high profits by the appreciative defense industry to the grateful and generous government eager to use them. To justify the enormous cost and the existence of forces dedicated to intervening hither and yon, policing the world, the next Hitler who pops up on the horizon nicely does the trick. The Western European elites were happy to play along so as to keep the gravy train in motion. This is why, seventy-five years after he blew his brains out with his Luger in the Berlin Fuhrer bunker, he keeps regularly auditioning for primetime reruns.

In order to understand the fundamental devious and duplicitous nature of what NATO was up to at this time in the Balkans, it helps to look at how the NATO propagandists would "spin" their war of aggression against a country that had attacked none of the NATO members.

Article 5 of the North Atlantic Treaty Organization

(NATO) alliance commits all members to participate in the defense of any single member that is attacked — the definitional core of NATO's purpose. NATO was conceived and justified as a *defensive* alliance of military forces. After 1991, a way was sought to escape from the constriction of Article 5. NATO's existence was premised on "defense." But the region was no longer under serious threat. So, in order to escape obsolescence, the ruse of "humanitarian intervention" was concocted. NATO had a new life and a much more robust mission.

A meeting was held. A wand was waved, and "*non-Article 5* crisis response operations" (NA5CRO, the abbreviation) were born. "War is peace — freedom is slavery — ignorance is strength," and now: Defense is offense. Article 5 became non-Article 5. Below, the tortured language shows how 1984 was replicated in 1999. It is a veritable word salad, painful to read. It is a leaden, impenetrable argot of "government-speak." Its purpose? To deceive the reader and cover up the criminality. It is a piece of writing at once so outrageously, audaciously stupid and dishonest one can only conclude that its authors had utter contempt for the intelligence of the reader.

> *The need for the North Atlantic Treaty Organization (NATO) to be capable of responding to a crisis beyond the concept of 'collective defense' under Article 5 of the North Atlantic Treaty was first identified in the 1991 Strategic Concept and reiterated thereafter at the 1999 Washington Summit.* [The illegal bombing of Kosovo triggered this "need"]
>
> *Washington Summit recognized that future NATO involvement in non-Article 5 crisis response operations* [Article 5 is hereby annulled] *is needed to ensure both the flexibility and ability* [maximum "flexibility" meaning "no obstacles to our interference"] *to*

execute evolving missions ["evolving missions" meaning "military actions that increasingly escalate the bombing of civilians"] *not described under Article 5, including those contributing to effective conflict prevention.* ["conflict prevention" meaning "picking a 'victim' we can use as an excuse to interfere in a domestic conflict"]

The Alliance's military mission of NA5CRO is focused on contributing to effective crises management [meaning "interfering in places you don't need to"] *when there appears to be no direct threat to NATO nations or territories that otherwise would clearly fall under Article 5 'collective defense.'* [Which was the major purpose of NATO, which now has no purpose unless Article 5 becomes non-Article 5]

NA5CRO are a major part of the Alliance's contribution to effective crisis management. NA5CRO are intended to respond to such crises in a timely and coordinated manner where these crises could either affect the security of NATO nations, or threaten stability and lead to conflict on the periphery of the Alliance. ["periphery" meaning "a place where NATO has never had a legitimate basis to intervene"]

NA5CRO encompass the Alliance's conduct of and participation in the full range of operations [bombing civilian targets, if necessary] *as directed by the North Atlantic Council (NAC) Also, NA5CRO may be conducted by NATO in any part of the world* [NATO now can go anyplace, anywhere, anytime it pleases] *as opposed to the specific Euro-Atlantic area defined for article 5 operations; this implies that NA5CRO may have an expeditionary nature.* ["expeditionary nature" meaning "to open a Pandora's Box with no unpredictable, disastrous surprises"]

Try not to gag on this crude confection of systems-analysis-sounding, "efficiency"-themed mumbo-jumbo and anodyne, do-gooder, humanitarian hoo-ha: the ghost of Robert McNamara colluding with the super-ego of Jimmy

Carter to produce a masterpiece of public relations bullshit drafted by anonymous scribblers on the NATO payroll. You need to run this stuff through my proprietary hermeneutical decoder-decryption device to finally get to that "duh" moment: heavily-armed, fake-moralists desperately grasping for that fig leaf that gets them off the hook for bullying whoever they want anywhere in the world. Expensive weapons systems to be tested on folks who can't fight back. "Who is going to stop us?" They don't even bother to ask.

The NATO "crisis response operation," for the folks in Bosnia four years earlier, turned out to be a roaring success, at least for some — Brown & Root. That American engineering, procurement, and construction company, formerly a subsidiary of Halliburton, was awarded a substantial contract to provide "emergency support" to U.S. military operations there. "Emergency" and "crisis" are the well-worn triggers that get things going — things that never seem to end or don't end well. Emergencies and crises are amazingly routine and frequent, especially in those parts of the world where American oligarchs want to install another control center to complete the pacification of the native populations and the eventual colonization.

The much-ballyhooed Dayton Accords of 1995 turned the NATO-bombed-Bosnia into an American colony ruled by a non-Bosnian, appointed by the U.S. and the EU with complete dictatorial power over its imposed division into separate Croat-Muslim/Serbian Republics — another piece of the world under American rule, with American military power securing its corporate interests and doing its bidding.

U.S. military-corporate collusion never draws deserved attention, at least not enough to offset the hyped up, moralized "human rights" propaganda that gets the intervention machinery going in the foreign countries whose people supposedly need our protection. The installations, lucratively run by the defense industry, become permanent.

CHAPTER FORTY-THREE

Kosovo Catastrophe

Kosovo — the site of a genocide that never was — is now a violent 'free market' in drugs and prostitution. What does this tell us about the likely outcome of the Iraq war?

John Pilger

B y 1999, the Norwood ex-pat community was in anguish over the growing turmoil in Kosovo. We watched the inevitable step up to what would be the seventy-eight-day NATO bombing campaign against the Serbs, launched by my old money-laundering business partners from the Little Rock days. The bombing campaign was never authorized by the Security Council of the United Nations and, therefore, a violation of international law. Law, supposedly, had given way to the higher calling of "morality." And where would one find higher standards of probity and morality than those employed throughout their personal and professional lives by Bill and Hillary Clinton? Word was that Bill was not so keen on it, but his co-president was up for obliterating the Serbs — a disposable, little-people commodity for the First Lady. She was planning the next "Clinton Presidency," and being a gal, her testosterone had to be shown to exceed Bill's.

Kosovo was an ideal place for the Devious Duo to

overlay a fake moralistic narrative steeped in a simple-to-grasp Good-Muslims/Evil-Serbs narrative of the violence. Holocaust and genocide analogies from WWII were unleashed to stoke moral outrage and raise public support for a blank check to launch a fake "humanitarian" military intervention. Kosovo was far away, in a part of the world with a tortured, complicated history that few Americans had any familiarity with, much less an understanding that could shift through the confusing propaganda barrage. Distortions, lies, and pumped-up body counts were laid down to ratchet up the official drumbeat to send American pilots to drop bombs on helpless civilians.

The American-led NATO bombing, you might say, was a "rouge" operation. No American boots on the ground, however: Our soldier-boys coming home in body bags would start to look too much like a replay of Vietnam and remind folks of the lying, deception, and treachery that made that epic fiasco happen. Bill would begin to resemble ole LBJ. "Democracy," we were supposed to believe, would sprout up magically from the rubble and corpses converted by American bombs.

Jano had an extensive reach into the political circles in Belgrade. He was in Dayton, Ohio, near Wright-Patterson Airforce Base, in 1995, monitoring the progress of the negotiations run by Clinton consigliere Richard Holbrooke that led to the Bosnia treaty. Jano had been a political opponent of Slobodan Milošević in the early 1990s, but, knowing how heavily slanted against the Serbs Western opinion had been manipulated, he came to Dayton to provide him with support in his negotiations with the Croats and Bosniaks. Jano put aside politics to attend to the precarious state of his fellow Serbs in Yugoslavia.

When I arrived at Norwood, in 1998, from Seoul, Jano

was actively maintaining close contact with an intelligence network out of Belgrade. The members were desperately working to try to avert the approaching disaster for the Serbian minority in Kosovo, then under assault from Kosovo Liberation Army (KLA) thugs. KLA guerrillas, condemned in 1998 by the United Nations Security Council as a terrorist organization, were being armed and trained by Military Professional Resources Incorporated, a "private" security company used by the CIA as a cutout in order to maintain "plausible deniability" for The Company. The State Department had already decided to back the KLA against the Serbs, looking the other way for the magical conversion — "terrorists" to "freedom fighters."

In February 1999, the Western powers, France and Great Britain, led by U.S. Secretary of State Madeleine Albright, convened a meeting of the conflicting Kosovo parties in Rambouillet, a city outside Paris, near Versailles, supposedly to negotiate a settlement. The meeting was a disaster for the Serbs — an orchestrated and premeditated charade by you-know-who. I know that for a fact. Thanks to Father Dragon, I was there and observed first-hand the rigged outcome. Jano headed up a contingent of Serbian ex-pats from North America, including his sister Petra, who brought her expertise in international law to advise Milošević and the Serbian negotiators.

We flew into Paris a couple of days ahead of the conference. Milošević feared for his life — an assassination-attempt by CIA operatives or their proxies a distinct possibility. I came along as backup, to provide security-protection for Milošević, entering France on a falsified Serbian passport. At the meeting, I was Stefan Popović, a retired sergeant from the Serbian Special Forces, recently recovering from a minor throat operation, which explained why my ability to speak was somewhat impeded, a cover for my limited Serbian language ability. I wasn't needed for making conversation: Rather, I was one of three bodyguards assigned to Milošević, who spoke very good English, which made my job easier and enabled me to get to know him and appreciate the horrendous challenges he was facing. Milošević, I realized, was the David; the U.S. was the Goliath.

Albright's MO, and that of the U.S. State Department at Rambouillet, was to hand the Serbs an ultimatum that would have them relinquish any political say in the long-historic Serbian territory. It would put the Serbian minority there in a defenseless position against the KLA. Worst of all, it would give NATO the authority to establish a virtual military occupation of Serbia with dictatorial powers and no accountability. It was a setup from the beginning, calculated to dismantle the remainder of Yugoslavia and turn its parts into U.S. vassal states. First, they had to destroy Milošević. Then, they would scapegoat him.

The Western powers knew Milošević could not accept the ultimatum. His attempts to negotiate were scorned: "Sign it, or NATO starts bombing," a diktat. John Richard Pilger, an Australian journalist who, along with our delegation, witnessed the travesty, wrote that it was nothing other than "surrender or destruction." It turned out to be both. The Americans, as we observed, made no secret of their backing for the KLA. The Muslim majority there was the designated "victim" needing the protection of the U.S. Madeleine Albright was not even embarrassed to be photographed giving a hug and a kiss to KLA Chief Hashim Thaci, known by his colleagues as "The Snake." His long career as a drug trafficking, terrorist thug was apparently forgiven. Recently on the Interpol's and FBI's watch lists for organized crime, he now was a highly favored client of the CIA.

Following the disastrous meeting in Rambouillet, our entourage flew to Belgrade with Milošević. His setup by Albright and, ultimately, Bill Clinton to be the chief villain in the Kosovo conflict was now complete. The Western mainstream media would pile on.

Jano and I then drove from Belgrade to Pristina, the capital of Kosovo, in early March. He had a network of friends and associates there who had been pressed into acting as private security forces, trying to protect Serbian families from KLA robberies, assaults, and vandalism against Orthodox churches. Also, Jano hoped to act as an observer of and witness to KLA violence, reporting the rampant criminality to international news organizations and independent sources that, perhaps, could exert some countering influence on public perceptions outside of the region and add some balance to the heavily-slanted anti-Serb coverage.

Early the second evening after our arrival, we met with a small group of security-force volunteers in an Orthodox church on the outskirts of Pristina. The meeting broke up after several hours. The discussions were difficult and frustrating. They dealt with the escalation of KLA-armed attacks on Serbian communities. Consistent, non-corrupt law enforcement in Kosovo was at third-world standards — nonexistent. What protection could we arrange for the Serbs there? The challenges were enormous; the outlook dismal.

Jano and I walked out of the church toward the parking lot and headed toward our car. With us was a local Albanian Kosovar, Gezim Bytyçi — a friend and supporter of the Serbians of Kosovo. He was looking out for our safety and walking about ten feet behind us. A few steps before we got to our car, three torpedoes slipped out of an alley next to the church and came straight at us across the dirt parking lot.

They came shooting, and Gezim went down right away, hit with five or six shots to the chest and abdomen before he could react. I dove behind the car, trying to force Jano down as I went. He was too big for me to get him to the ground in time. He caught slugs in the stomach and shoulder and collapsed next to me. I got to my knees behind the car, pulled out my semi-auto 9mm Glock, and waited for the gunmen to come around. The shooters must have mistakenly thought they had hit me, too, because when they came around to my side of the car, they hadn't quite expected that I'd be waiting and ready to open fire, which I did. As they came around, reloading, I emptied my eight-shot clip into the two of them. They went down. The third shooter, who had stopped to finish off Gezim, then came around the car and was suddenly standing above me, his pistol inches from my face. He pulled the trigger at point-blank range, but his gun jammed. Fortunately, he was wearing open-toed sandals, so I slammed the butt of my pistol down hard on the top of his foot, which took his mind off me for a few very precious moments. I jumped up and stomped on his knee. I heard it break, and, as he doubled over in pain, I got behind him and executed him with the neck-throttling technique I had learned from Elsa in our Havana days. *Vielen Danke, meine lieber,* Elsa! I had practiced it many times and knew someday it would save me. The dude also had a knife on his belt. I took it off him and drove it into the middle of his chest as an exclamation point — for Gezim.

The three, now-dead bastards were KLA assassins. Gezim, father of three daughters, bled to death in the parking lot. People coming out of the church got an ambulance to come — it took an hour — and we finally got Father Dragan to a hospital. The hospitals in Pristina were awful — few doctors and drugs, and medicine were scarce. Three hours later, he died from complications of the horrific gut wound.

The Pristina police were in cahoots with the KLA. They arrived at the hospital and immediately arrested me. They put me in one of their interrogation rooms in the city center headquarters. The interrogation unfolded as a vintage third-world mix of terror-torture. A black hood over my head, the racking sound of an automatic pistol readied for firing, some blows to the head and groin. Killed in Kosovo by the KLA — whatever. Alliteration always had an appeal for me.

It worked to my advantage that I could not speak good Serbian and neither Gheg nor Tosk, the two dialects of Albanian. *Jebi se* (roughly translated, "Go fuck yourself") was my only answer to their questions — well, for the first ten minutes or so of the interrogation, until I realized how impolite I was being. One of the interrogators did speak limited English. He finally concluded that I was an American renegade and should be turned over to the NATO authorities for further questioning. Let them deal with me, he must have been thinking. I didn't need to be his problem. After a few more slaps and punches, they dragged me off to a cell. When they got me there, they pitched me onto the floor. One of the interrogators unzipped his fly and pissed on me before leaving. There I was in my finest hour: sprawled on the floor, waiting and expecting to be arrested by the NATO operatives the next day.

Lying in the cell, thinking about what had just happened, it suddenly hit me like a cement truck: like father, like son. My father had gone to a foreign land, a troubled place where he had no financial, material, or practical interests — where he had "no business" being, as my mother tried to convince him — in order to serve a "higher" spiritual purpose. "Higher" met lower in the DR, and lower — all muscle, no virtue, and full of fury — won. I had vowed to live differently. After a long, circuitous journey, however, I found myself in Kosovo. Just like my father in Santo Domingo, I had experienced a brutal interrogation by police thugs. Dad came to the island believing he was doing "the Lord's work." I had come to Kosovo thinking I was going to help the "good guys." It was scripted; they were going to lose. Leonard Cohen's words kept reverberating:

> *Everybody knows the war is over*
> *Everybody knows the good guys lost*

I knew it from the beginning — the confirmation came with serious pain.

The corruption of the KLA Pristina police was rampant, which turned out to be a stroke of good fortune for me. Father Dragan's Serbian-Kosovo friends bribed a couple of the jailers early in the morning. It didn't take much. They smuggled me out of the jail, cleaned me up a bit, and loaded me into a van — also with Jano's body — and took me out of Kosovo. I was driven to *Topčidersko Brdo*, a neighborhood of Belgrade, where Petra was waiting.

Normally, it would be about a six-hour ride. This one took nine because I had to stop frequently: From the beating, I was vomiting, had lost control of my bladder, and was pissing blood.

CHAPTER FORTY-FOUR

Lieberman's Lesson

*The store is called Hillary; it's near Bill Clinton Boulevard,
and it's packed full of pantsuits.*
Petra Živić, on a visit to Kosovo

I brought Petra her brother's body and the terrible news of his murder by the KLA. She was inconsolable. I had gone with him to Kosovo and failed to protect him. She didn't blame me, and I knew there was nothing I could have done to save him from the attackers. Still, I was alive, and Jano was dead. Nothing I would say or do could stem the grief. Her first husband and now her brother had been murdered by anti-Serb thugs. No retribution.

The next two weeks, I helplessly watched her feeble battle against despair. Late one evening, I had gone to meet with Milošević and his advisors. Petra downed a tall glass of *Šljivovica*, a strong, traditional Serbian liquor, along with the contents of a bottle of a morphine-derivative pain medication I had been taking. I found her dead when I returned.

That was on March 23rd. The next day, NATO launched "Operation Noble Anvil," a massive bombing campaign, including cluster bombs, which typically inflict heavy casualties on civilian populations.

Delenda est Carthogo
(Carthage must be destroyed)

Marcus Porcius Cato

General Wesley Clark was the NATO commander in charge of this modern-day Carthaginian decimation by an Imperial power. Clark was eager to expand and complicate the conflict, since expansion and complication in warfare means the whole business gets to go on longer. He insanely ordered NATO soldiers under British Commander General Mike Jackson to fire on Russian soldiers guarding the Pristina International Airport. They were there as a part of an agreed joint NATO-Russia peacekeeping operation supposed to police Kosovo. Jackson refused the order, telling him: "I'm not going to start the Third World War for you."

Operation Noble Anvil also featured some "Three Stooges"-like pratfalls. The Americans bombed the Chinese embassy in Belgrade — mistakenly, they said — killing three Chinese journalists. CIA Director George Tenet "took full responsibility" for the diplomatic fiasco. Before a House Subcommittee, the head of the world's top intelligence agency made what must have been one of the more humiliating and comical confessions on record: The CIA's database of "off-limit targets," Tenet admitted, did not have the up-to-date address for the relocated Chinese embassy. Imagine: You are bombing the bejesus out of a foreign capital, and you lose track of probably the single most important building you should *not* touch.

U.S. House Committee Chair George Harris: "Director Tenet, I'm not sure I heard you correctly. Can you speak up and confirm what you just said, that the Chinese embassy was mistakenly bombed because the CIA address book was not up to date?"

Tenet, conferring with aide, who shuffles through papers: "That is correct, sir."

Harris: "Is your microphone not working, Director Tenet? I'm waiting for a response. Please speak louder and confirm."

Tenet: "Sir, that is correct. Very unfortunate: The bombing was a result of a technical error. I take full responsibility."

"Taking responsibility" is another thread in the fabric of word-corruption that serves the interests of the powerbrokers and protects their minions when they get caught fucking things up or breaking the rules. It is a nod to accountability and restitution that, actually, translates: "Yeah [sigh, shrug, smirk], it didn't exactly work out the way we planned. So, what? Waddya going to do about it"

The Chinese journalists got killed; Tenet kept his job for another five years. Maybe it took him that long to get his address book in order.

The bombing campaign lasted a God-awful seventy-eight days and forced the withdrawal of Yugoslav armed forces from Kosovo. The United Nations Interim Administration Mission in Kosovo then took over to make everything right. You can't help but appreciate the rich irony: "Noble Anvil" echoes Plato's "Noble lie" — the lies the "Philosopher Kings" use to manipulate the little people they rule over. "Noble" attached to "Anvil" (morally-legitimated violence), the pinnacle of cynically inspired "humanitarian"-cloaked euphemisms to cover up the "punching down" the big bully boys do to get what they've been after, knowing they were going to get it all along. NATO bombed Milošević's home to smithereens, along with other strictly civilian targets.

The future Vice-Presidential candidate, Senator Joe Lieberman, by pure coincidence, was shilling for the

American Albanian lobby during the bombing. He appeared on a "Meet the Press" interview, where he attempted to justify NATO's bombing of non-military targets in densely populated suburbs of Belgrade — apartments where women, children, and old people lived — somewhat reminiscent of the Allied bombing of Hamburg and Dresden during WWII. I don't recall that it was one of his better efforts, though he was, apparently, pleased with himself. Maybe his wife, Hadassah, forgot to remind him at breakfast that blowing up toddlers and retirees hadn't suddenly come back into fashion. He must have skipped his Yeshiva class the day they covered that item.

Questioned about the civilian bombing, he had this to say: "I hope the air campaign, even if it does not convince Milošević to order his troops out of Kosovo, will devastate his economy, which it's doing now, so ruin the lives of his people that they will rise up and throw him out...We're not only hitting military targets...We're trying, through the air campaign, to break the will of the Serbian people." For me, there was a kind of perverse satisfaction in hearing this U.S. Senator, a man who loves to put on public display his religious piety, braying before the world his enthusiasm for war crimes — no nuance or pretense. "Might makes right" was the message.

The Connecticut Senator was reputed to be a deeply moral man. Maybe the bags of money he took and put under his pillow helped him sleep at night. But, in broad daylight, however, he was playing the unabashed enthusiast for ethnic cleansing — no nuances or subtleties to get in the way. The Senator was celebrating the bombing of civilians, bragging about his country's violation of international law, extoling the misery of innocent people whose lives were being wrecked. None of his interlocutors — those pretend truth-to-power boys in the press corps — bothered to ask him the glaringly obvious question: How is "ruining the lives" of people living under the rule of a supposed brutal dictator anything other than piling more misery on helpless people? With a suck-up-to-the-powerful press corps firmly in place, we can be assured that the high-placed pretend-moralists like Lieberman can be easily purchased.

Advancing "human rights" and "promoting democracy" formed the moralistic core of self-congratulatory propaganda campaigns that rationalized the U.S. destruction of Serbia and ruined the lives of its people. You might also wonder why the world's most powerful country committed to democracy and human rights could, with consistency, support a brutal and corrupt feudal autocracy like Saudi Arabia. Consistency, however, is an expectation that applies only to the little people.

Twenty-years later and still in place, the United Nations Mission is still the "Interim Administrative Mission." In eastern Kosovo, the Americans built a 1,000-acre military base, Camp Bondsteel, estimated to be the largest U.S military base on foreign soil since the Vietnam War, all its services provided by Halliburton — history repeating itself.

Some years later, the grateful KLA mafia, now installed and ruling Kosovo, erected an eleven-foot tall, 2,000-pound bronze statue, high up on a pedestal, of their *Patrón*, Bill Clinton. It could be found on Bill Clinton Avenue, in the center of Pristina. A few yards away, a women's clothing store called "Hillary" adds a fashion touch. For gauche, no one surpasses the Clinton vainglorious and insanely egotistical — Bill and Hill were still doing what they were always best at: self-promotion, making their mark from Little Rock all the way to Kosovo. *Plus ça change, plus c'est la même chose.*

The KLA-gratefuls couldn't possibly grasp that a huge

"Bronze Bill" in the middle of one of his "liberated" vassal states might appear as a grotesque irony. Maybe the Kosovo ladies stuffed into Hillary pantsuits were enough of a distraction. Some Readers from an earlier generation might be reminded of the "Bronze Joes" that Stalin had ordered put up in the Red Army-liberated cities like Budapest and Warsaw.

CHAPTER FORTY-FIVE

Nuremberg Two

For my friends, anything; for my enemies, the law.
Oscar Benevides, President of
Peru, 1933-1939

To continue with and bolster the WWII narrative: In the aftermath of its massive bombing and destruction in the Balkans, NATO needed a patsy. Someone had to play the part and take all the blame. The NATO guys who had been killing civilians and "ruining their lives," as Senator Lieberman blithely announced, would be the judges and jury — not exactly how you were taught in school how "justice" is supposed to operate. Call this "Lieberman jurisprudence."

What better than a WWII-style "war criminal," someone to put on "trial," a choreographed ritual, a faithful imitation of the original, Nuremberg, with all the familiar memes in play — "war crimes," "crimes against humanity," and, of course, "genocide." Slobodan Milošević had been long set up by the American ruling class to play the lead role and be the fall guy in the ongoing fake morality play.

I grew up holding the Nuremberg trial in spiritual awe — a monumental reckoning — cosmic justice dispensed, condign punishment meted out to the men in the dock who were evil incarnate.

"When I was a child, I spoke as a child, I understood as a child, I thought as a child; but when I became a man, I put away childish things."

Putting away "childish things," I saw it as a high-posturing exercise of moral pretending. Nuremberg, as Senator Robert Taft decried it, was an ad hoc "Victor's Justice," drenched in hypocrisy. Robert Jackson, Chief Prosecutor for the Americans, had falsely promised that no rules would be applied that could not be applied to the Allies. The Soviets murdered 15,000 Polish officers at Katyn, located twelve miles west of Smolensk, in April-May 1940. They persisted in blaming it on the Germans. Not until 1990 did Mikhail Gorbachev, pushed by his own much publicized policy of "openness" in Soviet politics, publicly admit Soviet culpability. "Openness," as we saw with the Gorbachev version late in the last century, can have fatal consequences for the ruling class. Our own observed and took notes.

By the end of the war, the Americans and Brits knew the Soviets were behind this heinous war crime. For obvious reasons, they pretended otherwise. They gave Stalin a pass and so put the stamp of duplicity and hypocrisy on the entire proceedings. Katyn was a huge embarrassment, particularly for the Americans. They desperately wanted Nuremberg to be a symbol of the reign of international justice in a new era. It turned out to be a giant legalistic fig leaf to cover the crudely expedient nature of the war-time collusion with Stalin, who murdered innocents in numbers equal to or greater than Hitler, and a scheme to make the hanging of the defeated enemy German leaders look like something resembling an impartial legal proceeding that dispensed justice.

A minor, temporary problem confronted the Americans: They needed to get Milošević to the Hague in order to get the show-trial started and continue the phony "America to the rescue of oppressed people" storyline. They were going to follow the same script proposed by Stalin's very own show-trial stage manager from the 1930s, "Prosecutor" Andrei Vyshinsky. At Nuremberg, he told the Americans: "Don't worry [wink-wink], only the guilty will be put on trial." Unlike the Americans and British, the Soviets were refreshingly candid.

Unlike Germany in April 1945, Serbia was still intact as a sovereign nation. Milošević was not about to sign his own extradition papers. Legally, there was no way for the International Criminal Tribunal for the Former [sic] Yugoslavia (ICTY) to get him there. But legality was not to interfere with the staging of Nuremberg II, with a Serbian in the lead role.

Milošević was still in power. I talked with him briefly, after Jano's funeral. He was now under tremendous pressure, brought by the U.S. and NATO, with almost no means to resist their efforts to finish destroying him. He was overthrown in a coup in 2000. Imprisoned in Belgrade on corruption charges that were never confirmed, the ICTY continued to demand his extradition to the Hague. With Serbia decimated from the bombing and its economy "devastated," as Joe Lieberman had candidly announced was the U.S. objective, the U.S. blackmailed the new government. It conditioned its releasing of aid to war-wrecked Serbia as a quid pro quo for the turning over of Milošević to ICTY for trial. The new Prime Minister, Zoran Djindjić, eager to be a NATO lackey, decreed Milošević's extradition order. It was blocked by the Federal Constitutional Court. I was at the proceedings that handed down a rejection of the extradition orders. Nevertheless, Djindjić, in 2001, ordered the police to force him into a helicopter. They took him to a U.S airbase, then to the Hague. To administer justice to this "war criminal," they kidnapped him.

Karl Marx famously remarked that history repeats itself, "the first as tragedy, then as farce." The celebrated Nuremburg trial took a mere ten months to dispose of twenty-two top Nazis. Milošević's trial at the Hague was the longest criminal trial in history. The replay as farce began in 2002 and was dragged out until 2006. An embarrassingly botched-up show-trial, it was rigged from the beginning to produce the "guilty" verdict and thus secure Milošević's place in history as "Hitler, Round II" and Serbia, though having done none of the massive bombing, as a criminal aggressor-nation, alone responsible for the war's terrible destruction. I followed it closely; it was a travesty.

The proceedings, four years in the making, were never brought to conclusion because the defendant died in his cell, an outcome highly convenient for the prosecutors, who were making this odious business into their life's work. Conducting his own defense and under tremendous stress, with seriously high blood pressure, diabetes, and a heart condition, Milošević's requests for medication and medical assistance were either ignored or deliberately fouled up by the ICTY. The prosecutors were unable to convict the defendant with a fair and expeditious proceeding. They must have realized that the Western audience now contemplating the American-made disaster unfolding in Iraq was rapidly losing interest in the frame up. Yet, they continued to drag it out until he died from the clearly intended medical neglect. What good is Nuremberg II if nobody who was supposed to care about the outcome cares? A tragedy should be long remembered; a shameful farce, quickly, conveniently forgotten. The latter applied.

CHAPTER FORTY-SIX
Escape and…

The only difference between Detroit and the Third World in terms of corruption is Detroit don't have no goats in the streets.

Charlie LeDuff

The end of the seventy-eight-day NATO bombing campaign in 1999 found me in Belgrade. Jeno was dead. So was my wife, Petra. Milošević was in Belgrade. It was under siege. His country was physically destroyed. I remained in Serbia until the early Spring of 2001, a few months before Milošević was abducted and sent to the Hague. It was not safe for me to be there, but serious complications were in place that made it difficult for me to find a way out.

I was in Belgrade, with a false passport as Stefan Popović, the retired Serbian Army Sergeant. The real Sergeant Popović, it just so happened, had been killed in one of the NATO bombing raids, along with his wife, two sons, and ten other civilians when a cluster bomb advancing Bill Clinton's humanitarian mission hit their apartment complex. NATO Command, however, did not know they'd killed him and had issued an arrest warrant for him — now me — as a "war criminal."

I had taken my American passport with me to Serbia, but it had no entry visa stamp. So, even if could get out of Serbia on Popović's passport, to try to use my own for reentry to the U.S., with neither an entry nor an exit stamp, would give me big problems. I would be detained, interrogated, and searched. Immigration officials would find and seize my false passport and uncover my extensive criminal past. However, if I stayed in Serbia, sooner or later, I would be arrested and in store for a very long prison term. I was in, you might say, some very deep shit.

In desperation, I called Sun in Seoul. She wired me money for a plane ticket to South Korea. With her connections high up in the government circles there, she was able to arrange for me to get an entrance visa on my American passport. I used it when I arrived. Compared to where I was coming from, South Korea was an oasis of public order and tranquility: no bombs, no terror, no masses of desperate, war-shaken, and shattered people.

What a mess I was, physically, from the beating I had taken in Kosovo. Mentally, I was broken from being hunted by NATO Police, living through the months of the terror bombing, the threat of capture, and the grief and depression from Jano's murder and Petra's suicide. At night came the nightmares, panic attacks during the day. Shortly after Petra's burial, the cemetery was blown to pieces by the NATO bombers, an exclamation point on its "democracy-importing" mission. It was also tearing me up that Milošević' had been sold out, shanghaied, and on his way to a phony trial. The U.S. and NATO had their "Hitler" in tow to justify seventy-eight days of bombing a country that had threatened none of the NATO member countries.

Upon arrival in Seoul, I discovered Sun to be about as magnificent an ex-wife as anyone could imagine. She put me up in a beautiful apartment near the one she lived in upscale Myeongdong, Seoul, near the Namsen tower. She also arranged for medical attention and spent long hours with me, diverting my mind from the recent Balkan horror show to her entertaining adventures in the treacherous shoals of South Korean politics. We reminisced about our "diversity" days at BGSU. How, we wondered, were we able to sustain such a duplicitous front for so long?

I was crumbling. My thoughts had been toward taking the same route as Petra. But, after a couple of months, the raw and desperate emotions were churning slower. From Sun's extraordinary kindness and wonderful ministrations, my instincts for survival gradually began to take hold of me. I had to go back to the States. My family, I hadn't seen in decades. My next destination had to be Michigan. With some financial assistance from Sun, I got a direct flight out of Seoul to Detroit. It was a sad and soulful departure. I knew that I would never see her again.

Upon arrival at the airport, I rented a car and headed into a gigantic slum — once, Motor City; now, Mugger City. In the 1950s, when I was a kid growing up in Michigan, Detroit was a muscular, industrial, blue-collar home to two million people, a production powerhouse for the WWII military machines and weapons, and, for a long season, the car-producing capital of the world. Now, I sloughed my way through a skid row of 700,000 people — mostly on the dole — scattered across massive swatches of abandoned houses.

I drove along, reliving a long-ago afternoon from downtown Detroit. I was a twenty-year-old university student. On a lovely, sunny July afternoon, I was with three college friends in a car on Livernois Avenue. We were coming back from Tiger Stadium, where we had spent the afternoon watching a doubleheader with the New York Yankees. I remember watching one of my boyhood baseball idols, Micky Mantle, who was playing in two of the final games of his career.

Heading into the Detroit downtown, we had no clue about the chaos that had been boiling in the works for the last twelve or fourteen hours. It was the summer of 1967. Race riots had become popular summer recreation in American cities. Detroit's was epic. It began with a run-of-the-mill police bust of a downtown blind pig. That routine bust was a spark that exploded. A massive and catastrophic tumult erupted that presaged the collapse of this once-great city.

We were just passing through, on our way to get out of town and head home to Grand Rapids, on the west side of the state. Downtown appeared normal at first glance. Strange things began to happen. For no apparent reason, traffic suddenly came to a halt. We sat at a traffic light. It would change — green to red to green, back to red. No movement. Then, the picture came into focus. My buddy, the driver, was the first to notice. At first, it was disbelief at what we were seeing, then horror: cars on fire; the sidewalks, mobs in motion, not single individuals. In the middle of Livernois Ave stood a big white Detroit cop, motionless, helplessly watching swarms of black looters spilling topsy-turvy out of shops and stores — they were closed; it was Sunday — with their windows broken out. They were loaded down with TVs, liquor bottles, clothing, and other stolen stuff. The looks on the faces of the looters were unforgettable — happy people no longer bound by silly laws, they were "helping themselves" to free stuff, enjoying the Sunday romp on a sunny afternoon. This was a good thing for us, I guess, since they left us alone in the car.

This Sunday outing turned out to be something quite other than a romp. That day in Detroit began one of the worst riots in American history. Detroit and the Michigan State Police were unable to contain the mobs who were looting stores, torching buildings, and, in some cases, sniping at firefighters. Governor George Romney called Lyndon Johnson and pleaded for federal assistance. It took us hours in congested traffic to eke our way out of the city that was coming apart. On the incoming Interstate I96, we watched the Michigan National Guard, ordered by Governor Romney, rolling toward the chaos, bumper-to-bumper in their military transports. Shortly later, the 82nd and 102nd Airborne Divisions arrived, courtesy of LBJ. Five days later, the riot officially ended, with forty-three dead, 1,189 injured, over 7,200 arrests, and more than 2,000 buildings destroyed. Only the 1863 New York City draft riots during the American Civil War and the 1992 Los Angeles riots were greater.

Who knew it at the time? This was the beginning of the end for Detroit as a great city — well, even as a "city," in the normal sense of the word. Most of the stores and businesses that were destroyed in the riots belonged to Jews and other non-black ethnic people. Rebuilding them in Detroit was not a winning move. White Detroiters cleared out. In 1974, the rabble-rousing, community organizer Coleman Young was elected mayor. He reigned, so to speak, for the next twenty years, Detroit's first black mayor. Young didn't bother to hide his hatred of white people. Eight Mile Road became the boundary that separated an almost completely black and increasingly poor and violent Detroit from the white Detroit affluent suburbs.

Coleman Young ran Detroit like a Robert Mugabe prototype, a crypto-communist lusting for racial revenge. Put in charge of a rich and vast social-cultural-political asset that took hundreds of years to create, he managed, in just twenty years, to turn it into a crime-ridden, third-world hell-hole that became a worldwide symbol of political corruption, urban blight, and destitution. The productive, taxpaying, property-maintaining Detroiters left *en masse*. In moved the drug-dealing gangs, who laid waste to the neighborhoods — robbery, assault, arson, and murder part of the daily routines. Vast tracts of the city became too dangerous to inhabit and, eventually, uninhabited. Block upon block of homes were hopelessly abandoned. Mayor Young infected the dwindling residents with his poisonous racial resentment, rendering them indifferent to his accountability for the rampant waste and corruption that engulfed the city. Content to play the role of victim and embrace their moral superiority, they blamed white, racist America for the city's poverty and misery. Detroit became a massively subsidized, highly dysfunctional urban jungle, from which most anyone who could escape would. Driving through, fifty years later, I could not help feeling that I was looking at the remnants of an epic national tragedy.

CHAPTER FORTY-SEVEN

Homecoming and...

You can't go home again

Thomas Wolfe

With the fifty-year-old events replaying in my memory, I drove out of that shell of a city northwest to Lansing, where the politicians who "governed" the state probably, secretly, wished that Detroit could be deeded over to Canada and join up with Windsor just across the Detroit River — maybe as "Windsor West" or Upper Windsor." Not that the Canadians could be persuaded to attach themselves to that sorry pockmark on North America.

At Lansing, I turned north and began my approach to the small town where I grew up. I had last visited my parents there thirty years ago. The last time I had seen Dad was when he made a long drive from Michigan to Mississippi, to see me when I was a prisoner in Parchman Farm — a very long trip for a two-hour visit that further broke his already-breaking heart.

I pulled into the gravel driveway, shut off the engine, and remained immobile in the car for a long time. They didn't know that I was coming. I saw a curtain in the house move. The front door opened, and Dad came out, stood on the stoop, and stared intently at the car. I got out and stood beside the car. I watched the recognition slowly, physically take over his entire body. First, his eyes as they focused on me and connected the now fiftyish man standing in his driveway to the person whom he had last seen as his young son. Then, his mouth, as it opened slightly; his whole face, as it tightened to control a surge of emotion. Finally, his entire physique, as he halting approached me.

I spent two weeks in my boyhood home with Mom and Dad. They now were old and infirmed — my mother with Parkinson's Disease, my father with a heart condition. My father and mother both broke down and wept when they first saw me. Dad blamed himself for my disordered and dissolute life. "I should never have taken you to the Dominican Republic," he told me. Well, probably, he shouldn't have, but how could he have known? "Dad," I said, "for whatever it's worth, I never blamed you. No one could blame you. You were a good guy. You always have been. I've never stopped believing that." I played Merle Haggard's "Momma Tried" for my mother. "Well, I didn't try hard enough, I guess" was her response. "No, Mom," I said, "don't forget the key line in the song: 'No one could steer me right.' I was incorrigible."

Both my sisters came with their husbands to spend some time with me, and they were eager to hear tales of some of my adventures, suitably edited to reduce the shock and disgust they would likely feel with some of the more dark and shameful pieces of my history. My younger sister, Dorothy, had gone from social work into the shadowy world of state politics. She had risen from a State Representative to State Senator to Lieutenant Governor, as a Republican. As a teenager, I remember, she had worked for Lenore Romney, the wife of the ex-Michigan Governor and mother of Mitt Romney, in a Senate campaign against the highly popular

Phillip Hart, who crushed her in the election, with sixty-seven percent of the vote.

My older sister, Jeannette, who had introduced me as a little kid to root beer floats, had recently achieved local heroine status in her hometown of Three Rivers. She was coming out of a local drugstore, a mile or so from her house, one evening. On the edge of the parking lot was a huge, raging twenty-something-year-old guy, Brent Bremer. Brent was whacking away on a skinny young woman. He had pushed her up against her car, screaming obscenities and threatening to kill her. My seventy-year-old sister, a retired librarian, at 5'2" and 120 pounds, just happened to be in possession of the "woman's equalizer," a snub-nosed, .38 caliber Colt Revolver loaded with six hollow-point rounds. After pulling the pearl-handled pistol out of her purse, she yelled at the guy to stop and "Get the hell away from that woman!" Brent ignored her and continued to flail away on that poor, skinny gal. Jeannette yelled again, this time threatening to shoot him if he didn't stop. He whirled around and came charging at her like a bull, from about forty feet away. It took four rounds from the "equalizer" before this crazy, 270-pound shit-heel collapsed to the asphalt, about five feet in front of her. He arrived DOA at the local hospital: One of the slugs had severed his aortic artery. His blood alcohol level was measured at 0.22. The woman he was beating on, it turned out — you will be shocked to learn — was his ex-girlfriend. She had frequently been on the receiving end of his massive fists, with multiple trips to the ER. The court restraining order she had gotten was, of course, worthless, and if my sister hadn't come out of that drugstore then, the ex-girlfriend would have been back in the hospital or dead.

Days later, the dead guy's father, Burt Bremer, stormed into the county Prosecutor's office to complain about how the shooting had gone down. My brother-in-law, a retired Kalamazoo County police detective, told me that Bremer senior was a local hothead and bully who always seemed to be pulling his son, Brent, out of trouble and blaming it on someone else. Burt was also, it turns out, the brother of Arthur Bremer. Arthur was the busboy from Milwaukee who shot George Wallace on the Presidential campaign trail in Laurel, Maryland in 1972. Arthur Bremer was currently a guest resident of the incorrectly named Maryland Correctional Institution in Hagerstown, Maryland. Bent on shooting somebody important, Arthur had initially fixed his murderous sights on Nixon. He got discouraged and settled on trying to kill Wallace. A few days before the Laurel shooting, he took the six-hour ride on the ferry from Milwaukee to Ludington, Michigan and was stalking Wallace at his campaign stop in Kalamazoo. My brother-in-law, as a police detective, questioned him after he had been reported as a suspicious-looking character hanging out at the National Guard Armory. The cops had no handle to detain the would-be assassin. He moved on and, a few days later, put Governor Wallace in a wheelchair for the rest of his life.

Burt Bremer was clamoring for my sister to be charged: "She didn't need to have shot him four times," he yelled at the Prosecutor. I was impressed with his response: "If it were me," he said, "I'd have emptied the gun on that worthless son-of-a-bitch. I wish I could clone Jeannette. She saved that girl's life. Get the hell out of my office!"

I could not stay long in Michigan. Still a fugitive, if I was caught, my sister Dorothy's political future would be crushed. Briefly, I considered a return to Chicago, to live in Norwood Park with the Serbian ex-pats. One of my Serbian friends was working as a U.S. House of Representatives legislative staffer in Rod Blogojevich's Chicago office. In 1996, Blogo jumped out of the State House and, in a U.S. House election, beat Pat Flanagan, a conservative Republican who had taken the seat of the powerful but massively corrupt, high-ranking House Democrat Dan Rostenkowski. Danny-boy ended up in Federal prison after conviction on mail fraud charges — from one of the loftiest perches in the DC Power Region all the way down to the slammer. High office to the penitentiary seems to be the career path for many Chicago politicians. Blogojevich himself would follow the same course. I suspect, however, that only a few of the really deserving ones make it to the Big House in Jolliet or the Federal Penitentiary in Leavenworth.

I had met Blogo briefly, in, of all places, Belgrade, in 1999, shortly after the bombing there stopped. He had come with none other than the Publicity Hound of the Windy City, Jesse Jackson, to meet with Milošević. Their goal was to negotiate the freeing of three American servicemen prisoners. Blogojevich had been approached by Serbian-American leaders who had contacts placed high enough in the Milošević government to be able to help free the American soldiers. It was Blogo's Serbian connections that made the deal possible: Jackson made it into a self-promotional photo op and, of course, took all the credit.

My contact suggested that I might be able to get a job in Blogojevich's office, working for the Congressman. But, with the deaths of Petra and Jano, it would be too painful to go back to Chicago and get immersed in the politics there. Given where Blogo was headed, it was just as well. I needed to get far away from the Midwest, not anywhere near Arkansas, and not to California.

To Alaska — a place I'd never been, where no one remotely connected with my past would be likely to appear — is where I finally decided to go. Dad gave me his 1989

Toyota pickup truck and then made another sad, tearful goodbye.

CHAPTER FORTY-EIGHT

Blown away
in Bozeman

I never believe anything until it is officially denied.
Otto von Bismarck

I set out for Alaska. Taking a leisurely pace on Interstate 90, I made it as far as Bozeman, Montana. Sitting in a restaurant booth, drinking strong black coffee after a massive breakfast of steak and eggs, and almost ready to hit the road, I heard some of the other customers, suddenly agitated, loudly carrying on. They were reacting to what they had just seen on the television screen located above the lunch counter. Glancing at my watch, I wondered what could be going on so early in the morning: It was 6:43 a.m. Mountain Time; the date was September 11, 2001.

The north tower of the New York City World Trade Center had just been crashed into by a jet passenger airliner. I got up and moved over to the counter to join the group glued to the television screen. Twenty minutes later, we watched a second plane slam into the South Tower. Throughout the entire morning, I stayed with the television and watched with astonishment the chaos unfolding with the collapse of both towers and following the reports of the other soon-to-come astonishing Kamikaze crashes. The third one hit the Pentagon at 7:30 MT. Then, the fourth hijacked plane, supposedly headed for the U.S. Capitol, at 8:02, was forced to crash in a field in rural Pennsylvania by group of passengers who launched a spectacularly courageous revolt against the hijackers.

By the early afternoon, I'd had seen as much as I could endure. I drove out of Bozeman in a state of shock. It took almost another week in my old Toyota pickup truck to complete the journey to Juneau, where I had planned to settle — at least for a few months — until I could get a feel for what life in Alaska would be like. All the while driving, I was highly agitated, mulling over what had happened and struggling to come to grips with and figure out what was really going on.

By the time of my arrival in the capital city of Alaska, the 9/11 master narrative had been crafted and well established by the highly invested organs of government and the mainstream media to (a) explain who was behind the attack and why, and (b) more importantly, shape (manipulate?) public opinion and mobilize the country to support a really big government response. Just how big, I was wondering, would it be, and where would it hit?

Now, the course of my life from my "adventure" in the Dominican Republic at fourteen years old through the bombing of Belgrade and the NATO-instigated abduction of Milošević had turned me into the most suspicious, cynical person alive. Nothing is what it appears to be on the surface, particularly when that "surface" is put in place by government agencies and the talking heads from cable networks. What I observed unfolding from the machinations of the powerful propaganda organs in our country in their efforts to manage perceptions of the of 9/11 attack should have made the most innocent and naive of people highly suspicious of where the country was going.

With memories of the recent military intervention in the Balkans in the back of my mind, I kept asking myself three related questions: Where is this going? Who wants us to go there? Cui bono — to whose benefit?

To the first question, quickly, the answer was one word: "war." "Another Pearl Harbor," loaded up with traumatic memories and potent, revenge-themed imagery, seemed to be the dominant motif in the media's framing of this event, perfectly done to make that one-word answer stunningly obvious. The talking heads disseminating "the news" were in non-stop heated debate. What should be the "appropriate" response Americans should make to this attack on "our values" and the threat to "our way of life"? The scary stuff kept getting scarier, with existential consequences and always with the "we," "us," "our," those insidious pronouns disguising the manipulation and keeping the "herd" moving in the same direction.

Zbigniew Brzezinski, Jimmy Carter's national security advisor and a long-standing foreign policy "genius," remarked that "9/11 is more murderous even than Pearl Harbor, and the psychological impact is the same." Really? The "same," Zbigniew, or is it "should be the same"? The latter will require a similar response to Pearl Harbor — next step, WWII. The media, too, was quick to jump in with the Pearl Harbor meme. *Time Magazine* wrote: "What's needed is a unified, unifying, Pearl Harbor-sort of purple American fury — a ruthless indignation that doesn't leak away in a week or two." Purple fury or purple prose? All this had the disagreeable odor of the worst sorts of organized, hyper-emotional propaganda and mass manipulation, aimed at spiking individual feelings of vulnerability and gearing up the masses for self-justifying military-style revenge.

With the patriotism and let's-go-get-em feelings revved-up and on the front burner, you don't have to be much good at analogies or have a solid grasp of WWII-era history to figure out what our powerbrokers had in mind as a follow up. From President Bush and his supporting cast? Real simple. The world, as they now seemed to want us to experience it, was remarkably like America on December 7, 1941: Us, the Good Guys, just minding our own business and being wonderful Americans, hit in a "sneak attack" by Them, the Evil Guys. This is from Propaganda 101, on the first day of class: Us-Good blindsided by Them-Evil, the formula for mass-hysteria.

But in 1941, the Evil Guys were from an actual country, Japan. FDR, behind the scenes, had been working hard to goad the Japanese into the attack by hitting them with crippling economic sanctions embargoing their oil.

In 2001, the attacker-profile was a bit more complicated — messy, actually. Osama bin Laden, who had masterminded the operation, and most of the attackers were from Saudi Arabia, a major Middle East U.S. Ally — a brutal, Islamic theocracy, by the way. So, what was with that? There were also credible rumors that bin Laden had been funded and trained by the CIA in the 1980s to bring down the Soviets in Afghanistan. The hijackers, we were supposed to think, were some scheming Muslim fanatics who "hate us." But, somehow, prior to the attack, these fanatics with questionable backgrounds were given visas, unimpeded travel in the U.S., and access to flight training schools. Neither was it clear why, all of a sudden, this "hatred" had exploded in such a dramatic and lethal fashion and why these guys who hated us so much had such an easy time getting here and getting trained for their mass-murder plans. But action, not questions, was the order of the day.

Against these shadowy haters of "our way of life," Bush proceeded to declare a "war on terrorism." We were now lurching into a life-imitates-art scenario, resembling a blockbuster Hollywood-scripted thriller, heavy on the alien, sinister *appearance* of the villains — bin Laden's image, with the flowing robes, long beard, and the stony stare was the perfect picture of cosmic malevolence to put us all on high-alert, itching to go out and bomb somebody or other. The collective enthusiasm for it, I must say, was completely and depressingly predictable.

Alan Jackson, a loveable, popular Country Western singer, recorded a song, "Where Were You (When the World Stopped Turning)," that captured his feelings immediately after the 9/11 attack. It went to the top of the charts. Some of the lyrics were genuinely moving, but:

> *I'm just a singer of simple songs*
> *I'm not a real political man*
> *I watch CNN, but I'm not sure I can tell you*
> *The diff'rence in Iraq and Iran*
> *But I know Jesus and I talk to God…*
> *Did you burst out with pride for the red, white, and blue?*

This entire verse struck me as a nutty, sappy non sequitur: from a simple guy to an ignorant guy to a prayerful guy to…finally? A guy bursting with patriotism? The direction was all wrong and the conclusion a head slapper. No, I didn't "burst out with pride." Pride was the last goddamn thing I was feeling. Suspicion was what I was seized with.

One can certainly appreciate this initial expression of humility and sincerity, but what to think about Jackson's painful confession of ignorance and naivete? Unfortunately, its popularity meant that it resonated with millions of

Americans, for whom an establishment propaganda machine like CNN, peddling the "wisdom" of manipulators like Brzezinski, was the go-to source to try to understand what was going on. Comprehending "The diff'rence in Iraq and Iran" seemed to be a challenge and less a priority than "talking to God." CNN's blow-dried talking heads milking the interviewed establishment plants with the scripted talking points are "Big Brother" in constant motion. They are everywhere. You can't even escape them at the airport.

Listening to this song, I thought: "Wow, with pride bursting out for the 'red, white, and blue,' plus the down-home religiosity, plus frank admission of no clue about the composition of the Middle East and what motivations might have been involved in the attack. These are the sort of lyrics that must give the Maestros running the intelligence community and the military-industrial complex multiple orgasms, thinking: 'Christ, this couldn't have been easier.'"

This was when a healthy dose of cynicism — taken seriously — would have saved Americans and many people in the Middle East agony and grief. Some brave soul from the Church of the Latter-Day Cynics needed to step up and say: "Hold on a goddamn minute: Everyone hates something or someone. 'Terrorism,' in case your reasoning faculties are on vacation, is an abstraction. And now, our leaders have declared war — are they kidding — on an abstraction? An abstraction that, somehow, connects to the vaguest of collectives — 'people who hate us, who don't embrace our values.' Which, when you think about it, could be at least half a billion people, worldwide. This doesn't begin to pass the sniff test. Just how, my fellow citizens, does one make war against an abstraction, and how do we sort out those who hate us from those who don't? Do we ask and believe them if they say so? Abstractions don't declare war. They don't sue for peace, negotiate terms of surrender, lay down their arms, give up, make restitution, and pay reparations. We, the United States at war, have defeated Germans, Italians, Japanese, and Spaniards — not Vietnamese, however — but we've never in the country's history defeated an abstraction because…well, think about it! It's just impossible to do. What the hell is going on here? I smell a rat!"

CHAPTER FORTY-NINE

The War Party

It's my party, and I'll cry if I want to…
You would cry, too, if it happened to you
                    Lesley Gore, "It's My Party"

So, war, of course, *was* "the answer." "Make love *and* war" was the new chant. Poor John Lennon. Good thing he wasn't around to hear everyone singing: "All we are say…ing is give war a chance…" Which takes us to the second question: Who wanted us to go there — to war in the Middle East? Well, duh: the War Party, of course, with the support of a citizenry that didn't know Iran from Iraq but was on a first-name basis with Jesus.

The United States had and still has the biggest, most powerful military force in the world. When the Soviet Union, as mentioned earlier, went kaputski, a decade or so before 9/11, America lost its scariest enemy — that big hammer and sickle tattooed galoot firmly in place since the end of WWII, propping up its lackies all over the planet to cause grief for ours. Immediately prior to the 9/11 attack, there was no enemy big and badass enough to justify the existence of our own immense military force, with hundreds of installations in seventy countries spread across the globe — at an enormous cost — to hold that enemy at bay.

The War Party remained all dressed-up formally for the big dance. But there was nobody now to take to it. With 9/11, though: Bingo, thank God, an enemy had suddenly materialized, and not just some pissant, "junior-league-type" Hitler like Slobodan Milošević, whose country and people could be blasted into mangled cadavers among the rubble in a few months by American pilots high up, in the safety of their airplanes. No, we now had ourselves one unique doozy of an enemy, the best imaginable, an abstract evil — terrorism, an illusive, protean "ism."

The War Party honchos were wetting themselves in excitement because war against an "ism" can be launched anywhere and go on pretty much indefinitely. Got it, Reader? "Old Isms never die, and…they don't *just* fade away." They last forever, which, for the War Party, means a *permanent* war, a war against an enemy that can be forever and anywhere — even better, "everywhere" as in here, at home, even.

Now, we've arrived at a place where we should be able to get at some answers to the third question: Cui bono? Let's turn that pesky cynic loose again to ask: Who benefits now, in this post-9/11 world, with America's "war on terrorism"? For President Bush, it was terrific. Bolstered by his down-home spiel, with its earnest, personal resolve about those "killers" he promised to go after, just like Clint Eastwood tracking down and dispatching one-by-one — "Make my day" — the sleazy low-lifes in one of those 1970s spaghetti westerns of his that I loved to watch. Bush's poll numbers shot up from a positive 55 percent the day before the bombing to a whopping 90 percent the day after — the highest such measurement for any U.S. President. This "war on terrorism," we were supposed to believe, was for us, the American people, the "we," who need it to protect "us" from "them," the guys with the long beards and the robes way over there in Central Asia.

Where was that pesky cynic to step up again and say: "Our country already has the biggest, insanely expensive, most powerful military establishment in the world, and it couldn't defend us against an attack by nineteen palookas armed with…box cutters? Now, the Commander in Chief of his multi-billion-dollar, awesome military force that a generation ago couldn't beat a bunch of sandal-clad, Vietnamese peasants and failed to defend us against those box-cutter hijackers wants to start up a war against an abstraction?"

That's correct. So, off we go like a bunch of drunks piling late in the night out of the Last Chance Saloon, forming a posse to follow this folksy, four-flusher President down a crazy path with no clear direction, no end in sight, no containment of cost. Does this sound like a recipe for epic disaster? Perhaps, the most powerful, expensive military force in the history of the world, financed with a no-cap credit card, is not the way to go. Do you think? But go, it does, and where to? Wherever it wants. In this case, some primitive, God-forsaken mountainous death trap on the other side of the world, inhabited by some of the toughest, most fearless motherfuckers on the planet. It's a place nobody here gives a shit about, a place where all this hatred for us was supposed to be fermenting. Of all the countries in the world it makes absolutely no sense to go to, *this* is the place…hands down.

So much absurdity to digest. The box-cutter boys got the red-carpet, warm American hospitality and the high-tech training at a Florida flight school that gave them the tools to kill 3000 Americans. Yet, somehow, that didn't catch the attention of our sophisticated intelligence professionals, who struggled to update their "address book" and mistakenly bombed the embassy of a world power. But the guys who represent an existential threat to "our values," we're going to find holed up in caves on the other side of the world. How many of our guys are going to get killed or crippled? What is it going to cost? Who cares? Not to mention, two other imperial armies, the British and the Soviets, didn't perform so well in this mountainous graveyard for powerful invading forces."

The cynics and critics, however, at the time, were flying into the fierce headwinds of reflex-patriotism, media hype, and manufactured paranoia. They made little headway. The answer to the cui-bono question of this proposed "war on terrorism," which should have been stunningly obvious, seemed to escape most of us. The Bush-Cheney-Halliburton cabal, just like LBJ and Systems-Analyst Bob a generation earlier, was dealing the cards from the bottom of the deck, working furiously to implement a formula to ensure that the guys in the War Party got to run the show in perpetuity — *perpetual wars for unachievable peace.*

Were our cynic able to jump into a time machine and fast forward eighteen years, he could crow: "I told you so." At eighteen years and counting, the Afghanistan war, launched in 2001, continues — unfinished — by far the longest war in American history. It's been going on so long that public attention to it has lapsed, and many Americans probably don't realize or care that it is still going on. The anti-war aphorism of the 1970s — "What if they gave a war and nobody came?" — has slowly morphed into "What if the war went on and nobody cared?"

But, back to the cui-bono question. It's clear that whatever "good" that comes from the war on terrorism goes to a small, select, war-vested collection of folks high up the food chain, with their snouts thrust deep into the trough —

like the Halliburton corporate contractors. The American Embassy in Bagdad turned into the biggest one in the entire world, built at a cost of $750 million to the American taxpayer. Covering 104 acres, it is replete with a shopping mall, food courts, an Olympic swimming pool, basketball courts, and a full-size soccer field. The empire must spend generously to provide the appropriate comforts for its occupiers. All of that for a cobbled-together, unstable little country like Iraq.

War-theater experience is a career-promotion booster for military brass — more impressive and much better than paper-pushing desk assignments on the home front. Retired Generals step up to lucrative consulting with the Defense contractors.

Defeating terrorism abroad was a great pretext for high-ups in the intelligence community to ramp up the surveillance state against "domestic terrorists" here at home — in your backyard. Note the imprecision of "terrorist" and appreciate how flexibly it can be used. The FBI's official definition is thus: "the unlawful use of force or violence against persons or property to intimidate or coerce a government, the civilian population, or any segment thereof, in furtherance of political or social objectives." Sounds like a perfect description of standard CIA operations. It describes exactly what my colleagues and I were doing in Chile back in 1973, not to mention what went on in Guatemala, Iran, Vietnam, and many other places in the world.

This war was also useful as a testing ground for weapons development — Predator drones, for example — and as a training ground for the techniques and tactics to import to an increasingly militarized civilian police force back home, to terrorize the little people whose taxes paid to develop them. You've probably seen some of the local news footage of platoons of what used to be the trusted policemen in blue. Now, it is a SWAT officer in Level IV body armor, Kevlar, carrying M-4s with thirty-round magazines and EOTechs (electro-optical products and systems, such as holographic weapon sights for small arms). Up he rolls with his unit in an MRAP and crashes down the doors of some old Hippie couple reported to have drugs in the house. Sometimes, these SWATs get the wrong address: a terrorized mother and father, with a traumatized kid, get dragged out of their beds at 3:00 a.m., thrown around, threatened, yelled at, then…oops…a belated, half-assed apology. "Sorry, our database wasn't up to date." Hey, it worked for George Tenant.

The "war on terrorism" never had anything do with defending the American people from hostile foreign powers: We were way over-capacity in that regard, given that there were no foreign powers that were actually threatening us. 9/11 was about expanding the power and wealth of the ruling class and reducing the status of the average American citizen to contented, distracted helotry.

The "War on Terrorism," being a war against an abstraction, meant that there could be no end to it. It was not a real war: Real wars come to an end. That doesn't mean there were no winners and losers with this fake war. The losers were the American soldiers and the Iraqi civilians who died there — also, the American taxpayers, who were going into hock trying to pay for it. The winners were the oligarchs who got us into it. For them, it was a triumph of public relations.

The Viennese-born Edward Bernays was the inventor of advertising and public relations and might, justly, be viewed as a kind of evil genius. In 1928, in a book called *Propaganda*, he wrote:

The conscious and intelligent manipulation of the organized habits and opinions of the masses is an important element in democratic society. Those who manipulate this unseen mechanism of society constitute an invisible government which is the true ruling power of our country.

He was talking about the mediators of "the news" — modern journalism, a massive industry that exercises enormous power through its manipulation of public opinion. At the age of one-hundred years, still mentally acute, Bernays let slip in a documentary interview what a deceitful, manipulative character he really was, what he was really about, and whom he served throughout his long career.

His work, he told the interviewer, was "propaganda," as he openly called it in the 1920s. But the Germans, he conceded, had given propaganda a "bad name." He needed a euphemism; hence, "public relations." This is particularly disturbing when you think about the power of the media to manipulate public opinion in a direction that the ruling class wants it to go. Advertising and public relations were destined to become the industries of political manipulation.

Bernays, then, had a long career, putting his knowledge helping hidden power centers like the CIA "engineer consent," — that is, launder pro-war, interventionist propaganda. Among his most notable and influential publications were *Public Relations* and *The Engineering of Consent*, two titles that should send chills down your spine, particularly the last one.

One of his more notorious "successes" was with the United Fruit Company, during the 1950s. He designed a highly sophisticated public-relations campaign that was instrumental in destabilizing the Arbenz regime and providing congressional support for the U.S. overthrow of a democratically elected president. Early in the post-WWII years, he worked for the tobacco companies, designing advertising to entice American women — at the time, mostly non-smokers — to light up. In the 1960s, when the health-hazards of cigarettes came to light, he worked on anti-smoking public-service messaging. He was always for sale (Verkäuflichkeit) to the highest bidder.

By the time of 9/11, Edward Bernays was dead, but he was probably perched on his comfortable cloud, admiring how adroitly the Bush Gang had engineered the consent that made the war in Iraq possible. What a masterful job they did making the little people think that the foxes were all about the safety of the chickens in the henhouse, whom they were looting.

Less than a fortnight after 9/11, the Cabinet level "Office of Homeland Security" was conceived by coincidence just when the collective angst was moving toward peak. Its purpose, officially stated, was: "to oversee and coordinate a comprehensive national strategy to safeguard the country against terrorism and respond to any future attacks." Note: "future attacks" are anticipated — plant that in your already agitated psyche.

"Oh, God! Who? When? Where? How? My kids will never be safe anymore!"

In the course of a single day, "terrorism," an abstraction, had hit the top of the charts as existential enemy *numero uno* — permanently, no less. What would be the best way to combat a deadly abstraction that threatens us forever? Bring on Dr. Federal G.D. Jekyll to create a vast Mr. Surly J.C. Hyde governmental bureaucracy. This newborn joins the family of deformed, deranged siblings — you know, the other agencies, departments, divisions, etc. that failed to protect us from the box-cutter gang. This one will be an "ism"-focused, monster-sized agency to match any "ism"-enemy that might appear anywhere. Think about that for a minute, and then, think about the "limited government" you've been told ad nauseum that you live under. Someone's been pulling on your leg, among other less appropriate intrusions into your life.

What did Mr. Homeland Security Hyde, once he got going, actually do that would make us appreciate how necessary he was and how much more secure we would feel? The "henhouse" needed more surveillance, the chickens more plucking.

Here is a novel idea: Why not make regular airline travel for ordinary Americans as demeaning, frustrating, and miserable as possible. It used to be relatively easy and sometimes pleasant. I vaguely remember that. But the government "guardians" had to look like they were protecting us from something. So, they concocted humiliating and stupid rituals that had nothing to do with security. Their secondary purpose was — and continues to be — to harass and intimidate the average law-abiding American citizen, which underlies their primary purpose, which is to make everyone clearly understand that the government can do *what* it wants, *whenever* it wants, to *whomever* it chooses, Clyde.

Mr. Hyde's airport "security" bullies, unleashed on us by 9/11, is government coercion ratcheted further up. It's what those of us who are ruled over must endure and have come, helot-like, to expect. Complain and see what happens to you. The rulers themselves, of course, never have to experience these indignities, submitting to the gropers and having their possessions handled by the rubber-gloved crews. And why should they? They make the rules for the little people to follow. For them, beings of superior virtue and wisdom, they are not necessary.

CHAPTER FIFTY

Juneau Tops Little Rock

*The men the American people admire most extravagantly
are the most daring liars; the men they detest most violently
are those who try to tell them the truth.*

H. L. Mencken

Upon arrival in Juneau, the capital city of Alaska, I rented an apartment and returned to my old profession of bartending. As a state capital, Juneau, you'd probably guess, turned out to be a rather different experience than Little Rock under the Clinton Regime. For starters, Juneau, by land area, is the third largest city in the United States, at 3,255 square miles, larger than the state of Delaware. Little Rock, by comparison, is a shrimpy 116 square miles. Because of the extremely rugged mountains surrounding the city, it is the only U.S capital with no roads connecting it to the rest of the state, which, transportation-wise, makes it an island city. While Little Rock had a somewhat tired, jaded, and lazy feel to it, Juneau struck me still as something of a frontier outpost whose inhabitants retained a bit of that hurry-up, gold-rush, entrepreneurial mentality. You could find a few people there with optimism, energy, rugged manners, and courage — in Little Rock, not so many.

I worked in a tavern close to the state government complex. It teemed with rent-seekers, job-seekers, and assorted lobbyists. All were mightily trying to latch on to and feed off one of the state's resource-lactating tits. Many of my customers were state government employees. They tended to favor a drink called the "Alaskan Gold Rush," a shooter made with a mix of Seagram's Seven, Crown, and Stolichnaya vodka. The adventuresome drinkers would chase it with a short glass of an Anchorage-brewed beer called "A Deal with the Devil," at 17.30 ABV. A round of this heady brew would loosen the tongues. The conversations after the booze had reduced the glutamate in the brain were predictably uncensored and full of enticing, evil gossip — graft, nepotism, transactional sex, shakedowns. They were not unlike the ones I had with the Singapore Sling-lubricated "public servants" from my Little Rock days. Many of these failed self-censored conversations would begin with: "You wouldn't believe…" My response was always: "Try me."

Absorbing the inside intelligence about the cockeyed machinery of Alaska's state government, I remained firmly convinced of the truth of my view that all governments, no matter how benign and gentle they seem, are either corrupt or on the verge. The explanation, I realized, is simple, really.

Because governments, by their nature, are coercive entities, and because people, by their nature, are coercion-averse, individuals are innately antagonistic to the institutions that attempt to govern them — that is, attempt to coerce them. This antagonism predictably works its way out in "work-arounds" of the sort intended to subvert or evade the imperfect rules or laws that are supposed to make everything for everybody fair and above-board. Corruption, in effect, is the inevitable trajectory away from "fair and above board," driven hard by this naturally entrenched human antagonism

— between the coercers (the rule creators and enforcers) and the coerced (the governed).

These "work-arounds" are collaborations (collusions) between the governors and a subset of the governed. The former grab and keep their power by doing "favors" for the latter — that is, the powerful, wealthy, influential ones — at the expense of those lacking the connections, resources, or inclinations to bid competitively for the favors offered. The ultra-cynic, the late H. L. Mencken, put it this way: "Government is a broker in pillage, and every election is sort of an advance auction sale of stolen goods." The rules and laws, as I mentioned at the beginning of my confession, are epiphenomenal. They are paid extensive and fulsome lip service — especially at election time — but amount to nothing more than useful, potent distractions that have little to do with the way things actually operate.

State governments are smaller and less powerful than the Federal Behemoth, so the corruption I've found in them is typically downscale. The folks who work at it are either ambitious minor leaguers, honing their skills and biding their time, hoping to jump to the majors, like Rod Blogojevich in Chicago and the Clintons in Little Rock. Those of modest ambition and limited abilities remain content to hunker down. They settle into a comfortable, well-lubricated operation, where they can ascend to the highest level of incompetence, one sufficiently compensatory but not overly demanding of exertion or accountability.

Big bucks and enormous power are behind the rampant corruption at the national level. They make this theater of warfare a densely populated, super-competitive jungle, where only the most ruthless, vicious, and cunning rise to the top. It's a high-stakes competition for the most psychopathic of the players, those with the fewest inhibitions for bribery, breach of trust, and profiteering. Its deceit and treachery are rampant; the effects are riveting and breathtaking to observe. The action is certainly more attention-worthy and attention-grabbing than what you usually see at the state or local level. 9/11, with its catastrophic, long-reaching effects, brought that home to me.

On arrival in Alaska, the "War on Terror" was taking on the smoke and mirrors features that I expected from an enterprise run by Big League slicksters like Cheney and Rumsfeld, with "W" as the managed, smiley front man. This "War," remember, initially was supposed to be all about defending Americans from terrorists. Right. Just as the Clintons, in the late 1990s, conjured up a Serbian Hitler in the Balkans in order to green-light an American bombing campaign of civilians and begin the colonizing of another part of the world, in the immediate aftermath of 9/11, in 2001, the Bush administration was planning to set up an Arab fall-guy as the excuse to launch a massive invasion in the Middle East. This "Arab Hitler" was no junior league type. By every popular account, he was the real deal. They used him, in Edward Bernays-speak, to "engineer the consent" for the launching of another military adventure in a faraway part of the world. "Vital American interests" were at stake, just as they were in the Balkans. These "interests" are routinely summoned to justify the military targeting of a civilian population deemed insufficiently enthused about the "regime change" the American oligarchs have decided they need.

By 2002, on cue, pushed on to the world stage was the Bedouin Hitler, mustache and all. This one disguised himself as an ambitious Ba'athist named Saddam Hussein, who, we were told, possessed "weapons of mass-destruction." Conveniently forgotten was that the U.S., in the 1980s, had instigated and supported the Saddam regime's massively bloody war against Iran. Roughly half a million Iranian and Iraqi soldiers, plus civilians, were killed. Saddam got several billion dollars' worth of economic aid, the sale of dual-use technology, non-U.S.-origin weaponry, military intelligence, and special operations training. That's ancient history that gets erased if it makes current plans look…well, a little suspicious. One day, you're the "friend" we load up with expensive weaponry; the next, you're Hitler. *Que sera, sera.* Which one you a happen to be on a given day depends on the calculations of our weapons contractors in cahoots with the current Quislings in the State department.

Hitler, loaded up with weapons of mass-destruction, anywhere in the world, as everyone knows, is a huge problem — something to get really worked up about. And the solution? A massive military intervention by the country that saved the world from the original Hitler seventy years ago and, more recently, from the junior-league-type in the Balkans. Saving the world from Hitler — whenever and wherever he happens to appear — apparently, is something that America is just supposed to occasionally do. Perhaps, it's whenever the accountants in the Pentagon get nervous about the bottom line. The families whose sons come home in body bags feel better about themselves, no doubt, and believe that it's all worthwhile. Why Hitler keeps reappearing when it always turns out so bad for him is a topic that never seems to get much attention.

From the initial 9/11 attack, over the course of a year or so, I noticed that the purpose of the "War on Terror" began to profoundly but imperceptibly shift: from "defending the American people against terror" to an offensive "save the world" operation, with the easily attainable goal of making the Middle East, politics-wise, resemble Vermont. American soldiers, one more time, were called upon to risk their lives to dispose of an arriviste Fuhrer. Boots on the ground, this time, with our guys coming home missing body parts or in coffins. Once complete, however, Iraq would become a "democracy" — just like us. Just like Vietnam did, in case you forgot.

Is there a pattern finally emerging here for you, Reader? In the 1990s, remember Slobodan Milošević, the Hitler of the Balkans? He was relatively easy to dispatch — too easy, apparently. Getting rid of the Balkan-Hitler in the late 1990s was the warmup act for the Big Show a few years later. Iraq was the new theater, and Saddam was the target, who, according to the first President Bush, was "even worse than Hitler." Some American Jews got their noses out of joint with this because "Come on, Dude, *nobody* could be worse than Hitler." He quickly apologized. "Jeeezzz, I forgot. I'm sorry. That wasn't *prudent*."

CHAPTER FIFTY-ONE

Que Será, Sarah…

But, obviously, we've got to stand with our North Korean allies.

Sarah Palin

In Juneau, I lived alone in a small apartment — no wife, no friends. I worked long hours in the restaurant-bar, doing everything I could imagine to make the customers come back for more. The owner of the tavern-restaurant was delighted with my single-minded devotion to his business, not to mention his expanded profits. He made me the day manager, with a nice raise. With it, I was able to rent a bigger apartment and share it with Jurgen and Habermas, my two black German Shepherds.

One of my regular customers in the bar was Zeke DuCaine, an old ex-Hell's Angel, originally from Los Angeles. Zeke had fled to Alaska from California to evade arrest after being charged with attempted murder. The incident that triggered his flight occurred at the Altamont Music Festival in Northern California, near the end of 1969 — that time period known as the Age of Aquarius, when the planets moved into perfect alignment to support our collective manifestation of love and peace. I remember it a bit differently.

Altamont was a rock extravaganza that did not exactly

exude "love and peace," certainly not as much as had been promised. Billed as the "Woodstock of the West," on the card were Santana, the Jefferson Airplane, Crosby, Stills, Nash, & Young, and the Grateful Dead, with the Rolling Stones coming in as the headline band. The Stones were finishing a nationwide tour. They had hired a Hells Angels chapter that Zeke was a member of as informal security detail, paying them "beer money" to keep the rowdies in place. Think about that for a moment, and you begin to grasp why no one in a rock band should be put in charge of anything remotely important, especially something as consequential as security and public safety.

When he got to Alaska, Zeke went underground to avoid apprehension and extradition. He worked as a day laborer in the oil fields for a few years. Zeke claimed that he had acted in self-defense, but he was not confident enough to submit to arrest and risk a trial. The statute of limitations finally put his arrest warrant in California to rest. No longer would he need to convince a jury that the guy whose gut he stuck his Bowie knife in had been trying to bash his head in with a crowbar. Once in the clear, however, Zeke realized that he preferred pristine Alaska over the tarnished Golden State. By the time I met him, he had been here for many years. Zeke owned and ran the best motorcycle repair shop in Juneau.

Now in his sixties, Zeke was a long-time alcoholic-in-recovery, and, while he was a frequent customer at my bar, he always restricted himself to Ginger Ale on the rocks. Zeke had gone through several wives and even more girlfriends. Alone now and done with women, he came to the bar for serious conversation, something I offered — professionally, of course — at no extra charge as I poured his Ginger Ale. He was a few years older than me, but we had come to share a strikingly similar view of the 1960s. Zeke had converted to

Christianity — not contemporary Catholicism, with its guitar-masses, love-is-the-answer music, bearded, sandal-clad priests dispensing liberation theology. His was rather an old-fashioned Protestant version that put a lot of stress on sin, punishment, and damnation. His antagonized reflection on the whole Altamont disaster and the way the 1960s had unfolded had driven him to look upon the human condition in a Calvinist, "total depravity" sort of way. "The heart is deceitful above all things and desperately wicked" was how the Old Testament Prophet Jeremiah put it. That was a piece of the OT firmly embedded in my memory from my "Sunday learning" childhood. As I aged, it had become the foundation of how I saw the world in its daily operations.

"Desperately wicked" brings certain events to mind. The Altamont Festival was unfettered decadence — a chaotic, violence-filled orgy that symbolized the collapse of the 1960s counter-culture and exposed the mindless, delusional nature of its self-worshiping rituals. The concert's next-to-last scheduled act was the Grateful Dead. But the Dead bailed at the last minute, threatened by the mounting violence, fearing for their safety. One of Zeke's Hells Angels amigos knocked Jefferson Airplane singer Marty Balin unconscious in a brawl while his band was performing. Stephen Stills, of Crosby, Stills, Nash, & Young, was stabbed several times in the leg by one of the stoned-out Angels with a sharpened motorcycle spoke. The Stones were the last act to take stage. A fight erupted at the foot of the stage when they launched into "Sympathy for the Devil." This added to the performance a hallucinatory-like dimension of the surreal and prompted the Stones to pause their set while the Angels restored order. Yes, you read correctly, the Hell's Angels "restoring order." How does that strike you? We had now arrived at a Fellini-style dark carnivalesque moment.

But the culmination of halcyon images betrayed by ugly, vulgar reality took place during the Rolling Stones' last set. Eighteen-year-old, gun-wielding Meredith Hunter was stabbed to death by Alan Passaro, another one of the Hell's Angels security detail. The killing took place twenty feet in front of the stage, where Mick Jagger was caught up in a performance of his sadomasochistic masterpiece, "Under My Thumb."

> *Under my thumb*
> *It's a squirmin' dog who's just had her day*
> *Under my thumb*
> *A girl who has just changed her ways*

Jagger danced and gyrated his way through the verses in his vintage pouty-lip, bad-boy style, completely unaware that, just a few yards away, a real "squirmin' dog" had "just had [his final] day."

The Rolling Stones finished their set, putting an end to a day of assaults, drug overdoses, brawling, and general mayhem. A woman was dragged across the stage by her hair. Another woman on a bad acid trip was kicked and stepped on. Someone at the Festival accidentally drowned in a nearby canal on a bad LSD-trip. *Rolling Stone Magazine* wrote of it: "rock and roll's all-time worst day, December 6th, a day when everything went perfectly wrong."

No, the entire decade had been "going wrong." December 6, 1969 was the symbolic consummation and culmination of the 1960s nihilism gaudily dressed up as liberation, a "celebration" of the groin in charge of the mind. Imagine the disappointment of Grace Slick: She had expected the "loving vibes of Woodstock, but that wasn't coming at me." No, Grace, it wasn't. I hate to break it to you, Sweetheart, but the "vibes of Woodstock" were a drug-induced one-off, highly overrated and over-hyped, at that. Woodstock was the second-to-last stop in a race to the bottom.

Zeke was old and absorbed with the past. Another one of my occasional customers at the bar was a guy named Todd Palin, who was focused on the future. He had worked for British Petroleum in the North Slope oil fields of Alaska. Todd was a friendly, amiable customer, and a frequent one. He would stop in, have a couple of beers — never more than two — and talk about current developments in Alaskan politics. This was of great interest to me, and even greater, personal interest to him. He was married to a gal named Sarah, his high-school girlfriend he had eloped with some seventeen years earlier.

In 2003, Sarah Palin had been appointed to the Alaska Oil and Gas Conservation Commission. The Commission had safety and efficiency oversight responsibility for Alaska's oil and gas fields — the State's economic engine. About oil and gas, she knew nothing, but she wanted to learn the industry. She got herself named chair of the ethics commission — a very good move for anyone who is politically ambitious. On an "ethics commission," in the midst of muck, you can become virtuously visible in a hurry, not to mention make your political rivals into "squirmin' dogs," more likely to fall in line with *your* plans, which, of course, follow the highest "ethical" guidelines — remember, Reader, what I said about "Government commissions?"

Sarah, I came to observe, was a politically ambitious young woman. She was positioning herself to take on the political establishment, a move that would bring her a lot of success. By November 2003, she had filed ethics complaints with the state Attorney General and the Governor against fellow commission member Randy Ruedrich. Ruedrich was a former petroleum engineer and, at the time, the chairman of the state Republican Party.

Shortly thereafter, Senator Ted Stevens appointed Palin as one of the Directors of the Ted Stevens Excellence in Public Service, Inc., an NGO that provided political training for Republican women in Alaska. Her star was on the rise. Her wholesome good looks and soccer-mom image did not hurt.

Todd, with wife Sarah, frequently dined at the restaurant side of the bar I managed, and it became one of their favorites. I like to think it was, in part, because I had worked so hard to improve the menu, the service, and the atmosphere. I got to know them as regulars and enjoyed the casual chatting that came out of their visits.

One evening, Todd and Sarah were dining in the restaurant with two of their older kids and Sarah's brother, Chuck. Chuck suddenly inhaled a half-chewed piece of steak when he started to laugh at one of Todd's jokes. It lodged in his throat. I heard the panicked screams, and when I got to the table, he had started to turn dark red. I got behind him and did the Heimlich maneuver, with my locked fists under his diaphragm, which popped that chunk of meat out of Chuck's windpipe. It went flying out of his mouth onto the floor. I know all about the terror of choking on a piece of food. I experienced it once myself when I was alone. I did the Heimlich on myself bending over a wooden chair, pushing the back just below my ribcage.

That I had saved her brother's life made quite the impression on Sarah, and, eventually, it made me a rather special person for her. Soon after, I spent an evening at the Palin home and, thereafter, became a frequent visitor to the Palin household. Then, at some point, I realized that I had been adopted into the family.

The Palin's were a pretty open and welcoming pair. My "adoption," apart from the brother-rescue, I think, was probably related to the fact that I lived alone, with no family or relatives that were anywhere in the picture. I seemed to be a lonely sort of person, who would do well with an adult adoption. I had also acquired a slightly mysterious but gentle older persona, bearing a wealth of experience and a kind of worldly wisdom that, for whatever reason, appealed to the very hospitable, younger Palins and their children. My cynicism, I carefully dissembled. I listened intently and attentively to the children, told funny stories, had loads of clean jokes, and was always humble — genuinely so, I should add. As I mentioned before, I've always bended easily to those around me.

As for my past: I told them that I was an only child who lost my parents at an early age in a car wreck. I was raised by an elderly Aunt in Cedar Falls, Iowa, who had died a few years ago. I now had no living close relatives in my life. Having recently retired from working, I had come to Alaska on an extended vacation with no intention to stay, but I had fallen in love with the state and, especially, the people — people like the Palins. With no children or relatives to go back to, why not stay?

On my employment history, I was, of course, vague. I said that I had graduated from the Michigan State University's Police Administration/Criminal Justice program. The reason I pulled out that particular program to embellish my fictional past is because it had a special, personal place in my inventory of institutional-government corruption.

One of my cousins on my mother's side went through the MSU program in the 1960s, when the leftist muckraking *Ramparts* magazine did an explosive exposé on the collusion of MSU and the CIA. MSU law enforcement professors had been training Diệm's repressive police force in South Vietnam. Diệm connection to MSU was through Wesley Fishel, an MSU political science professor and a secret military intelligence agent he'd met on a trip to Japan. Fishel was particularly impressed with Diệm's anti-communist fervor. He subsequently arranged for him to visit East Lansing and meet with MSU President John Hannah. Hannah had been an Assistant Secretary of Defense under President Eisenhower. So impressed with the future South Vietnam President was Mr. Hannah that he turned himself into one of Diệm's most adoring patrons. Hannah hired him as a consultant, gave him an honorary degree, and used his connections with the Eisenhower administration to lobby for MSU to work in support of Diem's corrupt South Vietnamese security service and secret police.

I had worked, I said, overseas for many years for the big U.S. defense contractors on the constabulary side in Europe and the Middle East. I had trained the security units and local police forces. I then moved over to logistics. There, I did provision of supplies at the Class V level: ammunition of all types, bombs, explosives, mines, fuses, detonators, pyrotechnics, missiles, rockets, propellants, and associated items. I also told the Palins that I had burned out on that sort of work and was happy to have a more post-retirement "normal," people-oriented job, with less worry and stress.

CHAPTER FIFTY-TWO

Sarah Barracuda

Line up all your demons
Little by the bigger
Get a bead on them
And then pull the trigger
Don'tcha let them last forever
Nothin' lasts forever
　　Delbert McClinton, "Nothin' Lasts Forever"

My relationship with the Palins over the next couple of years became warm and close. I spent lots of the holidays with the family. Todd and I became friends. Some of our leisure time, we went snowmobiling, hunting, and fishing. For me, it was reminiscent of growing up in northern Michigan.

Sarah focused herself exclusively on her political career. I shared with her my unique observations and perspectives on how to read the cues and clues of motivation — cui bono? — and how to look through the typical "public servant" *spin* that the politicos put on their self-serving agendas and professional resumes. My antennas were always up for corruption-detection, and I could barely keep up with it. I gradually insinuated myself as an informal advisor. She came to appreciate my grasp of where the worse sinkholes of corruption were in state government, who were the most vulnerable culprits for exposure, and when was the best time to strike. This practical approach to political survival and triumph was inspired by a couple of lines from Herman Melville's Ahab in *Moby Dick*: "All visible objects, man, are but as pasteboard masks... If man will strike, strike through the mask!" Having worn so many "masks" myself, I was good at calculating the likelihood of lethal penetration.

Alaska, of course, was a Republican state, and, as a young, ambitious politician — as I frequently hinted to her — she could do no better than to position herself as an outsider and attack corruption behind the ruling party's mask. Strike through the porous Republican mask!

Strike, she did. In 2006, she struck right through the masks of two of the top good-ole boys. First, it was incumbent Governor Frank Murkowski in the Republican gubernatorial primary, who went down from the strike. Then, and though outspent, she soundly whipped former Democratic governor Tony Knowles in the Fall election. In 2006, the forty-two-year-old Sarah Palin put on her own mask as the youngest and the first woman to be elected Governor of Alaska.

Sarah turned out to be a popular governor, and I was happy to see her seemingly hitting all the right notes, wondering, though, how high she would go. How long would it last? "Nothin' lasts forever," right, Delbert?

I couldn't help but think about and compare the "first Alaska" couple with the "first Arkansas" duo I had encountered twenty years earlier. The latter were naturals for the Big Show — Ivy league education, with the "connections" it brings. They were ruthlessly ambitious, ethically unencumbered, and secularly in tune with the rotted-out popular culture. Bill and Hill were the perfect pair of 1960s-era self-enamored radicals, now "mature." Like their more radical counterparts — the Weathermen, Bill and Bernardine — they had ditched the bell-bottoms, beard, and the more conspicuous counter-culture accoutrements, became lawyerly and put on business suits as masks of conventional respectability to hide their Bolshevik instincts. They had made all the right calculations and maneuvers to step on and over whomever they needed to and to boogaloo their way on up to the top. Once there, they would self-enrich and rule over us — pulling off their scam as the avatars of compassionate, progressive politics. The future they were leading us to? Guys-who-just-wanna-be-girls, transphobia, preferred pronouns, and the dictatorship of bathrooms. The ugly reality of their self-seeking, beneath the mask of "idealism," however, was simple and prosaic, summed up by Bill years later in just seven words. It was to Bob Dole, who complained to him about misrepresenting his Senate record in his failed 1996 Presidential election campaign — Bill replied: "You gotta do what you gotta do."

Sarah and Todd? Where to start? In contrast with the Clintons, you could not invent a more opposite pair, culturally speaking. Todd was a blue-collar fisherman — no college degree, with some community college coursework — who liked to fish, hunt, and go snowmobiling. Sarah, also with some community college courses, finished up at the University of Idaho with a degree in Communication. She was the mother of five children, who also liked to go hunting, and a professing conservative Christian. In high school, she was the head of the Fellowship of Christian Athletes. A more enticing target for eviscerating derision from the sophisticates cannot be imagined.

The Clintons were prestigiously educated, liberal, verbally agile, and sophisticated — in a certain way. Their dueling banjos of avarice and ambition pushed them toward the centers of wealth, power, and glamour. The Clintons loved the rich and beautiful folks in Hollywood, and the Hollywood glitterati loved them right back — a ton, in a fawning-over, groupie sort of way that included their admiration, money, and adulation.

The Palins were modestly educated, conservative, Christian, verbally unpolished, family people. They were unabashedly parochial — hicks, to put it bluntly — not the sort that Barbra Streisand — high-school educated — or George Clooney — suit salesman — would gush over. No Jeff Katzenberg, Steven Spielberg-hosted, star-studded fundraisers for a fisherman and a snowmobiling mom. For the smart and beautiful set, those who jealously guard their entitlement to govern the country, lay down the "moral" standards they exempt themselves from, and sermonize on what's wrong with the world, the Palins were the sort of folks for whom they reserve their barely concealed contempt. Sarah's ascent to the height of a state governorship could only have happened in a place like Alaska — an observation later confirmed by cruel experience.

The Palins, in 2007, moved into the Governor's mansion on Calhoun Avenue, and over the next couple of years, I was there often and got an earful about Sarah's efforts at being a reform governor. The Restaurant was booming, and I was busy serving lots of the customers from the Capital complex and absorbing their backchat. This was good, of course, for keeping the political-gossip pipeline open, an informal source of intelligence to assist the Governor.

Late in the afternoon of August 25, 2008, Todd and I were in the mansion kitchen, drinking some Artic Rhino Porter, when Sarah came tearing in from the garage. She had been at the Alaska State Fair. John McCain had just called her to ask if she would consider being his VP running mate on the Republican ticket for the upcoming November election. He had met Sarah earlier in the year in DC, at the National Governor Association meeting. He was said to be impressed by her. She was, needless to say, worked up and completely out of reach for a talk that would touch on the possible downsides of linking up with the Arizona Senator. I'm not blaming her. Who could resist? On the 27th, she flew to Sedona, Arizona to meet with McCain at his vacation home, where he offered her the VP position. He introduced her to the world at Wright State University's "Nutter Center" in Dayton, Ohio, the same venue where Obama had staged a big rally a few months earlier.

I had become attached to Sarah in a paternal sort of way. In this, I could see nothing but disaster unfolding for her. Moreover, I was astonished that McCain would pick Sarah as his running mate. As much as I liked her and her family, it was obvious to me that she was not remotely prepared to become the Vice President — even, given McCain's age, quite possibly the President of the United States. Her drive, accomplishments, and intelligence were impressive, but her age, experience, and understanding of the world and its complexities beyond Alaska were — how shall I say it? — understandably limited. She didn't know what she didn't know. This would guarantee that she was not even minimally prepared for the blizzard of scorn and abuse the opposition would pour down on her during the election campaign.

Sarah's degree from the University of Idaho in Communication, unfortunately, didn't do much in the way to prepare her for that big step. "Communication" is a soft, "media journalism" sort of college major. You will see it typically offered at mediocre regional and state universities. It's easy, popular, and "revenue positive," meaning that you don't need expensive professors — law, engineering, and business, for example — to teach the courses. Tons of tuition-paying students in large classes easily navigate the intellectually-light, modestly-demanding courses. Communication majors get trained for "public relations," mass media, and marketing jobs. The lucky grad might get hired as a perky "news reader," a talking head on a cable channel or network affiliate, or, someday, a producer who churns out programing for the local "disaster" and murder coverage and the fluff "feel good" morning-filler stuff. A typical communication grad doesn't know much — that is, hasn't grappled with the sorts of the intellectual challenging material that would substantially deepen his understanding of how the world operates scientifically, economically, commercially, or, especially, politically. He lacks the intellectual equipment to think and talk about complex subjects such as, say, an engineer, a chemist, or a lawyer would acquire from his formal education and experience.

Sarah, as I noted, was going to get eaten alive by the smart set who ran the media, not to mention the Democrats who would feast on all the parochial features of her background — a Pentecostal denomination Christian and a former beauty pageant contestant playing her flute in the talent competition, winner of "Miss Congeniality," a woman who proudly identified as a "mom." All of this was fuel for cruel parody in venues like *Saturday Night Live*. The sharks would not hold back; blood would soon be in the water.

CHAPTER FIFTY-THREE

Striking Through the Mask

Getting to know you
Getting to know all about you
Getting to like you
Getting to hope you like me…

Rodgers and Hammerstein,
"The King and I"

So, the obvious question: Why did McCain pick "Sarah Barracuda?" — a moniker that came from her aggressive basketball playing style. Rumor was that he had been leaning toward Joe Lieberman, a "conservative" Democrat who, as a crossover, would appeal to independents. Joe, you might recall, relished bombing the houses of women, children, and old folks on the other side of the world — a perfect fit for John. Their campaign slogan: "Attention all tyrants anywhere and everywhere — ready or not, we're coming to get you." McCain advisor Bill Kristol was said to have urged McCain to go with Sarah — her youth, outsider status, and reform background to offset McCain's age and insider image.

That was the media, talking-heads take on it. To get at the

real reason, you must ask yourself the cui-bono question. Why would Bill Kristol, a New York, Jewish, Neoconservative, culturally sophisticated intellectual, be pushing McCain toward someone as intellectually, culturally, and socially remote from Kristol and the Republican establishment as Sarah Palin? Bill Kristol's father, Irving, dubbed the godfather of Neoconservativism, was a Trotskyist in this youth, turned "conservative." He went on to be a professor, publisher, and public intellectual. As a converted anti-communist, he closely affiliated himself with the Congress for Cultural Freedom, a front organization for the CIA. Try to imagine a private little party where Irv, Bill, and a few of their Neocon pals, after a couple of cognacs, got themselves going on topics like biblical Christianity, gun control, and fishing — out would pour scorn, mockery, condescension, and malicious contempt in a fierce contest of one-upmanship.

The answer, then, to the "why Sarah?" question, I fear, shows how vicious and duplicitous was the soul of the Republican establishment. Two words are all you need to describe the Kristols — both *père et fils* — "treacherous" and "opportunist." Sarah was, for Kristol and McCain, election bait to seduce the base, the white, blue-collar working class they pretend to represent but actually despise and routinely betray. McCain needed the "rube" vote to get elected. Sarah, with her young, fresh, buck-the-establishment image, would help and — they seriously misjudged — also pull in the women. President McCain would continue the Neocon agenda of perpetual war under the guise of "human rights," the importation of cheap third-world labor, and moving factories and jobs to Asia. Blue-collar, rural, Christian American was dying. For Bill Kristol, John McCain, and the Republican establishment, that was more or less the plan, long-term.

Sarah had no clue of what she was in for, and McCain, for all his supposed political smarts, was stupid to pick her. He should have known what the establishment media and the powerful entertainment industry would do to her. It would be difficult to find a more carefully groomed, self-promoting servant of the political establishment than John McCain. His war-hero, straight-talking maverick image had not even the remotest connection to the reality of his personal and political corruption.

As I mentioned, I was shocked when Sarah returned from Sedona and told me that she was McCain's pick for VP on the ticket. Some years before, I had conceived an intense loathing for the man. Will Rogers once quipped of Calvin Coolidge's politics: "He did nothing, but that's what people wanted done." With McCain, it would be: "He did a lot, but, mostly, what people didn't want done."

McCain used the Kosovo crisis in 1999 to advance his Presidential aspirations the first time he made his push to occupy the Oval Office. Many of his Republican colleagues were on the fence for the bombing President Clinton had unleashed on the Serbs. McCain, however, broke partisan ranks, supported the airstrikes, and unsuccessfully pushed a reluctant Clinton to send in ground troops. Joe Lieberman's ghoulish exuberance for Serbian suffering was likely one of the reasons for McCain's consideration of him for the VP slot.

You could not find a war McCain was not gung-ho for. He was the War Party personified. There seemed to be no place in the world he was not eager to send the U.S. Military to intervene, to overthrow the dictators whom he had decided needed to be removed while killing lots of civilians in the process. Years before Bush II invaded Iraq, McCain was arguing for military intervention and urging opposition groups to overthrow Saddam Hussein. He had also called for "regime replacement" in Iran, Libya, North Korea, and Venezuela. McCain also sought to create an international, U.S.-controlled "League of Democracies," which would circumvent U.N. Security Council resolutions whenever Russia and China opposed the use of force, tough sanctions, or other actions sought by the U.S.

Remember the "workarounds" I talked about earlier, the collusion between governors and the governed that work exclusively for the advantage of the politically connected? John McCain and a guy named Charles Keating pulled one off. It was one of the more audacious, notorious "workarounds" in U.S. banking history, a particularly punishing piece of corruption for the unconnected, the little people.

When I was in Wapakoneta, Ohio, selling plots in heaven on my cable tv network, about 100 miles down the road in Cincinnati was Charles Keating. He had initially made a name for himself as an anti-pornography champion, founding the Citizens for Decent Literature advocacy body. That is hard to top as a moniker of unselfconscious, prim-and-proper self-righteousness. Imagine having to endure one of their meetings. Now, I am of the belief that the world would be much better off without pornography. I'm guessing that it is highly addictive and turns stupid those hooked on it. But I've never cared much for the "anti-types" who fancy themselves as being about "decency." I suspect that there is some sort of weird, pathological projection going on with the hyper-moralizing that animates them. It seemed to me that you might go to literature for many good reasons, but come on…"decency?" That's like looking for "satisfactory" in sex and "OK" on your annual job performance evaluation.

You might say that both Keating and I had deep

"religious" convictions — whether his were superior to mine, I leave for you, Reader, to decide. I met Mr. Keating once, at a fundraiser for Ohio congressional candidates, including Senator John Glenn. I was flush at that time and gave generously to both parties to cover the bases. I was impressed with how impressed he was, and I got a nasty whiff of that self-righteous, prudish side of his personality.

When I met Keating, he'd moved on from running off the pornographers to running Lincoln Savings and Loan into future bankruptcy. He was heavily investing the little people's money in junk bonds and other high-risk ventures and doing shell-game accounting. At the time of the fundraiser, he was getting a lot of attention from federal regulators. But this was no problem for the "decency in literature" sheriff. He was openly and indecently bragging about the five Senators he had in his pocket, who would be taking care of the over-zealous regulators making his life difficult. Senatorial friendship doesn't come cheap — about $1.3 million, it cost Keating, in the form of campaign contributions.

Of those five "friends," John McCain was by far his closest Amigo. Since 1981, the McCain family had made several trips — at Charles's expense — for vacations at Keating's palatial Bahamas retreat at Cat Cay. With McCain running Senatorial interference for Keating with those pesky regulators, the rest, as they say, was history — a sorry and stunningly corrupt piece of it. The federal regulators that McCain tried to fend off for his friend finally took control of Lincoln, which, by then, was insolvent. Its collapse meant that the Federal Savings and Loan Insurance Corporation (FSLIC) had to cover the massive losses. It was the largest of more than 1,000 failures in the savings and loan industry. The savings and loan crisis ultimately bankrupted the FSLIC and cost American taxpayers an estimated $124 billion. Two of the five Senator "friends" of Keating went down with it, but not the plucky ex-POW, McCain. Some 23,000 Lincoln bondholders were defrauded, and many investors lost their life savings. In the early 1990s, Keating was convicted on counts of fraud, racketeering, and conspiracy. McCain bobbed and weaved, counter-punching with the critics — some rope-a-dope — and, finally, slid off the ropes, politically unscathed. No doubt, he found equally luxurious vacationing and new well-healed friends who would advance his career.

Much more could be said that would give the worshipful picture of McCain's personality and character created by the establishment press organs — "The conscious and intelligent manipulation of the organized...opinions of the masses," as Bernays put it — a proper balance and a more accurate picture. Two words, however — "consummate opportunist" — could go a long way in making the necessary correction.

Shortly upon returning from his POW captivity in Vietnam, McCain met Cindy Lou Hensley, a blond beauty eighteen years his junior. Cindy was the daughter — and heir — of James Hensley, the mob-connected founder of one of the largest beer distributorships in the United States, plus one of the richest men in Arizona. Hensley's wealth stemmed from the bootlegging and racketeering empire built by Canadian Samuel Bronfman, founder of Seagram's. Bronfman was a business associate of gangster-extraordinaire, Meyer Lansky.

McCain's wife, Carol, had waited for him during his captivity, worked assiduously on the POW cause, and raised his three sons by herself. She suffered debilitating and disfiguring injuries from an auto accident, not long before his release from captivity. As you might guess, from a "what have you done for me lately" sort of a guy like McCain, she was unable to compete with the much younger, prettier, and richer woman whose resources — the fruits of organized crime — and connections would advance her husband's political career. "Adios, Carol, Darlin'. Thanks for waiting, but I've got a better deal now. You understand. Nice knowing you."

CHAPTER FIFTY-FOUR

Pain with McCain

Everybody has a temper, but mine was set on a hair trigger
Jake LaMotta

At least I don't plaster on the makeup like a trollop, you cunt

John McCain, to wife, Cindy

In early October 2008, Sarah was in St. Louis preparing for her upcoming debate with Obama's VP running mate, Joe Biden. Todd was in Juneau with the kids. Sarah was stressed out. She had called and asked him to come. She also wondered if I could come along, a friendly, familiar face she could trust, someone to offer some moral encouragement and emotional support. Todd and I made the flight. The next evening, I was in the audience at Washington University, St. Louis to watch the debate. It was not that far from where I had brass-knuckled Bill Ayers some years before at the Art Museum in Forest Park. As I had feared, Sarah did not perform well.

Late in the afternoon of the next day, I went to Sarah's suite to see how she was holding up after the prior evening's grueling debate. Todd was off to check on some transportation issues, and, for the moment, it was just the two of us in the room. She was upset with the coverage she was getting from much of the media, beating her up on her debate performance. McCain's staff, she claimed, was treating her badly, and she was in the grip of a paralyzing panic. I was trying to calm her down.

There was a quick rap on the door. It immediately opened. McCain charged in. He was by himself, looking angry as hell, and, of course, was startled to see me.

"Who's he?" he growled at Sarah, gesturing toward me like I was a fresh dog turd on the living room carpet.

"He's an old family friend from Juneau" she said, "just trying to offer some moral support. Senator, this is…"

"Out!" McCain snarled at me, turning away and walking over toward Sarah.

I shouldn't have, but I was unable to stop myself.

"What's the magic word, Senator?"

Sarah turned limestone pale. For a moment, I thought she was going to faint.

McCain's explosive, volcanic temper was not a particularly well-kept secret among those who had any dealings with him, personally or professionally. In an instant, he could go from calm to purple-faced fury, fists clenched and barking out in a rapid staccato series — "fuck, fuck, fuck, fuck" in a stormy crescendo, with each "fuck" getting louder until his head seemed about to explode. After the few seconds required for him to pause, jerk around, and digest my *lèse-majesté,* he twisted himself into a rage, stalked over to me, put his jaw about six inches from mine, and hissed, with his spittle hitting my face: "Get the fuck out of here, whoever you are. I never want to see your shit-festooned face again."

I took the hint and made an immediate exit, though fearing what was in store for Sarah. A couple hours later,

Todd found me in the corner of the hotel lounge, nursing a glass of ice and Jim Beam while feeling like three-day-old roadkill.

"Jesus Christ, John, what got into you? McCain was worked up even before he came into the room. Your smart-ass remark put him over the edge, and he took it out on Sarah. I hate to do this, but you have to be gone."

I didn't respond for a while, but, finally: "I'm sorry, Todd. It was really stupid. I fucked things up for her. I'll disappear."

I did. I flew that afternoon to Juneau and went back to work at the restaurant. The rest of the election campaign, I followed through the media. I avoided the Palins. McCain's campaign crashed and burned. Tina Fey, *Saturday Night Live*, and a hostile mainstream media had unleashed a storm of mockery and ridicule that pretty much ended any chance for Sarah to help McCain pull out of his nosedive. She had become a liability. Not that there was anything, really, that would turn it around. By then, Obama was "The One," the rockstar darling of the media, with maidens fainting at his rallies and the pundits one-upping each other in bizarre rituals of adulation. *News Week* Chief Editor Evan Thomas on television told Chris Mathews, whose leg kept getting thrills running up it whenever he heard Obama: "In a way, Obama's standing above the country, above the world; he's sort of God."

Well, you can't compete with "God" — whatever sort he is — and those thrills he sends surging up your leg. McCain and his own staff were trying to marginalize and distance themselves from her. I knew this would happen. I wasn't sorry to see McCain lose — not that I had any confidence in the thin man from Chicago peddling Hope and Change and being God for a while.

CHAPTER FIFTY-FIVE

In the Kingdom
of the Pretenders

Success without honor is an unseasoned dish; it will satisfy your hunger, but it won't taste good

Joe Paterno

In the Kingdom of the Pretenders, the fairest-haired boy is King

With the election over and the wreckage that it had left the Palin family in, I decided that it would be best to leave Alaska. My Alaska family had un-adopted me. Sarah's Presidential campaign debacle had changed her — not completely for the better.

I'd had enough of restaurant work. I missed the Midwest. My head bartender, Billy Donovan, was a recent transplant from Pennsylvania. He'd been a good defensive lineman at Penn State University — a Nittany Lion — and had hoped for a shot at the NFL. No go. Billy was a bit too small for the interior line and too immobile to be a linebacker. His major at PSU was Communication — watered down even more for the "scholar athletes" that Joe Paterno pretended to be all about. Upon graduation, not much in the way of opportunity seemed to be coming in his direction. Alaska, he thought, might be a good place for a fresh start. With his lineman size, rugged good looks, and a massive black beard, he was perfect as an Alaskan barman — Paul Bunyan in a plaid shirt serving up your screw drivers and manhattans. I'd hired him at the restaurant, showed him the ropes, and put him in charge of running the bar side of the business. We got to be friends. We spent some weekends together, hunting elk and fishing for salmon.

Billy, however, was missing his family, friends, and State College. He had gotten an offer for a low-level job in the office of the PSU's Athletic Director, and he told me he was leaving. He knew I was looking to get out — faraway, out of Juneau — and he said to me: "Why don't you come to State College? I might be able to help you get a job somewhere in the athletics side at PSU."

Yes, central Pennsylvania sounded like the right place to be. I was ready to bid farewell to the last nine years in the land of the midnight sun. It took me a while to wrap things up in Juneau, pack, and make the long drive to State College. By the time I arrived, Billy had set me up for a job interview as an assistant trainer to the assistant coach for the PSU football defensive backs. It was basically a gofer-position — in charge of towels, ankle wraps, and Gatorade — but perfect for me. It was offered. I took it eagerly. I have loved football since I was a kid and played it in high school. I was a defensive back — fast and a deadly tackler. The job didn't pay a lot, but no one paid much attention to me, which was perfect — attention was the last thing I wanted, and State College was a low-cost place to live, compared with Alaska.

I was happy to be away from the drama of national politics or politics of any kind. Now, I had ample time to hike in the beautiful hills, read, and to observe up close the corruption at work in Division I university athletics. I knew it was there: It was the sheer volume and brazenness of it that knocked me over. The athletic side of the university in the U.S. is fueled by prestige, money, and image promotion — less on playing the diversity moral-superiority game with its social justice mumbo jumbo, non-stop grievance-mongering, and self-righteous posturing that corrupts the little that's left of the legitimate academic side. The "diversity" industry concentrates itself on "losing-out" — the victimhood side of life. Athletics is about winning.

When I arrived at PSU in 2009, Joseph Vincent Paterno, the head football coach, was still king of the realm. JoePa, as they affectionately called him, was in his early 80s, and you might say he was living professionally on the fumes that his winning football legend continued to give off. He came to PSU to become an assistant coach in 1950, fresh out of Brown University, thinking it was a temporary stop before law school. It was just about the same time when I vacated my diapers at the ripe old age of three.

Sixty-one years coaching football at PSU — forty-five of them as the head coach — he had set the record as the winningest college football coach of all time. Now, that, I'd say, is unsurpassable, enviable longevity. Yes, but it comes with a truckload of informal power and the kind of arrogance that people inevitably exude when they cease, at some point, to be humanly flawed and are elevated to objects of worship. Problem is: Human nature is such that, when you put together longevity and the kind of power that JoePa had amassed with it — plus, the arrogance — corruption envelopes you. It gets increasingly heavy and cumbersome, and you must drag it along if you want to keep your momentum. Sometimes, it just gets too heavy and brings you down. I was there when it did.

By 2009, the octogenarian coach was thinking about

retirement…maybe — pushing back, however, against some folks on campus who thought that it was past time. There were problems. One being that it was a new era, with a lot more women everywhere on campus. They were coming from a generation more inclined to put up a fuss at being sexually harassed. That "fussing" had a close connection to PSU football.

A short while after I got there, one of the high-up women administrators mistakenly came to think that football players at PSU regularly sexually harassing and assaulting coeds was maybe a bit too "old school" and was urging for some changes to be made. Being relatively new, she was unusually and incautiously persistent. Finally, the President had to sit her down and explain that Coach Paterno was, well, a model old-school sort of fellow and understandably sensitive to any aspersions cast upon his players…oh…and that her contract for the next year had been cancelled. Ok, yes, "I am woman, hear me roar in numbers too big to ignore," but legends with Guinness record book longevity, who win record numbers of football games at big universities, "do not go gentle into that good night," no matter who happens to be roaring at the moment. What the President knew — what the lady administrator was finally brought to understand — was that JoePa, not the President, was the guy who called the shots at PSU.

> You don't tug on superman's cape
> You don't spit into the wind
> You don't pull the mask off that old lone ranger
> And you don't mess around with Jim
>
> Jim Croce, "You Don't Mess
> Around with Jim,"

Joe, instead of Jim, was the guy at PSU you didn't mess around with or tug at his cape.

Paterno's legend was built on the foundation of college football, and it's hard for me to conceive of any enterprise outside of big government that is more corrupt than college football. At big, nationally reputed universities like PSU, football is a highly sophisticated, huge-money, branding enterprise that gives the university its identity, visibility, and prestige. Throw out the names Ohio State University, the University of Alabama, or Notre Dame University. What first jumps to your mind? The philosophy, English, or sociology departments? The physics labs and women's basketball? Didn't think so. No one cares about them — least of all, the university administrators.

Football? In an entertainment-addled society, nothing tops football. It thrives on Mass Spectacle — helmeted, muscled-up gladiators, their cheering throngs amassed in huge stadiums, wearing the team colors and logo, vicariously sharing with the players the controlled violence of the game. For the university, it draws massive, television-generated revenue, attracting both big donors and prospective students. Football, unlike anything else, creates an image for the university of power, preeminence, and success. You'll be hard pressed to find a more bracing experience than a crisp autumn afternoon sitting with 110,000 of your best friends in Happy Valley, waiting for the marching band to burst into Beaver Stadium. Then, out onto the field storm the Nittany Lions, performing their frenzied preliminary rituals before they begin the crushing of the opposition. The man in charge — lean, unflappable, and determined — the weathered-face JoePa, with those piercing eyes behind the thick glasses, his stern, hawkish countenance and his unique presence of command — as always — pacing the sidelines.

Football, for the university, however, poses problems: Revenue and image-wise, its football program has to win;

losing programs are, well, the mark of losers. That is why winning coaches, like Paterno, command astronomical salaries.

Unfortunately, the lads who tend to be best at winning are, you might say, usually not well equipped to succeed in what most people traditionally associate with university's normal activities. These activities have measurable baselines that involve reading, writing, and arithmetic. The scholar athletes, as we are encouraged to think of them, also tend to come from somewhat less than nurturing family settings and settled, stable neighborhoods, where the means for effective socialization and encouragement to attain maturation are often not in adequate supply. Let's see: big strong guys + lower expectations for rule-conformity + immaturity and low impulse control + high self-entitlement + lots of cute girls. What do think might happen, Einstein? An appreciation of *Beowulf* and an acquaintance with organic chemistry are probably unreasonable expectations.

The solution to overcome this formidable set of obstacles, of course, is for the universities to pretend that it isn't a problem. The lady administrator mentioned above caught on too late about the pretending part.

> *Yes, I'm the great pretender*
> *Just laughin' and gay like the clown*
> *I seem to be what I'm not, you see*
> The Platters, "The Great Pretender"

Yes, sadly, we do see. I know all about pretending "to be what I am not" — I was highly skilled at it, since it was my life's calling. Some of it was pretty high risk. But, with college football, there is so much money, power, and prestige in play, pretending that this game has anything to do with education doesn't have to be all that good or even particularly convincing. It's another variant of Leonard Cohen's "Everybody Knows:"

> *Everybody knows that the boat is leaking*
> *Everybody knows that the captain lied*

Well, the PSU boat had sprung a leak, and everyone seemed to know the captains had achieved their ranks and fat salaries by shamelessly lying. About university football, everybody knows that "scholar athletes" are physically gifted but mostly functional illiterates enrolled in pretend academic courses, who, occasionally, get pretend degrees. In exchange for several years of free housing, debilitating, life-long injuries, and a miniscule shot at the NFL, they bring in millions of real revenue dollars for their "employers," who pretend to be educators. The university administrators pretend that their unpaid "employees" behave themselves on campus. Everyone pretends to be shocked when the usual rough-housing that the coaches pretend not to notice gets completely out of control and forces the university, reluctantly, to heave-ho one of its top "scholar athletes" for prison-bound behavior, usually of the assault kind. When you have pretending with this order of magnitude, a lot of corruption tends to be bubbling underneath.

CHAPTER FIFTY-SIX

Kingdom Crumbles

The minute you think you've got it made, disaster is just around the corner.

Joe Paterno

H ere I was in State College, winding down my days and immersed in yet another cesspool of corruption in 21st Century America. Still, I had settled into life in the small, big-university town, minding my own business and pretty much enjoying my gofer job for a couple of years in Joe Paterno's Football Kingdom, the bucolic Kingdom of the Pretenders. Outside of Beaver Stadium was a seven-foot, 900-pound bronze statue of the King, in front of which I would occasionally stop and pause to admire — another massive, bronze statue erected to keep the image of some pretend Immortal forever in our mind's eye, a grotesque physical prop intended to carry on the hoax. For me, it was an especially ugly reminder of the widespread human shortcoming for the credulous worship of powerful, corrupt men.

One day, I was working outside the football locker room when a sixty-something-year-old guy with a lineman's physique came in with a group of young teenagers — came in, that is, like he owned the place. He blew past me with barely a side glance and approached one of the other assistants near the entrance. After a brief exchange, in, he went, with the young guys trailing behind. I had seen this guy around a number of times but didn't know who he was and what his connection was to the football program. Also, I wondered why he had such easy, unimpeded access to facilities that Paterno was usually very strict about limiting.

When I went over to the assistant and asked him who the guy was, he looked surprised.

"You don't know who that is?" he asked.

"Should I?"

He looked slightly amused at this, like a guy who has to point a simple rube with a stupid question in the right direction.

"Well, he's Jerry Sandusky, an alum. He played defensive end for PSU in the early 1960s, when Rip Engle was head coach. For thirty years, Jerry was an assistant coach for JoePa, until he retired a few years back. He's a fixture around here, sort of a local celebrity."

"It looks to me like he's got the run of the place," I said. "What's with all the kids he has in tow?"

The young assistant again looked surprised.

"You don't know?"

"Should I?"

He hesitated, then relaxed a bit.

"He runs 'Second Mile,' a charity outfit for foster children. Paterno lets him bring the young guys from his program over, show them around the facilities, and, you know, sort of introduce them to a big-time college football program. It makes a real impression on them. They are in awe, and they really seem to be appreciative of the special attention. It's part of Sandusky's operation, for which he raises a lot of money. Don't get crossways with him if he comes in here when you're here alone and wants to go in. He'll complain to JoePa. You'll be gone."

That was all he would say. Talking about Jerry Sandusky seemed to be making this young guy uncomfortable, so I didn't ask more questions or attempt to continue the conversation in that direction. There were things operating underneath that I didn't need to know about and was happy not to.

Sandusky's charity work, I found out later, also impressed some high-ups besides his former boss. Jerry proudly displayed his letter of praise from Bush I, Sandusky's group being a "shining example" of how charity operations should run — one of those "Thousand points of light" Bush liked to talk about, a campaign meme that lent itself to some very creative mockery, such as "a thousand Bud Lites." U.S. Pennsylvania Senator Rick Santorum honored Sandusky with an "Angels in Adoption" award. Didn't we see something like this before, with the power-set slobbering all over the "humanitarian" Jim Jones? Perhaps, it can be expressed as a kind of "law" or adage: "To the perverts from the powerful goes the praise."

Shortly after that incident when I saw Sandusky invade the locker room with his kids in tow, the "things bubbling underneath" poured out in the form of a high-velocity shitstorm that hit PSU, its administration, its football program, and, most spectacularly, the Big Kahuna himself, Joe Paterno. A grand jury came in with a forty-count indictment of Jerry Sandusky for sex crimes against young boys. It followed a three-year investigation, with a lot to investigate. The grand jury indicted Sandusky for sexual advances and assaults that took place over years — some of them while he was still employed at Penn State. This PSU humanitarian and football fixture was subsequently arrested.

This "one thousandth point of light" was quite disgusting in its full illumination. Joe Paterno and his vaunted PSU football program was deeply mired in the scandalous criminality. Sandusky went to trial. He was convicted and sentenced to sixty years — his first parole eligibility date would be when he was ninety-eight years old.

My reaction to all of this? I was like Claude Raines in the scene out of the 1940s movie classic *Casablanca*, playing the Vichy police inspector who walks into Humphrey Bogart's casino and, as he collects his winnings, says: "I'm shocked. Shocked to find there's gambling going on here." Yeah, I was shocked by it all.

How much did Paterno know about Sandusky's extracurricular pursuits? I don't know. If he did, well…but, if he didn't, he probably worked hard at not knowing. In either case, he was way too long in the saddle — too much power, too much arrogance. The King is dead, long live…? Overnight he went from immortal to perishable commodity, from invincible to broken, from proud to pitiable.

The Grim Reaper turned out to be Joe Paterno's friend. Less than three months after the Sandusky scandal broke, JoePa died. He was rescued from having to contemplate the destruction of his legacy and participate in the *auto-da-fé* with the intense national media frenzy that plunged PSU into disgrace. Poof! Down came JoePa's seven-foot bronze statue — his golden reputation in tatters, the PSU football faithful distraught. There was, however, an upside for Paterno: His family got a $5.5 million settlement package from PSU. It included additional perks for the family, including the use of the athletic department's hydrotherapy facilities by his widow.

There were other casualties. Graham Spanier, the PSU President, resigned in disgrace and faced criminal charges, of which he was eventually acquitted. I was one of the lesser ones. The new administration cleaned out the football staff. I got a week's notice and no severance.

CHAPTER FIFTY-SEVEN

Disintegration

Thou seest the world, Volumnius, how it goes.
Our enemies have beat us to the pit.
It is more worthy to leap in ourselves
Than tarry till they push us.

Shakespeare, "Julius Caesar"

Everyone has probably made one of these, at some point in his life: a seemingly inconsequential, mundane decision that turns out to have monumental, life-altering consequences. Some are good decisions; some…not. Mine? The latter. It was the weekend after I had lost my job, when the mass expulsion of the PSU football personnel rolled through and over the program.

Bored and depressed, in the early Friday evening, I drove across town in my beat-up Honda Civic to a bar, Kelso's Karriage Haus. I liked Kelso's because, unlike most university town bars, it had some quiet charm — no loud bands and a well-behaved clientele, rather than the typical rowdy fraternity crowds. It was a good place to drink alone, think, contemplate the contours of your misery, and try to put your fears into a manageable perspective. I arrived, sat at the bar, and had a Bourbon — well, several. The place was full — unusually so. I think, perhaps, because the bar was hosting a lot of the local football faithful. They appeared to be in throes of the local epidemic: "Paterno Pity."

A male of my size metabolizes, on the average, alcohol at the rate of around one hour per one standard drink. The two Whiskeys I drank over the course of a couple of hours, roughly calculating, meant that I had probably metabolized enough of the alcohol to legally drive back to my apartment and finish reading "All Quiet on the Western Front." At this stage of life, I was pretty careful in this regard.

When I gestured for my check, the bartender sauntered over and grinned: "One for the road, Pal?" Ahh, that fateful decision I was about to make. I do wish I could rewind and have another chance. I didn't feel like going back to my apartment just then. So…I wavered, with an unconvincing "no."

The bartender, with a walrus mustache, a three-inch pompadour, and the physique of a PSU linebacker, cocked his head sideways, paused, and then said: "Sure?"

Remember what I said at the beginning: I obsessively need to conform to the desires and expectations of anyone and everyone I happen to be around…

"Ok. Why not?"

"A double?"

"Ok," I said, after hesitating slightly again, thinking, finally, that I'd nurse it a while and be fine. It was early. The "a while" turned out to be not quite enough of a while.

On my way back to my apartment, I blew through what I judged was a late yellow traffic light that was actually a lot redder than it was yellow.

A half block later, a State College city police cruiser filliped on his flashers and pulled me over. After I produced my license and registration, the officer went back to his car for a while. When he returned, he asked me to "please step out of my vehicle," which I did. At his request, I walked, with him following shortly behind, over to the front of his cruiser. I stopped and turned around. He studied me for a short time and then asked:

"Have you been drinking, Mr. Davis?"

"A little bit."

"A little bit?... Okaay. Well, don't take this the wrong way, Mr. Davis, but I'm going to ask you to take an alcohol breathalyzer test to confirm that it's been, uh, legally 'little' enough for me to let you go on your way with a citation for the traffic light violation."

Into the test devise he produced, I blew a .11 BAC. The legal limit in Pennsylvania is .08.

I was arrested for driving under the influence of alcohol and spent the night in the city jail. The personnel there were somewhat friendlier than the ones in Kosovo, a decade or so ago. No beating. No one pissed on me. Early in the morning, I was fingerprinted and ready to post the small bond for my release. It being the weekend, I was told that I would have to wait a couple of hours for the paperwork to be processed and a court date set.

The two hours turned into four and then into six. Finally, a tall, trim-looking city detective in a blue polo shirt and tan khaki slacks opened the door and slowly strolled into my cell. He had that slightly ominous air about him that my antennas — refined over of the years from all the trouble I've been in — are acutely sensitive to. The detective leaned back slowly and fixed himself against the wall, with his arms folded across his chest. He seemed to be curiously studying me, as if something was not quite right.

"Sorry for the long wait," he said. "I'm Detective Bill Ford. I've got some good news and some bad news for you, Mr....uh...Davis, is it?"

"Davis, yeah. [Long pause.] Maybe you could start with the good news, if that's ok, Detective?"

"Sure. Well, the good news is that we are going to drop the DUI charges against you" [a smile].

I let that sink in for a few seconds, knowing that the "bad," by comparison, was going to dwarf the "good."

"Oh, really...and so, on then, I guess, to the bad news?"

He paused and took a deep breath. The smile had disappeared.

"We ran your prints through the FBI database. At first, there seemed to be no problem, but there were some anomalies in what we were picking up. Normally, we'd let it drop, but it was a slow night, and this particular desk-sergeant is a very persistent guy — bad luck for you, I guess. Finally, after a deep dive into the fugitive database, he found some matches that went way back. I've been making some telephone calls this morning, which is why the long wait for you. You have quite a colorful history, Mr. Davis — quite a long history, actually, and it's of particular interest to the Federal government. Some of the curious folks over in Quantico, Virginia I talked to at some length this morning have been worried about you and wondering just where you have been these many years — and what you've been doing. They've been wanting to talk to you for a long time, as you can probably guess."

He paused, lowered his head a bit, and fixed his gaze on me intently, waiting for some kind of a response.

I had known this day would come. It was amazing to me that I had been able for so long to avoid a reckoning. I had dreamed about it often. Now that it was upon me, there was a slight feeling of relief. I looked up at the detective, his face still fixed impassively, staring at me. Shaking my head back and forth slowly, I was trying to come to grips with it all.

Finally:

"So, then, Detective, what's the next step toward this 'conversation' I am going to have with these curious folks who have been so worried about me?"

"We are going to be holding you here over the night — actually, through the weekend. Monday morning, a couple of Federal Marshalls will come and take you to the Federal Court house, over in Philadelphia. There, you will be interviewed by the FBI and, maybe, personnel from some other federal agencies. Not sure about that. Then, possibly, you will be arraigned on a number of violations of federal law. That's all, really, I can tell you at this time. Right now, I'm going to read you Miranda, and the Feds will do it again when they arrive, just to make sure law enforcement at every level is covered."

Well, that was a relief, of course. I certainly wanted no slip ups on their procedures that could keep them from locking me away for the rest of my life. When he left, I kept thinking about that bartender: "One for the road?"

The Feds arrived on Monday and read me Miranda. I told them I would act as my own lawyer. That took them back a bit. I spent three days at the courthouse in Philadelphia, under recorded interrogation conducted by a series of FBI agents who were patient and agreeable. After all these years of lying and deceit, I had no reserves of them left. I decided to tell them everything, beginning with the Parchment Farm escape. Before I launched in, I prefaced it with the words from the Bard: "It is more worthy to leap in ourselves, than tarry till they push us." They were impressed.

The FBI had been after me because of my Weatherman shenanigans. They had nothing in their files about my gig with the CIA in Chile. This turned out to be a bit of problem — for them — in so far as just what to do about it, criminal charge-wise. Officially, the CIA was never involved in the

Allende coup in Chile, which meant I couldn't be and, therefore, wasn't involved in it. So, I got a free pass on that piece of government-sponsored criminality. Ironic, no? The CIA had squashed the Parchment Farm extradition order for my return from Florida. So, as far as the Mississippi folks were concerned, I was never there. Besides, my escape was an embarrassment for them, and if they took me back now, as a "senior," I'd soon be running up their medical costs. Why bother?

As far as the Balkans business, that was not quite so happy an outcome. I was charged with:

- *18 U.S.C. 1542 False Statement in Use of Passport*
- *18 U.S.C. 1543 Forgery of a Passport*
- *18 U.S.C. 1544 Misuse of Passport*
- *18 U.S.C. 1546 Fraud and Misuse of Visas, Permits, and Other Documents*
- *18 U.S.C. 371 Conspiracy to Commit Offense or to Defraud the United States*
- *18 U.S.C. 1028 Fraud and Related Activity in Connection with Identification Documents and Information*

The passport and visa violations were associated with foreign terrorism, so there was no statute of limitations. For the bombing of the California Attorney General's Office, I was charged under Section 802 of the USA PATRIOT Act (Pub. L. No. 107-52) for an act of domestic terrorism. According to the law, a person is a domestic terrorist if they do an act "dangerous to human life that is a violation of the criminal laws of a state or the United States, if the act appears to be intended to: (i) intimidate or coerce a civilian population; (ii) influence the policy of a government by intimidation or coercion; or (iii) to affect the conduct of a government by mass destruction, assassination, or kidnapping. Additionally, the acts must occur primarily within the territorial jurisdiction of the United States, and if they do not, may be regarded as international terrorism." This pretty much describes what I was about at that time.

I was also charged with the Fugitive Felon Act (18 U.S.C. § 1073 — Unlawful Flight to Avoid Prosecution).

I think that you'd have to admit that this was a pretty impressive inventory of misbehaving. My interrogators were finally done with me. I was transferred to the Federal Detention Center in Philadelphia to await a scheduled hearing. My sisters had hired a lawyer, Robby Griffin, from Grand Rapids, to act now as my attorney at the hearing. He worked with me over the phone: Robby advised me to plead "not guilty" to the charges and attempt plea bargaining at a reduced sentence — otherwise, go to trial. I didn't want to go through a trial, and I didn't have much confidence in his ability to do much for me. I didn't have the money to pay him, and I certainly didn't want my sisters to wipe out their retirement savings.

As Gary Gilmore said to his jailers when they came to escort him to face his firing squad executioners in the Utah penitentiary: "Let's do it." Push gave way to shove, and I did it: I pled "guilty" to all the charges. The sentencing date was on my birthday: I was sixty-five years old — ironically, official retirement age and Social Security eligible. Well, I was eligible for an even more extensive kind of social security, which was generously awarded. The judge sentenced me to thirty years, with parole eligibility in fifteen. At age eighty, I would have a brand-new start on life. My two sisters were there for the sentencing. They sat and quietly cried when it was over. My parents had died ten years before.

CHAPTER FIFTY-EIGHT

Vindication

All my life, I wanted to be a bank robber. Carry a gun and wear a mask. Now that it's happened, I guess I'm just about the best bank robber they ever had. And I sure am happy.

John Dillinger

That invitation to my 50th class reunion that put me so badly out of sorts is, now, several years old. I still have it. I'm now grateful to my old classmates for giving me that kick in the behind to go back and try to put everything together and see what it all looked like in the rearview mirror. It took me longer than I thought to get through all the "bad" to which I always "kept on turning," and I lost track of time.

The confession: It is now complete. I think I've covered most of the "vile and despicable" pieces, but, unlike Rousseau, I'm afraid I can't claim to offer much in the way of the "good, generous, and noble." And I can't say with any confidence that my soul is better off for confessing, since I've never been able to get much of a grasp on what the original condition my soul was in when I started out.

What I can say is that, after having followed along patiently with my train-wreck of a life, if you are expecting an outpouring of self-pitying, self-flagellating, shouldn't-have-done-it moaning and groaning, you're going to be disappointed. I'll go with a verse from William Ernest Henley's "Invictus." My English teacher, Mrs. Williams, made us memorize it in eleventh grade.

> *In the fell clutch of circumstance*
> *I have not winced nor cried aloud.*
> *Under the bludgeonings of chance*
> *My head is bloody, but unbowed.*

I am content just to be "unbowed." I think about Arnoldo Ochoa, refusing the blindfold and commanding the firing squad himself. That was "unbowed" for the ages. I must say that I feel lucky — lucky that I didn't get killed in the many places I shouldn't have been and where I was doing things I shouldn't have done. Lucky, yes, that I didn't spend most of my good years in prison and, most of all, lucky I didn't kill one of the innocent little people while I was blowing up buildings on behalf of the psychopathic, moralist Weathermen. Better to be lucky than good, perhaps, is the wisdom to take away from this.

More to the point: I feel vindicated. That will probably register as arrogant and shocking for you. Let me explain, if I may. I am now convinced that my understanding of the world that came out of the aftermath of those three horrible days in the Dominican Republic at a tender age was a true picture of the human condition: "The heart is deceitful above all things and desperately wicked." I could have acted differently, and I should have. That is a given. I hereby repent and with sincerity; there you have it. But repentance is not where I want to leave all this — rather, it is my sense of vindication that I must explain to you. Take it or leave it, Reader, as you see fit.

Here it is: I saw and still see the world as it really is and not how the moralists think it should be. Truth is brutal and ugly. Facts are sharp and brittle. They seldom conform to our expectations. They make us miserable — thus, they are routinely shunned. Illusions are warm, soft, and comforting, which is why they are insanely embraced and why truth-tellers are routinely reviled. Everyone wants the world to be something other than what it is, which is why so many people are determined to remain blind to actuality. They are willing — no, eager — to believe comforting lies that conceal the corruption and reward the liars. Here, then, is why the biggest and most outrageous lies attract the greatest following.

I was and am a conman. But, by freely exposing the corruption in myself, the honesty that follows from the renunciation of self-justification and rationalization makes me unassailable and my confession devastating. In telling the truth about myself, I have nothing to defend and am, therefore, invulnerable. I am an accuser — a genuine truth-teller — fearless in facing the pervasive and relentless ugliness and brutality revealed by my accusations. In so doing, I also rise above the other conmen — some of whom I served — who still pretend to be something other than what they are — benefactors rather than predators.

I have, then, achieved that moral superiority that has alluded me for so long — a genuine, personally satisfying kind that sustains me and gives me comfort as I look unbowed toward the end — not the kind I made my living at for so many years, not the kind that animates those who act as our guardians. My truth-telling has vindicated me, and my confession forces you to confront a terrible question, one that I hope never stops disturbing your sleep and haunts you in your quiet moments: *Who will guard us from the guardians?*

It doesn't matter where I make my home now. What greater satisfaction can a man have than to approach his final years as a genuinely morally superior person?

> *There was a young man they called Steve,*
> *Who rejected what others believed.*
> *He saw through their reasons*
> *In all his life's seasons:*
> *By them, he was never deceived*

Further Reading
from the Good People at
Falling Marbles Press

NOT JUST A JOB
by Michael Long

A quartermaster's naval
misadventure, as served in the
1970s West Pacific

"The Navy. It's not just a job, it's an
adventure." So said the television ads,
and so, having graduated high-school
during America's withdrawal from
Vietnam, Gary Thorpe signed up. A
quartermaster, his job is to steer and
navigate the ship, but he learns
quickly that being in the US Navy
entails much more – and much less –
than advertised. *Not Just A Job* is sure to relate to anyone who has
ever found himself in a situation less than he imagined.

RAVENS ON A WIRE
by Andrew Bacevich

Vietnam's dark legacy, as faced on
the West German border

The first novel from noted historian
and author of over a dozen books,
Andrew Bacevich, *Ravens on a Wire*
chronicles a routine border incident
and its subsequent investigation,
during which the wounds of Vietnam
find themselves on the verge of being
reopened. For some, the regiment's
motto – "Duty, with Honor" – would
seem to demand this reopening, no matter how painful the results.

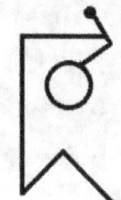